Herta Maria Moser lives in London. She was born in 1920 in Vienna, and brought up in Central Europe, where she witnessed much suffering in the aftermath of World War I. Many of her stories draw on these vivid experiences. Escaping the Nazi occupation of Austria, she moved to England just before the outbreak of World War II.

HERTA MARIA MOSER

THE SINGING CHAIR AND OTHER STORIES

Matador
9 Priory Business Park,
Wistow Road, Kibworth Beauchamp,
Leicestershire. LE8 0RX
Tel: 0116 279 2299
Email: books@troubador.co.uk
Web: www.troubador.co.uk/matador
Twitter: @matadorbooks

ISBN 978 1789015 065

British Library Cataloguing in Publication Data.
A catalogue record for this book is available from the British Library.

Printed and bound in Great Britain by 4edge Limited

Matador is an imprint of Troubador Publishing Ltd

CONTENTS

PART ONE:
A CENTRAL EUROPEAN CHILDHOOD

PART TWO:
STORIES OF LOVE AND LOSS

PART THREE:
INNOCENCE AND EXPERIENCE

PART ONE:
A CENTRAL EUROPEAN CHILDHOOD

THAT'S HOW IT IS

Even before she opened her eyes, Emma knew that today was different: no familiar street noises, only a faint swishing and scraping.

'Mother! It's so quiet. Is it Sunday?'

'No, darling. It has snowed all night. That's why all the sounds are muffled. Listen, they are still clearing the roads. Poor things, they've been queuing for their shovels since the early hours of the morning.' She sighed. 'And all to earn a few extra schillings for Christmas. She opened the shutters. 'Look at this.' Dazzling light flooded through the voile curtain with its lace insets of floral garlands and a lute-playing troubadour.

Emma rubbed her eyes and sat up. She laughed. The roofs across the street were wearing high hats of snow, and even the windows had white eyebrows and bibs. When her mother had freed the second window, the reflected light hit every corner of the room. Emma couldn't remember ever having seen it quite so bright.

Even her mother's thick plait, wound round her head like a crown, was glowing with the richness of gold. It had turned her into a queen.

'Stay in bed,' said the queen. 'It's too cold for you to get up. The tiles only just started to get hot. Later, I'll bring in a bowl and let you wash by the stove.'

Content, Emma slipped back, her goose-down duvet pulled up to her chin. 'Will you take me sledging?' she asked.

'Tomorrow, dear, when the snow has settled. Today we'll go and buy a tree. But first I must finish Frau Dr Windhaber's skirt. We'll deliver it after lunch on our way to the square.'

Now that the cold weather had started, and since father was no longer around, they slept in the large sitting room to save fuel. It had the additional advantage that mother, who also did her sewing there, could keep an eye on Emma day and night when she was ill. Unfortunately, this was all too often, for Emma was a sickly child. Having been severely undernourished in infancy, she had little resistance to any infections and diseases that happened to be going round. Vienna, capital of a defeated and truncated empire, was short of food long after the end of World War I. There had been no fair rationing, and very little found its way into the shops for the people who could not afford to buy on the black market.

Emma dreaded the frequent attacks of bronchitis and especially tonsillitis that left her prostrate and delirious with fever. On those occasions, the Biedermayer wardrobe in her range of vision used to terrify her. Its fancy walnut graining encouraged her vivid imagination to see all manner of threatening figures and faces, such as witches, gargoyles and fierce gorillas. When this happened, her mother would soothe her and quietly cover the offending piece of furniture with a sheet. The other ordeal was mother's well-tried method of bringing down a high temperature – wetting and wringing out a sheet, which was then wound round her naked body. Then she was rolled in a blanket, which in turn was covered by the duvet. Thus cocooned, she was left to steam. If the fever happened to be exceptionally persistent, a raw potato was grated and spread over two pieces of rags, which were then tied to the soles of her feet. She hated this remedy, but knowing from experience that it worked, meekly accepted her fate. Herbal concoctions too were part of the treatment since there was no money for calling in a doctor or for buying medicine.

This morning, however, Emma was well and eager to

go out and help mother buy the Christmas tree, which the Christ-child would come to decorate after she had gone to bed on Christmas Eve. Mother had warned her that the Christ-child was poor this year and unable to leave much of a present, but Emma felt sure that there would be something she liked. Last year, though the Christ-child had been just as poor, he had somehow managed to leave a little picture book under the tree. Emma had been content enough but couldn't help wondering why Karl Schulz, the greengrocer's naughty son, should have been left several books as well as toys. When asked about this, her mother had shrugged her shoulders saying: 'That's how it is.' The tone in her voice had stopped Emma from pursuing the matter further, though she had found the answer puzzling.

'You know,' she piped up now, 'the present I'd like best wouldn't cost the Christ-child anything.'

'What's that?'

'I want my hair to grow again.'

Emma saw that though her mother was smiling, her eyes had turned sad. They always did when Emma's baldness was mentioned. She sensed that her mother was more affected by this than she was herself. It was over a year now that the scabs of her scalp infection had finally disappeared. But so had her hair. She had learned to live with it. When going out, she would wear one of her fine jersey hats with a tassel. That was in summer. For winter, she had soft, woolly ones. To prevent itching, her mother had lovingly lined them with pure silk from an old chemise.

'It's this radiation treatment, we just have to be patient,' said her mother. 'Don't worry: it is bound to grow eventually. Who knows, it may come up suddenly, like new grass in spring. And once started, it will grow and grow.'

Emma sat quietly, as if listening to one of her mother's bedtime stories. She wanted her hair back more than anything: she desperately wanted to look like other children. Then they would play with her again instead of teasing and even bullying her. Most of all, she wanted to see her mother happy.

Later, washed and dressed, Emma was surprised to be given an egg for breakfast. 'Father managed to send us a little money,' explained mother.

'Where's your egg?'

'Oh, I've had mine. I had to get up early to finish Frau Dr Windhaber's skirt.'

'You should have woken me, then we could have eaten our eggs together.'

'I didn't because the room was still too cold for you. No good risking another fever. As soon as you have finished breakfast, I'll press the skirt and iron a few other things. By then all the pavements should be cleared of snow, and we'll be able to go out.'

Emma held the eggcup as she had been taught and carefully tapped the egg with her spoon. Then she picked off the cracked pieces.

'Shall I start it off for you?'

Emma nodded and, after watching her mother's expert topping of the white of the egg, opened her mouth to receive the first spoonful. After that she managed on her own, doing very well for a five-year-old.

She thought of her father and was pleased that he had sent some money. It meant that they could treat themselves to little extras. Apart from that, she was not interested in him. She hoped he would stay away forever. She did not actively dislike him, but was happier without him. She loved having her mother to herself. Emma had noticed other fathers fondle their children and play with them. She had also seen them hit their offspring and shout at them. Her father did neither. He had always treated her with good-natured indifference – like a grown-up who happened to be in the flat.

'Everything is still expensive,' mother sighed, 'but at least the goods are in the shops now.'

Emma knew that life was hard. Everybody said so: neighbours, people in the shops and her mother's customers who liked to gossip during their fittings. But it had been much worse when she had been a baby. Her mother, undernourished herself, had had no milk for her. And more often than not, after hours of waiting, she would return from the shops with only a little bread and polenta and an empty milk can. She had heard of the kind Swiss and Swedes who had sent food parcels to Austria, but none of those ever came their way. Mother had explained that unless one belonged to some official organisation or group, be it political, a union or church, one had no chance. 'Unless you carry a label,' she always declared, 'you're invisible.'

Emma could tell that 'more goods in the shops' was a good sign. She hoped that life would become easier so that her mother wouldn't have to work so hard.

'Before I start ironing, I must get some more coal.'

'Can I come, mother?'

'If you want to. But you must wear my old woollen shawl.'

Coal was kept in the cellar. Each flat owner had the right to one of the dank rooms that led off the underground passages. Mother always commented on how lucky she was to have a cellar just below the outside wall of the house. This meant that the fuel could be poured straight down through a trapdoor, instead of having to be carried though the house.

At the entrance to the cellars, mother lit her candle before stepping into the dark. It was like entering the catacombs. The flame, flickering in the dark, failed to spread much light, but mother and daughter were on familiar ground. Emma, very conscious of the musty smell, was counting the turnings as they passed the wooden doors on the way. All of them were heavily padlocked to protect the precious coal or coke from neighbourly thieving. Their door too had a padlock. Emma was given the candle to hold while her mother tried to deal with it. Alarm. Something was wrong. She wriggled the key about, but the lock wouldn't budge. Had someone tampered with it to get inside? Some more frantic wriggling. At last it clicked and sprung open. Panic over. 'Please remind me to bring the oil next time,' said mother as they entered. While she shovelled the coal into the buckets, Emma tried to stand as still as she could to keep the light steady. There wasn't much for her to see; in one corner, warmly wrapped in newspaper, the geraniums from the window boxes were still deep in their winter sleep. In spring, mother would re-pot them and coax them back into growth.

There also were some washing utensils, as the communal laundry was also here underground. Because washing day was a major operation, most residents could only face it once every three or four weeks. Emma hated it, because mother wouldn't let her stay with her, considering the laundry too unhealthy for a delicate child. She was therefore left in the care of Frau Vratni, a neighbour. She didn't like the old woman, who had a nervous tic and suffered from nervous itches which she couldn't help scratching. Emma thought she was not at all 'nice', even though she kept on about God, telling her how God would punish just about everybody for everything. In the end, Emma had come to the conclusion that God wasn't very nice either.

On the way back from their cellar, Emma went proudly ahead with the candle. It was her lighting the way that gave mother a free hand for the second bucket, thus saving her an extra journey. They were just about to pass the laundry, when they heard a loud clatter and shouting. Mother set down the buckets and went in. The steam was so dense, one could hardly see the other side of the room.

'What's the matter? Are you alright, Frau Binder?'

The woman addressed answered with a curse. *'Verfluchtes Klumpert.* The damned thing's fallen off and knocked the bloody tub over. Just look at the mess.' Her hair, wet and dishevelled, stuck to her face. She looked exasperated. 'On top of that, the bloody boiler's playing up.' She went over to the iron stove, opened its door and started to prod its inside with a poker. Flames started to shoot up, so that the surrounding steam acquired an evil glow.

'Can I help?'

'No, I can cope.' Frau Binder, recovering, smiled. 'Thanks for the offer. You had better get out of this hell's kitchen. You'll see enough of it when your turn comes round.' She sighed. 'There ought to be an easier way. It's not just the washing, there's the bloody drying too. Four floors up to the loft, I ask you! This lot here will take at least four trips.' She winked at Emma. 'That, my little one, is why we're called the weaker sex.'

Back in the flat, mother prepared for the ironing.

Emma noticed that she would be using the large tailor's iron, because she was piling pieces of charcoal over the lit gas ring. It didn't take long before they started to glow, ready to be picked up with the iron tongs and transferred to the inside of the iron. Then the lid snapped down to be safely hooked shut. First came the already dampened sheets. The iron was now hot enough to glide over the wrinkled fabric, leaving it straight and smooth. Emma sat on the kitchen stool, enjoying this efficient creation of order. It made her feel calm and relaxed. On these occasions, mother would often tell her stories of times gone by, or better still, of the wonderful things that could happen in the future. Sometimes, they would sing together while the iron did its job.

The charcoal had turned black. It was time to revive the glow. Mother, standing astride in the middle of the kitchen, firmly gripped the handle and swung her arm backwards and forwards, so that the iron could receive the maximum draught. With its side holes and the deeply serrated edges of the lid, it seemed all eyes and teeth. Emma imagined it to be the head of a dragon that was writhing and rearing up, getting more and more angry as the charcoal started to glow. But, of course, her mother was in full command of this wild creature and forced it back to the ironing board to resume its duty.

At last came Frau Dr Windhaber's skirt. Mother explained that the fabric was pure woollen worsted, specially imported from England. 'Very, very expensive,' she stressed, 'but the Windhabers have oodles of money.' She tested the temperature of the iron by holding it close to her cheek. Then, after having spread a dampened cloth over the skirt, she started to press it. It wasn't just a gliding over. Oh, no. She seemed to be putting all her weight onto the iron, as if to make sure that these pleats would stay in forever. At last it was done. She gave the skirt a little shake and held it up before Emma.

'What d'you think?'

'Oh, it's beautiful! Clever, clever you.'

'And now,' said mother happily, 'I'll get us an early lunch. Then you must have a little nap before we set off.'

Emma was able to dress herself, but leggings, which she would have to wear when going out into the cold, were beyond her. Even with her mother's help it was quite a performance to get them on and off. She was therefore not surprised when her mother told her to go to the toilet first, to save trouble later. Then she had to put an extra cardigan on before being stuffed into her winter coat. It was last year's, with the hem let down, originally made from an old jacket. But clever mother had made it look like a new, expensive one, by adding a silver-grey fur collar with cuffs and muff to match. The muff was on a cord that went round Emma's neck. She squeaked with delight when she discovered it had a pocket, large enough to accommodate a handkerchief and a little purse. For her own old coat, mother had also made a new fur collar and a splendid fur hat to go with it. These pelts had been given to her by a grateful customer whose husband kept rabbits. Though this lady had a twisted back and was difficult to fit, mother always managed to style the garments so as to minimise the deformity.

Emma watched her mother get ready. Turning this way and that in front of the large full-length mirror, so beloved by her customers, she examined her appearance. She turned to Emma.

'Am I beautiful?'

The little girl did not notice the mocking undertone, and considered the question most seriously. She had always taken it for granted that her mother looked 'nice'; the slim figure curving in and out in the usual places, the straight legs, the oval face with the clear complexion and the honest grey eyes. They all seemed quite ordinary. The one exception was her wealth of dark blond hair. Emma was very hair conscious, having none herself. She always liked to watch the way her mother brushed hers; bending at the waist and throwing it all forward so that it nearly touched the floor. With her long-handled hairbrush, she would brush it vigorously till it was silky smooth. She would then dress it in a variety of styles. The one Emma liked best, was simply wound round the head like a wide band. No other mother had such wonderful hair.

'Yes,' she pronounced solemnly, 'you are beautiful.'

The question settled, they went out.

A few metres from the main entrance they met Frau Kummer, who lived on the ground floor. She looked somewhat tidier than usual, her straggly hair having been pushed under her woolly hat. She was wearing a fringed shawl that hung loosely down her front. It was obviously meant to cover the gap in her coat, where her advanced pregnancy made buttoning up impossible. Leaning backwards to counterbalance the weight in front, she passed them with slow, heavy steps. When mother and child greeted her with a friendly 'Guten Tag', she replied politely enough, but quickly turned her face away. She obviously didn't wish to talk.

'Poor woman,' said mother, out of earshot, 'her

ankles are terribly swollen. It must be albumin.'

'No, it isn't,' Emma objected firmly.

'Good heavens, child. What makes you say that?'

'It's because she is too heavy. She's eating too much. She always grumbles how dear everything is, but they have plenty of money for food and drink.'

'You don't know that.'

'Oh yes, I do. I heard them say in the shop that he spends a fortune on drink. And you can see for yourself, she is fatter every time we meet her. I think she shouldn't be so greedy.'

The mother, somewhat disconcerted, gave her judgemental little daughter a searching look. After a lengthy pause she said: 'You know, Emma, it isn't our business what people do and how they spend their money. They can please themselves, as long as it doesn't affect others. We mustn't interfere. That's how it is.'

The high piles of snow that had been cleared from the pavements glittered in the bright light. Mother and daughter, hand in hand, were walking through these wintry canyons, momentarily preoccupied with their own thoughts. The mother felt somewhat anxious. It would take at least half an hour to reach the Windhabers' flat. Was she overtaxing the child's strength? When they got there, however, Emma was still perky, eagerly absorbing the new impressions.

It was a beautiful old house. Dr Windhaber was an internist, specialising in kidney and bowel complaints. Since he had moved his practice to one of the more exclusive parts of town, his wife's self-importance kept increasing in proportion to her husband's success.

They were admitted by the caretaker. Emma, squeezing her mother's hand, drew her attention to the glowing stained glass of the vestibule door. Walking up the wide stone stairs, she was intrigued by the red carpet, kept in position by polished brass stair-rods. No peeling paint to be seen anywhere. The Windhabers had the whole of the first floor. To the right of the stairs were the consulting rooms, to the left, the private flat. The mother pointed to the bell, and Emma pressed it.

A maid opened the door. 'Oh, you're delivering Frau Doktor's skirt.'

'Don't let her in. Just take the parcel,' came a sharp voice from inside. The maid looked embarrassed and, apologetically, reached out for it. But instead of the parcel, the mother handed her the bill. 'Please tell Frau Doktor that I must be paid now.' The maid took it and disappeared, leaving the door ajar. Alarmed, Emma looked up at her mother. The shrill voice, far in the interior, sounded very angry. Then they heard footsteps and the door was flung open.

'So you don't trust me to pay you. You think...'

'Frau Doktor,' interrupted the mother, 'your credit-worthiness is not in question. It's just that I need the money to live.'

Stony-faced, Frau Dr Windhaber handed over the cash and took the parcel. 'I hope you realise that there are people who charge a lot less than you do.'

'I know. And so they should,' came the prompt reply. 'Have you seen their frumpy styling and shoddy workmanship? Their garments are just thrown together, so that even the best fabric looks cheap. This skirt is expertly cut with a haute couture finish; good seat lining and real silk binding on all seams. And look at the top of the pleats. All with hand-embroidered crow's-foot tacks. You don't get that from your cheap jacks.' Her voice had been low but firm. Taking Emma's hand, she walked off.

Frau Doktor shouted after her: 'I warn you. If this skirt doesn't fit, you'll be in trouble.'

Having reached the stairs, the mother looked briefly back. 'If your measurements are the same as last week – it will fit.'

When they were on the street again, Emma asked: 'Why didn't the lady want to pay you? Why was she so cross?' The mother looked at the little, troubled face and realised how deeply this unpleasant scene had affected the child. She bent down and hugged her. 'Don't worry, my angel, some rich people just are like that. There's nothing one can do. That's how it is.'

Just then, an elderly lady with a white poodle on the lead was about to pass them. The mother, anxious to divert Emma's attention, pointed to it. 'Look at this lovely little dog! And look, he's wearing a blue knitted coat.'

Emma's eyes lit up. She smiled, first at the dog, then at the old lady who had stopped. 'You can pat his head if you like,' she offered, 'he's quite safe.' Turning to the mother, she explained: 'He always plays with my granddaughters when they are visiting me, so he's used to little girls.' Emma shyly stroked the woolly head. 'What is his name?'

'We call him Hansi. He's very gentle and good company; someone to talk to when I'm alone.'

Emma turned to her mother. 'Can we have a dog too?' she pleaded.

'I'm afraid not. I wouldn't have the time to walk him regularly. Besides, feeding him would also be a problem.'

'I'm lucky,' confided the old lady, 'all my family are saving their scraps for him. Even so, I'm glad he's only a little one.'

While the two grown-ups walked slowly on, chatting amiably, Emma kept bending down to Hansi to stroke him and talk to him. When they reached the corner where the shops started, the old lady said goodbye and turned off. They waved to her till she and her little dog were out of sight.

The child's interest was now in the shop windows, the skirt episode apparently forgotten. The mother breathed a sigh of relief and drew her attention to the various decorations that tried to entice the passers-by. Christmas trees, garlands of greenery covered with fake snow, parcels and boxes wrapped in bright colours, and glittering tinsel just about everywhere – it seemed an almost hysterical effort to persuade the careworn public that the long time of hardship was finally on the way out.

They were attracted to a fashion window, where three mannequins in party gowns had been arranged in a group. Wine glasses had been fixed to their hands and, against a background of elaborately draped fabrics, they were supposed to be gaily socialising.

'Oh, aren't they pretty!' exclaimed Emma.

The mother did not want to dampen her daughter's enthusiasm but found it important to make her aware of inferior quality. You can't start too early to cultivate good taste. 'Yes, the colours are bright, but just a bit too gaudy, don't you think? And the material's pretty poor. See how creased it is. Just imagine how crumpled it would look with a real person sitting and moving about in it. And, good heavens, the hems have been machine stitched. Very down-market, I'm afraid.' Relenting a little, she continued: 'There are two things that can be said for them; they're relatively cheap and can be bought off the peg.'

After a few moments of hard thinking Emma asked: 'If your ladies were to start buying from the shops, you wouldn't have any work. How would we get the money to live?'

'A good question,' admitted the mother, but she was taken aback. The last thing she wanted was to have the child worry about their finances. Of course, it was her fault. Working alone at home, she had slid into the habit of talking to Emma as if she were an adult. Without thinking, she had shared some of her worries with her. And what was even worse, her customers too found relief in unburdening their troubled minds in her presence. Hardly any of them were aware of the little girl in the corner, sitting on her little stool with a picture book, sometimes turning a page, but all the time paying attention to every word that was spoken. By confiding in the mother, who was not only a discreet listener, but also capable of giving the occasional, sensible advice, they inadvertently revealed to the child the desperate struggle of an impoverished community.

'Don't worry, darling,' the mother said as casually as she could, 'I have little to fear. Most of my customers come to me because their figures are unusual in some way or other. You know, for instance, that Frau Brauer has very large hips, that Frau Heilmann has a very long neck and hardly any bosom to speak of. Fraulein Stein has short arms and a high waist, and, you will remember, Mrs Ebert has one shoulder higher than the other.'

'Yes,' Emma interrupted, 'that's why you always pad the left.'

'You see, Emma, shops cannot stock fancy shapes and sizes of every dress they make. Their sizes cover a small range of standard measurements only. That's why practically none of my people could wear them.'

'What about Fraulein Bertolini and her friend? They have lovely figures.'

'Yes, they could buy ready to wear sizes, but they won't. They prefer to get their own material and choose their own personal style. In short, pay a little extra for a bespoke garment. Luckily, they're a bit better off and can afford it.'

'I heard Miss Bertolini say that your work is high class,' Emma added. 'That's very good, isn't it?'

'Yes. Both ladies know that I worked for high-class salons before I had you. By coming to me direct, they're actually saving money.'

They started to move on, when Emma skipped excitedly. 'It's him. Look, it's Herr Dr Steif!'

She was about to run across the road, when her mother grabbed her and jerked her close. 'Be quiet,' she hissed. 'Don't attract his attention.'

As it happened, the gentleman in question had his head turned away, looking at the shop windows on his side as he went. He carried himself well. His self-assured, easy stride proclaimed a man in good physical condition, just as his stylish astrakhan hat and quality coat spelt financial prosperity. Emma tried to free herself for another attempt at crossing the road. She was about to call out, when her mother's hand clamped across her mouth. She found herself lifted and, within seconds, stood beside a stationary delivery van that hid them from the road.

'Don't you dare make another move!' Her mother sounded cross. Very cross. Though Emma's face had been freed, her hand was still in a tight grip. She didn't understand. What had she done? 'I only wanted to say hello to him,' she whimpered.

The mother made sure they were standing in line with the back wheels, so that their legs could not be seen from the other side. The two horses at the front stood patiently waiting, their steaming breath escaping in regular bursts. Blankets had been thrown over them, which meant that this was a lengthy delivery. At the back of the van, only the half on their side was open, so that the mother could safely watch the road through the hinge-side gap of the door. Rigid with tension, she waited for the man to draw level, and then pass on away from them. At the same time she listened to Emma's chatter.

'He's such a nice man, mother. He always talks to me when he sees me waiting for you outside the shops. And he's not only friendly, he's kind too. He gives me ... that is, he wants to give me things.' Her mother's silence made her uneasy and she started to babble at top speed. 'Yes, he says he has presents for me – and for you too, mother. There's a lot he can offer you. You'd only have to ask. He says that if you would be kind to him, he'd give you a much larger flat than we have now. It has a beautiful chandelier, and lovely furniture and rugs. And he says there is a special room for me, and that I could choose my own colours. I think I'd like pink curtains and a pink and white bedspread. And we'd have plenty of food and new clothes and shoes and all sorts of things ladies like. And I could have as many toys as I fancy. And, mother, you wouldn't have to work any more. All this for just being kind to him. Please, mother, do be kind to him.'

Dr Steif, unaware of the agitation across the road, sauntered nonchalantly on. The mother followed his progress while listening with increasing indignation to her daughter's enthusiastic chatter. She could hardly believe her ears. That cunning dog, that evil bastard – tempting her child, corrupting her for his selfish ends.

Her cheeks were flaming with shame and anger. He was now crossing over to their side but, luckily, continued to walk away from them.

Emma, completely bewildered, felt she had to convince her mother that Herr Dr Steif really was their saviour. She played her trump card. 'He asked me not to tell you yet – but he loves you and wants to marry you. He said I would then become his darling daughter. I'd love to be his daughter. Father won't be coming back to us, I'm sure he won't. So you can marry him. You will marry him, mother, won't you?'

'No. Be quiet.'

'Oh, mother, please! Why not?'

The mother exploded. 'Because, you stupid little know-all, he's already got a wife – plus three little darling daughters of his own.' She was outraged, ready to dash after him. She would slap his face, spit in that smart mug of his, and make a scandal that'll ruin him. But even as these thoughts crossed her mind, she knew it to be an indulgence she couldn't afford. It was she who would be the loser. He, the clever, ruthless lawyer, would crush her like an insect. With her reputation damaged, many of her straight-laced customers were bound to shun her. Her livelihood was in jeopardy.

The realization of her helplessness made her tremble with anger. How she hated him! Her head was throbbing. She had to get away – get away before he looked back and saw them. Without further thought she rushed off, unaware that she was practically running as she pulled the child along.

Emma tried to keep up with her. Running, sliding, stumbling, she did not dare to protest. She feared that drawing attention to herself would provoke some terrible punishment. She had never seen her mother so wild and distracted; not even during the last big quarrel with father, when he had left them for good. Her chest was hurting as she panted and gasped for air. When her mother rushed on, even after having turned into a quiet side street, Emma's strength left her. She cried out and collapsed. It took two, three steps more, before the cry penetrated the mother's consciousness, before she felt the extra weight she was dragging along. In turning, she let go of Emma's hand. Oh, my God, what had she done? How long had she been dragging her? She saw the child struggle to get up. 'I'm sorry, mother,' she sobbed weakly, 'I'm sorry, I can't ...'

'My poor darling,' exclaimed the mother, 'are you hurt?' Bending down to pick her up, she was dismayed when the little body stiffened under her touch, and the usually so trusting eyes stared at her with apprehension.

The mother was conscience-stricken. How could she have bolted as she did, mindlessly, without thinking of her vulnerable child? She should have controlled her rage. But then, that's how she was. As her cousin used to say: 'You're a true Taurus – patient and placid like a cow most of the time, but when roused, oh boy, you see red and charge without thinking.'

As she carried Emma in her arms, she was painfully aware of how small and light she was for her years. 'Hush, my love,' she tried to comfort her, 'I'll find us a warm place to rest before we go on to buy the Christmas tree. They were now in the Ritterstrasse, flanked by upper middle-class houses that proclaimed their importance with ornate facades, liberally embellished with wrought iron balconies. The street was too exclusive for shops, but further on, she vaguely remembered, should be a coffee house that would serve their purpose. She walked slowly and carefully in order not to slip. In contrast to the main street they had just left, and which had been completely cleared of snow, the pavements here had been inadequately scraped and were lumpy underfoot.

She was worried. What damage had been done to the child's health and, equally important, to their relationship? How could she repair it? She decided to be as truthful as possible. 'I'm sorry I frightened you,' she started, 'but I wasn't cross with you. I was angry with Dr Steif for going behind my back and telling you lies. He really is married. I have seen his wife. She's a very nice lady and their three little daughters are charming. So he can't marry me without committing bigamy.'

Emma looked puzzled. 'Bigamy is when someone is married to two people at the same time. It's against the law and people go to prison for it. Believe me, darling, Dr Steif isn't planning to go to prison for us, nor will he risk a divorce. He's an ambitious lawyer and his reputation comes first.' Emma listened attentively. 'However,' continued the mother, 'he does want me to be kind to him and, I dare say, give me some of the things you mentioned in return. But I won't, because it would upset his wife and make her and her children very unhappy. You can see that it would be wrong, don't you?'

'Yes,' whispered Emma.

'So let's forget Dr Steif and his tricks. And we won't mention the naughty man again.'

The mother could feel her relax, and when the little head snuggled up against her, she could have cried with relief.

The Erzherzog was one of those solid, old-fashioned coffee houses, with a regular clientele that looked upon the place as their second home. The waiter happened to be near the door as they entered. His experienced eyes noticed the child's poor condition and the mother's initial bewilderment. At first glance, it struck her as a very opulent place. The multiple reflections in the large, gilt-framed mirrors magnified the size of the long room with its high stuccoed ceiling, and made one believe that there were many more chandeliers than just three. Oh, my God, she thought, this will be an expensive do.

But as they followed the waiter to the far end, she saw that the Persian runner was threadbare, and that the green velour curtains and leather upholstery had long since passed their best. The splendour of the Austro-Hungarian Empire had given way to a dignified shabbiness which, she noticed, was reflected in the appearance of the clientele. She thought that most of them looked as if they were here in order to save heating their own homes. As she passed groups of card players, elderly gentlemen engrossed in newspapers, and several students too preoccupied with their paperwork to look up, she felt as if she had strayed into a time capsule where she and her child were invisible. Even the middle-aged ladies, gossiping intently, never saw them walking by.

When they reached the end of the room, she realized why the waiter had taken them there. An upholstered bench ran along the wall and looked very comfortable; just the place for Emma to have a nap. He took their coats and hung them up, then waited for the mother to remove Emma's leggings, which were wet from having been dragged on the pavement. All this took place in silence, but the eye contact between the child and the tall grey-haired man had sparked an instant recognition and empathy.

Then, the amazing thing happened. Emma, who never bared her head in public, who even insisted on wearing her silken hat at home when customers came for a fitting, now slowly and deliberately pulled off her woollen bonnet to reveal her bald head. Her eyes never left the waiter's face. It was a challenge, a test. She had found it hard to accept that Dr Steif was a bad man who had lied to her about his intentions. He had also told her in a dramatic outburst of pity, how sorry he was about her loss of hair. But then he had quickly reassured her that she looked very pretty as she was. Those statements too must have been lies. Did most men lie?

The mother, unaware of the chemistry between them, was fascinated: what did Emma expect him to do? How would he react? She looked at him more closely. Of late middle age, pale, with sharp features, he had the air of a man who had seen better days. He neither appeared shocked when the bonnet came off, nor did he pretend that everything was normal. Instead of some gushing remarks of sympathy, he asked Emma in a matter-of-fact voice when she had lost her hair.

'About one-and-a-half years ago,' came the dry reply. 'Do you think it will grow again?'

'I don't know,' he said after a moment's reflection, 'but a neighbour's boy, who had been bald for nearly three years, now has a very good head of hair. He had some sort of pernicious scalp disease. I suppose it's hard to be patient, but these things take their time.'

'Did it grow the same as it was before?'

'It's the same colour. The peculiar thing is, that it used to be straight, but has grown back curly.'

'He's a very lucky boy,' Emma said thoughtfully.

The waiter gave her a little smile, then turned to the mother. '*Gnadige Frau* wishes to order?'

'A glass of warm milk and a small black coffee, please.' She stood up. 'Do you need the toilet, Emma?' The child shook her head. 'In that case, stay here, I won't be long.'

'I had an egg for my breakfast,' boasted Emma when her mother had gone.

'Lucky you. Do you often have egg for breakfast?'

'No, I haven't had one for a long time. Mother had to have hers very early in the morning, because she had to finish a skirt. Actually, we just delivered it. And you know what? The lady was annoyed because mother wanted her to pay straight away. We need it to live on, she told her, but the lady was cross just the same.'

'Did she get her money?'

'Yes.' After a little pause she continued, 'my mother makes beautiful clothes. She makes all mine. Did you like my coat? It's from an old jacket, turned and re-cut. I think it looks like new. Don't you?'

The man nodded. 'Very stylish, especially with that fur collar. And what does your father do?'

Emma shrugged her shoulders. 'I don't know. They separated. I don't want him to come back, but it makes it hard for mother. She often has to sew till late into the night.' She sighed. 'But that's how it is.'

'Yes, indeed.' His expression of sympathy was

muted. Then, bending down to her, he asked with the waiter's professional attentiveness: 'Would you like something to eat with your milk? We have a beautiful chocolate cake.'

Emma's eyes lit up. They were a deep violet blue and looked enormous in the pinched little face. But then she lowered her eyelids and said primly: 'No, thank you, I'm not hungry.'

When he saw the mother return, he left to execute the order. It was not long before he was back with his silver tray. In addition to the ordered drinks, there was a plate with a broken piece of chocolate cake and two forks. '*Gnadige Frau*, please excuse me. Our clumsy cook has just dropped this piece on the counter. There is nothing wrong with it, but we're not allowed to sell imperfect goods. I thought, and I hope you don't mind, that since you and your daughter are here for the first time, you might agree to taste it as a sample of our patisserie.'

'What a friendly gesture of goodwill,' exclaimed the mother, and gave him one of her heart-warming smiles.

The waiter bowed and left. From the distance he surreptitiously watched their enjoyment. They were not wolfing it down, but were slowly savouring it bit by bit. Neither of them guessed that he had conjured up their treat by carefully dividing the cake into nine instead of eight portions. He had then broken the extra piece with a fork. Robbing eight future customers of a tiny quantity of cake didn't seem to trouble his conscience.

The mother put three spoonfuls of her black coffee into Emma's milk to flavour it. She then sipped from her cup. Emma caught her expression of delight.

'Is it good?'

'This, my love, is what real coffee should taste like. Not like our malted grain concoction with chicory.' Concentrating on this rare experience, they ate and drank in silence.

Later, Emma put her head on the cardigan her mother had folded into a pillow, and wriggled her body into a comfortable position on the bench. What an unexpected treat this chocolate cake had been. She'd enjoyed every morsel of it. She would tell the Godwoman, as she secretly called Frau Vratny, all about it. And she would try hard to make it sound as mouth-watering as possible. With a sweet tooth like hers, she was bound to feel envious. And envy, Emma had been told, was a sin. So what would God say to that? According to the Godwoman, God knew and saw everything. He was everywhere, even in the lavatory. Emma hated God watching her wipe her bum, and she wondered whether the Godwoman minded. Being so old, she reasoned, she probably had got used to it. Closing her eyes, Emma let herself sink into a cosy world of semi-consciousness. Her thoughts drifted to the waiter. It was kind of him to tell her about the boy. He understood without making a fuss. And she could tell he liked looking at her beautiful mother ... How tired she was. So very, very tired.

Seeing her daughter safely asleep, the mother allowed her thoughts to wander. She was alone on this side of the room. The other customers seemed to prefer the entrance end with the display counter of cakes and pastries. There too, the waiter hovered, ready to spring into action when required. She observed him in a detached sort of way, thinking vaguely how odd it was that he hadn't made the mistake of underestimating Emma's intelligence. Most people did, because she was so small and frail. She noticed his slight stoop and signs of tiredness, and wondered whether his feet were aching. Poor old boy. She felt sure he hadn't been a waiter before the war. Like so many others, he probably would have had to reconstruct his life in order to cope with the disastrous effects of the defeat.

Karl, her divorced husband, had never managed it. He seemed to have lost his moorings and couldn't settle down to anything. She sighed. The marriage had been a mistake from the start. They had never really been in love, but had liked each other enough to settle down together. Both had been in need of an emotional anchor and a home. She still liked him; he was civilised and pleasant to be with. But his inability to knuckle down to a steady job and provide for his family had destroyed their marriage. Their constant quarrels had been about money – always, always about money. She thought of Dr Albrecht Steif and sighed. Steif, in contrast, had plenty of money and could keep her and her child in comfort, should he wish to do so.

They had been seeing each other for some months, usually in coffee houses, restaurants or other public places away from their home grounds, where they could chat discreetly for an hour or so. At times, when Emma had been to Schönbrunn and the zoo with them, he had gone out of his way to charm her. The little girl had loved his attention and found it hard not to be allowed to boast about him to the neighbours or anyone else. It had to remain a secret. The mother too had enjoyed these short escapes from her humdrum life but couldn't help wondering where all this would eventually lead.

At their second meeting, she had asked him to tell her something about himself. For a man with such obvious self-assurance he had seemed somewhat reluctant at first. 'My family is actually Armenian,' he'd explained. 'They were astute enough to leave the Ottoman Empire when the first massacres threatened to start. That's how they managed to bring some of their money with them. Unfortunately, the bulk of their wealth had to be left behind. We changed our name to Steif.

'Then, with the help of some old contacts, my father succeeded in establishing a new business in Austria. Being a shrewd and practical man, he encouraged me to study law, which has proved of great help to him. Subsequently, when I went into real estate, I found it invaluable. When one's working in the world of business, finance and property, there's nothing more useful than knowing the legal ropes.'

'Were you hit by the war?' she asked.

'In some ways. But on the whole,' he grinned, 'things went in our favour. There, dear lady, you have my background.'

So that explained his rather foreign appearance, his strong, prominent features with the bold, curved nose and full lips. From under his bushy brows his dark eyes focused on her with what looked like a mocking expression. 'Any more questions?'

'Are you married?'

He gave her a quizzical look and smiled. 'Yes.'

Though she had half expected this answer, she was taken aback. 'Oh, this puts me in an awkward position. We'll have to stop meeting.'

He protested. 'Please, don't be alarmed. You must understand that my wife and I are estranged. We go our separate ways. I agree not to question her private life, and she doesn't interfere with mine. However, we decided to continue the appearance of family life while the children are still young. Later on, you can rest assured, we're bound to separate. So you see, whatever you and I do or don't do, it won't affect my marriage.'

He had leaned forward as he spoke, every pleading word charged with sincerity. 'Meeting you and talking with you means such a lot to me. There's no harm in that? Is there? As long as we're discreet enough to stop evil tongues from wagging, why deny ourselves the pleasure? I hope I'm not assuming too much. I really hope you like me enough for our little rendezvous to continue.' He had looked deep into her eyes, willing her to agree.

Since then she had met him nearly every week. To her surprise, he had remained the perfect gentleman. Could he really be content with a little light conversation and the pleasure of looking at her? But since she enjoyed her outings and he was kind to Emma, she told herself to be satisfied with that. Yet once in a while, for a few moments, his gaze would embrace her like a caress and the timbre of his voice would acquire a disturbingly sensuous depth. Since she hadn't been sure how to react to such indefinite signals, she'd pretended not to have noticed.

'I'm not born yesterday,' she thought, 'it's obvious he's a virile man after sex. So why isn't he making a proper move?'

All her life she had tried to be as honest as possible. She found the telling of lies demeaning. Perhaps it was a sort of pride: take me as I am or leave me. Above all, she felt, one had to avoid self-deception. In considering her relationship with Steif she was brutally honest. She was flattered by his attention, she found him physically attractive, and she wanted him to take Emma and her away from their life of poverty. But she had to be sure that he genuinely loved her. She didn't want a short-term affair. If she agreed to be his mistress, it would have to be understood that he would marry her as soon as he was free. She took care to leave the initiative to him. He should never be able to reproach her that she had thrown herself at him. But she was getting impatient.

Then, about three weeks ago, he had made the long awaited offer. It had been his first dinner invitation and she had asked Frau Vratni to look after Emma and put her to bed.

Steif had booked a table at The Golden Grape, an up-market wine cellar in Grinzing. The lamps, almost obscured by garlands of vine leaves and grapes, shed their subdued light over the secluded alcove, creating a feeling of cosiness and intimacy. A *Schrammel* trio was playing in another room, and fragments of their folksy ditties and syrupy Viennese songs came drifting in. She couldn't help but realize that he intended to take their relationship further. She was in two minds. If he was going to make some sort of proposal to her, why did he think it necessary to make it in this setting – wining and dining her, like in a third-rate seduction scene? On the other hand, maybe he was being genuinely romantic, feeling that the occasion required a special background.

The food was delicious. During the lengthy inter-vals between courses, he had entertained her with amusing anecdotes while plying her with wine. At last they reached the last course. The waitress in her dirndl costume winked at her as she set the *Nusschaumtorte* and yet another jug of wine before them. Steif left his chair and sat on the bench beside her. Not being used to such a quantity of wine, her cheeks were glowing and a comforting wooziness lulled her into a state of contentment. But when he took her hand into his, her pulse started racing. And when he kissed her, she felt like melting in his arms. What a man. Yes, she wanted him alright. She had no doubt about that.

'I want you to be mine,' he whispered and his breath caressed her ear. 'I love you – and your little Emma. I want you both with me, always.' Then, almost soberly, he explained that in one of the blocks of flats he owned, an apartment had become vacant. It was lofty and large, with a balcony overlooking the park – the ideal home for them. He would decorate and furnish it to her taste. She would give up her work and just be there for him. For the time being he would have to continue living at home with his family, but would spend a lot of time with her and Emma. 'Please say yes,' he pleaded. 'I will treat you like a queen.'

She was overcome. It was her dream come true. Well, not quite. She and Emma wouldn't be his official family. They would have to wait for that. But from now on her life would be easier. She'd be able to give her little girl the nourishing food she needed, even try to find a specialist to do something about her hair.

'Come, say yes,' he urged.

Looking up at him, she gave him a radiant smile. 'Your offer is wonderful. But please, give me till Sunday for my final answer.' She didn't know what had made her say that. Had an innate pride prevented her from instantly falling in with his wishes, or had she been reacting to a subliminal warning?

He was slightly taken aback, but then, knowing that the dice were loaded in his favour, accepted her reply as typically feminine.

The next day was full of inner turmoil and excitement. Of course, she would have to give up her flat and sell her furniture. They were bound to be unsuitable for the posh park-side apartment. If she wasn't working, she'd have quite a bit of spare time. She'd be able to take a course of study and work towards a degree, something she'd always dreamt of. All sorts of ideas and possibilities went through her mind. This was the gateway to a new life.

'Are you alright, mother?' asked Emma, noticing her

mother's preoccupation.

'Yes, my sweet. I'm just thinking of a suitable coat design for Frau Gerner.' She had decided not to say anything to Emma before most details of the change were absolutely clear to her. 'After lunch, I'll have to make a delivery in Erdberg which is too far for you. So I'll take you over to Frau Vratni and you can have your afternoon nap there.'

Emma had pulled a face, but knowing that a protest would be useless, said nothing.

Later, on the way back, the mother met Frau Lieberman almost outside her block. She was shocked to see the distraught look in the old lady's face, her unnatural paleness and red rimmed eyes. She did not wish to be dragged from her emotional high, but in all decency, she could hardly walk by with a simple 'hello'.

'You don't look well, Frau Lieberman, is anything the matter?' she asked.

At the sound of sympathy, the old face puckered and her eyes filled with tears.

'Come up with me and tell me all about it.' She took her arm. 'We'll be alone. Emma is not there.' Having put a mug of weak chicory coffee in front of her guest, the mother waited. Frau Lieberman collected herself and began.

'You met my great-niece Gabriela – the pretty one with the auburn curls. She's a language teacher but had been out of work for quite some time. She really hated being dependent on her family. You see, they find it pretty hard to make ends meet. Then she met a man who courted her and offered to keep her. He told her that his wife was in the process of divorcing him. Of course, the family were against it, but she went to live in the flat he'd provided for her. But please, don't get the wrong impression. Gaby wasn't selling herself, she really was in love with that man.

'For well over a year she was very happy. But then she became pregnant and he told her to have an abortion. She refused. He made her life hell till she gave in. And, would you believe it, when it was all over, he turned her out of the flat.'

Frau Lieberman started to cry again. 'Silly little innocent. She'd thought her new home was hers, that it had been a gift from him. You see, he's very well off and could afford to be generous. But everything was in his name and she didn't own a thing. He offered her a sum of money if she accepted a job in Switzerland, which he'd arranged for her.' The old lady sobbed. 'Poor Gabriela. She couldn't face the family, so she accepted. I can't tell you how much I miss her.'

The mother had listened with increasing interest and sympathy. 'I'm so sorry, Frau Lieberman. What a terrible shock. But please remember, the young are resilient and can overcome traumatic experiences better than we imagine. I'm sure she'll make friends who will help her. But this man is a monster,' she exclaimed. 'He should be reported and made an example of!'

Frau Lieberman sadly shook her head. 'You can't get at the rich and powerful, they know the ropes. My niece just missed being a minor. Dr Steif waited with his seduction till she was of age.'

The mother gasped. Her heart missed a beat or two. Steif! It couldn't be Steif.

The old lady, preoccupied with her own woes, did not notice the mother's reaction, and carried on. 'He's a handsome devil, full of himself. He's a lawyer, knows exactly what he can get away with. You see, Gaby wasn't his first unfortunate mistress. We know now that he had several. And his poor wife, as usual, will be the last to know.' Sighing, she gave the mother a wan smile. 'I must go now. Let's hope you're right. Let's hope Gaby will make friends out there who'll help her forget. Thanks for letting me talk to you, my dear. You're very kind.'

Alone, the mother sat staring into space. She was stunned – numb. Gradually, she managed to gather her thoughts. The monster, the vile deceiving monster! His weeks of gentlemanly reticence – just tactics to play her along, keep her interest alive while he made arrangements to get rid of Gabriela. He'd made quite sure the young girl was well out of the way. He was utterly ruthless.

Suddenly, the full implication hit her. She felt a tightening of her chest, a sharp pain in the pit of her stomach. Oh, my God, this could have been disaster. It was a one in a million chance that she'd met Frau Lieberman and, that by good luck, she'd fought her own exuberance to listen to her troubles. If Steif had abandoned all these women, she was surely destined to share their fate. Having by then given up her flat and her customers, she would have been homeless and without means. What extra privations that would have spelled for her poor child. She couldn't stop shaking. Thank God, she had avoided disaster. Slowly, she made her way to the kitchen cupboard, to her special bit of luxury – a half bottle of rum. Sometimes, she would allow herself one or two teaspoonfuls in her cup of tea. Now, she grabbed the bottle and took several good swigs. She had to rest a while before collecting Emma.

Her outrage could have filled pages, but in the end her letter to him just said: 'I know all about you. My answer is no.' In the following fortnight, he had tried to waylay her and persuade her to change her mind. 'You have been misled – let me explain – you must listen to the truth ...' But she had refused to listen or have anything to do with him. Of course, he could have sent her an explanatory letter, but he was too smart to put anything on paper.

What she hadn't guessed, was that he had thought it worthwhile to lobby her little daughter. Did he really think that she would listen to Emma and be influenced by her wheedling and badgering? But what had affected her more than anything, was the humiliation of having been so infatuated with him. She, who was supposed to be so bright and practical, had taken all his statements on trust. It had never occurred to her that she should check him out. She had totally succumbed to his male magnetism. No wonder she went mad when she saw him saunter self-confidently down the street, and then found Emma fighting her to join him.

She looked up. The waiter stood before her. He cleared the table but left a little silver tray with a fresh glass of water. He obviously expected her to stay longer. She gave him a smile. 'The bill, please.' It amounted to less than she had expected. She paid and included the usual tip. She than sat for quite a while longer, wondering whether to waken Emma. Light was turning into twilight. The waiter appeared again, this time switching on the wall lights as he went. The one beside the mother was the last.

Emma opened her eyes, stretched, and sat up. 'I had a lovely sleep.'

'I'm sure it's done you a world of good,' said the waiter. 'You look much fresher and rested now.' They smiled at each other. It was a relaxed, companionable smile, as if they had known each other for ages. He returned to his place and the mother started to dress Emma. Then they too followed the long threadbare runner to the other end of the room. The mother caught several reflections of herself in the many mirrors, and was surprised how good she looked in her new fur hat. When they reached the door, Emma insisted that she could walk, but her mother picked her up, promising, 'later, when we get to the trees.'

The waiter bowed and opened the door for them.

When Emma looked back over her mother's shoulders, she saw him standing by the window, following their progress. She raised her hand and gave him a little wave.

Once again, the mother walked along the Ritterstrasse. The blue midday sky had given way to a solid, low mass of gunmetal grey that seemed to threaten the roofs and chimneys. She looked up. Some of these roofs were supported by draped, dignified females – caryatids, who had performed such duties since antiquity. For this was the noble end of the street. Upper middle-class flats had been followed by rich men's town houses, which in turn had given way to these aristocratic palaces. She had just passed a portico that rested on the muscular shoulders of two nude giants. She could not help wondering whether their ostentatious size and display of strength could be taken for a sign of the original owner's hidden fear. A case of trying to intimidate the common masses, who could turn dangerous, rather than just wantonly showing off.

How empty the street was: no traffic, no sight or sound of any living creature. But for the odd strips of light escaping from the gaps between closed shutters, it could have been totally deserted. Vienna pavements were made from large cubes of granite, which were expected to last forever. Hard on the feet at the best of times, with their slippery winter surface they were positively dangerous. Holding her child close, the mother took care not to fall. She was feeling low. Back at the Erzherzog, trying to recall her past life as objectively as she could, she had found little to please her or to be proud of.

Why was she like a magnet always attracting trouble and difficulties? It seemed to her that up to now, her personal life motto had been: 'Everything the Hard Way'! She suppressed a sigh. No good alarming Emma. But in truth, it had been a frightful, upsetting day. Hadn't she been confronted with a bad omen the very moment they set foot outside? On seeing that poor, pathetic Frau Kummer, pregnant once more against her will, her heart had ached for her. Throughout the day she had been haunted by that lost, despairing look. Then there was that mean Windhaber bitch refusing to pay, followed by the sighting of Steif, and her stupid, hysterical reaction which nearly injured Emma.

The child looked up: 'Mother, why does the sky look so heavy?'

'Because it's full of snow. I shouldn't be surprised if it started to come down before we get home.'

'Wasn't it lovely and warm at the Erzherzog, mother?'

'Yes, that's why so many people sit there for hours.'

'Shall we be going there again?'

'I'm afraid not. We can't afford to go to coffee houses.'

'But Dr Steif could take us.'

'Emma!' the mother exploded. 'I told you he's a wicked man. You're not to mention him again, or I'll be really, really cross.'

'Sorry, mother,' Emma whispered meekly.

When they reached the end of the street they met the lamplighter with his ladder and pole. He had just finished his round of the square, so that they could clearly see the magnitude of the invading forest of Christmas trees. In the centre, the basin of the fountain was almost completely screened by the tallest pines. But through a few narrow gaps, one could glimpse a wooden structure, shaped like a bell jar. Emma remembered that inside it, three mermaids were frolicking with leaping dolphins. But in winter there was no water, and they would have to manage in the wads and wads of straw that protected them from the frost. The size of the trees decreased the nearer they were to the outer edge of the circle, so that the impression was of a green, spiky hill. And over it all, in the absence of a breeze, hung the strong, wild scent of pine needles and resin.

Having put Emma down, the mother squared her shoulders and lifted her head. With closed eyes she inhaled deeply. Emma, watching, felt that her mother was far away. A man in large fur boots, who had been stamping to and fro, was now approaching.

'Are you alright, lady?'

The mother opened her eyes. 'Yes, thank you. It's just that the fragrance of the trees is taking me back to my homeland.'

'Where's that? If I may ask.'

She smiled at the old man who, in his many layers of clothes, looked almost as round as a ball. Between the earflaps of his fur hat stretched a large, grey walrus moustache.

'Czechoslovakia,' she replied. 'The highlands of Moravia.'

He looked interested. 'My family are from Croatia, came here a long time ago. I myself was born in Vienna – so you can tell how long ago. We have a farm now, just outside Floritzdorf.' Pointing at Emma, he said: 'I've got four little grandchildren like this, and one on the way. Now, little lady, I expect you've come for a tree.'

Feet firmly planted a little apart, hands in her muff, Emma looked up at him. 'Are you the tree man?' Seeing him nod, she continued. 'Yes, we want a Christmas tree, but not one of those big ones. We want one that is just half a metre taller than I am. Actually, I'd fancy one of those silver-blue pines, but they're too expensive for us. I'm afraid we'll have to content ourselves with a spruce, but it must have a good triangular shape with evenly spaced branches.'

The man looked at her with increasing amazement. 'Well, I never! Just listen to this little dolly. She's talking like a book.'

The mother laughed. 'I'm afraid this is my fault. As a fairly recent immigrant, I only speak High German. I can't do dialect or baby talk. No matter. Once she goes to school, she's bound to pick up the local Viennese.

Now, to business please. Can we see what you have on offer?' They walked along his section and he pulled out a number of trees for display. Though the mother had to agree that they looked good, some of them even splendid, she couldn't make up her mind to buy. Eventually, he got the message.

'If I may ask,' he said diplomatically, 'in what sort of position will you be putting it? Free standing?'

She shook her head.

'Well, if it's going to be against a wall, you don't need a perfect all rounder. This one for instance. Two of its branches are broken on one side, but you wouldn't need them anyway. If I knock off a schilling, or say, one schilling fifty, would that be of interest to you?' He watched them look at each other, and then at the tree. 'It's fresh and green,' commented Emma with the air of an expert. 'And it's nicely symmetrical,' admitted the mother. 'Yes, we'll have it. I'll pay for it now and collect it tomorrow midday.' Seeing his questioning look she explained. 'I can't take it now because I have to carry my daughter. She had a bad fall earlier on.'

'I was thinking,' said the man. 'Where do you live?' She told him. 'Well, in that case, I can deliver it.' With that he wrote the address on a piece of cardboard and wedged it between two branches.

The mother was delighted. 'Oh, this is kind of you. Are you sure?'

'Don't worry, lady, it really is on my way. But it'll be well past six o'clock. You see, I've got to wait for the late trade – workers and overtimers shopping on their way home.'

Emma was glad to be picked up again. Even the short time of standing had made her feel tired: also, her chest was aching. Safe in her mother's arms, she relaxed. It was almost dark now and their progress seemed to be measured from one street-lamp to the next. Large, loose snowflakes were floating in the yellow lamplight, like petals drifting down from a tree in bloom.

Such a lot had happened today, Emma mused. She'd loved stroking that adorable little white dog, and seeing the pretty shop windows with their colours and glitter. And hadn't the chocolate cake been absolutely wonderful? On top of all this, they had bought a beautiful Christmas tree, which that kind old man had promised to bring right to their door.

'Mother, will it still be warm at home?'

'Yes, dear. I filled the stove to keep it going. You'll be able to sit on your little stool and warm your back on the warm tiles. And for supper, we'll have slices of *Extrawurst* on our bread.

'Oh, lovely, another treat. It's been a good day, hasn't it mother?' She snuggled closer and sighed contentedly. 'What a lucky girl I am.'

Technology

The other day I was watching a young boy play with an electronic device. Since I don't know the name of any recent gadgets I am unable to tell you what it actually was. It appeared to be some sort of screen that produced certain pictures when touched in the appropriate places. I am aware that this naive description is bound to betray my vintage.

Well, this little lad was sitting alone on the sofa, away from the rest of the company, oblivious to what was going on around him. I couldn't help noticing his concentration and eagerness to achieve some particular result as his finger kept stabbing at the device. Though he didn't smile or display any outward sign of pleasure, I felt justified in assuming that he found this activity satisfying. One thing, however, was obvious. He showed no awe or sense of wonder that such a toy even existed, no realisation that it was a miracle of technology. He was taking it all for granted.

This took me back to my childhood in Vienna a long, long time ago, when radio was generally unknown and the cinemas screened only black-and-white images that moved silently to the accompaniment of tunes bashed out on an old warhorse of a piano. But please, don't believe that this was our only experience of music. Far from it. People sang or played instruments and made their own entertainment. My mother and her friend, a soprano and contralto respectively, would often sing for hours as they got on with their needlework. It was a repertoire of popular songs, ballads, lieder and even arias from operettas. The streets too were full of music which, strangely enough, was a sign of poverty. This was the time when Austria, having lost World War I, and with it its vast empire, was still suffering from the disastrous economic consequences. In desperation many people had to resort to begging. Offering some sort of performance in return was an attempt to diminish the shame. So, hoping for generosity, they would go from courtyard to courtyard within the blocks of flats that still provide Vienna's main living accommodation.

Every day, when returning from shopping, my mother would transfer the small change from her purse to a cracked cup which was kept in the kitchen drawer. It was my task to wrap three groschen in a piece of paper and throw it, at the end of the performance, down into the yard. Mother insisted that everybody received the same, from tone-deaf single vocalists to the sometimes brilliant professional singers and musicians. When I remarked that three groschen was very little, she explained that it would add up and that by the end of the day they could have enough to make some difference. Out on the streets, small professional bands would treat us to waltzes and rousing marches, one of their members usually joking when holding out his cap for contributions. I suppose experience must have taught them that an amused, happier public is inclined to be more generous. This also was the heyday of the barrel-organ. Some afternoons we would have several in succession in our street. Their offerings ranged from popular concert pieces to music from operettas and operas.

One day, my father came home with a mysterious parcel. From his expression mother and I gathered that something important was about to be revealed. It turned out to be a little square board with some peculiar attachments. He then put a half-hoop over his head that carried two discs that covered his ears. He began to move the board's lever. Attached to it was a short piece of wire. With it, he kept touching the small, jagged stone in the middle of the board. Mother and I watched this delicate operation in silence.

'That's it,' he exclaimed at last and passed the hoop-contraption, which he called earphones, to mother. I watched her face as she listened intently. She handed them back. 'That's amazing. It's ever so clear.'

'Yes,' said father with pride as if he had invented the thing. 'This is only the beginning. Mark my word. In the fullness of time this invention will connect us with other countries. The whole world will wing its way to us through the ether.' Mother, being used to father's histrionics said simply: 'Well, I'm looking forward to that.'

'Can I listen?' I cried. 'Please, father, let me listen.'

'I have to go out now. But of course you can listen. Here, put the earphones on. If you lose the sound, just move the lever and search for another connection.'

This was exciting. My first contact with cutting-edge technology. I wonder how many people can remember the first sentence they ever heard on the radio? Mine was uttered by a child in despair. Though there was a slight vibration of sound, I heard it quite clearly.

'Oh, what shall I do, what shall I do? My cap, my beautiful new cap has fallen into the well. Oh how terrible! It has disappeared in the water! Oh, whatever shall I do?'

Gripped by the poor little boy's misfortune, I

spontaneously leant forward, knocking the table in the process. Instant silence. The connection had been broken. Frantically, I got hold of the little lever and moved the wire from place to place on the crystal. No luck. I was losing precious time. However I tried I couldn't retrieve the sound. I called mother for help but she too seemed to lack the magic touch.

'Now I shall never know what happened,' I lamented. 'You see, mother, there is this little boy who lost his new cap in the well. I'm sure he'll be beaten. Oh, the poor, poor boy!'

Mother tried to comfort me. 'The cap probably fell from his head as he was bending over to look down the well. Or perhaps he had taken it off and accidentally pushed it over the edge. He obviously didn't do it on purpose. So I'm sure he won't be punished.'

'But he will, he will. He sounded so frightened.'

'Look here,' mother said firmly. 'Have I or father ever punished you for losing something?'

'No,' I admitted. In fact I had never been smacked. My parents believed in reasoning and I happened to be a sensible child.

'But other parents aren't like you. Egon Weber and little Karl Braun always get beaten, even when they haven't done anything wrong. And Hilda, who is ten, gets shoved and pushed by her father when he's drunk.'

Mother sighed. 'I know, I know. This is wrong, very wrong. But, darling, there's one thing you must consider. What you heard was only a made-up story – like a fairytale. The people in it tell what happens to them and try to make it sound as real as possible. It is called a play or a theatrical performance. The boy in the play you heard is meant to sound upset, but when he finishes what he has to say, he'll most likely be praised for his good performance and end up enjoying a lovely afternoon coffee with fancy pastries.'

Mother managed to convince me. Later, when my friend Trudi came round I showed her the gadget and treated her to a performance of what I had heard. I contrived to reproduce the vibrations of the sound by speaking through a piece of toilet paper stretched over a comb. 'Oh, what shall I do, what shall I do? My beautiful new cap has fallen into the well ...' and so on. Trudi was suitably impressed and my poor mother subsequently had to endure quite a number of repeat performances. And you know what? I still wonder how the story really ended.

THE NEW MAN

You would never have noticed him in a crowd. That you did, was mainly due to the fact that he wore a cassock.

I can well remember the first time I saw him. I was about ten years old and, like the rest of my schoolmates, eager to know what the new catechist would be like. In Austria, being a Catholic country, religion was taught in schools by Roman Catholic priests. Our last one, a moody old man who frequently lost his temper, had suddenly been taken ill. We understood that he would have to undergo a serious operation, followed by a lengthy period of recovery.

We were sitting at our desks, eagerly waiting for the new man. Speculation was rife. The school bell rang. Nothing happened. Just as the suspense was becoming unbearable the door opened at last, and there he was: a tall young man carrying a shabby leather bag and a violin-case. We rose as we always did when a teacher entered. He greeted us and bid us sit down. Then he busied himself with the paperwork on his desk, giving us a chance to observe him. He was thin to the point of boniness. We were surprised to see that his closely cropped hair was of a pale auburn, which was very unusual in our experience. His very pale complexion seemed to have the fine, almost translucent quality of china, but was partly covered by freckles.

When the whispering and tittering had subsided he stood up and surveyed the scene. His eyes appeared to be slightly protuberant behind the thick lenses of his spectacles; they were of a pale blue. Everything about him looked pale and pastel and it he gave the impression, on first sight, of an insipid personality. Yet as soon as he started to speak the image changed. His voice was warm and resonant and the richness of its timbre seemed to colour his whole person.

'I am Father Renner,' he said, then asked every girl in turn for her name and received the answers with a show of approval. 'Mary. Yes, that is a most beautiful name. She was the mother of Jesus, as you know. And you, you say you are Elisabeth, this too is a beautiful and holy name. And you are called Barbara. Well, as you will be aware of, this is after Saint Barbara, the gentle saint ...' and so it went on. So far, every girl could boast the possession of a saintly predecessor, but when my turn came and I said 'Herta', there was a noticeable pause. 'This is a very attractive modern name,' he hastened to say, 'but so far there has been no saintly Herta. But you know, that doesn't mean there couldn't be a Herta soon, holy enough to be sainted.' He looked at me kindly, as though he thought there may be a chance for me to become the first St Herta. I felt he had taken special notice of me and that there was now an invisible bond between us, hidden from the other girls.

Having completed the naming round, he produced a violin from its battered case and bid us sing a popular hymn, which we did with gusto. We watched him accompany us and later on expressed our unanimous opinion that he couldn't be more different from grumpy old Father Putz. I cannot remember whether he played well or not, but I shall never forget the movement of his hands. They were decadent hands, white and slim with long fingers, and exceedingly elegant in action. As I discovered later, he was quite conscious of their beauty and vainly kept his fingernails just that little bit longer than most men did.

Having thus put us at ease, he proceeded to give us a short lesson, then finished off with a story containing a religious moral. Father Putz used to almost bludgeon us with weighty, pious morals. But Father Renner's gentle moralising, being subtly camouflaged, went down very well.

Subsequently, we used to look forward to these lessons, particularly the stories. In fact, the new man had become our special favourite. Girls from other classes used to tease us about him but then, of course, they couldn't understand. They had neither seen him play the violin, nor had they had occasion to experience the uncanny charm of his voice.

There were also the odd religious services we attended as a class in church. On those occasions I managed to steal a little extra attention from him by pretending to have lost my place in the hymn-book. He would then bend over me and his beautiful hands would turn the pages and point out the correct place. I don't know whether he guessed what I was up to, but he always remained solicitous and patient. When, afterwards, he would leave his hand for a few seconds paternally on my shoulder, or even give my hair a little pat, I was in heaven. I suppose this was the first romantic crush of my young life.

Alas, it was too good to last. To our great disappointment, Father Putz recovered much earlier than expected. It is hardly surprising that our thoughts and wishes regarding him were far from Christian. Now, in retrospect, I feel sorry for the old priest. I realize that he had been a square peg in a round hole, and most likely had felt frustrated and deeply unhappy.

The farewell to Father Renner turned out to be a sad affair, the majority of us being dissolved in tears. I imagine the other girls too must have been in love with him, each thinking to have had a special contact with him. As he went through the rows, gently consoling us and smiling, he must have felt both amused and flattered. When he stroked my hair with his beautiful hand, saying: 'Now, now, little one, cheer up!' it was a major experience to be pondered over romantically for a long time.

My sentimental memory of Father Renner was finally expelled by a boy who moved in next door and who could perform acrobatic tricks on his bicycle.

Even so, I have not forgotten him. I wonder now whether he would have been shocked or disappointed to learn that I had become an agnostic by the time I had doubled my age, and that by the time I had trebled it, I was a fully fledged atheist. But one thing is certain: he has left me with a soft spot for red-headed men.

YOUNG LIFE

At the end of the track, we met the farmer's wife. She smiled at us and bid us a good morning. She was carrying a rucksack and we noticed that a baby goat's head was sticking out of it.

'Oh, look,' I cried, 'isn't it sweet?' The woman stopped and let us stroke the little white head. I ran my finger up its cheek, and was delighted when its little pink tongue licked my hand.

'You can see it's enjoying the ride,' I enthused. 'Look at its bright intelligent eyes.' Indeed, it displayed a lively curiosity for everything around it: the clear blue sky, the mountains, and us, the newcomers. Here was the essence of the joy of living, the hunger to experience the world.

'Where are you taking it?' I asked.

The woman stopped smiling. 'I'm afraid he's a billy. I'm taking him to the butchers.'

WILD STRAWBERRIES

Having stepped out of the dark pine forest, they had to adjust to the bright sunlight that dazzled their eyes. They had been foraging for mushrooms which filled a large canvas bag whose weight was now pulling heavily on Emma's arm. But she was pleased: what a haul. That'll show them that a town girl can turn her hand to anything. Of course, she'd been lucky; the warm spell after the soaking rain had brought up fungi in abundance. Actually, she'd been surprised the grown-ups let her go on her own and, what's more, take little Masha with her. Of course, she had been taught to distinguish between edible and poisonous mushrooms. In any case, Aunt Lisa, who was the undisputed expert, always checked every lot that came into her kitchen, no matter who had gathered them. As for the possibility of a thirteen-year-old girl, new from the city, getting lost in the vast, rolling pine forests of Moravia, they were remarkably unconcerned.

'You can start from the river road outside the village,' they said. 'It runs for some kilometres along the edge of the forest. You can enter anywhere along there and work your way up into the hills. When you come across the main track that cuts through the woods, just walk down it till you hit the road again. If, by any chance, you come across any other track, remember the village is in the west so, this being afternoon, you'll have to walk facing the sun. Just use your common sense.'

Emma had found this trust in her intelligence both flattering and daunting. Of course, she didn't let them see that she wasn't quite as sure of herself as she pretended to be. But so far, everything had gone smoothly. They had entered the old wood where the pine trees stood so densely together that their tops, high above, were fighting for light. Of course, she knew that this close planting was deliberate, that all these forests were here to satisfy a commercial demand. The lack of space and light encouraged the upward surge of straight, branchless trunks that were suitable for the industrial market.

Emma found the silent ambience pleasant as they walked soundlessly on the springy layers of pine needles. The occasional diagonal beams of light reminded her of holy pictures where some angel, the Holy Spirit or even God-the-father himself was sending divine messages to mankind. She could never fathom how this should be interpreted but in her case, it seemed, God was sending almost solid-looking shafts of light to point the way.

Often, they illuminated a patch of yellow chanterelles, which ordinary folk called egg-mushrooms, making them look like a hoard of gold.

Little five-year-old Masha could have been a hindrance but turned out to be an efficient helper. She picked cleanly and quickly and Emma realized that she must have done this many times before. Emma was not used to young children but she liked her little cousin well enough. They were bound to get to know each other better in the course of her holiday on her aunt's farm. She guessed that some family member had hastily cut her hair, leaving a spiky, copper-red halo to frame the little, freckled face. Though not pretty in a conventional way, she more than made up for it with her sweet nature.

'I'm looking forward to supper', she said. 'Are you, Emma? Our family fry this kind of mushroom with lots of eggs and parsley and caraway seeds. How does your mother cook them? And where do you find them?'

'Living in town, we have to buy ours. They're quite expensive. You see, we have to pay people for gathering them and then for bringing them in from the country. But we grow parsley and other herbs on the window-sill.'

'It's funny you having to pay for everything. You should live with us and get things for free.'

Emma laughed. 'I don't think your parents would like that. Now, in summer, during the school holidays we're helping with the harvest and are so to speak earning our keep. But later on there wouldn't be enough work for us. I'm sure they wouldn't want to feed us for doing nothing.' 'Oh, I'm sorry,' sighed Masha, 'I would have liked you to stay for good.' Emma was touched.

'Come, let's get a move on. We have a long way to go and I want to be out of the forest before dusk.'

But Masha kept falling behind and Emma realized that the child was tired. She was therefore relieved when they reached the track. Taking Masha's hand, she helped her down the steep bank and led her between the high ruts of dried mud that must have been caused by the loggers' heavy vehicles.

'Let's go further down,' she said. 'I want to find a more level margin. I think we could both do with a rest.' The churned-up ground made their progress slower than she had wished. Eventually, they did find a pleasantly wide strip with a gentle gradient, wide enough to be called a woodland glade. They sat down after Emma had carefully leaned her bag of mushrooms against the stump of a tree.

'My sandals are uncomfortable,' Masha said reluctantly. Emma unbuckled them for her and took them off. They were full of pine needles. Emma appreciated that another child would probably have whined all the way and made a fuss.

'You should have told me sooner. I don't want you to get blisters or sore patches. Let me see your feet.' Luckily, there were only a couple of not too angry red marks.

Although the forest comprised a vast monoculture of pine trees of various ages, its severity was hidden from any road or major track by borders of graceful larches and a variety of deciduous trees. Between them nestled wild bushes, and large clumps of foxgloves glowed there in upright dignity. Too tired for sustained conversation, the children just sat there absorbing the pleasant warmth, letting themselves be soothed by the natural life around them. There were little secret noises in the bushes, and on the thyme-covered bank, butterflies, bumblebees and other insects were feeding on the scented vegetation, going diligently about their everyday business.

Then Masha pointed to the other side of the track. On the somewhat steeper slope, almost under the low dipping branch of a larch, a sparkle of bright red seemed to wink at them from between the familiar pattern of dark green leaves. Wild strawberries – lots and lots of them. The memory of their delicious taste and fragrance enhanced the children's eagerness to harvest this special treat. They wanted to get there as quickly as possible. Emma rose and helped Masha into her sandals. They were about to run over there when a shrill alarm-call stopped them. Above, a large, brown bird, with neck outstretched, was flying across the glade followed by at least a dozen more. To Emma's surprise they were not a flock of the same kind but looked and sounded like an exodus of a variety of birds eager to get away.

As soon as they had disappeared from sight, Emma became aware of the sudden stillness. She couldn't hear a sound. She also noticed that there was no movement. No twig, no leaf stirred and even the insects had fallen silent and were not to be seen. The air was heavy now and the pleasant warmth had given way to aggressive, oppressive heat.

Though the hot air weighed down on her, Emma felt a cold shiver run down her spine: she was suddenly afraid. And when she looked at Masha's little face it was obvious that she too was aware of the threatening malevolence. She tried to put on a bold front to reassure her.

'It's a pity we have nothing to put all those strawberries into, but at least we can eat a good lot of them.' Anxiously, she looked for the child's reaction.

It was then that the wind arrived. It came whistling down the track, pulling at every upright bush and plant. It shook the twigs and branches till the hard poplar leaves produced a myriad of uncanny little metallic sounds that seemed to combine into a rattle of doom. The strange thing was that though the wind had come down the track, it did not carry on but appeared to be circling round and round the clearing. After the excessive heat, its cold bursts of contact on their hot bodies felt like being manhandled by icy hands. Emma stood rigid, not knowing what to do. It was a relief to hear Masha cry out: 'I want to go home. I want to go now.'

'I suppose you are right,' admitted Emma in a forced matter-of-fact sort of voice. 'There's certainly been a sudden change of weather. We had better get moving.' She picked up the bag of mushrooms, took a firm grasp of Masha's hand and, making sure the child was well within the ridges of the ruts, they ran down the track. In spite of the wind buffeting them from all directions, they safely reached the end of the clearing. As soon as they entered the narrow continuation they found themselves back in normal conditions. The air was calm, the sun gently warm, and nature here appeared to be unaware of the uncanny upheaval in the upper reaches. With every sign of life, their confidence grew: the red squirrel crossing in front of them and running up a tree, the two rabbits, disturbed in their browsing, scampering into the bushes, and the many butterflies in search of nectar.

They were tired and walked along in silence. Emma felt rather shaken by the unusual experience and was trying hard to make sense of it all. This had been no ordinary heat or wind. Reluctant as she was to admit it, even to herself, it felt very much like one of those supernatural phenomena you read about in cheap fiction. There was no doubt, it had been real enough, but what had caused it? Recreating the sequence of events in her mind, she came to the conclusion that it all hinged on the wild strawberries. Every time they had mentioned them or got ready to harvest them, something or somebody had made a great effort to prevent them. But whoever that may have been, it was not the spirit of the strawberries, assuming there was such a thing. Nature study was one of Emma's favourite subjects and she knew that plants were eager to propagate their species. Why else would they go to the trouble of producing fruit with tempting looks, scent and flavour? Even if they could propagate by layering, they still wanted the chance of animals eating their fruit and spreading the seeds further afield. So what ghostly creature had caused all this upheaval? Really, the whole idea was ridiculous. It must have been some freak atmospheric happening that could be explained by science. Well, for the time being she had to leave it at that.

When they finally reached the village, Masha perked up. She walked a little quicker and started to chat. 'Won't they all be pleased with our mushrooms?' And indeed, they were. Masha told them how they went from one golden patch of chanterelles to another and how they had been able to observe all sorts of birds and animals. Emma was expecting her to talk about their frightening experience, but she did not mention it. As for the wild strawberries, she seemed to have forgotten all about them.

BANNER-MAIDEN

When the Deutsche Mannergesangsverein – the German Male Voice Choir – in Vienna had a special anniversary to celebrate, they decided to make it into a grand affair. The production required four attractive young girls to carry the traditional banners and to look decorative in the procession and during the ceremony. Our neighbours, the Schnitzlers, longstanding members of this choral organisation, thought that I would be suitable. When they approached my mother for permission, she told them that, in view of my tender age, she would have to give it some thought. Actually, she wasn't at all keen on letting me take part.

'Why not?' I asked. 'Don't you trust me with a bit of flag-waving?'

'It's not you, darling. It is the choir. There's a rumour that the members are all underground Nazis, or at least have connections with them.'

'Oh, come!' I protested. 'The government would be sure to know. Everyone says they've got their spies all over the place. They'd not allow a do like this if it were true, especially with all that public razzmatazz.'

Mother looked at me surprised. 'I didn't think you were interested.'

'But I am. It would be a little adventure – something different.'

After a lengthy pause, mother gave a sigh. 'I suppose the Schnitzlers have always been good to us. I know Frau Schnitzler is very fond of you: she always wanted a daughter, you know. Well, if you really want to join this jamboree, so be it.' I suspected that, faced with an insecure political future, mother probably thought it expedient to keep in with all parties. So it happened that at the age of sixteen I was recruited for the honourable position of Gesangsverein banner-maiden. But even at that age I was aware of the ever-present dangers. During the last few years I had witnessed Engelbert Dollfuss' rise to the chancellorship of Austria. He, the friend of the ultra-conservative Horthy of Hungary as well as of Mussolini, had boldly suspended Austria's parliamentary government. When left-wing workers dared to demonstrate, he ordered the army to bombard the socialist housing estates in the suburbs. After five days of fierce civil war the social democrats were vanquished and a new, fascist constitution was imposed on Austria. Dollfuss now had to fear the pro-Soviet Marxists, as well as the National Socialists, the underground Nazis, who plotted for unification with Germany. The subsequent Nazi coup d'etat failed but Dollfuss was murdered in the process. Since then, a paranoid, dictatorial government had enforced order. I did therefore understand my mother's concern. But being young, I longed for a break in my humdrum life. A celebration was just the thing.

My silk confirmation gown still fitted me. It was ideal for the occasion, as the maidens had to display themselves in virginal white. Vienna's famous baroque Karlskirche was the venue of the main celebration, and the more informal programme and dinner were to take place in the Rathauskeller, the basement of the town hall.

Herr and Frau Schnitzler took me to the meeting place, where I received a friendly welcome. When the banner was presented to me, my heart sank. 'I'll never be able to carry this huge thing,' I thought, but after being shown how to handle the long pole I realized that it was manageable.

'Isn't it a magnificent banner?' exclaimed Herr Schnitzler. 'We've got an enlarged photograph of it at home. You must come over and I'll explain it all to you.

The historical and mythological details are fascinating, full of meaning, you know.' Indeed, the embroidery was splendid, an arrangement of fantastic figures and objects in glowing colours, enriched with lots of gold. I was interested but didn't relish the prospect of the old man close to me, breathing his peppermint breath into my face and down my neck. I hoped his wife would be present.

At last we started, making our way from the quiet side street to the large square, the Karlsplatz, dominated by the beautiful verdigris cupola of the Karlskirche. The column was quite a long one. There were a number of people about and most of them stopped and watched us pass by. In Vienna, and the whole of Austria, one often came across groups celebrating in this fashion. It wasn't just tradition: in those grim times, any excuse for a procession and a knees-up was welcome. Taking part instead of just watching was a first for me and I felt somewhat disconcerted to find myself observed by so many eyes. It was no better inside the church. A space had been cleared to accommodate the choir, and we four maidens, with our ornamental banners, were placed right in front for the delectation of the congregation. Needless to say, a lot of singing accompanied the service.

I felt sorry my mother wasn't present. Being a Czech from Moravia, where music always played an important part in life, she would have appreciated the performance. I certainly did. The singers had been well drilled and their beautifully blended voices seemed to fill every nook and cranny of the church, soaring right up into the lofty cupola. I thought how strange it was that a little, insignificant man like Herr Schnitzler should be part of such a wonderful performance. But as the concert went on and on, I was ashamed to admit to myself that I now wished for it to end soon. Although we were allowed to rest the banner poles on the ground, we were expected to stand completely still, which I found uncomfortable. Besides, the temperature inside the church was much lower than outside and my lovely silk gown afforded little protection against the cold. I started to shiver and longed to be outside in the sunshine again.

It was then that a lady in the front row got up and, beaming at me benevolently, stepped forward to drape her silver-fox cape around my shoulders. Evidently, for her the cape was purely decorative, since her plump body was already generously insulated, but to me it was like a lifeline. Gratefully, I snuggled into the cosy, pre-warmed fur and fancied I looked as glamorous as a film star. If my impression of being watched by everybody had been fanciful before, now it was fact. Intensive listening does not dim the desire to look and behold. The hundreds of eyes that had been contemplating the baroque interior with its holy paintings, marble pillars, statues of saints, angels and chubby little putti, must by now have become tired of their immobility. Even the singers in their uniform dark suits stood still, only their lips moving.

Then, to the sound of a rousing crescendo, the visual boredom was shattered by an almost ritualistic scene. A virgin in white, trembling as if apprehensive of a terrible fate, was suddenly rescued by a symbolic gesture – the donation of a protective cloak!

Relaxed and cocooned in warmth, I started to take closer notice of my surroundings. Were the audience really just music lovers or did they come in support of a Nazi underground movement? And what about the singers themselves? Was my mother right? Looking at them in turn I thought them a very mixed lot. They varied in age as much as in appearance. There was Herr Schnitzler with his narrow shoulders and receding hairline, and next to him, almost dwarfing him, an athletic looking young man with a wealth of blond hair. Turning to look more closely at this handsome giant, I was shocked to find him staring at me. With studied nonchalance I continued my survey of his singing companions, but every time I risked a fleeting glance back, I found him still looking at me. Since he was constantly singing I was unable to detect any facial expression that would betray his feelings. I felt unsettled, almost flustered – yet at the same time strangely pleased. I wondered whether he would seek me out after the performance and how I should behave if he did. Luckily my suspense did not last long: a short, rousing march and the concert was over.

Having regretfully returned the fur cape, I found my previous place in the procession. As soon as everybody had arrived, we set off towards the Ringstrasse and on to the Rathaus. It was exhilarating to be outside again. The air was pleasantly warm and the late afternoon sun spread its golden light over the splendid buildings we passed. This broad street, flanked by avenues of trees and bordered by a number of parks, had been built to show off the power and culture of the Austro-Hungarian Empire. It had replaced the old wall that encircled the inner city until the mid-nineteenth century. Here, dozens of imposing buildings – including the opera house, the gigantic art and natural history museums, the parliament, the state theatre and the imperial palace – vied to impress the world.

More people were now watching our festive procession and I realized that I was enjoying myself. By now I had got the hang of the pole-carrying business and started to manipulate it to impart some movement to the banner. When we arrived at our destination, Frau Schnitzler joined me and waited with me until one of the organisers appeared to collect my banner and to thank me. Her husband had preceded us into the cellar and reserved our seats.

Though I can no longer remember the precise look of the vast dining hall, it was something like a cross between ye olde cellar and a Lyons Cornerhouse dining room. I don't think I was impressed. I was about to take my place between Herr and Frau Schnitzler when my heart stopped: the blond young man had approached our table, to be invited by Herr Schnitzler to join us. To my dismay his wife suggested that I should change places with her so that I would sit next to the newcomer. She introduced us. His name was Gunter. It took me quite a few seconds to collect myself. Obviously, I was expected to make conversation.

'I enjoyed the concert very much,' I said. I realized I had to be careful not to sound either condescending or gushing. 'Since you were standing next to Herr Schnitzler,' I continued, 'I assume you too are a baritone.'

'Yes, I am what is called a lyrical baritone, that is neither a heroic nor a bass baritone.'

'Oh,' I exclaimed. 'You surprise me. I would have put you in the heroic bracket.'

He laughed and I had to admit to myself that it was warm, pleasant laughter. I noticed that he had blueish-grey eyes and a good, slightly tanned complexion.

'Do you sing or play an instrument?' he asked.

'I play the piano, but my performances are very mediocre. As for singing, that is even worse. Nevertheless, I do love music but my only chance of hearing it is on the wireless. I'm afraid my mother knows quite a lot about art but not much about classical music.'

He listened to me intently, and his even more intent examination of my person somehow made me feel vulnerable. 'What else do you like? What about sport?'

'Well, like my mother, I like art. That is, painting and sculpture. As to sport, I dislike ball games and any cutthroat competitions. I'm quite a good swimmer and enjoy walking in the countryside or in woods and mountains if I get the chance.' I could see that he liked what he heard. 'What about you?' I asked.

'Like you, I like swimming and walking. And I've done some sailing and rock climbing. My latest passion is going out into the country on my motorbike. Have you ever made trips on a motorbike?'

'No. My mother wouldn't allow it. She'd think I'd be too young for that. I'm still a student, you know – only just sixteen.'

He looked genuinely surprised. After a little pause he said with a smile: 'In that case, you'll have a lot of good and interesting things ahead of you.'

Of course I knew that I looked and sounded more mature than my years, a consequence of having spent more time with adults than with my peers. Amongst strangers I wouldn't have admitted my age, but with the Schnitzlers present I couldn't afford to pretend. Gunter continued to be attentive and charming as if my revelation didn't affect him. Every so often our conversation was interrupted by speeches, thankfully fairly short ones, and by bursts of singing. Then there was the food and, of course, the drinking. I was only sipping from my glass but in the course of the evening I would have expected the level of wine to get lower, but it never did. It seemed that everybody within reach had a go at topping it up. At home I sometimes had the odd little glass of wine, but only because my mother thought it would give me an appetite.

I rose, asking Frau Schnitzler whether she knew were the ladies' toilets were. Gunter immediately got up and offered to take me there. As we walked along the maze of corridors I was conscious of being light-headed and not all too steady on my feet. When I came out of the ladies', Gunter was waiting for me. He got hold of my elbow and I was content for him to lead me. After having turned one or two corners, he stopped and put his arms around me. This sudden move came as a surprise but I didn't resent it. In fact I found it exciting and rather pleasant. And when he started to kiss me, I found that pleasant too. After a few minutes we heard approaching footsteps. It was time to go back.

On our return Frau Schnitzler gave us a quick, searching glance. Had she noticed that my face was flushed? Gunter and I continued talking but I have no recollection what about. Then, a flower seller approached our table, carrying a basket of red roses. Gunter beckoned to her and to everybody's surprise bought the lot. There I was with an armful of roses, feeling touched but also embarrassed. When I looked round I saw, as if through a mist, the smiling faces of our table companions. I was ready to go home, but the others, deciding they had a bit more drinking to do, lingered on. It was well after midnight when the Schnitzlers delivered me and my roses to my mother's care.

Next day, being Sunday, my mother let me sleep. It was nearly eleven o'clock when I woke and got up. It took quite a few seconds before I remembered what all the roses were about. They had filled not only all our vases but also the kitchen jugs.

Mother appeared. 'Did you have a good time?' she asked. I nodded.

'Who gave you all those roses?'

'A young fellow called Gunter. He must have been drunk.'

And that was that. My mother never raised the subject again, and I, though I had hoped for a continuation of my relationship with Gunter, eventually forgot all about him.

It was many years later that I learned the truth. I had married a British-born man and spent the war years in England. On my first trip back to Vienna I naturally asked my mother what had happened to all my friends and acquaintances. Some had had a very bad time, some were dead. The Russians had sent their eastern, Mongolian troops to capture Vienna. They did so with rape and plunder. When the Allies partitioned Vienna into four zones, mother found herself in the Russian zone. It meant that the population there was being watched and dictated to as they had been in the Nazi eara. It still was a very hard time and she had much to tell me.

'How did the Schnitzlers get on?' I asked at last.

'He died suddenly – a heart attack. Frau Schnitzler then went to Styria to live with her sister. You know, she turned out to be a good friend to me. When I was arrested by the Gestapo, she ...'

'Good God' I interrupted. 'Why were you arrested?'

Mother smiled. 'You know me. I always have to say what I think. Only I did it once too often. I was talking to a few neighbours, making some remarks about Hitler and the regime. You see, I believed they were like-minded. But one of them denounced me.'

I was shocked. 'What happened then?'

'Well, as soon as Frau Schnitzler heard about it she went to the Gestapo and asked them to release me. She and her husband had been underground Nazis for years, so they couldn't ignore her. Besides, as you will remember, she was a very determined woman but charming at the same time. She told me that she convinced them that I was a silly old woman who didn't know what she was talking about and that I was completely harmless.'

'That was very courageous of her. But why did she take that risk on your behalf?'

'Because she was fond of you. She would never have forgiven herself for causing you the pain of me having been sent to a concentration camp if she could have prevented it. Besides, she still felt somehow responsible about the banner-maiden do.'

'What do you mean?'

'She thought you might have been fretting over Gunter.'

'Good God, no. That was just a flash in the pan – on both sides.'

Mother gave me a somewhat sheepish look. 'Not on both sides, dear. He was deeply in love with you. He wanted to marry you.'

I burst out laughing. 'What gives you that crazy idea?'

'Not my idea, but fact.' She was watching my face.

'The very next morning, when you were still asleep, he called on Frau Schnitzler. He told her that he was seriously interested in you. He said he knew you were only sixteen but he was prepared to wait till you were ready. Further, he didn't mind if your family were not well off, he wasn't bothered about a dowry. But before taking any further steps he had to make sure that you were Aryan and of pure Germanic origin.'

'So you knew all about this before I even woke up?'

'Yes.'

I couldn't believe my ears. 'But mother, this was two years before Hitler marched into Austria!' I protested.

'Yes, Gunter was an underground Nazi. Nearly the whole male-voice choir was. Of course, Frau Schnitzler had to tell him that I was Czech, a member of the despised, so-called inferior Slavonic race. And she couldn't even vouch for the Teutonic purity of your father.'

'But mother, that means that even then he must have expected to rise to great heights in the party. I wonder whether he became a Gestapo officer – one of those who were prepared to sacrifice their integrity for the sake of position and power.' In my mind's eye I could see him in the smart, black uniform that was so becoming, especially for blond men. I wondered whether he had had anything to do with concentration camps. 'Good heavens,' I thought, 'had I been a pure Aryan, I could have been the wife of an extermination-camp commander.' I shuddered. I was letting my imagination run away with me.

Aloud, I said: 'For him it was a choice between love and ambition, and the latter won. I'm sorry if Frau Schnitzler thought I was fretting, but really, mother, as I told you before, for me it was just a flash in the pan.'

THE TRUANT

'Cowards!' cried Jan as he ran along the lane. 'None of you sods dare to fight me alone.'

He looked back. The boys were gaining on him. Still, he might yet reach St Nepomuk's before them. Though hampered by the can of milk he was carrying, he tried to run as fast as he could without spilling the contents. He would hide it in the church and deliver it later.

Hens flapped cackling out of his way and a cat, ambling home from its nightly prowl, jumped aside in alarm. The air was still and cool. In the morning haze the whitewashed cottages of the Moravian village bore a mellow look. Later on they would dazzle the eye with reflected sunlight. Dogs were barking all along the lane now, and some people, already busy outdoors, looked over their gates and fences. They saw what was happening and knew what it meant. But none of them tried to stop the chase.

Jan saw their faces in passing, immobile faces with suppressed smiles and glints of malicious joy in their eyes. 'Cowards,' he cried again and it was meant for them too. These grown-ups were worse than the boys, he thought, they'd love to join the hunt if it weren't undignified. Theirs was a deep-rooted hatred born of ignorance and envy. The boys only reflected their parents' prejudices. As rage surged within him, his power increased. He was now widening the gap between himself and the mob.

Suddenly, a gate opened and Jaroslav Sukov, the baker's son, dashed out and barred his way. Before Jan could avoid him, Jaroslav had kicked the can so that its contents splashed over both of them. Encouraged by the shouts of his approaching friends, the aggressor tried to tackle Jan, only to be repulsed by a blow on the head with the can. The hollow clang sounded like music in Jan's ears. No longer held back by fear of spillage, he gained the end of the lane well ahead of his persecutors. Their shouting grew shrill with disappointment as he entered the sanctuary of St Nepomuk's.

The coolness of the church comforted his heated body. He stepped behind one of the columns near the entrance and waited. Panting and tense, his hand gripping the handle of the can, he swore to crack their skulls if they dared to come in. There was no one about. Through the narrow windows, the trees outside cast strange shadows that moved about randomly and seemed to people the gloom in the church like a ghostly congregation. Jan was too preoccupied to be affected by the eerie ambiance. He considered his situation. It appeared that his pursuers would refrain from fighting in church. Apart from the front, there was also a side and a back entrance. Since there were seven boys, he had to reckon with two or three of them, whichever way out he took. Meanwhile, he might as well take a short rest. He relaxed, dipped his fingers into the font of holy water and crossed himself. Then he turned to the side altar where Saint Nepomuk, carved in wood and splendidly painted, stood in silent dignity. Jan put down the can, sank to his knees and folded his hands.

'Look, sir,' he said to the holy image, 'they've wasted a whole litre of good cow's milk, and they've mucked up my clothes. Mother will be cross. And ... and, sir, they won't fight honestly.'

He stopped his address. How could he best explain to the saint that he didn't mind a straight fight, that it was the unfairness of being faced with an overwhelming number of enemies that enraged his sense of justice. More than that, it hurt him deeply. After all, barely two years ago, these very enemies had been his friends. Together they had fooled about on their way home from school, had fished for sticklebacks and had shared many adventures. He had been their leader, but now...?

Why should he be punished for the turn of events? He thought of his father, whose helpfulness to a neighbour had started the trouble. He recalled how people used to call his father 'Merry Svoboda' or 'Strong Svoboda'. Now they referred to him as 'the Squeezer', the man who had squeezed his neighbour out of his property.

Jan drew a deep breath and looked defiantly towards the main exit. Whatever the villagers called him, his father was still champion amateur wrestler of Moravia, 'Pavel Svoboda, the strong one', who couldn't be thrown by anybody and who still was merry at home.

It had to be admitted that his father had gone into this with his eyes open. Jan often remembered the night when he had overheard his parents argue about lending Josef Stanek the money. 'It's too risky,' his mother had said. 'Let him go to the bank. Why doesn't he want to go to the bank?'

'Because he doesn't trust them. They're too strict. If he didn't pay back in time, they wouldn't wait till he recovered. They'd grab his land on the cheap and sell it for good money.'

'And what would Mr Svoboda do for him?' His mother's voice had been sarcastic. 'I hope generous Mr Svoboda isn't thinking of lending him the money without guarantee? I hope Mr Svoboda will remember that not only he, but also I and even the children had to worked hard for every krona we've saved. What happens if he doesn't pay back?'

His father had given one of his hearty laughs. 'Of course, he'll pay back. Josef Stanek is an honest man. We've been friends for years. Surely, you know him as well as I do.'

'No one can foretell the future,' his mother had replied. 'If he's so safe, why won't his other pals chip in as well?'

'Cause they're a mean lot. Look, love. I know it's hard earned money, but I can't let an old pal down.'

There was quite a pause before Jan had heard his mother again. She had spoken with deliberation, her voice revealing an unfamiliar hardness. 'Very well, Pavel. Lend him the money. But I insist it is done through a solicitor with the same conditions the bank is asking for. If he defaults, he loses the land. Don't look so shocked. If you're not thinking of your family's future, I must.'

His father had sighed: 'I suppose it'll be better for him than the bank. If the worst should happen, at least we could give him breathing space.' And then he had laughed again. 'You're such a pessimist, my love. Always expecting trouble.'

This had been two years ago. Jan still remembered how proud he had been of his father's generous support of a friend in need. In contrast, how petty and mean his mother had seemed. Unfortunately, time had proved her right. Stanek couldn't pay and, after a lengthy period of grace, the Svobodas had taken possession of nearly half of his land. After that, Stanek had lost his nerve. He had started to drink and his position had rapidly gone from bad to worse.

About a year later, Jan had witnessed another momentous scene. He had been in a back corner of the barn, tidying up a toolbox. His father and Josef Stanek had come in, too deep in conversation to notice him. He had known that he should have revealed his presence but curiosity had held him back. What's more, he had quietly moved behind the threshing machine from where he could observe without himself being seen.

Stanek, a large, well built man, at least half a head taller than his father, seemed now to have shrunk to the same height. His jacket was hanging loosely from his bent shoulders, and his face, Jan had been shocked to notice, was haggard yet strangely puffy. The sight of the bloodshot eyes that expressed such depth of dejection had almost made him gasp. How could a grown man be in such a state of despair?

'Come, sit down,' his father had said. 'Tell me what's the matter.'

Stanek's voice, though audible enough, had seemed strangely frail. 'Frantisek left last week, and now Petr too has gone. Both got jobs in Blansko.' He had sighed, shaking his head. 'Just think, Pavel, to have four sons and not one of them willing to stick it out; not one of them interested in the farm. How can I run it without more help? They know I can't pay for extra labour with all those bills overdue.'

'What does Bozena say?' his father had asked.

'She's had enough. Too much worry and no reward for hard work. She says, that if I sell out now, there'll be enough to start a new life elsewhere. But if I hang on, she'll leave me.'

Jan had seen his father spontaneously put his hand on Stanek's arm. 'What are you going to do?'

'What can I do? She's right. I'm near the age when I should be handing over to my sons. I've no longer the strength to fight on. But to quit like this, after so many years!' His voice had broken into a sob. 'It's hard, Pavel. A lifetime's work wasted.' Then he had pulled himself together. 'She says we could get a little smallholding and grow enough to feed ourselves and just a little extra for sale. She wouldn't mind getting the odd job in a shop or factory to help things along. She's made up her mind, Pavel, she can't face any more hassle here.'

'So you want to sell the farm?'

'Yes ... I want you to buy it. I know you'll give me a fair price. But that's not all. You're a good farmer and you've always been good to us. It'd be a comfort to me to know it's in your hands.'

As Jan listened, he had felt so sorry for old Stanek that tears had trickled down his cheeks. He watched his father put his arm around the older man's shoulders. There had been quite a pause before he answered. 'Josef, old friend, I want to do the right thing by you. But you know how the villagers feel about all this. They're land-hungry and anxious to grab the fields for themselves. They already resent what I've got now. They're already whispering that I tricked you out of half of your property and that I'm out to ruin you. So far, they didn't come out into the open because you were here to deny it and stand up for me. But imagine what they'll be like if I get the lot and you're no longer here? I've got to live here, Josef. I must think of my family. I don't want them to be outcasts.'

This time, there had been an even longer silence. At last Stanek answered. 'I know what we'll do. At the time of sale I'll make a declaration. I'll explain how the road downhill started and developed. I'll make it clear that everything you did was at my request and for my benefit. It'll be a document certified by a solicitor. Then, if any of the bastards make false accusations, you can take them to court. That'll stop them. And if I'm still alive, I'll testify for you.'

Jan had been moved but also excited. He had known how sorry his father felt for old Stanek and, at the same time, how tempting the acquisition of more land must have been to him. He understood, because he felt the same. Young though he was, he too had that passionate love for the land, that possessive hunger that only those born to the soil can understand. He stood in his hiding place, gripping the machine's metal bar, willing him to buy. When at last his father agreed, Jan had felt as relieved as Stanek. The men had risen and Stanek, emotional and grateful, grasped his father's hand in both of his. 'God bless you Pavel. You're not only good, but also brave.'

Alone again, Jan had sat down, feeling quite weak. The tension and emotion had been overwhelming. In the still comfort of the barn, hardly aware of the outside noises, he had let his thoughts drift. Then, suddenly, he realised with awe that the new, combined Svoboda Stanek farm would be the largest in the area and one day, it would all be his.

Now, a year later, he was in church, another silent place, trying to recover from one of the consequences of that eventful day. 'Holy Saint Nepomuk', he whispered, 'you know what it's all about. I thank you again for making the takeover so smooth. Father got a mortgage for improvements and has already started to pay back. He's engaged a lot more men from other villages – good workers who have nothing to do with our malicious lot. The harvest is super. Everything's running like clockwork. But you know what's wrong. Our villagers are getting more vicious by the day. Please, sir, calm them down, make them forget their envy, make them normal as they used to be.'

He sighed. He felt lonely. He needed a pal. If only he could make friends with Karel, who had just arrived from Prague to spend his holidays in the village. That was why he had to meet him today, before the other boys got a chance to tell him about 'The Squeezer'.

'Dear Saint Nepomuk,' he prayed, 'let me have Karel as a friend and, please, give me strength to beat up those dogs outside.' Piously, he crossed himself and rose.

The two boys fell upon him the instant he left the church. Jan pushed the little, thin one aside, who stumbled and knocked his head against the wall. He staggered back only to be pushed again, this time by Jaroslav who bawled: 'Out of my way, I'll deal with that mean little squeezer.'

'You stupid crumpet!' gasped Jan at the baker's boy who, bent on personal revenge, had gripped him by the throat and was trying to force him down. Jan stepped back as far as he could before digging his knee into Jaroslav's groin. With a curse, Jaroslav let go and somehow managed to avoid the can, which then clanked loudly against the wall. They came to grips again, fighting each other with all the fury of their young bodies. They were about equally matched, the farmer's agility making up for the baker's greater bulk. They separated, only to take breath for another tussle. Out of the corner of his eye, Jan saw the little boy run away to fetch the others. At that moment Jaroslav charged at him again. Jan clenched his teeth. He had to work fast now. With one lightening movement he tripped up his attacker and, with a blow that felt like having cracked his knuckles, struck him to the ground.

Hearing the approaching voices and footsteps of the other boys, he made a quick dash through the yew hedge, then ran across the churchyard, jumping over flower borders and graves as he went. Panting, he reached the gap in the wall that gave onto the lane leading to Willow Farm.

His mother's eyes widened. His scratched face and torn and bespattered clothes felt so much worse under her silent gaze.

'I'm sorry I spilled the milk,' muttered Jan.

'Are you hurt?' she asked with that peculiar flatness of voice that a stranger might have taken for indifference, but which to him betrayed her suppressed emotion.

He shook his head.

She took the can and, throwing a fleeting glance over its dents and patches of chipped enamel, turned towards the kitchen.

Jan darted across the yard to reach the pump in the kitchen garden before the farm hands could see him in this state. He had just stripped off his shirt when Lidka, his elder sister, arrived with soap and towel and clean clothes.

'Oh, what have they done to you,' she cried, throwing her arms around him. She was two years older than he and buxomly pretty. He freed himself. Although he loved her, her demonstrative display of affection always embarrassed him.

'Don't worry,' he said gruffly, trying to make his voice sound as masculine as possible, 'I gave as good as I got.'

As a special concession he let her examine his scratches, but would not allow any further fussing, afraid it might encourage her to mother him for days on end.

She worked the pump, and he put his head, limbs and torso in turn under the icy stream. Then he went behind the blackcurrant bushes to dry himself and change, throwing his dirty shorts back at her.

'Don't be long,' she called, 'we'll be leaving soon – we're cutting on the forest side today.'

Jan worked with quiet efficiency, spreading the corn for drying as it fell from his father's scythe. He was used to manual labour and expected nothing else, not even during school holidays. It was harvest time. Every hand was needed. Later, when they had saved enough money, they intended to buy one of those modern harvesting machines. Until then they had to carry on in the old way. He looked ahead to where Vaclav and Manil, the hired hands, were wielding their scythes with rhythmic precision. Behind them worked his mother and Lidka, their red underskirts showing as they bent over the corn. He continued to labour steadily, giving no hint of his inner turmoil. Today he would run away and not return until dusk. He glanced at his father's muscular body and brawny arms. This time, he feared, it would cost him a thrashing.

Jan listened, then stood up. The others too stopped working and watched the 10.15 express train thunder along the high bank that bordered the far side of the fields. Then they turned and, carefully avoiding the cut corn, walked across the stubbles towards the edge of the wood. There, little Mara was skipping about, her thin voice greeting them with excitement. Barely seven years old, she was minding the cows grazing on the grass verge, at the same time keeping an eye on their baby sister Resa.

'Look,' she piped, 'isn't it lovely?' All of them, as they stepped from the vibrating heat into the shade of the woods, had to admire her treasure. It was a little skull, gleaming white between her grubby fingers. Jan had found a dead squirrel the week before and they had put it on their favourite ant-heap to be eaten to the bone.

'The other parts have come unstuck,' she complained, 'and I've been ever so careful picking them up. But the head's alright. Look, sir, the head is lovely.'

'Yes,' smiled Svoboda, 'they've made a clean job of it.'

Jan had seen other fathers spoil their children's joy with words of impatient indifference. 'He's kind, but he won't be kind to me tonight,' he thought. He wondered whether he should ask for permission to spend the day with Karel, but felt sure it wouldn't be granted. And why should he be let off? Every one of them had to work: even little Mara was tied to her duties. Well, he would steal the time and pay for it. But he had never before had a serious beating and he was afraid. Worse still, he knew that running away like this would deeply upset his parents. Yet Karel was worth it. Surely, he couldn't break his promise to a new friend.

Jan settled with the others round the basket of food and the large can of malt coffee Lidka had brought from the wagon. Meanwhile, his mother had fetched the baby from its hammock of sacking slung between two pines. Feeding it, she sat turned away from the family. Munching his black bread and dripping, Jan looked at her broad back. She wouldn't understand him either. None of them would, except perhaps Lidka. They didn't realize how desperately he needed a friend. Being fond of one's sisters wasn't the same. Absentmindedly, Jan took the mug of coffee passed to him. It was lucky he had overcome his shyness and had spoken to Karel straight away. It had not been easy, for in his long trousers and townish jacket Karel had looked very smart and much older than fifteen. But Jan had matured a lot during this last unhappy year and it was difficult to believe that he was only just fourteen.

'Fields and miles and miles of woods!' Karel had exclaimed. 'What on earth can one do in such a place?' Incredulously, he had listened to Jan's assurances that one could spend a whole day in the forest without a minute's boredom. They had agreed to meet today.

The mother turned round and buttoned her blouse. She passed the baby to her husband who held it upright against his shoulder and patted its back. It burped contentedly while staring with large, blue eyes at the surrounding faces. Jan asked for another piece of bread. He was no longer hungry, but this would probably be his last meal today. He looked at each one in turn. They appeared happy enough, or was their cheerfulness only a veneer, like his own? Their relationship was warm and close, closer than it had ever been. Was that because of village hostility?

Jan waited for his elders to break up the mid-morning rest. He looked at the field and noticed with pride that his father had already cut more wheat than the men. In two to three years' time he too would be mowing and little Mara would be old enough to spread the cut wheat for drying, assuming they were still without a harvesting machine. They always worked in teams of two. The thought, that his absence would disrupt the smooth flow of the reaping routine, made him feel guilty. Vaclav and Manil knocked out their pipes. Jan rose but didn't follow them back to the field. Nobody took any notice as he strolled into the wood.

When he arrived at the bridge, Karel was already waiting for him. Jan had been a little awed by the town boy's smartness the previous day. It was a relief to find him now in shorts and a faded blue jersey. Karel's long legs too, white and thin, restored Jan's self-confidence: they were so obviously inferior to his own firm calves and tanned thighs. He was a little late, but Karel just smiled and said 'hello'.

'God be with you', replied Jan in the manner of the Moravian country folk. Both felt a trifle shy and hardly spoke as they followed the rough cart track deeper into the wood. For the first ten minutes they walked through the fir tree nursery in the bright heat of the morning. The trees there were not tall enough to cast any useful shade.

'Look!' cried Karel as a streak of brown flashed past them. With excitement he watched a fluffy white tail bob up and down before disappearing in the undergrowth.   'Gosh, I've never seen a live hare before.' Jan smiled. It had only been a rabbit, but he said nothing and walked on. Barefoot, he seemed to glide along the dry mud-ridges of the track. Soon, they were more at ease with each other. Together they watched a squirrel, inspected a fox's earth and tickled crickets out of their hiding places.

Karel shuddered as they entered the old wood. It was dark and eerie. The bare trunks of the firs, tall and austere, supported a canopy of green that almost shut out the sky: the carpet of needles absorbed every sound, and the stillness seemed sombre and solid. When their eyes became accustomed to the dark they noticed bright patches of fungi that challenged the gloom.

'Company charge!' shouted Karel and stormed towards the first group of toadstools. With a mighty war cry, Jan too went into battle. Their yells echoed in the wood as the red caps of the fly agarics rolled like bloody heads in all directions, their compact little stronghold utterly shattered. The heroes revelled in the glorious slaughter and, drunk with victory, routed every garrison on their way. Karel was about to crush another colony of fungi when Jan stopped him.

'Not those, leave them alone!'

'Rubbish. They're all enemies.'

'No, they're not. They're edible mushrooms.'

'Bad luck for them. They're innocent victims of war then.'

'Stop!' shouted Jan. He wasn't going to let a townie ruin their food. 'These mushrooms are good to eat. Besides, some of the poor folk gather them and sell them to make a little extra money.'

Jan could see that Karel was annoyed, but he stood his ground. 'Come on,' he said. 'Let's make for the opening, there may still be some wild strawberries.'

Sunlight greeted them as they approached the glade. Here, on the edge of the wood, they came upon a giant anthill. They stopped and watched. 'Rush hour in Wenceslas Square', commented Karel and, before Jan could intervene, he had thrust a stick deep into it and then churned it round to produce a crater. The resulting panic delighted him. The ants were frantically darting about, trying to save their treasured eggs. Karel picked up an even thicker stick and beat it down onto the teeming life.

'What the hell are you up to?' yelled Jan.

'Killing the enemy!' And down came his stick again with a thud.

Jan caught his arm. 'Stop it.'

'What're you freaking about? They're only insects. Insects are bad news. You've got to kill them. Kill the lot. Kill, kill, kill,' he chanted, ready to carry on.

Jan went for him. 'Don't be an idiot. Ants are useful.'

'Are they?' challenged Karel. 'You tell me how.'

'They clean up the place.' Jan spoke with cold disdain. 'They strip carcasses on the spot or drag small dead creatures into their ant-heap. You wouldn't want to be stepping into rotting flesh everywhere, would you?'

'I see,' said Karel sulkily and threw the stick away. He resented having his fun spoiled again. For some minutes they walked in silence till they came to a decline made slippery by layers of dry pine needles. When Jan slid down, Karel followed and thought it great fun. They clambered back and did it again and again. The ant contretemps was forgotten. They found pinecones and held a lengthy competition pelting them at each other that left them happy and exhausted.

'Let's sit down,' said Karel.

'Wait, there's a brook further up.'

This clearing was large and partly overgrown with blackberry bushes. Four larches cast lacy shadows onto the moss-covered ground, just above the brooklet that seemed to be inviting them to rest. The boys settled down. First, they drank from the cool water, then splashed their arms and faces and finally dipped their feet.

'I don't know how you manage without shoes,' said Karel.

'You get used to it,' replied Jan. 'Look, my soles are like leather by now.'

'But you wear shoes in winter?'

'Oh, yes, and to school, and to church on Sundays.'

'You go to church?'

'Of course.' Jan was surprised. 'Don't you?'

'No. None of us go, except when there's something on. A christening or a wedding.'

This seemed strange and sinful to Jan but he did not voice his disapproval. Karel unwrapped his sandwiches. 'Where are yours?'

'I've forgotten mine.'

'Here.' Karel held out half of his, and Jan, who was hungry, accepted gladly.

For a while they ate in silence and Jan thought of his family, who would also be eating their midday meal: plum dumplings with crushed poppy seeds and soured cream. Never mind, the egg sandwiches too were quite nice, even if not enough. He imagined his mother and sister talking about him in subdued voices while his father swore to whip the skin off his back. Jan wondered about the instrument. Would it be a stick, a brush, or a belt? The thought of it scared him but he hoped he'd be able to endure the pain without crying.

'Have you any brothers and sisters?' he asked, mainly

to divert himself from his apprehension.

Karel nodded. 'A brother – Vasha. He's a trained mechanic. Doing his military service now.'

'Does he like it?'

'Not much, but I shall. I'll join the tank corps. It's a man's life, and once the war has started I'll soon get promoted.'

Jan marvelled at Karel's self-assurance. 'But why another war?'

'Because they're all against us.' recited Karel. 'The Austrians, the Germans, the Fascists, the Jews – everybody. Masaryk's achievements after the Great War and our newly won liberty are at stake.'

It sounded grand to Jan, though he didn't really understand what it was all about. The other boy seemed so grown up, braving a hostile world.

'You too will have to fight when it comes to it.'

'I should like to,' said Jan, 'but they need me on the farm.'

Karel snorted scornfully. 'They'll have to do without you. It's time the women worked.'

'But they're working already,' exclaimed Jan, 'and jolly hard too.'

Karel was nonplussed. Not knowing what to say, he changed the subject. 'Our Vasha,' he boasted, 'is interested in the country's economy. He's been looking at agriculture. He says our farms and smallholdings are badly run. He says it's time we had collectives.'

Jan flushed. He didn't know about collectives, but he was a farmer's son. He could overlook Karel's lack of religion, but he would never tolerate this. 'Our farms are perfectly run,' he said sharply. 'We don't need mechanics to tell us what to do.'

'Don't take on,' joked Karel after an embarrassed moment. 'I don't mind who runs them, as long as there's enough grub.'

Jan was pleased that his protest had been effective. He picked up the empty sandwich bag and disappeared in the jungle of blackberry bushes. While gathering the fruit he wondered whether he should take Karel to watch the red deer. He had come upon their favourite glade during one of his lonely rambles, and their grace and beauty had repeatedly lured him back. Nobody knew about this special grazing ground except, he supposed, the gamekeeper. On Saturday afternoons, when the other boys met for games, he would return there and with great patience get as close as possible. This time of the year the deer were very shy, and to be near enough to see their eyelashes and quivering nostrils gave him a thrill of achievement.

No, he decided. Karel was a city boy whose clumsiness was bound to alarm them. Even if all went well, could he be trusted? He was bound to hear about 'The Squeezer'. He might then join the other boys and betray him. Jan decided not to take the risk.

It took quite a time to fill the bag. On his return he found Karel fast asleep. He sat down and relaxed, watching the brooklet, the clouds and a hunting dragonfly. He thought how strange it was that Karel and he lived in the same country, yet hardly knew anything about each other's background. He realised how very little he knew about people, about life and about the world. What were all those threatening dangers Karel had talked about? Those mighty forces that were determined to destroy their lives? With some effort he pushed these depressing thoughts aside. What was the use? He hadn't a clue what it all meant. There was nothing he could do. He started to nibble a few more blackberries, when Karel woke up. He stretched himself with a sheepish grin: 'I must have dropped off for a few minutes,' he said.

Jan laughed and pointed at the long shadows. It was getting late. Since it would take well over an hour to reach home, they decided to make no further detours. Yet they couldn't help lingering on the way, since everything was new to Karel, and at every turning there was something to be inspected and explained. Walking along, their chatter never ceased. Karel described his life in Prague, the flat he lived in, what his family did and how he spent his spare time. He made everything sound grand and exciting and basked in Jan's admiration.

When they reached the slope that had been deforested the previous year, they had an open view of the village below. Dusk was deepening and a number of lights shone through the evening mist. Willow Farm too could still be seen, a large, squat building dominating its surrounding out-houses and stables. The sight of his home returned Jan to reality, and with it fear. Fear of punishment, and more still, fear of losing his new friend.

'I shan't be free again till Saturday afternoon. There's a lot of work at harvest time.'

'Oh,' said Karel.

Jan hesitated. 'In the meantime you'll be meeting the village boys. They ... they'll stop you from seeing me again.'

'Stop me!' exclaimed Karel. 'Like hell they will. Why should they, anyway?'

This wasn't easy. Why was he so ashamed of being an outcast, when it wasn't his fault? He took a deep breath and started on his father's story. Though he had rehearsed it many times in his mind, he still had to concentrate to report the events clearly and objectively without being side-tracked into emotional justifications.

He threw a sidelong glance at his companion. Karel, his thumbs in his belt, was walking slowly beside him, watching the track for obstructions as he listened. When Jan had finished, he kicked a lump of soil and whistled. 'Frankly, I can't see why they're making all that fuss. Seems your old man bought the land right enough. If they missed their chance, that's their silly fault.'

Jan rejoiced over Karel's reaction, and yet, barely admitting it to himself, he was dissatisfied. Karel's attitude was not a proof of friendship. The land meant nothing to him. He wasn't involved. His tolerance was the fruit of indifference. They were silent again, each in thought. Reaching the end of the High Street, they stopped in front of the cottage that belonged to Karel's aunt.

'Mind you,' continued Karel as if there had been no pause, 'I know what the boys are up to. It's the fun of the hunt. There used to be a little yid down our street, a weedy, scraggy lad. We other kids had a rare old time chasing and threatening him. The more he got scared, the more we enjoyed it.'

Jan was taken aback. 'But why? What has he done?'

'Nothing. It's enough him being a yid, a Jew. Jews are bad news. You know what they're like.'

Jan didn't know. As far as he was aware he'd never seen a Jew. He supposed there must be a good reason. He didn't want to betray his ignorance but couldn't help saying: 'If he deserves to be punished, it should be one to one. Ganging up is cowardly. I've got to keep facing the mob and, believe me, it takes guts.'

'Alright, you win,' conceded Karel. 'Next Jew boy I come across, I'll tackle all by myself.' He slapped Jan on the back. 'I can see you're tough. You've got what it takes. It'll give me quite a kick to be on the other side for a change. You wait, we'll lick them proper.'

'Thanks,' said Jan. They grinned and shook hands. 'See you Saturday.'

'Till Saturday,' Karel called back as he walked down to the cottage.

By the time Jan reached the farm, it had become quite dark. A wedge of light fell across the yard and onto the chained-up mongrel. He wagged his tail but did not bark as Jan approached the kitchen window. The light from grandmother's old table lamp was warm and friendly and caught the fair hair of the three people sitting silently at the table. It meant that work was done and the evening meal was over. His mother and sister were sewing and his father, with wrinkled brow and severe expression, was bent over a book. Jan watched for a while. There was no sign of the usual friendly atmosphere, and he knew it was on his account. Suddenly, his father looked up and their eyes met.

Svoboda rose slowly, unfastening his belt as he went. Jan waited in the yard. For a moment he saw Lidka's face at the window, tense but controlled. 'Oh, God,' he thought, 'don't let him use the buckle end. Not the buckle end, please.' He faced his father.

'Take them off. Over the block.'

Svoboda did not use the buckle end, but he was a powerful man and did not spare his arm. High sang the strap into the night before biting into the tender flesh. Jan could not stop his tears, but he clawed the block and bit his lips and never gave a sound. When it was over, he drew up his pants with difficulty. His limbs were weak and shaky.

'Well,' asked his father, 'have you anything to say?'

'I'm sorry. I ... I didn't run off to dodge work ... I was meeting the new boy from Prague. Mrs Suk's nephew Karel. I had to meet him before the others did. He's my friend now.' Jan's voice had recently broken and it kept snapping with emotion.

'And you didn't even bother to ask my permission.'

Jan hung his head.

'You'll sleep in the stable – without food, of course.' This was the routine punishment for disobedience, and had been uttered crisply, almost cheerfully. After a few steps towards the kitchen Svoboda turned round. 'If you like, you can invite that boy any evening, as long as it's after work.'

Jan waited till his father had shut the kitchen door, then wiped his eyes with the back of his hand. He felt ravenous now. He would have sucked some eggs, but the henhouse was locked. Slowly, he made his way to the stable. In the far corner was a pile of spare hay and, as he pulled it into shape to make his bed, his hand touched something hard. It was a tin basin, turned up over a plate to protect a slab of bread and a piece of smoked sausage.

'Lidka,' he thought gratefully.

He settled in the hay, easing himself gently onto his side. All was quiet, bar the occasional tinkling of chains and swishing of tails. As he chewed his supper, he could feel the steady burning of the belt-marks. He gave a little sigh: it had been a wonderful day.

TOTAL RECALL

There are things I should prefer to forget. Yet they keep floating to the surface of my consciousness like dead fish on water. Other memories, though anxiously courted, stubbornly refuse to reveal themselves.

I know old people who can recall their childhood in great detail, and who will happily recite the endless ballads of their youth. My mother, at the age of 90, bereft of health and confined to her bed, sang to me: '*Freiheit die ich meine ...*', a passionate song that cries out for freedom. Her sightless gaze fixed on the distance, she sang with a still sweet voice stanza after stanza and I found it hard to hold back my tears. I too had learned this song at school but had retained none of it.

Even one of my early thespian triumphs defies recollection. The occasion: an end-of-term performance when I recited 'Merry Augustin', a poem based on a supposedly historic character. Augustin was a harmless rogue, a dissolute entertainer and bagpipe player who roamed the streets of Vienna at the time of the great plague in 1679. According to my mother, several women in the audience wept, and the one next to her declared that cold shivers were running down her spine. What a dramatic ballad! Yet I can't remember a single line of it.

Then there are the children's games; those enactments of arcane rituals, passed on from child to child. I enjoyed singing and dancing with my peers and it never occurred to me to question the stories or their meaning. There was comfort in unanimity of action. The herd instinct, I suppose.

To begin with, the Florian game. The children hold hands, walk round in a circle and sing. Translated, the verse goes: 'Florian, Florian, he has lived for seven years. Seven years have gone and little so and so (naming one of the children) turns round.' The named child faces out from the circle and the walking resumes. Then the name of the seventh child from the previous one is called out and they too turn to face outwards. When the whole circle it turning outwards, the game is over. Simple enough, but what does it mean? Was this turning a turning away from this world, a symbol of death? Poor little Florian, why was he destined to die so young? No one knew. Fatalistic acceptance and no questions asked.

Another game. A girl sits in the middle of the circle. A boy enters and mimes the story as the children chant:

'Mariechen sat upon a stone, upon a stone, upon a stone. Enter brother Karl now, Karl now, Karl now. He stabs Mariechen in the heart, in the heart, in the heart'. Try as I will, I cannot remember what came before or after this scene. But I can't help speculating. Was this Mariechen's punishment for a misdeed? Disgracing the family honour perhaps? Or was it sibling rivalry pushed to the extreme? Or, shame on me for such suspicion, was it the tragic outcome of an incestuous affair? Whatever it was, the little girls didn't break rank to lynch brother Karl, but placidly accepted the deed and sang on.

The next game too is shrouded in mystery. The verses go:

'Machet auf das Tor,

machet auf das Tor,

es kommt ein gruener Wagen.

Ja was will er, will er denn,

ja was will er will er denn?

Er will die Tochter haben.'

It could be translated as: 'Open wide the gate, open wide the gate; a green vehicle is approaching. Say what does it, does it want? Say what does it does it want? It wants to have the daughter.'

To start with, there is the word *Wagen*, vehicle, the generic term for anything on wheels. In view of the game's age, we can assume it to be horse-drawn. Judging by the imperious call for entry, it isn't any old cart, but most likely a carriage of some importance. Further, there is the feeling that it had been expected. No mention of a passenger or a coachman. So, there we have this carriage in green, driving up empty like the *Marie Celeste*, and what happens? It – *it* mind you, wants to have the daughter. Not collect her for a party, or pick her up for a little spin. It wants to have the daughter.

We have all heard of mighty Zeus, the randiest of Greek gods, who thought nothing of adopting the oddest disguises for the sake of gratification. Now, a bull, swan, or shower of gold is weird enough, but a green carriage! No, the line has to be drawn somewhere. The truth may be much more sinister in spite of the declared greenness. In fact, I think it is the word green that points to the horrific end.

Just imagine the scene: the ghostly carriage arrives. The girl, a virgin, of course, dressed in a pure white shift, is led out. There is a wide circle of onlookers. They stare, motionless. The girl is silent and pale with fear. But she has been prepared by her elders and knows her duty. Without the razzmatazz of *The Rite of Spring* she enters the green carriage, which takes her away through the barren winter landscape. Is it not obvious that she will sacrifice herself? That she will pay with her young blood for the fertility and growth of the coming year?

I turn with relief to the last fragment of my recollections. A single-stanza game – and a life philosophy in a nutshell.

The children form the traditional circle. They stand in pairs, the boys outside, the girls inside. A boy dances round the inner circle singing:

'Thief, oh thief I ought to hate you,

since my girl you did steal.

Never mind, I'll let you keep her

and I'll find another soon.

Tra-la tralala, tra-la tralala, tra-la trala ...' and so on.

The other children join in while the boy picks a girl and

dances round with her before settling in his vacant space. Whereupon the bereft partner in turn dances round and steals a girl to fill his space. And so, tralala, it goes merrily on. A foretaste of the permissive society, I wonder? But thank Zeus, there's no aggro, no bitterness, no histrionic show of grief. What a lesson: accept your situation, find a remedy and get on with life.

As to all the missing verses and possible wrong interpretations, I could undertake some research. But somehow I doubt whether I'll ever get round to it. I wonder, is there anybody who goes back to the mid-1920s in central Europe who could enlighten me?

PART TWO:
STORIES OF LOVE AND LOSS

THE SINGING CHAIR

When Quentin York came to the gate he stopped. He had never seen it open. In fact, he knew it as permanently locked. After parking his Bentley in the side street he had frequently walked along the iron railings of this town square garden and, on occasions, had given way to the impulse of trying the handle. Always in vain. Why was it open now? Something prompted him to enter and close the gate behind him.

Once past the bushes that obscured the view from the gate, he was delighted to see a long lawn with beautiful old trees. On the far side a short herbaceous border flanked an open-fronted summerhouse. Automatically he walked towards it. 'I haven't time ... that blasted meeting,' he reminded himself, but carried on nevertheless.

Seated on the bench inside, he enjoyed both the suntrap effect and the view. This was glorious weather for mid-October. The coloured foliage had only just started to fall in any quantity. In front of him, a magnificent beech tree seemed to release its copper treasure with an almost languid air. He watched the leaves float and spiral to the ground. In the treetops the birds went unseen about their business. Judging by the uncut lawn and drifts of fallen leaves, maintenance was infrequent. But since his ideal garden was a barely controlled wilderness, it was a point in its favour.

This idyllic interlude, bursting so unexpectedly into his hectic morning, suddenly seemed significant and precious. How did he get caught up in this frantic go-getting, money-grubbing mode of existence? This wasn't what he had wanted from life. He supposed that he had taken the line of least resistance and let himself drift. His father, an academic, had never taken the trouble to teach him anything. But young Quentin, living in a world where literature, music and the arts were taken for granted, and where a facility for discussion and debate was essential to hold your own, had, without conscious effort, absorbed the values and skills of his milieu. And yet, though the acquisition of wealth had been far from his mind, he had, almost accidentally, found himself in a job demanding financial acumen. It probably was his relaxed, detached attitude to money that had made it easier for him to judge opportunities more clearly and to take inspired risks. He had been sought-after and headhunted. He had become the man with the Midas touch. Eventually, he had set up his own company with the intention of retiring in affluence by the time he was forty. For years he had been ignoring his birthdays but now it suddenly struck him that he actually was forty today.

'I could go anytime,' he mused. 'Could start phasing out now. I really must stop wasting my life. Why should I feel guilty about sitting here, for instance? Hell, I'll tell them I can't make it. Get them to carry on without me.' As he reached for his phone, he accidentally pushed his briefcase down the back of the seat, dislodging an accumulation of leaves. As he picked it up he noticed a partly exposed rectangular object which turned out to be a book. He could not tell how long it had been there but it appeared to be unharmed. The long dry spell had been in its favour.

He made a quick call to cancel his business appointment before continuing his examination of the book. This elegant, slender volume, he was surprised to discover, was a collection of poems by Rainer Maria Rilke: the *Duino Elegies* in the original German. Yet the dedication on the flyleaf was in English: 'To dear Eugene from his loving aunt Elvira. September 1951'. He ran his hands over the cover. It was of dark blue leather, beautifully inlaid and embossed in a simple, abstract design. The gilding too was still in good condition. Eugene, whoever he was, must have taken good care of it – apart from losing it. Quentin was intrigued. What had aunt Elvira been like? The large bold handwriting pointed to self-assurance, and the ornate copperplate style led him to assume that she had been an older person even then. The unique binding revealed not only good taste and affluence but seemed to indicate affection for what must have been an unusual young man. In his late teens, Quentin himself, in spite of his declared agnosticism, had been captivated by Rilke's spirituality and otherworldliness. And he still had a soft spot for him. Of course, by now, this Eugene was bound to be an old boy; mid-eighties, most likely. Quentin stroked the covers with the appreciation of a connoisseur. He liked the feel of the book, its very size and weight. It seemed to snuggle into his hands as if it were at home there. He wished it were his.

As he flicked through the pages, he came across a bookmark, a folded piece of paper. It turned out to be a bill of recent date for a bespoke silk shirt and two silk cravats. It was made out to E. Kalinsky Esq. Well, that was that. The address was number 25 in this very Georgian square, so he had no excuse for not returning the book.

Why was he so loath to part with it? Not only did he own a copy of the same poems, but was also sufficiently well off to commission any number of art bindings if he wished to do so. His thoughts turned with pleasure to his book collection, now splendidly displayed in his new flat. He had moved only recently and everything was still fresh and exciting, especially the view across the Thames. It had always been his dream to live by the river.

There had been an additional reason for moving. Samantha. He didn't actually want to break with her. She was good in bed and, to give her her due, she never let him down in public. Not only was she attractive and stylish, but also intelligent enough to keep quiet when the conversation went above her head. But she had become increasingly more possessive and interfering.

He regretted ever having given her the key to his flat, for not only had she taken it upon herself to rearrange things there without consulting him, she seemed to take it for granted that she had the right to know all about his affairs, including his business. Though her snooping had been annoying, he had so far been able to frustrate her efforts. However, what riled him most were her constant attempts to pry into his mind and very soul. It seemed she could not bear the fact that parts of him were inaccessible to her, that she could not get at his innermost being. She had even tried to research his past and questioned his friends and acquaintances. Though she did so with discretion, he had been incensed when he found out. At first, assuming that she loved him, he had felt somewhat guilty for shutting her out, but soon realized that her attempt to get so close to him was her craving for control. In fact she was calculating and manipulative.

As with so many things in his life, he had drifted into this relationship and let things take their course. He knew he did not love her but it seemed pleasant and convenient to have her company when going about. He did not resent her constant demand for expensive presents; he knew she was out for what she could get and thought it was a fair exchange. But, obviously, she wanted more.

'Quentin, darling,' she had said one day, with that little-girl voice she used when asking for something special. 'Wouldn't it be lovely if I didn't always have to leave you and trudge home to my place?'

'You never trudge, I always take you home.'

'But darling, think of the time and effort we could save if we were together. Also, I'd love to look after you.'

'You know my housekeeper does all the looking after I need.' Alarm bells had seriously started to ring. One fine day, he'd felt sure, he would find her installed with her possessions, presenting him with a *fait accompli*. This had made him decide to move, and he did so quickly, without consulting her. He had also taken the risk of losing her altogether by refusing to give her a key to the new flat. She had kept her anger and frustration under control and accepted the situation without comment. He realized that she thought him too good a catch to give up. He had to hand it to her; she was a sticker and a trier.

He sighed and watched a squirrel run across the lawn. The trees and shrubs seemed ablaze in the morning sun. He couldn't remember ever having experienced such a magic display of autumn colours. And still he was the only person in this idyllic place. He just had to stay and savour every minute. He relaxed, letting his thoughts drift. One day, he hoped, he would find a woman whose close interest he wouldn't resent, with whom he would be in tune and eager to share everything. They would truly love each other and she would be the centre and anchor of his life.

'Romantic fool!' he said out loud, convinced that this was only the stuff of literature. Yet sometimes, sleepless in the small hours of the morning, he ached with a vast inner loneliness that only a miracle could cure. And he, in desperation, had longed for and tried to make himself believe in this miracle.

At last, he roused himself to seek number 25. It was a fine Georgian town house. Four steps led up to the pillar-fronted porch. A female voice on the entryphone asked him to come up to the first floor. He found the door ajar, knocked and walked in. To his surprise the rooms leading off the hallway were empty.

A voice called: 'In here!'

Entering, he faced a woman in her late thirties. She wore an apron and rubber gloves and he guessed she was the caretaker or cleaner.

He took the book out of his briefcase. 'I found this. From the invoice inside it I'm assuming that it belongs to Mr Kalinsky'. He handed it to her. She was thin and bony with a long, unremarkable face. He watched her turn a few pages and wondered whether she would notice the quality of the paper and the beautiful font and layout. When she looked at him again he knew that she was fully aware of its value.

'You're too late. Poor Mr K. He passed away ten days ago.' She registered his shock, then handed the book back to him. 'You'd better keep it. The flat's been cleared.'

'But shouldn't it be forwarded to the heirs?'

She gave a little snort. 'It'd mean nothing to him. Him with that fancy name. He never came to visit Mr K. Not ever. Didn't even come to the cremation. Next day he turned up here to have a butchers, then flogged the lot to a dealer.' Her resentment was evident. Then her expression softened: 'Mr K loved his home, you know. He had a lot of books and real nice furniture and things. They took it all, bar that shabby old chair there.'

Quentin turned round. The old-fashioned wing-chair by the window must have looked splendid in its heyday, but now the once dark green leather was faded and cracked, even split in places. There were old scuffmarks and scratches that the high polish could not conceal.

The woman sighed. 'He loved that chair. Used to sit in it a lot, often with his eyes closed. But he wasn't asleep. Now and then his lips was movin' and his head nodded, like to a tune. I was allowed to polish it but he wouldn't hear about having it repaired.'

Quentin barely heard the woman's voice as he felt himself drawn towards the chair. He touched one of the side wings and a strange sensation overcame him. He just had to sit in it. The chair fitted him perfectly. It was like entering an embrace. He became aware of strange, subtle waves or vibrations entering his being and becoming part of him. He would have been hard put to to describe the feeling of serene stillness that flooded his consciousness. A consciousness that seemed suspended in a rarefied sphere of its own. It was as if a long denied inner void was about to be filled. Then, something made him return to normality and he realised that the woman had stopped speaking and was watching him. How long had he been sitting like this? Probably only half a minute, though it seemed much longer. He smiled a little awkwardly and got up.

'I should like to buy this chair. It feels comfortable; seems to be the right shape for me.'

'It would be, sir. You've got the same figure as Mr K. Though the last few years he was kind of frail. But no, you can have it for nothing. Saves me the trouble of having it took away or else it would have to be cut up for the bin. I ain't got the space for it.'

Quentin sensed that, apart from her declared reasons, she was actually keen for him to have it.

'Thank you. I'll send someone to pick it up after lunch. About two o'clock. Will that suit you?'

She nodded and he noticed that she had a rather pleasant smile.

On impulse he asked 'Tell me, please, what was Mr Kalinsky like?'

'He was foreign, Russian. And he was a real gent. Treated everybody with respect.' She gave him an odd look. 'He was quite a toff hisself, but la-di-dah didn't count with him. He looked for the person, even behind this 'ere plastic apron. Yes, he was a kind man.' She paused, and Quentin was in no doubt about her genuine affection for the old man.

'He had a baby grand, you know, used to play real beautiful till the arthritis stopped him. They say, years ago he played in concerts.' She sighed. 'I'll be missing him, that's for sure.'

Quentin thanked her, said goodbye and pressed a fifty-pound note into her hand.

As he walked along the square, the experience in the armchair still clung to him like a lingering fragrance. He felt elated and happy. 'Anybody would think I'd struck a multimillion deal,' he thought, 'not saddled myself with a tatty old chair.'

Impatience made him return home by mid-afternoon. Mrs Bedford, his part-time housekeeper, was bound to have arranged the collection of the chair as instructed. She was a woman in her fifties, reliable and efficient. Her husband, a retired bank clerk, spent most of his time on his allotment growing prize vegetables which benefited all their family and friends including Quentin. Though she had worked for him for many years, they still addressed each other as 'Mrs Bedford' and 'Mr York'. Their formality masked a deep understanding of and liking for each other of which, had she perceived and understood it, Samantha would have been jealous.

When he caught sight of the chair, he had to smile. In this minimalist setting it looked even more incongruous than he had expected. No wonder Mrs Bedford had put it in his bedroom. Knowing him as she did, she appreciated that he would not want to be forced to explain this acquisition to his visitors and friends. The fact that she had placed it by the balcony door in exactly the same position and at the same angle as it had been in Eugene's room, struck him as a good omen.

He strode over to it, ignoring his beloved river view. But then, strangely inhibited, he stopped two paces before it. What made him think it could be more than an inanimate object? Could it be like a creature with consciousness that may well resent having been taken high-handedly from its accustomed environment?

When at last he sank into the chair, the longed-for contact was like a reassuring embrace. He felt as if a long and frustrating journey full of restlessness and disappointments had at last brought him into a harbour of peace. What's more, he knew that no criticism or judgement awaited him: he was being accepted with all his imperfections and faults. He wondered whether his empathy with the late Eugene Kalinsky or his fervent longing for some sort of fulfilment had qualified him for acceptance to this other dimension.

He closed his eyes. The faint noises of the street and river traffic from below faded away and an ethereal melody took their place. He was unable to recognize any instruments but as the approaching sound swelled and vibrated around him he became certain of its human quality. Gradually, a female voice, a rich contralto, rose to prominence. Its enveloping warmth felt personal, almost physical. It was Eugene's aunt Elvira. Quentin could not have said how he knew, but he was certain. He remembered her dedication on the flyleaf: 'To dear Eugene from his loving aunt Elvira'. Fleetingly, he wondered about the nature of their love when, once again, he experienced the sensation of floating and drifting high above, cradled in a comforting embrace that rocked him gently to the wordless song of these mysterious voices. All earthly care vanished and he basked in a sensation of contentment and peace.

Gradually, the sounds of everyday life returned and he became aware of the warm sun-rays on his face and body. He opened his eyes. He was back in his room.

During the next three weeks he treated himself to one or two daily sessions in the chair. He felt he had to ration himself if he wanted to remain active. Of course, he did not accept this experience without curiosity and wonder. Actually, he thought a lot about it. His inclination was to reject fancy psychobabble and quasi religious influences. The explanation, he felt sure, lay in science. Strange as this phenomenon was, it had, like everything else, to be subject to the scientific principles that governed this world. But what principles? He was only too aware of his ignorance in this field. In any case, the so-called Renaissance man and genuine polymath no longer existed. In view of the wealth of discoveries during the last decades alone, there was too much for one man to know. His approach to the question had to be on the schoolboy level of his past.

If you mix certain chemicals together they will, according to the laws of chemistry, produce other chemicals or gases. And if you release an object from your grip, it will be subject to the rules of physics: gravity will make it drop. But what rule was controlling the happenings produced by the chair? It seemed to Quentin that it must have absorbed some waves or arcane matter that had emanated from Eugene. Any person with the appropriate qualities would then be able to, so to speak, plug into the process and receive the message.

We know that the brain sends out electric pulses that can be monitored with the right equipment, and these pulses can even be harnessed to operate certain mechanical objects. Sitting quietly in one's room one is not aware of the hundreds of sound and TV waves that fill our space, unless we have the right devices to connect with them. Quentin speculated that the human brain must be sending out other impulses apart from electrical ones. Though they have as yet remained undiscovered, they may be sufficiently substantial to be absorbed by physical matter, like the chair, ready to be released when the person with the appropriate receiving facility makes contact. Quentin thought, judging from the things he knew about Eugene Kalinsky, that it was likely he possessed sufficient empathy with the man to make this connection.

In any case, whatever the cause of the phenomenon, there was no doubt – so far the effect had been beneficial. He was more relaxed, and since his chronic resentments and frustrations had been reduced, he enjoyed a clearer and more positive outlook on life. He decided to make a new start. He would dispose of the major part of his business and reorganize the rest so that it would function with the minimum input on his part. Four or five weeks in America would be necessary to make most of the arrangements. He would stay with his cousin Denis who played an important role in the organization of world wide charities. This kind of activity appealed to him. He had considered it before as worthwhile work that would be emotionally rewarding. Denis could help him to find the satisfying career he wanted.

His second resolution was to end his relationship with Samantha. She was like the grain of sand in an oyster-shell; she constantly irritated him but failed to inspire him to produce the pearl. Instead, she drew out the worst in him. He did not blame her. His liberal attitude had always made him accept that people are what they are. Though his common sense told him that a sudden, brutal break would be the most effective – perhaps a letter of farewell after his departure – his conscience did not allow him to take this cowardly way out. Since he did not wish to hurt her feelings he would try a gradual loosening of the ties. His five weeks of absence would be a good start, allowing her to get used to being on her own or even, with luck, to find someone else to console her.

As a consequence he was now sitting with her in a

new little Italian restaurant where they were unknown. He thought it wise to take this precaution in case she decided to make a scene. With her new hairstyle and beautiful lace shawl draped over her bare shoulders she looked very attractive against the background of all the bright ethnic tat. Quentin noticed the admiring glances from the neighbouring tables and so, of course, did she. It put her into a good mood. After a couple of glasses of wine, between the main course and the dessert, he told her that he would be going to the United States for about four to five weeks. She reacted instantly.

'Wonderful! How exciting! You will take me with you, won't you?'

He had half expected this. 'Sam, dear, I'm not going on a holiday. This is a business trip.'

'But darling, I wouldn't be in your way, and it would be nice for you to have me to relax with in the evenings and between appointments.'

'It doesn't work that way. I am sure to be caught up in a programme of corporate entertaining which is invariably for men only. In any case, since there is a lot at stake for me, I will have to use all my spare time gathering information, reading up on things and checking contracts. I cannot afford to be distracted by concerns for you. I must keep on top of things.'

'But darling ...'

'Don't you understand? I said NO.' He realized he had to be firm or all was lost. 'And what's more, even on my return to London I'll be very busy. You'll have to get used to seeing a lot less of me in future.'

She looked at him with her beautiful grey eyes and pouted a little. He expected her to protest again but she didn't. Of course, she understood what he had said but he wondered to what extent she was aware that this was the thin end of the wedge for the final break-up. To soften the blow he promised to give her a substantial cheque for the expensive handbag for which she had been hankering. He continued trying to maintain a light-hearted conversation during dinner. Afterwards, he dropped her off at her house, promising to write to her, time permitting. He watched her totter up the steps on her ridiculously high-heeled shoes, wave back at him and disappear in the doorway. Suppressing the faint nigglings of doubt at the back of his mind, he gave a sigh of relief. It had all turned out better than he had expected.

Quentin's negotiations in the US had gone without a hitch and he had been able to complete his arrangements in good time. In fact, he was returning to his flat more than a week early. He did not expect to see Mrs Bedford, since she had arranged to visit her sister in Gloucester during his absence.

He unlocked the door and was surprised to be met by a strong odour of paint. Seconds later he gasped and dropped his travel bags. There, thrown over the hall chair, was Samantha's fake ocelot coat with an ostentatious red handbag towering above it on the half-moon table. In front of it were two keys on a ring. He picked them up, recognizing them to be his house and flat-keys.

'What the hell!' he shouted and started to move towards the noise from the spare room. Samantha came running, ready to embrace him but he pushed her away, dangling the keys close to her face. 'What's the meaning of this? How did you get them?'

'Quentin, darling, please relax. I intended to give you a wonderful surprise. You see, I always heard you praise people with initiative. Well, knowing how demanding your business has become I used my initiative to relieve you of a lot of work.'

'Don't waffle. How did you get the keys?'

'Well, on my last visit here I had left my mystery novel in your study. So I called when your Mrs Bedford was here and asked her to get it for me. I noticed her open handbag on the hall table with your keys on top. I quickly took them, then followed her to help with the search. I just had time to put my gloves on your computer desk when she found the book. I thanked her and left immediately. You know the little shoe-repair shop round the corner. They also cut duplicate keys. I returned to the flat within twenty minutes, apologizing for having left my gloves in your study. While she retrieved them I had plenty of time to return the original keys to her bag. I knew, of course, that like you she would be away for at least a month which gave me time to bring some order and style into your place.'

'And what the devil did you ...'

'Please, please,' she interrupted, 'let me tell you what I've been doing. You'll be delighted. First of all I rearranged your furniture and pictures, which is a great improvement. Then I got a man to repaper and paint the spare room. It is such a lovely, large room that I decided it would suit me very well. My furniture and things will be arriving tomorrow.' Quentin could not believe his ears. He was too shocked to even blurt out his objections.

'I know,' she continued, 'that you thought of it as a guest room. But really, darling, you wouldn't be using it very often, not for that purpose. And on the rare occasion when your parents come up from Torquay, they can stay at the Pension Belmonte which is quite near and inexpensive.'

Outrage made his blood boil. She could see his angry flush and threatening stare. Now, full of apprehension, she tried to present her next revelation with an exuberance she no longer felt. 'And now, darling Quentin, you'll have the most wonderful surprise of all. I have been able to give your tatty old wing-chair a new lease of life.'

'You what?!' he cried almost in anguish.

'Yes, I examined it and found the manufacturer's label on the underside. Gifford and Fraser. A very prestigious firm, as you know. You'll be amazed to learn that Mr Gifford's grandfather had made this very chair many decades ago. What's more, they just recently happened to have come across a few hides of the very same leather and also enough of the same old studs to recreate the original effect.' His look of anger and hatred terrified her and, without thinking, she continued with the verbal flood she had practised it in her mind. 'Of course, it isn't cheap. You may wince when you see the invoice, but it's worth every penny, darling. It really, really looks classy and spanking new.'

At last he exploded. 'How dare you! You bitch! You greedy, interfering, manipulative bitch!' He had grabbed her shoulders and shook her with all his strength. When he saw the terror in her face, her eyes bulging, her mouth gaping and gasping for air, he realized that his hands were now around her neck and that he was squeezing.

He froze. 'Oh my God!' The moment he released her she stumbled to the door and within split seconds out into the corridor. Not waiting for the lift, she'd kicked off her silly shoes and ran barefoot down the stairs.

'Don't you ever dare show your face here again!' he roared and threw her coat and handbag after her.

For two long minutes Quentin leant against the door. He was trembling, trying to regain his breath. He felt both sick and dizzy. Though drained of all energy he started to drag himself along. He had to find Eugene's chair. Where was it, where had she put it? As he hurried through the rooms he took only fleeting notice of Samantha's so-called improvements.

In truth, it didn't mean all that much to him. It was her interference, her attempt to impose her will he could not bear. Surprisingly, he found the chair in his bedroom occupying its old place by the balcony door. He approached it, one slow, hesitant step after another, searching for familiar signs, at least for a faint aura of welcome. There were none. And yet it was the same chair – the chair Eugene Kalinsky had commissioned to be made for him over half a century ago, to rest and dream in, to be his emotional sanctuary. He speculated that, obviously, in addition to the leather, all the webbing and soft padding would be new. But perhaps the old horse-hair stuffing had been cleaned and re-used. And, of course, the wooden structure would be the same. But could any fragments of Eugene's feelings and emotions have survived this thorough refurbishing?

Gone was the relaxed, shabby look, the homely ambience that allowed one to seek its comforts without inhibition. Instead, here was a piece of furniture that commanded admiration, even respect. It was now a thing of beauty, its old shape having been enhanced by superior upholstery. Yet it was not entirely aloof. The plump sleekness and subtle sheen of its green leather curves, melting warmly into their buttoned depths, had a very tactile appeal. No doubt, young Mr Gifford had done the memory of his grandfather proud. It was an aristocrat of a chair.

Quentin was exhausted. He let himself sink into it. There were no familiar hollows and bulges moulding themselves around his body. Yet it was comfortable enough. To be honest, it was very comfortable in a neutral sort of way. He waited to experience some of the old sensations – the subtle vibrations, the transcendental floating, the heavenly voices. Nothing. The magic had gone. Weak and exhausted, he was suddenly overcome by an overwhelming sense of loss. Tears started to stream down his cheeks, turning into a veritable flood that soaked the front of his shirt. Last time he had cried was as a boy in his early teens, and now he seemed to be making up for decades of repression. Gradually, his sobbing stopped, the torrent turned into a gentle flow. With it flowed all the anger and frustration and all the deep fears he had never allowed to surface. It was an easing that allowed him to drift into unconsciousness.

It was dusk when he woke. He realized that he fallen into this long sleep without having recovered any of the old, yearned-for sensations. It had been just a natural, refreshing sleep. And now, with his dizziness gone and some of his strength restored, he had to admit that tapping into Eugene's comforting legacy was no longer possible. He had lost this crutch and there was a world to be faced.

First of all, Samantha's arrangement of his flat had to be reversed. It was a task that could be left to Mrs Bedford. He himself would concentrate on following up the letters of recommendation Denis had so obligingly written for him. There was so much trouble and suffering on this earth that an experienced man, prepared to work hard for very little remuneration, was bound to find his niche. He made a resolution to live life to the full. But he would use his new chair to rest, nap and dream. Gradually, as it got older and shabbier, it would start to sag with his, Quentin's, body indentations as it previously had done with Eugene's. And over the years it would, in whatever mysterious way it was achieved, absorb and store his memories, feelings and emotions just as it had done Eugene's.

Quentin was conscious of the comfortable way his head was supported by the wing of the chair, and the faint, sensuous smell of leather. He stroked the arm on which his hand was resting: it felt silky-smooth. He gave a sigh of contentment. He felt sure that, in the fullness of time, his chair would sing again.

DEMETER

She literally looked like a bundle of rags when we picked her up. So you see, there was no question of love at first sight. And yet ...

Well, this story goes back to immediately after World War II. Though some of the background facts have become somewhat hazy, the main events are still vivid in my memory.

We happened to be on our way back to Neuberg, the regional HQ of the British Control Commission in Germany, known as CCG. We were tired, and there was another two hours' journey before us. Wilkins, our ex-army driver, took the long day in his stride. He considered himself lucky to have landed this job: regular work with decent pay. Besides, he enjoyed driving and was devoted to his boss, Don Wilberforce.

Don sat beside me in the back of the car. Though we had long since stopped discussing the conference we'd attended, we were still thinking about it. He was looking straight ahead, his stern features in profile against the passing landscape of neglected fields and pastures. It seemed a comparatively pleasant view after our drive through war-damaged towns. At times, the ruins had looked like stage sets, fantastic constructions created to intrigue the eye. Then one would spot the narrow, trodden paths that wound their way around stacks of debris, only to disappear behind some dramatic cliff of rubble. Over and over again it was hard to accept that this was real and that people were still living there – the old, the sick, the weak, a damned population of secret troglodytes.

As the Russian army advanced into East Germany, thousands had tried to escape retribution. Then, after the victory of the Allies, Germany was divided into four areas of military administration. We, the British, weren't happy about having to cope with the additional burden of refugees that were still making for our zone: neither were the West Germans. Their homes were already overcrowded and food was scarce. Many East Germans found themselves shunned, and sometimes even driven away.

Nowadays, films and TV have made us familiar with the plight of desperate people trudging in convoys along endless roads. But to us, immediately after the war, this was a new experience. Don and I couldn't help being touched, but Wilkins, though not actually gloating, felt no pity.

'They're Germans,' he'd say. 'They've started the war and lost. They made millions homeless. Now they're refugees. Let them whinge. Let them take some of their own bloody medicine.'

We didn't argue. Fighting in France, he'd been in the thick of it. He'd been injured. His mother had been killed in an air raid. His emotional wounds were still very raw.

Don turned towards me. 'That thin man, John, the one with the scar. Professor Miller, was it? What'd you make of him? He must have been a Nazi of some rank to get that position.'

'Not necessarily. They probably picked him for his qualifications, same as we'll have to. He may not even have been a Nazi but, like so many others, just hadn't the courage to refuse to join the party. Willing or not, as long as he toed the party line and did his job, they were content.'

'You're sure he'll toe our line?'

'Intelligent man like him? Sure to. And he's got the right personality to push things through.'

'Hmmm.' Thoughtfully, Don stared ahead again. He was a good-looking man in his early thirties, with regular, slightly heavy features. Being blond and tall, he went down well with the Germans. He had the air of a man who was used to seeing his orders obeyed. Ex-RAF and with a good education, he was determined to make his mark in the CCG.

He had revealed his ideas to me the second time we met in the officers' mess. With great charm he'd offered me a drink, separated me from the others, and steered me to a quiet table. He seemed to take it for granted that I too believed that it would be a good thing if Germany returned to the democratic system of the old Weimar Republic.

'With your legal experience, Dr Prentice,' he said, 'you'll realise the importance of establishing the right political structure. But creating a sound basis isn't enough. It has to be a lasting transformation. For that we must build on the youth of the country.'

I thought I guessed what he was leading up to. 'I see you've already checked me out,' I joked. 'By the way, call me John. Yes, I'm also interested in re-educating the young. I already spend most of my spare time talking to youngsters, encouraging them to discuss and to question. I feel it's important they learn to think for themselves. At the moment, our group comprises seven British and two Canadian CCG chaps, as well as two co-opted anti-Nazi Germans. If you want to join us, you're very welcome.'

Don didn't accept immediately, as I'd anticipated, but started to talk about a structured plan encompassing the whole area and involving an almost official recruitment of lecturers working a set circuit. It became clear to me that he intended to set this thing up and that he expected us to work with him. I had already heard about Donald Wilberforce on the grapevine. He was considered an idealist with enthusiasm and administrative talent. He'd impressed the top people and they'd entrusted him with a certain amount of power to negotiate with the existing education authorities.

'Look here,' I said. 'We're a small band, steadily gathering volunteers as we go. It's an ad hoc thing, which is its advantage. Nobody is tied, everything's informal, and we approach the youngsters with a low profile so they don't get scared off. They don't need rigid, structured tuition. They've had plenty of that.'

'But John,' Don interrupted me. 'They'll have to be taught in an orderly fashion.'

'Yes, in school. But what we're doing, Don, isn't school. These are people of fifteen plus, ready to go out into the world; finding jobs or continuing studies. This is a spare-time activity for us and for them. You'd be surprised how quickly they open up in a relaxed atmosphere. Sympathetic listening and occasional help work wonders. They're starting to trust us. They've gone through hard times and have seen their old gods tumble. Believe me, they're more than ready to absorb new ideas. I'm sorry, Don. I'm not interested in turning this into an official activity. It would put them off and I, for one, should hate the restrictions of an indoctrination programme.' Don was obviously disappointed but gave in with good grace. He would join us and see how it worked.

From then on, we spent a fair amount of time together. For security, we were encouraged to go at least in twos. Also, cars had to be requisitioned from the pool, and petrol was scarce. Don settled in well. He proved to be popular and seemed to enjoy himself. But I wasn't fooled. He was an empire builder, biding his time.

The previously mentioned trip had nothing to do with these spare-time activities. Don was on a job and his regular interpreter had been unable to come. Feeling the need for a little change, I'd agreed to help him out. Normally, I worked for Colonel Gifford, an army man of the old school, the commanding officer for the whole district. Though he demanded discipline, life had mellowed him sufficiently to take a tolerant view of somewhat unorthodox methods, as long as they achieved the desired results. Being a linguist, I acted as his interpreter. I also had to liaise with the German public in case of serious difficulties or disputes. Press and theatre matters too were within my brief.

The Commander demanded regular reports on the state of public opinion, on the principle that it is useful to know whether one is sitting on a powder keg or not. He therefore encouraged any activities that would allow me to monitor German feelings vis-à-vis the CCG administration. He knew I gave him straight, unsanitized reports, covering tacit tolerance to angry, rebellious resentment. The informal mixing with German young people was one of my dual-purpose operations. It was surprising how much one could learn from them of the attitudes and prejudices of the parents. That was why I could always claim use of a car for my spare time activities. Don, on the other hand, had a regular car and driver for his daytime work only. The complementary nature of our mobility was an additional reason for working together.

We drove on in silence. More fields, copses, scrubland. For some time now, the Russians had stopped the mass exodus of refugees, but the odd stragglers still managed to get through. Though the roads happened to be empty that day, we couldn't drive very fast – too many bumps and potholes. Dusk had started to close in when we came across some ruined houses. We hadn't noticed the bundle of rags on the pile of bricks till it was caught in our headlights. Drawing level, we realised it was some huddled-up creature.

'Stop,' said Don. We got out of the car to investigate. It was a woman. She didn't move as we approached. When we addressed her in German, there was no response. She sat with her head buried in her arms that were folded over her knees, so that her long tangle of hair hung over the front of her legs. She must have chosen this prominent spot in the hope of being picked up. So why didn't she react? Her clothes, not much more than rags, were still wet from the afternoon rain. 'She must be freezing,' I thought.

We went up the mound and I tried again: *'Guten Abend, können wir Ihnen helfen?'*

No reply. Don looked genuinely worried. 'Hell, we can't leave her here like this!'

I got hold of her under her arms and tried to raise

her. Unable to co-operate, she was just so much dead weight. Even with Don's help it turned out to be tricky, because of the insecure foothold on the rubble. Wilkins was watching us from the car. Don got angry.

'You! Lazy bastard! Get off your arse!'

The man jumped to and, together, we got her down. I nearly laughed at Wilkins' expression of disgust. But in truth, she didn't just look filthy – she smelled it.

'Let's wrap her up before we put her in the car,' I suggested. We used our two travel rugs and except for her face, covered her completely. It had become obvious that she was but skin and bones. We decided that Don would take care of her in the back of the car. But first we gave her some coffee from our thermos. We watched as Don put the cup to her lips. Her face wasn't just dirty; it looked as if it had been smeared with soot and mud. It was impossible to guess her age or what she would normally look like. The touch of the cup and the strong odour of the coffee must have reached her consciousness, for she took a few sips.

Then she opened her eyes. They looked enormous in that emaciated face. They were young eyes, blue – the deepest, most beautiful violet blue I had ever seen. I swallowed and heard Don catch his breath.

She looked at us in turn and, with what sounded like a sigh of relief, fell instantly asleep.

'Make a detour to the hospital, sir?' asked Wilkins. Don and I looked at each other. I'm sure it was the impact of those eyes that decided us to take on the responsibility of putting her into private care.

'No,' said Don, 'we'll take her to Frau Berger, 17 Altdorfer Platz.' He turned to me. 'Or d'you think the Lederer family would be more suitable?'

'No. Berger's the better choice,' I agreed.

Don grinned. 'Especially as she owes me.'

It was dark by the time we arrived. Wilkins almost leapt out of the car. Don and I followed quickly. We were eager not only to stretch our legs, but to escape the unsavoury odour of our unconscious passenger. Don promised to be as quick as possible in preparing Frau Berger for the arrival of her unexpected guest.

No 17, a large, detached house, possessed the same self-conscious dignity as its neighbours in the square. The small town of Neuberg, though affected by all the usual privations of war, had remained physically almost unscathed. Apart from lack of lighting and the disappearance of iron gates and railings, it had preserved its pre-war look. The operative word was 'solid'. And what could be more solid and exude more gravitas than a pyramid of steps in the centre of the square, topped by a grandiose plinth on which the archducal effigy stood silhouetted against the sky.

It was a starlit night. The moon, though waning, was bright enough to illuminate the square with a cool light that seemed to enhance the overall stillness. We watched Don approach the house, mount the three steps up to the massive door and strike the brass knocker. The ratatat rang out like pistol shots and almost made one wonder why the dark windows, like shut eyes, weren't instantly lighting up in shocked surprise. Even when the door opened there was no burst of light, only a faint, reflected glow from somewhere in the interior. When the door closed behind him, I felt as if he had been swallowed up: as if, hero or victim in some arcane ritual, he was going to meet his destiny.

'What utter rubbish!' I mocked myself and joined Wilkins who had lit a cigarette and was thoughtfully strolling to and fro.

'It's incredible,' he mused, 'that any woman could let herself get into such a state. I mean, I know soap is hard to come by, in her case most likely impossible, but she must have passed some streams or pools with the chance of an occasional wash. Let me put it this way, sir. Whatever else the krauts are, they're known to be clean.'

'Well, Wilkins,' I said after a pause. 'Let me put it to you another way. There is this female on her long trek to safety. She's alone, weak, and getting weaker. You've come across her and got her cornered. You've left your conscience in England, and this is defeated Germany. You happen to be desperately randy. Are you going to rape her?'

'Yuck! Crikey! This bundle of shit?'

I didn't react. Two seconds later the penny had dropped.

'I see what you mean, sir,' he said sheepishly.

Time dragged on. I was getting impatient. Should I follow Don and support him?

'Don't worry, sir. Frau B. is sure to take her in.' Wilkins was getting his own back by being condescendingly soothing. 'If she'd wanted to refuse, the boss would have been back long ago. Shouldn't think he'll be long now.'

As if on cue, a wedge of light fell across the square as Don and a female figure emerged from No 17. They were carrying a makeshift stretcher. The woman turned out to be Elsie Pickering from the school for English children of CCG personnel. Though we tried to transfer our patient from car to stretcher as gently as we could, she moaned softly without opening her eyes. Back at the house, we were met with what looked like a reception committee. There were two CCG women, Elsie and Betty, whom I knew quite well; Magda, the general factotum; the two thirteen-year-old twin granddaughters of Frau Berger; and, of course, the lady herself. What with the addition of Don, Wilkins, me and the stretcher, the hall was crowded. After the initial hush, a hubbub of voices demanded information. There was a pushing forward to see more of the mysterious stranger.

Frau Berger, a tall woman, heavy-boned but well proportioned, assumed command. I knew that her only daughter had been killed in an accident before the war, and that her two little granddaughters were now in her care. Spacious houses near the CCG headquarters had tended to be taken over for staff families but, probably by pulling the right strings, she had been able to hang on to hers. She was now making a living by accommodating and looking after single CCG women. She ordered the stretcher to be taken upstairs.

'I have telephoned Dr Raimund,' she announced. 'He is on his way. After the examination, Magda and I will do all that is necessary. So please, return to whatever you were doing.'

Watching her, I realized how much she was enjoying this. Organizing and giving orders was just up her street. She and Don could have been mother and son. She had studied in England after World War I, and her English was still near-perfect. No doubt, having to deal with English lodgers must have helped to refresh her facility.

The hall cleared. Don and I were ushered into the salon, a glorified German version of the English front parlour. It was cold and stark. There were none of the artefacts and ornaments this type of room would normally have had on display. We could see from the unfaded patches on the walls that pictures had been removed. I could only speculate what sort of art would have been at home here. The polished parquet floor was bare, the furniture looked as if it had come from a much more modest home. I learned later that all good and valuable possessions had been spirited away to safety: Frau Berger had used her organizing talent to avoid the risk of war damage and looting.

Don and I sat in silence. We were both tired and

there was no point in speculating. Yet I couldn't help wondering who the young woman was. What had she been through? I had no doubt that she was young, not after having seen those amazing eyes.

Dr Raimund lived nearby, so it wasn't very long before he and Frau Berger came in to see us. He was an old man who must have been very well nourished in his prime. Now, the loose skin on his face and neck gave him something of a bloodhound look. He reported in German and I translated for Don the parts he couldn't understand. It appeared that the patient had no physical damage but was suffering from starvation and total exhaustion. Food would have to be introduced carefully – first, light digestible food, gradually progressing to good and nourishing fare. 'Just as well we brought her here,' I thought, 'she'd never get that at the hospital.' At least Don and I had the connections to lay things on.

'Excuse me, gentlemen,' said Frau Berger, 'I must attend to my charge now. If you would care to call again tomorrow evening, I hope to be able to tell you more. We can then discuss further arrangements.'

If Don was put out at being dismissed, he didn't show it. I thought she had handled the situation well and that we could trust her. She definitely got her priorities right.

Next day I happened to be very busy, mainly with discussions with the Intendant of the local state opera and theatre. Even in those days, a lot of effort was put into the production of entertainment. Neuberg had a predominantly middle-class population, who seemed to need a weekly fix of culture to remain sane. Since goods of all description were scarce, shopping and trade were based on barter. The Reichsmark was practically worthless, the only reliable currency being cigarettes. The theatres, however, accepted Reichsmarks, so it was not surprising that most performances were sold out. Dr Karl Friedrich, the Intendant, was not only the manager, but did at times himself direct productions that interested him. His reputation in the theatre world stood high, and his new *Antigone* by Jean Anouilh was eagerly awaited at the time. He was also a distinguished art historian. Dealing with a man of his calibre was a pleasure. We soon became friends. When I wasn't out on youth work, I would often spend my evenings in Karl's book-lined study, after having picked up a bottle or two at the NAAFI. His wife, Johanna, who had been an actress, would join us, together with one or two other friends. Our discussions would go on well into the night. I discovered later that Johanna possessed an extensive wardrobe. Since she was slim and tall and had excellent taste, I was pleased when she agreed to let me have some outfits for our foundling, for which I would pay her with cigarettes and Nescafé.

After our meal at the mess, Don and I walked over to Altdorfer Platz. I must admit that although I had had an interesting day, my thoughts had kept straying to our mystery girl. I was surprised when Don admitted that he, too, had been wondering about the consequences of our commitment. 'Oh, well, we'll soon know the score,' he muttered.

Magda received us. She was a plain looking, middle-aged woman who was obviously used to keeping her feelings and opinions to herself. 'Frau Berger won't be a minute,' she said laconically and, once again, we found ourselves in that awful salon. Frau Berger did indeed come without delay and sat down opposite us. Her fine, grey eyes gave us a lightning once-over. Not being given to small talk, she immediately tackled the subject in question.

'Her name is Demeter Ellenburg, she is eighteen, born in Koenigswalden. Now, according to Dr Raimund's instructions, we are giving her slightly enriched liquids every three hours, which she has swallowed without actually being fully conscious. We are to let her sleep without bothering her. This means, that so far, we have only been able to give her a cursory clean up.' She looked at us like a teacher expecting questions.

'If she hasn't been awake, how did you find out her name?'

Frau Berger allowed herself a little smile. 'Fraulein Ellenburg wore a large kerchief round her waist, like a body-belt. Folded into it were her personal documents and two photographs.'

'Let's see them,' said Don.

The lady shook her head. 'Sorry, they are her own private things. It is up to her whether she wants to show you.'

It was obvious that Don was taken aback, but his next question was quite controlled. 'Can we see her?'

Another 'sorry'. Frau Berger felt that the young lady should not be seen until she was completely conscious and presentable. 'You must respect her dignity,' she said firmly.

So that was that. I gave Frau Berger one of my best smiles. 'Surely, you can't be surprised that we are interested. At least tell us what she looks like.'

She gave a deep sigh that made it clear she thought us a nuisance. 'She is tall. Long legs. Painfully thin. Face oval. Cheekbones look high over sunken cheeks. Good hairline. Hair in a tangle, will take ages to sort out. Its colour, when clean, probably dark blond. That's it. Oh, and her hands and fingernails are beautifully shaped.'

'Thank you, that's something,' acknowledged Don. His expression, however, revealed that he thought she hadn't told us much that was new. He then proceeded to discuss expenses and remuneration with her. I left the business side to him, having already agreed to equal shares of whatever it amounted to.

From then on, we received regular reports about the patient – brief, bare facts. When she had first woken up, how long she'd managed to stay awake, when her diet had changed to solids, her first few steps, and so on. It was over three weeks later when Frau Berger invited us to tea on a Sunday afternoon. At last we were to meet Demeter Ellenburg.

Her name had made us speculate about her background. Demeter, the Greek corn goddess, associated with the Great Mysteries of the ancient world and rituals of death and rebirth.

'I can't imagine working-class parents christening their daughter Demeter,' said Don. 'More likely to be some middle-class people with a smattering of classical mythology, or perhaps some gentlefolk farmers trying to placate the gods? Interesting, eh? Anyway, I'll be calling her Dem.' He grinned at me and, for one moment, I saw the mischievous young boy he must once have been.

I had been dreading that front parlour, but Magda led us past its door and up the stairs to a room at the back. Bright light dazzled us as we entered and it took us a few seconds to orientate ourselves. It was quite a large room, charmingly furnished as a bed-sitter.

'Ah, here you are,' said Frau Berger, stepping forward. 'Gentlemen, let me introduce you. Demeter, dear, your two rescuers, Dr John Prentice and Mr Donald Wilberforce. Gentlemen, Faulein Demeter Ellenburg.'

Somehow, I had expected her to receive us sitting up in bed. But as we entered, she rose from a sort of wicker armchair by the window.

'Don't get up, please,' Don and I burst out in unison, which sounded funny enough for smiles all round.

She made a few steps towards us. 'I am delighted to meet you.' Her voice was weak but had a pleasant timbre. 'Dr Prentice, Mr Wilberforce, the very first thing I want to say to you is "thank you". Thank you for everything you have done for me.' She shook hands with both of us and returned to her chair. Frau Berger had been right, she had beautiful hands. What she hadn't told us was that our foundling was potentially a beautiful girl. I am of above average height, and she was nearly as tall as I. Though obviously weak, she carried herself well, her head poised gracefully on a long, slender neck. A pale yellow dress, which I recognised as one of Elsie Pickering's, hung loosely from her shoulders. It was not fully opaque and revealed her skeletal state against the strong light from the window. Even so, one could appreciate the promise of a fine figure. But what fascinated me again were her wonderful eyes. It had been the memory of their deep blue that had made me eager to see the whole person. Her hair, shoulder length, was light brown with a rich, golden sheen. In fact, I remember thinking that it seemed in incredibly good condition, despite its owner's frail state of health. Her facial expression was difficult to read. Considering that our position as benefactors was at that stage ambiguous, and that she didn't know our intentions, I thought she struck the right note by being politely welcoming and friendly, at the same time maintaining a certain reserve.

'Frau Berger never told us you spoke English,' I said. 'And such good English at that.'

She smiled mischievously, displaying a perfect set of teeth. 'We kept it as a surprise. You see, for about three years, my brother and I had an English au pair. Dear Alice! She had to leave us when the war started. We had been very fond of her and made a point of speaking English among ourselves so as not to forget. Being here with Frau Berger and the CCG ladies also helps to keep my English going.' She looked tired and leant back against the cushion.

To give her time to recover, I recounted in detail how we had found her and had decided to take her with us. She listened intently. I had the impression that whatever I said, she would remember verbatim. I therefore chose my words carefully and made it clear that the decision to save her was Don's and mine in equal measure. I didn't want the lion's share of the credit, nor was I willing to allow her to be indebted to Don more than he deserved. She looked mainly at me while I spoke, but every so often she would glance at Don, who sat beside me on the two-seater sofa.

In contrast to me, lazily lounging as usual, with legs outstretched and supporting my narration with the occasional gesture, Don sat stiffly upright without any movement whatsoever. Even his eyes didn't move, being solely fixed on her. I had expected him to make interjections to fill out my story, but he seemed content to let me carry on. I wondered what impression we made on her. Don, undoubtedly handsome and provocatively masculine, always, as I knew from past observation, drew many admiring female glances. Would she be able to see beyond his appearance and evaluate the whole man? As to myself, I too was quite a good looker in those days – very slim, sharp featured, with a full head of wavy brown hair.

When I had finished, she sighed. 'By the time you found me, gentlemen, I had been travelling for many weeks.' She then told us that, originally, she had fled from the Russians. She had been with a group of other refugees when they were attacked by a marauding gang. In addition to robbery, they started to rape the women. She, being quite athletic and a good sprinter, managed to escape into the nearby woods. 'There were those beautiful old oak trees,' she recalled. 'I climbed up into one of them. Then I wrapped my dark patterned dirndl skirt all around me, so as to cover my scarlet blouse. Huddled high up in the fork of a branch, I saw two of the men come looking for me. I was paralysed with fear as they passed underneath, at times even glancing up. Because they were probably looking out for something red, they never found me.'

She had escaped but had lost her belongings, which included a small reserve of food. From then on, she made herself as disgusting as possible, and walked only at night and alone. Her only food was what she could steal from fields and farms. Her energy was ebbing away and she realized that death couldn't be far off. 'When I dragged myself up onto that pile of bricks, I hoped that I was well within the British zone.' She smiled. 'Thank God, I was.'

All this had been revealed in a question-and-answer dialogue. Although I asked all the questions, her replies were addressed to both Don and me. Frau Berger, of course, already knew her story. She was sitting behind us on the bed and we had almost forgotten her presence. Yet Don still sat there as before, looking at Demeter, hardly saying a word. His behaviour confirmed what I already knew. He, who was so self-assured and competent in dealing with men or groups of people, was awkward when it came to making relaxed, personal contact with women. He was a man's man, most at ease when entertaining and manipulating men. I, on the other hand, never had much time for male bonding. In fact, I always found the endless sports arguments and inane salacious jokes extremely tedious. Whenever I could, I avoided those convivial gatherings at the bar, or slunk away to escape all that back-slapping and guffawing. The truth is, I prefer the company of intelligent woman. That doesn't mean that they have to be highly educated. I find that most women are open to new ideas. They try to empathize and understand. They are capable of reasoned argument and do not suffer from the male notion that acceptance of other people's ideas amounts to weakness and is somehow demeaning.

I should have liked some information about Demeter's family background but Frau Berger stepped forward to put an end to the conversation. Regretfully, we had to agree. It must have been quite a strenuous session for our patient.

The door closed behind us. We stood on the top step overlooking the square. All was quiet except for someone on the other side sweeping the drive. I turned to Don. 'Well then, old man. What d'you think?'

He cleared his throat and gave me a hard look. 'I've decided to marry her.'

My surprise was genuine. All I could say was: 'Oh! Really?'

I don't know what my facial expression was, and what he read into it. He stepped close up to me. 'You didn't by any chance have the same idea? Do you want to marry her?'

Suddenly, the situation struck me as utterly ridiculous. 'No, I don't', I chuckled.

His face now came even closer to mine, the implication of menace unavoidable. 'You're quite sure?'

'Positive, old man,' I said and walked down the steps. Of course, this would have been the perfect occasion to tell him that I was already married. Happily married at that. But he had rubbed me the wrong way. I kept mum. Let the bastard sweat.

I was not surprised when a message from Don arrived the next day. Something had cropped up. He was unable to come to the brains trust we had arranged. I guessed he didn't trust himself to be civil to me and wanted to avoid an unpleasant confrontation. Luckily, Elsie Pickering was willing to take his place. As I mentioned before, she was a seconded CCG teacher, living at Frau Berger's. She also was a former school friend of my wife's. I liked her. With crisp, dark curls and lively brown eyes, she was attractive in a bouncy sort of way. She was also intelligent and not afraid to speak her mind. Coming from a puritanical home, she now made the most of her freedom from restrictions. But she was discreet, and only close friends had an inkling of her amorous adventures.

This first youth brains trust turned out to be surprisingly exciting. It was well attended, and we four old 'brains' were at times hard pressed to give adequate answers to all the questions. After a short period of shyness, many of the young people took courage and spoke up. We were surprised at the keen thirst for knowledge. Questions like: 'how could we square the possession of colonies with genuine democracy?' had been unexpected, to say the least. On our drive back, Elsie and I discussed the individual youngsters and their attitudes to the new, post-war world. Who could tell how they would develop? 'Most of the influences are beyond our control,' sighed Elsie. But she was hooked, and subsequently became an active member of our group.

When Don turned up the following week, we were both at pains to carry on as usual. But there was an undercurrent of tension of which, as I learned later, Elsie was fully aware. We also resumed our visits to No 17, chaperoned either by Elsie or Frau Berger. On one occasion, even Magda was roped in to take a turn. The good lady was at great pains to preserve the respectability of her house. No wonder, her livelihood depended on it.

Little by little, Demeter started to gain strength and put on weight. Her figure was no longer quite so bony, and her face in particular started to acquire a pleasant oval shape. She still had some way to go but, no doubt, she was going to be attractive.

As usual, I did most of the talking but Don had advanced to making the odd remark, or even to giving an account of things he thought might interest her. She remained as friendly as before, but her even-handed politeness towards us was obviously intended to keep us at a distance. Apart from that, it was impossible to guess her thoughts regarding her situation. But she had started to speak about her family. Both her parents were dead. Her father, a surgeon, had been sent to the Russian front, where he was killed by a direct hit on his field hospital. Her only brother too, had been drafted to fight in Russia, where he had been reported missing. The poor girl was hoping that missing didn't mean dead, that one day she would see him again.

I remember her sad look when she showed us her two photographs. One was of her parents, an attractive couple in their mid- to late thirties. The other was of her grandfather in riding habit, his arm around the shoulders of a good-looking young man who was obviously her brother. We learned that her grandparents had owned a small estate, given over to farming. Hence her fancy name of Demeter, the corn goddess. At that, Don and I exchanged glances: his joking guess had been right.

In the course of our conversations it also become clear that Demeter had enjoyed a good education, and that her family had expected her to go to university. Somehow, this fact hadn't registered with Don. He seemed to see her as a weak, lost girl, too young to make up her mind about serious and important things. Considering that she had decided to flee on her own, and that her manner of travel must have required considerable courage and determination, I just couldn't understand his blinkered attitude.

'She's coming along nicely,' he said to me after one of those visits. 'Frau Berger is taking good care of her. I think she should stay there for the time being. Later on we could probably get her a job in some office or other. Could be part-time to start with.' This sounded pretty useless to me as a basis for a career, but at least it would give her an outside interest, get her into circulation and help her to integrate into local society. So I agreed.

'As soon as she is strong enough,' he continued, watching me closely, 'I shall gradually make her aware of my intentions.'

'She's very young,' I said.

'I know. I consider it an advantage. She's had a traumatic time, and having entered a new, strange world, she'll be glad of my protection and guidance. She's fundamentally strong and of good stock. I'm sure she'll be happy as my wife, and mother of my children. And I intend to have a lot of them.' His features seemed to soften to an almost dreamy look. 'A large family has always been my ideal.' Remembering his reserve in Demeter's presence, I was surprised at his confidence. How could he be so self-satisfied? But his intention of becoming a pater familias on a grand scale was true to character. I could imagine him as the patriarch of a large clan, revelling in the power over his tall, blond tribe.

I would have found it difficult to explain my own feelings towards Demeter at that time. In fact, I deliberately avoided any serious thought on the subject and told myself that my motive for contributing to her maintenance was purely philanthropic. I was helping to save a worthwhile life.

That was also what I told Emma, my wife. After a period of romance, Emma and I had settled down to a relationship of deep friendship and affection. We understood and complemented each other to such an extent, that neither of us could imagine ever being without the other's support. After war work, she'd decided to finish her studies, while I put in my stint at the CCG. We let our house and she went to live with her parents for the time being. I wrote to her every day;

sometimes just a few lines, sometimes pages, which were posted once a week. She did the same. She was interested in Demeter's fate, and I don't think it ever occurred to her to be jealous.

Some time later, I was having a drink with Elsie at the club. She'd become quite a pal and we enjoyed the occasional gossip together. I must explain that, for social purposes, the CCG had taken over the ducal palace. It was quite modest, as palaces go – a heavy, solid interpretation of neo-classicism. The reception rooms, however, were reasonably suited to our purpose. If the original curtains, antique furniture and wall hangings had given them elegance and style in the past, they had long since vanished. I felt that the ambience of our post-war décor, comprising what looked like randomly assembled bits and pieces, couldn't even hold its own with a Lyons' Corner House. But the entrance hall with its marble pillars and its inlaid ducal weapon in the centre of the floor, was quite splendid. A balustraded, round opening in the middle of the ceiling allowed one to view proceedings from above. On special dress occasions, I used to linger there with my drink, looking down on the dolled-up CCG ladies parading in their party gowns. They obviously felt glamorous and romantic as they tried to flirt with the Allied officers, who looked so handsome in their various gala uniforms. These could have been scenes from some syrupy Viennese operetta, especially since waltzes and polkas seemed to be the obligatory accompaniment.

Elsie had chosen a table as far away from the bar as possible. We watched a bunch of middle-aged men knocking back one drink after another. 'That's the only reason that lot joined the CCG,' she said with disgust. 'For most of them it's booze, or getting away from the missus.' She gave me one of her bright smiles. 'There aren't that many like you with a sense of mission. Or like Don, to do him justice.'

'Talking of Don,' she continued, 'he seems to have fallen for Demeter in a big way, but tries not to show it.'

'Is she aware of it?'

Elsie laughed. 'How dumb do you think she is? But she's not interested in him. She fancies you.'

'I am afraid, Elsie, dear, you're letting your imagination run away with you. I think it's just that we're on the same wavelength, and that she trusts me.'

She shook her head. 'I believe it's more than that, John. I know about these things.' She sighed. 'I'm afraid you'll call me an interfering bitch, but I told her that you were married. You see, I don't want either of you getting hurt. And that goes for Emma too. These sorts of complications mess up lives.'

I was annoyed but had sense enough to see that she was right. Being honest, I had to admit that there was some sort of electricity between Demeter and me; a certain emotional empathy, spiced with a soupçon of sexual awareness. Aloud I said: 'I can't speak for her, since she's been consistently reserved. As for me, well, I'm interested in her and her development. You know, when I was a little boy, my father used to give me flower seeds to grow on the windowsill or in the garden. Sometimes he told me their Latin names but refused to describe the mature plants. It was tantalizing to have to feed and water the things and having to wait for the results. The process stimulated and excited my imagination. When the flowers finally came, I would experience either disappointments or thrills. The same with Demeter. She is like one of those unknown seeds – a mystery.'

Elsie gave me a quizzical look. 'Ten out of ten for effort. By the way, I know you like to remain a bit of a mystery yourself. So I've asked Demeter not to tell anybody else, especially Don.' She noticed my doubtful look. 'I know she won't. It wouldn't be in her interest.'

I understood. In these difficult times when both food and a roof over one's head were hard to come by, especially for a refugee, a CCG officer could be regarded a good catch. If Don was to be her only choice, she would want him to think that she had chosen him in preference to me.

As it happened, I needed an operation on my left hand, which had to be performed in the UK. I decided to take my three weeks' leave and add it onto my sick leave. This would give me a good break. I knew Emma would be delighted. As I learned from my secret sources, so was Don. It wasn't only a question of having Demeter to himself without fear of any implied criticism on my part, but rather that he had started his big intrigue. My connections had told me that Don was trying hard to influence the powers-that-be to convert our successful voluntary youth re-education set-up into an official body under his control. With me away, the takeover would be so much easier.

When I discussed this with my commander, Colonel Gifford, he was entirely on my side. 'Don't worry, old boy,' he said, 'it's not going to happen. You can safely push off to the UK and leave the matter with me.' This was a load off my mind, for I knew the man was as good as his word.

An unexpected change of arrangements forced me to leave the following day. Though I knew that Don was at work, I went alone to say goodbye to Demeter. It was Magda who opened the door. Her surprise was obvious.

'You can't see Demeter now,' she blurted out in a panic. 'I'm the only one here, and I'm in the middle of baking.'

'Look, I just want a little chat with her before I go on leave. Let me make a suggestion. We put the garden table and chairs on the lawn, where you can see us from the kitchen window. We won't know whether you are watching us all the time or only now and then. So we're bound to play it by the book.' I went up to her and, with an encouraging smile, slipped a packet of cigarettes into her apron pocket.

'I suppose that'll be safe enough,' she said grudgingly, and let me in.

It was my first time alone with Demeter and, as it turned out, my last. We sat in the middle of the lawn, facing each other across the table. The late afternoon sun shimmered through her hair, pink and white blossoms blended with the primrose yellow of her dress, and a blackbird sang in the neighbour's orchard. She was looking at me, her hands limply folded on her lap.

I pulled myself together. 'I'm going on leave.'

'I know,' she said.

'I'll be off tomorrow – for about four to five weeks.'

'A lot can happen in four weeks.' She said almost tonelessly. My chest tightened.

'Don's been visiting me without you. Did he tell you?'

'No.'

'Three times, so far. But Frau Berger was present.'

'I expect you'll see a lot more of him now,' I said dryly.

Silence. I concentrated on her every feature. 'She isn't Demeter,' I said to myself. 'Not the solid, matronly goddess of harvest. She's Demeter's daughter, lovely Persephone, harbinger of spring and joys to come.' Aloud I said: 'You are beautiful.'

'I know.' There was no false modesty, only an acknowledgement of fact. She gave me a searching look.

'What do you really see, John?'

'What do you mean?'

'Sometimes you look at me as if I were a picture, or even part of a picture. Now, here in the garden with all the flowering shrubs, do you see me as part of an Impressionist painting? A Monet, Renoir, Pissarro? Or perhaps a Berthe Morisot? When we're indoors, do you evaluate the light that falls on me and say to yourself, ah, Vermeer!?'

I was shocked. Shocked, because there was some truth in it. 'Demeter, dear,' I burst out,' you're not suggesting that I see you only as a two-dimensional thing? You can't believe that is all you mean to me.'

She shook her head. 'I'm sorry, John. That was unfair of me. You of all people, who's been trying to contact the real me. Oh, John, I'm so tired of being just a face and a figure, something men want for sex, for showing off, or for breeding beautiful offspring. Hardly any of them care whether there is anything more behind the shell.'

'And Don?' I asked.

She gave a sad smile. 'At the moment he's playing

Pygmalion, shaping my character and personality. Being thorough, he's taking his time. When he thinks he's completed his masterpiece, and considers me worthy, he'll surprise me with a proposal of marriage.'

'And you? What will you do?'

'I'm his Galatea. I shall do what is expected of me … to begin with.'

She must have been aware of the misery I felt, for she leant forward and said quickly: 'Don't worry about me, John. I'm tough. But you see I have no choice. At the moment you and Donald are keeping me, and I'm helping Frau Berger in the house and kitchen. But now that physically I'm nearly recovered, you'll have to stop your philanthropy. I wish I could repay you.' She gave a deep sigh. 'Am I wrong in not wanting to be a domestic drudge for ever? You know that for refugees from the east, there are no jobs with a future. I certainly won't sell my body piecemeal to the grubby little men who've run away from their wives. And since I don't have the connections for becoming a high-class prostitute, Don will have to do. It'll give me the chance of continuing my studies.'

'But Demeter, he intends to have a large family.'

Her lovely eyes narrowed, and there was a strange coldness in her voice as she said: 'Does he?'

Magda came to see me out. She obviously thought that I had had more than my ration of time. When I walked down the drive and looked back, she was still standing in the doorway, her rough hands folded over her stomach. There was a softness in her face I hadn't seen before.

Nearly six weeks had passed by the time I returned. The operation on my hand had been successful but had taken longer to heal than expected. This had cramped my style as far as holiday activities were concerned, since I should have liked to do some swimming and sailing. My wife Emma and her mother were happy enough to look after me and spoil me. I was very fond of my mother-in-law. A warm-hearted woman with common sense, she would put on the brakes when Emma was in danger of fussing too much. I visited friends and family, went to the theatre, exhibitions and concerts, and found that time passed very quickly. But I didn't forget Demeter. I often wondered how she was getting on with Don.

It was agreed that Emma would visit me in Neuberg over the summer holidays. She was looking forward to meeting Demeter and Don, and all the people I had mentioned in my letters.

When I arrived back at my Neuberg digs, I found a large piece of paper on my table. It said: 'VERY URGENT! Please ring me immediately. ELSIE.' Fearing that something had happened to Demeter, I did.

'Thank God you've come in time,' she exploded. 'We'd no idea when you were due back.'

'What's happened?'

Elsie's voice changed and I had the impression she was feeling uncomfortable. 'Well, John, I don't know whether this comes out of the blue for you, but Demeter and Don got married. Actually, about three hours ago. The reception at No 17 is nearly over and the couple are due to leave any time. I will ask them to wait for you. Thank God you're here. I was afraid you wouldn't be back in time. So, please John, come straight away.'

She was waiting for me at the door. 'Demeter will be so pleased to see you,' she gushed.

I was bewildered. 'Elsie, old girl, why all this drama? She'll see me after their honeymoon.'

'She won't. They're not coming back. Don had some setbacks; rubbed certain high-ups the wrong way. So he's quit and got a better job in Berlin. I understand they gave him good references to get rid of him.' As we made our way through the house to the back lawn, Elsie told me that Don had wanted a big church wedding with a showy reception at the club in the palace. Demeter, however, had insisted on a simple registry office wedding with a modest gathering to follow. Elsie stopped and faced me. 'And you know what? Registry wedding – means easier divorce. There's more, John. Demeter asked me to instruct her about birth control. As you can guess, there isn't much on that subject I don't know. Rest assured, I gave her the lot. Did you know she's still a virgin?' All this came bubbling out at top speed. My head was buzzing. When we reached the French window, she left me.

There were several decorated tables with food and drinks on the lawn, and about thirty guests milling about in between them. And there was Demeter, wearing the Nile-green silk suit I had bartered for her from Johanna. It was a pre-war haute couture model she couldn't possibly have bought with her new British clothing coupons. Not at the NAAFI or anywhere else. In my six weeks' absence she'd recovered completely, looking stunning in her elegance and beauty. She was Don's now and I wouldn't see her again. I hadn't expected it could hurt that much.

Then she spotted me and came towards me with long and eager strides. She stood before me, her back to the guests, smiling. Her eyes seemed unnaturally shiny, and I realized she was near tears. For a few moments she forgot herself and I couldn't help but see her pain and longing. 'John, dear,' she said softly, 'this is goodbye. Thank you for everything. I shall never forget you.' People were approaching. She swallowed, then exclaimed with exaggerated brightness: 'You see, John, I'm starting a new life – new adventures – the sky's the limit.'

Don, Elsie and Frau Berger joined us. After some small talk came the final farewells. The party made its way to the car, where Wilkins was waiting at the wheel. As the couple came towards him, he winked at me and held his nose. He was reminding me of the dirty bundle of rags. Elsie stood beside me, having slipped her arm through mine as a gesture of comfort and support.

Before getting into the car, Demeter looked back. Though she was a picture of radiant happiness, I knew her chest was as tight as mine. Don helped her get in, brimming with possessive pride. One last, self-satisfied look back and he too stepped into the car. As he did, I remembered the moonlit square and my pangs of premonition, when he had stepped over the threshold of No 17 to meet his destiny.

Elsie squeezed my arm and sniffed. 'The poor sod.'

ꟼORTRAIT OF A MAN WITH RED HAIR

I tried to remember when I had last stayed in a private house with such a splendid staircase. My old canvas holdall, leaning against the carved end post, looked forlorn and out of place.

Thomas Lancaster picked it up. 'Come, Laura, I'll show you to your room.'

His wife, Joanna, still on the right side of fifty and attractively plump, winked at me. 'You're honoured. He isn't so keen to show everybody up himself. But then, you're so much better looking than most of our guests. By the way, dinner's at eight. Come down any time. There's always a cup of tea to be had for the asking.'

Halfway up the stairs I looked back. Her gaze was still on us. Something in her expression puzzled me. Was there a trace of anxiety, or even jealousy? Instantly, she smiled again and gave me a little wave.

Considering that I was a stranger and that my visit had been sprung on them, the Lancasters' reception couldn't have been warmer. I had recently split up with my partner. The fizz had gone out of the relationship. I was resentful when Trevor started to use our home like a hotel, all services laid on, including occasional sexual ones. I'd felt exploited. In the end, when he had found someone else, it rankled that I hadn't had the courage to end it all before. Though there'd been no traumatic bust up, the parting had caused a lot of change and stress. I was feeling low. Then my childhood friend Rosemary came to my rescue. She invited me to stay with her and her family in Upper Wrenford. But, as sod's law would have it, on the morning of my arrival their plumbing had gone berserk, flooding bedrooms and kitchen.

That was how the Lancasters, Rosemary's neighbours, had got landed with me. She'd told me that Thomas Lancaster had retired two years ago after making pots of money in the City. This always sounds like magic to me. How on earth do they do it? Since then he had apparently devoted himself to the restoration of the house. It was at least three times the size of Rosemary's and, of course, much grander. I've always been sensitive to the atmosphere of a place. I only have to step over the threshold and know whether I like it or not. This, I felt, was a happy house. A cursory look revealed nothing unusual or exciting – just safe, good taste with the odd touch of ostentation. It seemed to reflect the owners' relaxed attitude to life.

'Well, Laura, here you are.'

'Heavens!' I exclaimed, 'what a size for a bedroom.'

Thomas chuckled, gratified. 'Plenty of space for your keep-fit routine.'

'Oh, I only do yoga and that doesn't need much space.'

He then explained to me that in the old days, when large families and lots of servants inhabited a house, privacy was at a premium. Only the most important members of the family were allowed a bedroom to themselves, which would also serve as a private sitting-room.

This one was really spacious with good antique furniture in all the right places. The huge double bed was covered with a beautifully worked quilt that matched the material of the canopy above the head end. All the room's colours were subtle, blending discreetly with the somewhat faded blue of the silk damask on the walls. Yet the ambience was not genteel but unobtrusively masculine, helped, perhaps, by the absence of bric-à-brac and any personal trifles.

As if on cue, Thomas said: 'You know, I asked Rosemary whether you would mind a bedroom that's not traditionally feminine. To my relief she assured me you weren't a frilly girl.' He lowered his voice conspiratorially. 'I shouldn't really tell you this. Joanna insisted that you should have the Primrose Room. But I did something I very rarely do – I put my foot down. You see, since I've only just finished restoring this room, we call it the Blue Room, so I naturally wanted a visitor to try it out.' He laughed. 'If you've got it, flaunt it! Believe me, in comparison, the Primrose Room is pokey. And it only gives out onto the orchard. But look at this view.'

I did. The garden wasn't very large. Its flowerbeds and paths had been designed by someone with a fine sense for movement and proportion. It was, however, the view beyond that caught one's breath: incredibly green hills rolling in waves towards a cerulean sky. There were islands of trees and, in between, grazing cattle and a flock of sheep.

I promptly expressed my admiration and was again touched by his response. No blasé pretence. He took delight in his possessions and didn't mind showing it. Altogether, he struck me as an honest, straightforward sort of person who would never willingly deceive anybody. How this could be squared with his success in the City, I didn't ponder. But I did think that Joanna had absolutely no reason to be jealous. His attitude towards me was that of a benevolent uncle. If he had put his arm around me and given me a squeeze, I would have seen it as a friendly, innocent gesture.

'I'd better show you where all the light switches are.'

It was then that I saw the picture. Being on the same wall as the door, opposite the dramatic bed, it had been behind me as I surveyed the room and the garden. I was startled by its amazing three-dimensional effect. It was a full-length, life-size portrait of a Victorian gentleman. In his early forties, I guessed. He stood at the top end of three carpeted stairs, one hand resting on his silver-handled Malacca cane, the thumb of the other nonchalantly tucked into the pocket of his waistcoat. His stance was not that of a cautious man pausing before the descent, but of an alert male deliberately taking his time.

The first thing I had noticed about him had been his red hair and, a split second later, his eyes. They were looking at me. I moved a few steps to the right. His gaze followed me. In years of art-gallery visits I had come upon this phenomenon before. Sometimes, a painter will let his model look out at the observer. It doesn't happen often, as the effect can be rather disconcerting. It was now. Those dark blue eyes under their copper-coloured lashes were definitely making contact.

'My great-uncle Maximilian,' said Thomas, watching my face. 'I see you're impressed.'

'Well, it is an impressive portrait. Who's the painter?'

'I haven't a clue ... Nor do I know the name of the model.'

'But you just said ...'

He chuckled. 'I was only teasing. Actually, I bought it at a country auction. It was one of a job lot of two. "Storm Clouds over the Fens" and "Portrait of a Man with Red Hair". The latter title intrigued me because my mother's family was ginger-headed. You wouldn't believe the state they were in. The frames were dilapidated, and the paintings themselves covered with grime. No wonder I got them for a song.'

'So you guessed the potential and had them cleaned and restored?'

'Yes. The funny thing is, this man really does remind me of my mother's uncle. Judging by the only photograph we have, he was quite a good-looker. He emigrated to Australia and died there comparatively young.'

'I noticed the Fen painting in the hall,' I said. 'It cleaned up beautifully. And this one is even better.' I knew that my appreciation would make him feel good. Though my taste favours more modern artists like Matisse, Klee or Kokoschka, I wasn't blind to the excellence of this painting.

'Just look at the textiles,' enthused Thomas. Indeed, the cloth of the suit, the velvet of the waistcoat and the silk cravat were almost tangible.

'See that Persian runner on the stairs?' he continued, 'you could stroke the pile, it's so real.' I looked at the runner, then at the rug that covered the low chest just below the picture. Thomas grinned. 'Another lucky buy. Perfect match. What? It brings the stairs right into the room. Did you notice that the light on the figure comes from the direction of the windows? I like these touches of reality. That's why I kept the frame unobtrusive.'

'Never mind reality,' I said dryly, 'you obviously have a penchant for drama.' He accepted this as a compliment.

During all this time I was aware of the red-headed man watching me. When Thomas started to analyse and discuss him I began to feel strangely ill at ease. 'He's got a strong, lean face but his features are irregular. Don't you agree, Laura? See his nose veering to the right? That means he's right-handed. Uncle Max's features were more regular and he was left-handed. But this one has more personality. In fact, the bearing of a patrician.' He gave me a cheeky look. 'Whether he likes it or not, I've adopted him as my honorary uncle Max.'

I had to agree that he had the presence of a man who would stand out in a crowd. Encouraged, Thomas carried on and I was too put out to know how to stop him politely.

'Just look at the treatment of the skin. Masterly. You can almost feel the flesh and the bone underneath. There, look at the veins on his temples.' Again, I had to agree. The translucent quality of skin, peculiar to some very fair and red-haired people, had been skilfully captured. Of the moderns, Lucien Freud came to my mind. Yet his flesh, superbly painted though it is, often strikes me as unappetising and morbid. In contrast, Uncle Max's flesh looked fresh and alive: it would be a pleasure to touch it.

'Well, well,' said a light baritone voice in my head, 'this looks promising.' I flushed. Did I see a faint mocking smile on those lips? This was ridiculous. I must be hallucinating. I was trying to find my mental balance when Thomas turned to me: 'Well, Laura, it's such a pleasure to have you here. I leave you to do your unpacking and freshening up. If you're interested, look into the other rooms, poke about a bit and generally make yourself at home.'

When the door shut behind him I felt he had deserted me. The temperature seemed to have dropped a degree or two. I was alone with Uncle Max.

I stood rigid. The atmosphere was charged with an indefinable, eerie something. I thought I could sense his presence behind me, but dared not look round. I gasped. Was that a breath at the back of my neck? I tried to call Thomas back, but no sound came. Desperate, I swung round. The room was empty. No movement, except for the curtains billowing gently in the breeze. Panic over, the tension eased. My saner self asserted itself: 'For heaven's sake, woman, it's only a bloody picture. Just clever daubs of paint on canvas. Get that into your silly noddle.'

Of course, I had been stupid. Nevertheless, feeling as I did, I should have preferred to change rooms or leave. Yet how could I, without making myself and Rosemary look ridiculous? My only option was to curb my sick fancies and act normally. And that, I realised, had to start right now. Resolutely, I went up to the picture and faced it like an objective critic. I looked through the lashes of my narrowed eyes to check the tonal values. Tried to evaluate its proportions, and the shapes of the negative spaces. What did I think of the colours and glazes? Heavens, who did I think I was kidding? Not myself, and certainly not him. All I could really take in was the glorious copper of his hair. I tried to evade his eyes. Too late. His gaze had captured mine and I felt him willing me to acknowledge his existence. 'This is a painting,' I said aloud, 'a good painting, but ONLY a painting.' If only this had been a magic mantra capable of helping me. I struggled. I really did. With a great effort I turned my attention to the impressive signet ring. I tried to study its engraved design but was distracted by the shape of his hand. Narrow and sinewy, it showed the veins pulsing under the skin. His impeccable shirt cuff reminded me of my grandfather – he who took pride in always being fresh and dapper.

I sniffed. Surely, this was eau de Cologne. Just like granddad's. Return of childhood memories and the old man's fragrant embrace. He had bravely continued to use what many called 'that sissy perfume', when 'real men' wore short-back-and-sides and fancied that the odour of stale sweat was a turn-on. Here it was again. Definitely cologne. Where did it come from? I scanned the room for a likely source. Perhaps a bowl of potpourri? There was none. But there were flowers on the windowsill. I went to check. Some were indeed scented but the combined odour differed from cologne. Surely, I couldn't have imagined it? Frankly, I was confused. What had come first, my awareness of the scent or my memory of granddad? Somehow, this point seemed important but I decided to consider it later.

Clouds had started to drift across the sun, creating changing shadow patterns on the hills. How peaceful this room and its view would be, I thought, but for that unsettling painting. I decided to ignore it completely and unpack. I had only brought the most essential things, since Rosemary, who was my size, would be able to lend me garments from her extensive hoard of clothes. I laid out what I needed for immediate use.

Resolutions are one thing, sticking to them another. Whenever I risked a sidelong glance at Max, our eyes met. His was an intimate, sensuous gaze. But his faintly mocking smile, which I had noticed before, betrayed an irritatingly male self-assurance. It asserted that HIS will and not mine would prevail. As a modern woman I found this offensive. And yet, my general resentment and apprehension was, I must admit, tinged with a certain pleasurable frisson. God, what a disturbingly fascinating man he was. His air of sophistication bordering on decadence, combined with male animal energy, was irresistible; perhaps the magnetism of a satyr manqué?

Not wanting to change in front of him, I picked up my things and fled into the bathroom. It was brand-new and a dream of white marble. A full-length mirror reflected an arrangement of exotic foliage. All the latest equipment had been unobtrusively incorporated, leaving one with the impression of streamlined elegance. With Max shut out, this was sanctuary. I felt safe to relax and luxuriate.

By the time I returned to the bedroom I had regained much of my confidence. I knew I looked good in my new short dress and pretty shoes. Had I expected Max to react? Believe it or not, he seemed to be moving. It looked as if he were shifting his weight, preparing to descend the stairs. 'Don't start being silly again,' urged my sober self. 'It's only the clouds affecting the light.' But my other half was alarmed: was he up to something? 'Don't you dare,' I snapped, as I hurriedly left the room.

Outside, I decided to take the Lancasters at their word and do a bit of exploring. I had to take my mind off that man. Cautiously, I knocked at every door on my floor before opening it. There were two rooms in the process of being redecorated, then came the master bedroom and, next to that, the Primrose Room. It turned out to be chintzily pretty and not to my taste at all. Then I found a panel door that opened into a walk-in cupboard. Cleaning materials and dusters on shelves gave way, on one side, to a vacuum cleaner and an assortment of brushes and mops. When I saw a very long-handled one, I had an idea. But did I have the nerve to execute it? It could be the answer to my problem. I had to try. I grabbed the mop and returned to the Blue Room. There, I pulled the quilt off the bed and, with my heart pounding, stepped onto the chest in front of the picture. Mustering all my courage, and concentrating exclusively on the frame, I managed to lift the material with the aid of the long handle and to tuck it over the top corners. Hurrah! Success. 'That's taken care of you,' I said, relieved. Before closing the door I looked back. Good God. The quilt. Did it move? 'Another trick of the light,' I thought, 'or perhaps a draught from the window.' But deep down I wasn't so sure.

When Thomas caught sight of me, he gave a little whistle. Joanna reprimanded him. 'You are embarrassing Laura.'

'Nonsense, a girl likes to be appreciated. I am a leg man,' he explained. 'And that's far less embarrassing than being a bum and breast man like your brother, Joanna.' The banter continued over aperitifs. Thomas handed me my drink. 'Tell us if there's anything you need. We want you to be comfortable.'

'Thanks, everything's just perfect. I count myself

lucky to have landed here. Such style and luxury. The bathroom is fabulous. I like the idea of the built-in dressing table and the cosy chair. In most bathrooms one has nowhere comfortable to sit. I find that most frustrating.' I didn't want to be too gushing, but a little praise, I thought, wouldn't come amiss.

Joanna smiled. 'I'm pleased you like it. But I must tell you the latest about Rosemary. Poor girl, she'll have her hands full. The damage is absolutely ghastly. It seems now that the whole house will need new plumbing.' 'Costly business,' interjected Thomas. 'And messy,' Joanna continued. 'We had ours done before we moved in. Plumbing and rewiring. And, of course, there were the structural repairs.' While Joanna was talking, I resolved to go and see Rosemary next morning. Right from childhood on she had been level-headed and competent. In fact, a good coper. Still, she may be glad of some help.

'Thank God, we've got all that behind us,' said Thomas. 'I can now concentrate on the enjoyable jobs; the decorating and furnishing. It appeals to the artist in me.' Lounging in his armchair, sipping his whisky, he radiated contentment and bonhomie. He was obviously on to his favourite subject. 'You know, I love going to auctions, or poking about in antique shops or even car boot sales. I've picked up some amazing bargains over the years. Haven't I, Joanna?'

'Yes, dear.' Her tone was that of a patient parent humouring an over-enthusiastic youngster. 'Some of your finds have turned out to be quite attractive, though it isn't always easy to place them.'

'Like Uncle Max, you mean?' He sounded a trifle reproachful.

I pricked up my ears.

Joanna sighed. 'I know it's a fine work of art, but you were trying to pass him off as your genuine uncle. Believe me, Laura, once he gets hooked on an idea there's no stopping him. I can see myself surrounded by a rogues' gallery of adopted ancestors. I just couldn't live with that. Besides, I think it is pretentious to claim descendance from picturesque characters picked up in a sales room. So you see, I had to nip this thing in the bud. That's why Uncle Max is now out of bounds upstairs.'

She had spoken with charm, making light of her subject. I was, however, aware that she was watching me closely. Smiling, I gave nothing away. I couldn't help wondering how Max had affected her. Surely, as a woman of taste she wouldn't exile such an elegant painting unless she had a very good reason. Somehow, her ancestor aversion didn't ring true.

'So he went straight to the Blue Room?' I asked.

'No, we had him down here for a couple of days till I managed to persuade Thomas.'

I was curious. 'How did you do that?'

She laughed. 'I made him an offer he couldn't refuse. Either you move Max or I plaster the walls with posters of cute little puppies and kittens.'

'To look at her,' said Thomas, 'you wouldn't think she could come up with such a fiendish threat. Even so, I'm determined to discover the identity of the artist and his patron. How would you set about it, Laura?'

'I'm afraid I'd start the lazy way. Send a good photograph to the National Portrait Gallery in London and let them get on with it. The experts should be able to find your society painter from the period of Uncle Max's clothes. Then you'd have to take it from there.'

'Thanks, I may do just that, especially as I shall be tied up for some time to come.'

'Is there still a lot to be done?' I generously gave him the chance to go on.

'Enough to keep me going for another two years. I haven't started on the top floor yet.' He gave Joanna an affectionate look. 'You see, Laura, I go to a lot of trouble not to get under Joanna's feet.'

She responded with an amused smile. I had the impression that all was well between them.

'We're lucky we've still got good craftsmen in the village,' he said. 'And, of course, Stanley is a great help.' He explained that Stanley was the live-in gardener and handyman. His Spanish wife, Juanita, looked after the house, with part-time help from the village. Joanna herself, he said with pride, was actively involved in local life. She had recently become a JP.

Two aperitifs on a more or less empty stomach had made me feel somewhat light-headed. Thomas was trying to press a third one on me, when the sound of the gong came to my rescue. We went in to dinner.

It turned out to be a candlelit affair. Not just a candlestick here and there, but four massive candelabra that seemed to have found their way from some Orthodox church. How does he persuade her to use all these things, I wondered.

I don't know what the candlelight did for me, but it flattered Joanna no end. She wore a little black number that set off her ornate jewellery. Opals set in diamonds swung sparkling from her ears, and a large opal of exceptional fire drew one's attention to her décolletage. Another bargain, I supposed. She looked opulently glamorous.

Juanita served at table. A wholesome, middle-aged woman, she was friendly without being servile. Neither did she efface herself but quite openly looked for our reaction to the food she had cooked. In contrast to the table with its fancy cut glass, ornate silver tureens and serving dishes, the food was simple. It was well cooked, with touches of refinement that did not disguise the excellence of the ingredients. I voiced my appreciation.

'All our own produce,' said Thomas proudly, 'including the duck.'

'You keep ducks?' I was surprised.

'And geese, and hens.'

'Doesn't it break your heart when it comes to killing them?'

` 'Stanley does the killing. Yes, we are sorry, but you get hardened to it.' He grinned. 'We no longer give them names. That helps. I mean, it seemed ghoulish to be nibbling Agatha's breast or Jenny's leg.'

He told me that he had recently bought a large stock of wine from a man with acute money problems. And, surprise, surprise, paying instant cash, he had got those crates for a ridiculously low sum. He was determined to make this an occasion for wine tasting. Opening bottle after bottle, he cajoled Joanna and me to give our judgement on I don't know how many vintages. Noticing me looking concerned about the number of abandoned half-empty bottles, he seemed amused. 'Don't worry, this tipple won't get a chance to oxidise. Not in this household.'

'What a do,' I thought. 'Surely they don't dress up and booze like this every night.'

Once again, Thomas seems to have guessed my thoughts. 'Normally, we eat in the kitchen, but once in a while we like to put on a show. No point in having things if you never use and enjoy them. Now, ladies, let's taste this one.'

By the time we left the table I was thoroughly befuddled and unsteady on my legs. Joanna said she felt sleepy and soon went up to bed.

I hazily remember Thomas taking my arm and half carrying me up the stairs to my door. I must have just slipped off my clothes and dropped straight into bed. Before my head touched the pillow I caught a glimpse of the quilt still covering the picture. Then: instant oblivion.

Next morning I woke slowly, turning drowsily as if from an embrace. What an amazing dream. I had never experienced anything like it. The memory of it made the blood rise to my cheeks. Max. Yes, Max had been with me. With his caressing voice beside me, any thought of resistance had melted away. Helplessly willing, I let him do things Trevor would never have thought of, things that had been even beyond my imagination. It was with a feeling of both awe and elation that I recalled the incredible intensity of the experience. Not at all like a normal couple relationship. Truly, a satyr in action. I stretched voluptuously, vaguely aware of the scent of eau de Cologne that emanated from the pillow.

When I opened my eyes, I saw the quilted cover in a heap on the chest, and Max in his 3D splendour looking straight down at me.

'*Bonjour, ma petite*,' said his voice in my head. 'What a night!'

I was about to reply favourably when I noticed his expression. It was not one of adoration, love, or even affection, but of unadulterated self-satisfaction. I had been just one more conquest. He had used me.

'It was good, eh?' His voice was suavely insinuating. 'But tonight will be even better. It'll be ecstasy.'

'Like hell it will.' I jumped out of bed. There were stabbing pains in my head and my brain felt all sore and tender. Naked as I was, I stormed up to him. 'You supercilious, condescending bastard. You've taken advantage of me. Alright, I'm hot-blooded, on the rebound and pretty much run-down, but you wouldn't have got anywhere if I hadn't been drunk. Who do you think you are? Some fancy aristocrat or lord of the manor exercising his *droit de seigneur*? I tell you who you are. A bloody out-of-work bit-actor, too pissed to hold down a proper part. Only just good enough to pose in borrowed clothes. Fancy yourself as a bloody grandee, do you?'

He seemed to increase in stature. His face darkened to a superior, haughty stare. I cupped my breasts in my hands. 'Look, demon lover, that's the last you see of them. And now you can bloody well watch my arse, and that's the last time too.' I was using the most coarse and vulgar words I could think of on the spur of the moment. I was desperate to rile him and demolish his lofty composure. Wiggling my behind as I minced my way to the bathroom, I sang: 'I'm gonna wash that man right out of my hair.'

I slammed the door, then had to lean against it. I was feeling shaky. My heart was pounding and so was my head. I was sweaty, my mouth tasted foul, and my tongue felt like a blanket. What a hangover. Yet I was pleased with myself. I had shown that patronising bastard that, even in this poor shape, I was capable of holding my own.

If only my head were clearer, I'd be able to sort things out. I decided to clean my teeth, have a good gargle and then relax in a hot bath. Yes, that might do the trick. When I bent down to run the water I caught sight of a mark near my groin. Startled, I went over to the mirror. There was another below my breast, and another at the base of my neck. All vividly coloured and lozenge shaped. I knew what they were. A cold shiver ran down my spine. Considering their position, I couldn't possibly have made them myself.

My mind was a whirl. Thomas, I thought, had

made me drunk. Had he put something else into my glass? Had he given Joanna a sleeping draft so that she wouldn't miss him? Was all his attention to her a sham? 'Oh, no,' I sobbed. 'I can't, I won't believe it.' What about Max? 'Get a grip on yourself, woman. He's only the phantom lover of your imagination. Oil paint on canvas, remember?' But even at this stage, hating him like mad, I wanted to believe in his reality.

I stared at my reflection. The longer I stared, the more vivid the marks appeared to be. 'Like the stigmata of saints,' I whispered, 'only mine are the stigmata of lust.' It was a combination of horror and perverted amusement that set me off laughing. I laughed and laughed until I could hardly breathe. I started to choke. Though I was trapped in a cocoon of hysteria, there must have been a small, sane part of me still outside. Suddenly, I found myself in the shower cabinet, gagging under a burst of cold water. The panic was over.

Wrapped in a bath-towel, I sat and pondered on the immediate future. Whatever had caused these shameful marks, I had to leave. I felt that further exposure could seriously upset my mental balance. Not only did I have to leave as soon as possible, but I had to do so without upsetting anybody. I found my mobile and phoned my sister. Of course, she was curious. 'Please, don't ask questions now, just do as I told you. Phone in about an hour. And please, Mary, make it sound convincing.'

After that I had a bath and washed my hair. I took trouble over my make-up. I had to cover the pallor and camouflage the dark rings round my eyes. A blouse with a collar and a kerchief tucked inside hid the mark at the base of my neck. When I was ready, I walked straight through the room, looking neither right nor left. My next problem was facing Thomas.

I entered the kitchen. It was a spacious, rectangular room with a 'ye olde' rustic ambience. All the stock items were present: the solid table with Windsor chairs, the Welsh dresser, the wicker and rocking chairs. Old samplers and corn dollies adorned the walls, and strings of onions and garlic, as well as bunches of drying herbs hung from the beams. There were hand-made rugs on the old tiled floor, and on the threshold of the open door that led into the kitchen garden sat a black-and-white cat washing its face. Yet, corny as it all was, it felt homely and friendly and I loved it. No wonder the Lancasters took most of their meals here.

Juanita by the Aga was assembling a plate of breakfast fry-ups. She greeted me. 'Same for you, Miss?'

I had to refuse. Much as I would have loved it at any

other time, my stomach was too delicate this morning. I helped myself to muesli and asked for coffee.

'Ah, good morning, Laura,' boomed Thomas as he entered, bending down to stroke the cat on the way. By the time he reached the table, Juanita had put the loaded plate in position. 'I trust you slept well,' he said brightly, stabbing his fork into one of the yolks. I watched it weep and nodded. He wasn't really waiting for an answer. 'We're lucky. It's going to stay fine all day. Unfortunately, I'll have to meet my surveyor this morning, but I can show you round after lunch. There's lots I'd like you to see. Didn't you say you'd be looking in at Rosemary's after breakfast?'

'Yes,' I said as casually as I could.

'Pity you won't be seeing the kids. They're a grand pair. I'm teaching the lad to ride, you know. We offered to have them both for the time being to give Rosemary a chance to cope with the flood, but her brother beat us to it. He collected them last night.'

I didn't know what to make of him. He seemed so relaxed and unconcerned. Was he innocent or a consummate actor? While chewing, he grinned at me across the bunch of marigolds on the table, obviously expecting me to reveal more of my plans. At that moment, small talk was beyond me. 'I'm sorry, I'm not at my best this morning,' I said somewhat awkwardly. 'You see, I'm not used to sumptuous late meals and lots of drink.'

Instant sympathy. 'Oh, you poor girl. A little hangover. What about the hair of the dog? You know there's plenty of it.'

I was in the process of refusing when Joanna came in. Except for a touch of lipstick, she wore no make-up. Though she had drunk more than I, she looked fresh and alert.

'Ah, here you are, Laura. I hope you slept well.' This, I felt, was a genuine enquiry. Once again, I was aware of the searching quality of her look. I wondered what she was thinking. What did she know?

'You with your hair of the dog, Tom. Laura, if you like, Juanita can mix you a potion that always works with me.' Her expression became serious. 'I'm afraid I have bad news. Rosemary just phoned with a message from your sister Mary. Apparently she couldn't get through to your mobile. She has broken her ankle and her husband is away on a business trip.'

'Oh, my God!' I exclaimed, trying to make it sound

spontaneous. 'I must leave at once. She'll need help with the children.'

'Of course, you must, Laura. But I'm disappointed. I'd been looking forward to enjoying your company. Tom and I were going to show you all the local sights and take you to a couple of fêtes.' Her regret sounded sincere, yet at the same time, I sensed that she was relieved to see me go. In spite of this, I knew that I liked her. In the course of the previous evening I had come to appreciate her intelligence, good humour and womanly warmth. I felt we could have become friends.

I decided not to stay for lunch but to catch the next train to London. Joanna would run me to the station. There was just time to finish breakfast and do the packing, but not to call on Rosemary. Though I felt guilty about the deception, I just couldn't face her. Knowing me as she did, she would guess that something was wrong. But telling her the truth was impossible. Her solid, down-to-earth character would be incapable of accepting such a weird story. She'd think me mad.

It didn't take me long to stuff my few belongings into my bag. Whilst doing so, I ignored Max. I hoped that by deciding to quit and by making this decision irrevocable, I had put myself beyond his power. Before leaving, I cast a last look round. The room was still invitingly beautiful and the view as idyllic as ever. The cattle and sheep were still grazing on those emerald hills. Approaching the door, I glanced back at Max. I caught my breath. How impressive he looked, poised with such nonchalant elegance at the top of the stairs. Yet his relaxed body language was belied by his imperious expression. His stare was aggressive – it was his will against mine. The voice in my head commanded: 'Stay, Laura. Stay!'

'Piss off,' I said, and walked out.

It was early December when Rosemary came to visit me in my new flat. I could tell on the phone that something was wrong and that the shopping trip was just an excuse. We had been friends since primary school. Her steady temperament complemented my restless, impulsive nature. We had some happy times together. Later, separated by circumstances, we had come to a tacit agreement that an occasional contact would have to suffice. Both of us led busy, even hectic lives in different parts of the country. To keep abreast with day-to-day happenings requires frequent, regular contact for which neither of us could spare the time. Thus, our friendship went into periodic hibernation. Yet whenever we did manage to meet, we were as close as ever, able to carry on as if there had been no break.

She arrived punctually, looking pale and tired. We embraced.

'Here you are at last,' I said brightly. 'Well, this is my new place. I haven't done much with it, mainly because it may be only temporary. I've been going steady for the last three months. Paul is a widower, some years older than I, and he has a house in Pinner. I'll be moving in with him in the new year. He's as solid as you are,' I tried to joke, 'so he'll be good for me.'

I watched her glance round. She looked listless and her eyes were dull. I couldn't help feeling guilty for pouring out my good news when she was so obviously suffering from some worry or stress. 'If things work out,' I continued, 'we may consider marriage and even children in a year or two.'

I was pleased to see her eyes light up, if only momentarily: 'Laura, dear, this is wonderful. I wish you much happiness.'

We settled down and I poured her a cup of tea. 'Enough about me. I see you got rid of your long tresses. Short and straight suits you. And I like that fringe.'

'It's easy-care,' she said soberly. 'No time for fancy hairdos.'

'So. What about your news? I assume you recovered from the flooding. That really was a shame.'

'The last six months have been hell,' she sighed. 'It started with the flood and the replumbing of the house. Then Julian's father Joe, who had Alzheimer's, got worse and needed more care. For his mother's sake, we had an annexe built and helped them move and sell their property. Then Christopher caught meningitis. It was touch-and-go. A real nightmare. Joe died two months ago and at his very funeral mum fell and broke her tibia. It's been worries and rushing about for months.

'Julian's been a most supportive husband, but when his job took him away I had to cope on my own. Thank God, apart from Joe's death, everything is back to normal.' She had spoken in her usual matter-of-fact way without any trace of self-pity. She'd had problems, faced them and coped with them. So why did I have the feeling that something else was troubling her? I commiserated with her and, more to keep the conversation going than from any pressing interest, asked how the Lancasters were getting on. To my surprise, Rosmary frowned and bit her lip.

'It's a long story, Laura. Shortly after you left, Thomas fell seriously ill. Some sort of infection and inflammation to do with his heart, I believe. After he came back from hospital Joanna nursed him day and night. She wouldn't let anybody else take a turn, not even Juanita. She got so run down that in the end Thomas insisted that his worrying about her health gave him no chance of recovery. So they got a professional night nurse and Joanna moved out of the master bedroom. The nurse got the room next door for instant access.'

'The Primrose Room?' I asked.

'That's right.'

'Then where did Joanna sleep?'

'Two rooms further on. I think they called it the Blue Room.'

My heart missed a beat. Joanna in the Blue Room – with Max! I could visualise him following her with his eyes and making her hear his voice. Had he managed to do to her what he had done to me? What had been their relationship? I pulled myself together. That bloody painting! After all this time, and all my firm rejections of anything supernatural, I was still being dragged back into the orbit of that dark, mysterious figure. I hid my concern as Rosemary continued.

'You'd think that sleeping on her own and away from all the to-ing and fro-ing of serious nursing, she'd soon feel better. Far from it. She got worse. I was shocked when I saw her. She'd lost a lot of weight and looked haggard. I called on them a number of times but there was nothing I could do. Besides, I was up to my neck in troubles of my own. Gradually, Thomas started to recover and was even walking a few steps with a frame.'

Rosemary's eyes filled with tears and she shook her head as if trying to rid herself of a terrible vision. 'It happened on the day the nurse had left and Joanna was due to move back to the master bedroom. Poor, Joanna! It's incredible, Laura. She ... she went out of her mind.'

I couldn't believe my ears. 'What on earth do you mean? What happened?'

'I can only tell you what Juanita described to me later. She was crossing the hall when she heard shouting in one of the bedrooms. Thinking that Thomas had collapsed, she dashed up the stairs to find him leaning against the doorpost of the Blue Room. He looked horror stricken. Inside, Joanna was rushing about in a frenzy, screaming abuse and brandishing a dagger. Juanita noticed that Joanna had already slashed one of the pictures in the room. Afraid that her beloved mistress would injure herself, she stepped forward to get hold of the dagger. Thomas called out and Joanna froze. Staring at them, she gave a harrowing groan and, before anybody could react, she'd run to the open window and jumped out.

'Death was instantaneous. And then Thomas suffered a stroke.'

Rosemary looked at me. She was calm now. I wondered whether having got this terrible story off her chest had eased her mind. Listening to her, I had visualised it all, down to the oriental paperknife dagger from the marquetry escritoire. The most important question in my mind was whether Joanna had experienced what I had? Had she, run down in the extreme, succumbed to Max's seduction – and enjoyed it? Night after night? What would she have felt when return to the marital bed was imminent? Devastating guilt most likely, and resentment and hatred of the one who had manoeuvred her into this situation. Most of all, hatred of herself. I remembered my own rage. But I hadn't ended up on the terrace flagstones, mangled like a broken doll.

'What did she shout?' I asked, and managed to sound sympathetic but controlled.

Rosemary shook her head. 'Juanita wouldn't say. There was something peculiar in the way she refused to answer, almost as if she'd been told to keep mum.'

For a moment I wondered whether Max had tried to influence her too. But I felt sure that, with village helpers to call on, she would have avoided working in the Blue Room by herself. She may have been aware of him but she wasn't under his spell. It was more likely that Thomas himself had asked her not to tell anybody. It must have been an embarrassing tirade, full of shameful details that had to remain secret.

I was interested to learn that his stroke hadn't been severe, but that he wouldn't return to the house. It was now up for sale, including contents. I was surprised by my strong feelings of regret. All the excitement and enthusiasm for planning, collecting and creating had come to naught. Poor Thomas: with Joanna gone, it no longer made sense to him.

I thought this was the end of the affair, mistakenly as it turned out. Rosemary was staring into the distance. She was far away.

'Will you miss them very much?' I asked.

'Miss what?' She looked bewildered and I realised

that it was not the Lancasters she'd been thinking about.

'The day before yesterday,' she started, 'I went over to see how the house clearing was getting on. The place seemed deserted. Then I saw smoke rising in the back of the stable yard and went round. Stanley was feeding a bonfire. You remember Stanley, the handyman?'

'I heard them talk about him but I never actually met him.'

'Thin, wiry chap but very strong. He adored Thomas. He isn't much of a talker but he let me chat to him and answered the odd question. That's how I learned that Thomas was recovering and would be staying with his son near Winchester for some time to come. The son was making all the arrangements and he, Stanley, saw to the practical execution of them on the spot. Burning unwanted stuff seemed to be part of it. It was cold and we stood quite close to the fire. Then Stanley threw some more wood on it and a large roll. As it uncurled I saw it was an oil painting; the portrait of a man with red hair.'

Startled, I sat up but didn't interrupt. My apprehension grew as I watched her face. It bore an expression of dreaminess and longing.

'Oh, Laura, you can't imagine how fascinating he was. Not run-of-the-mill handsome, but compelling. I swear his eyes were looking straight at me. The contact was ... well ... almost physical. I felt he was alive. I just had to have this painting and take it home with me. The lower half was somewhat damaged, but there was enough space around the head and shoulders to have made a well-proportioned picture.

"'Don't burn it, Stanley," I cried, "I want it. Please fetch it out." There was still time but Stanley refused. "The master's special orders. The thing must be burned. I had to promise him to make a thorough job of it."

'Believe me, Laura, the man was looking at me even more intensely. His eyes were pleading, and suddenly I heard his voice in my head: "Save me, you must save me." Without another thought I stepped forward to pull him out. "Are you crazy?" shouted Stanley, and dragged me back. I struggled to reach the canvas but his grip on my arm was like a vice. I was desperate. I would have done anything to save him. The flames started to lick the edges of the canvas and then, suddenly, the whole thing flared up; puckering, blistering and distorting the face. My head was bursting with the sound of screaming and the roaring of the fire. I fainted.'

Rosemary shivered and for a few seconds buried her face in her hands. 'The next thing I saw was Juanita in the Lancasters' kitchen, putting a compress on my forehead. Eventually, Stanley took me home.'

It was clear to me that Rosemary had never seen the painting before nor had she heard anything about it. Even in Juanita's account the specific picture had never been mentioned. And yet, quite out of context, within the span of a few minutes Max had managed to bewitch this solid, pragmatic young woman. Thinking of Rosemary's description of the fire, I also remembered historic reports of the burning of witches and warlocks; the *auto-da-fé* of the Spanish Inquisition, the great public occasions where the population could watch the heretics roast till their skin turned to crackling and their eyeballs exploded. Yet most of them had been innocent. Had Max been guilty? Evil? Had he deserved his fate?

'Laura,' Rosemary said with some hesitation, 'I had the impression that, in the end, he was cursing me. Could that be possible? I can't get him out of my head.'

I put my arm around her. 'Don't worry, love. The reason you keep thinking of the portrait is because it probably was a very good work of art. It appealed to you and, coming across it in such a dramatic way, it captured your imagination. But even if there had been another dimension, he would have seen how desperately you tried to save him. He couldn't possibly have born you a grudge.' I had made a great effort to sound firm and self-assured. She seemed relieved and her smile showed that I had convinced her.

'Well, that's the end of that,' I said. 'Now you can forget all about it.'

But inwardly I wondered, can I?

THE THINGY

One fine spring day the old lady returned home from her early morning shopping to see a young man outside her block of flats. He appeared to be searching for something around the motorbike at the curb, scrabbling frantically among the dirt and grit in the gutter.

'What are you looking for?' she asked. 'Can I help?'

More to give vent to his frustration than in any real expectation of help, he told her that he had lost a small but vital part of his motorbike, and that without it he could not make it go. The problem was that he had an important appointment and that he wouldn't be able to get there in time. She realized that he was near to tears.

'What does this thingy look like?'

'Oh, it's just a flat piece of tin, shaped like a sort of fish.'

'Come on,' she said resolutely, 'follow me. I'll make

you another.'

Unbelieving but desperate, he was obviously clutching at straws, as he followed her up to her first-floor flat. She immediately gave him paper and pencil. 'Here, draw it for me.'

By the time he had finished, she had emptied a cocoa tin and flattened a piece of it on her chopping board. Having been artistic all her life, copying his drawing and cutting it out with her heavy-duty kitchen scissors took her half a minute. A hole was needed on one side which she made with a nail and hammer. The young fellow almost snatched the thing out of her hands, and shouting 'thank you,' dashed off. By the time she reached the window he had already belted up the road and was turning into the main street.

'Ah well,' she said to herself, 'it seems to have worked alright.'

Two days later her doorbell rang. It was the young man, grinning from ear to ear. He handed her a box of chocolates and a giant bouquet of lilac. He had reached his appointment just in time and they had given him the job. He was happy to accept a cup of coffee and some of her home-made biscuits. His name was Hans. They spent a pleasant half hour chatting; she telling him about her daughter far away in England, he explaining to her that his new job was not a dead-end affair, but an exceptionally good position with wonderful prospects. In a year or two he would be qualifying for an important managership abroad.

When they parted, he thanked her again and kissed her cheeks. She watched him from the window revving up his machine. He looked up and she waved to him. He smiled, waved back and drove away.

The room seemed empty without his youthful enthusiasm and hope for the future. Only the sensuous scent of the lilac remained, filling the air with a mysterious feeling of languor.

They never met again, the enthusiastic young man in his twenties and the lonely old lady well into her seventies. But I am sure they kept remembering each other with warmth for the rest of their lives.

FAIRCHILD & MORRIS

I was a boy of fourteen, straight from school, when my father apprenticed me to the firm of Fairchild & Morris. He impressed upon me the fact that I would never have been given this wonderful chance without the recommendation of Mr Wiseman, who worked for this venerable establishment. When I enquired why Mr Wiseman should have been so solicitous for my future, father only said, 'because I asked him. He owes me.' His forbidding tone denied any further questions.

It was understood that I would have to start at the bottom and work my way up. So I found myself in the basement, where the merchandise arrived, was checked in and allocated to its proper place for sale or storage. I also had to unwrap goods for immediate sale. Most of the stuff was strange to me, for my mother believed in meat and two veg and a homemade pudding. The most exotic foods she would allow on her table were a slab of cheddar cheese or a tin of pilchards or sardines. In fairness it must be said that in those early post-war years so-called fancy food hardly ever made an appearance in our little local shops.

Fairchild & Morris were purveyors of high-class victuals and delicatessen supplies, catering for the *crème de la crème* of society. I must, at this point, acknowledge Mr Wiseman's patience and tact. It would have been easy to hold me up to ridicule, for my ignorance in culinary matters was all-pervading. Whether his kindness was genuine or because he 'owed' my father, I shall never know. I soon learned that those weird looking sticks were in fact sausages called salami and came from various countries. The variety of cheeses was bewildering, and so were the tins with contents like lychees or water-chestnuts. What with patés, herbs, spices and lots of other things that were totally unknown to me, I realized that I was touching the edges of a wider world.

I kept my eyes and ears open and learned quickly. I had to work hard, but then so did everybody else. In this section of the business there were, apart from Mr Wiseman, two more men and one boy called Fred, who was a little older than me. During our lunch break we would sit on any boxes or packing cases that stood around, eat our sandwiches brought from home, sip our tea which was generously provided by the employer, and gossip. For a long time I only listened. I was particularly interested in anything concerning the firm. Mr Fairchild was obviously the boss who did the day-to-day managing. I had seen him from a distance and didn't quite know what to make of him. On my second day there, he was walking through the yard when I was helping with the unloading. He saw me and stopped in front of me, joined by Mr Wiseman.

'This, sir, is Arnold, the young lad I told you about. He's real keen, ready to give it his best. Aren't you, boy?'

'Yes, sir.' I came up on cue. Mr Fairchild was fair alright. Not in the sense of fair beautiful, but fair pale. His complexion was very light and so were his grey eyes. His hair, fine and silky, was so pale it just missed being grey. He was slim and only topped me by a couple of inches: but then I was a gangly youth, exceptionally tall for my age.

'I hope you'll find the work interesting, once you get some experience.' His voice was unexpectedly deep. There was self-assurance and authority, and I recognized immediately that his social background was very different from mine. 'You know,' he continued, 'there are many centres where the world converges. In a small way, our little firm here is one of those centres. Goods from all the continents arrive here. If you can't see the excitement and romance of this, you'd be a very dull lad indeed.' He gave me a benevolent smile and with a 'good luck, Arnold,' went into the house.

I could see from the expressions of those around me that I had received a lot more attention than I could reasonably expect. I kept a straight face and didn't let on how pleased I was. At lunchtime, I had to put up with a little teasing and, in due course, I picked up the courage to ask what sort of boss Mr Fairchild was.

'He's strict,' said one of the men, 'but he's fair. I really think he wants to do the right thing for us. We get time off for emergencies at home, and there are all sorts of little things that make life a bit easier. He's even given us Christmas bonuses. But he can only do so much. You see, there's Mr Morris in the background. He's the other partner who keeps putting his foot down. He's a tight-fisted, hot-tempered bloke. The times I heard him stampeding up them narrow wooden stairs to the office, like a bull elephant in musk, and then yelling at poor Mr Fairchild, is nobody's business. Then, one day, coming down in a temper, he tumbled half a flight and landed with both legs broken and some internal injuries. We haven't seen him since. Have we?'

The others murmured their agreement and there was a short silence during which I speculated what musk was. I felt too shy to ask and wondered whether it had something to do with mustard. I knew that some mustards could be very hot, so that the elephant would be raging with a fiery temper.

'Though he's an invalid at home, he's as good as here,' the man continued. 'He's got his fingers in every pie, wanting this done, stopping that, asking for constant reports. I don't know how Mr Fairchild puts up with it. He must have the patience of an angel.' The others nodded in agreement.

'Still,' said Mr Wiseman, 'he's been able to bring about some changes which I for one never thought possible. Like buying the house next door and using some of the extra space for starting up the wholesale import business, and opening the dining room leading off the shop to serve our delicatessen and tasty snacks to the public. With all them offices around here, it turned into a little goldmine.'

'I suppose,' mused one of the men, 'Mr Fairchild can be quite persuasive in his quiet way.'

During the subsequent years I had plenty of opportunity to see Mr Fairchild at work. He never just told you to do something without explaining briefly why it should be done. Even we boy apprentices had the feeling that we were an important part of a whole enterprise and that we mustn't disappoint his trust. Sometimes, faced with a sudden decision, he would sigh and say, almost reluctantly, 'I'm afraid I'll have to consult Mr Morris on this one. His input on matters like this is essential.'

I never heard him make a derogatory remark about Mr Morris and, as far as I can remember, none of the others ever heard him say anything disrespectful. Yet it must have been an awful bind to have to refer to the old termagant on so many occasions. I developed a theory of my own which was based on Mr Fairchild's good nature. I thought he felt sorry for the old boy, invalided now and stuck at home without anything interesting to do. By involving him, he gave him some feeling of self-worth and importance. Of course, there were quite a number of things Mr Morris would not sanction. Sometimes, Mr Fairchild would react by looking pensive, saying, 'Maybe I can work around this one.'

And now, I must admit to a little underhand operation which had been triggered by curiosity. By then I had been with the firm for about three years and had worked my way up to the extent that I would be called to Mr Fairchild's office to give him certain progress reports and to receive follow-up instructions. On more than one occasion I had watched him dial Mr Morris's number to get the usual 'input'. In fact, I'd watched carefully enough to get the number and memorize it. I had been dying to hear Mr Morris's voice but realized I couldn't phone from a call box, which would have sounded suspicious. So I waited till I knew that Mr Fairchild was busy downstairs and not likely to come up for some time.

Hearing a woman's voice answer with the telephone number and the subsequent question 'Who's speaking, please?' threw me a little but I was sufficiently prepared to say 'I'm Mr Cox from Wainright & Masters' import department. Could I speak to Mr Morris, please?'

'He is not available at the moment. Can I give him a message? I am his daughter.'

'I am sorry,' I said, 'I really must speak to him personally.'

'In that case, I'll see what I can do.' After a few minutes Miss Morris picked up the phone again. 'Mr Cox,' she said in her mellow voice, 'would you please leave me your telephone number and Mr Morris will ring you back this afternoon.'

'Thank you,' I said. 'My number is...' and then, after quoting the first two digits, I put the receiver down to make it sound as if we'd been cut off.

I felt duly sorry for Mr Morris's gentle daughter and wondered what she looked like. Being young and impressionable, I couldn't help being romantically stirred by the idea of a mysterious female being in the power of this ogre – a sort of classic damsel in distress story. Except that she didn't really sounded distressed. She must have her method of handling him, I thought, otherwise, how could she possibly bear it?

If Mr Wiseman had imagined that I would understudy him in order to step into his shoes when he retired, he was very much mistaken. I soon left the receiving and stockroom work behind to join the elite in the selling department. There, I learned really fast, especially since nobody seemed to mind if I snatched a little taste here and there. I can't remember who prompted me, but I decided to attend evening classes. I chose German and French, since they were sufficiently different from each other to avoid confusion. To my amazement I found it easy to remember the vocabulary and, as everybody told me, I had a surprisingly good ear for correct pronunciation. In fact, I was a talented linguist.

My languages helped me a lot to get the hang of the international foods that came flooding in during those post-war years and which became increasingly more varied as time went on. I also had the opportunity to serve foreign customers and converse with them.

This brought me quite a bit of kudos but also, I'm afraid, a little jealousy from some of the staff. Since I had passed my French exams with flying colours, I went on to study Italian. During those years I was like a sponge, soaking up knowledge, experiences, impressions, in fact everything that came my way. The wonderful thing about it was that it made me feel good. Life was fun.

It didn't escape me that Mr Fairchild was taking an interest in my progress. Now and then he would have a little chat with me, not only about the business but also about things in general. When I asked my mum 'why on earth does he want to know what I think about Britain's relationship with France, or the rail strike, or how the local council handled Sainsbury's new planning application?' she was delighted.

'Don't you see, Arnold? He's is interested in you for higher things, not just slicing salami or weighing out cheese. I bet he's got you in mind for some sort of executive position.'

'Oh, mum, you're fantasizing!' Though I protested, I somehow felt she was right. I had noticed that, as time progressed, Mr Fairchild, when talking to me, had dropped his faintly condescending way of addressing juniors, and spoke to me in almost a man-to-man kind of way, which I found very flattering. My mind was made up: my career in the firm would lead me to the very top. This, I must now confess, wasn't just due to business ambition, but also because of my admiration and love – yes, love – of Imogen Fairchild.

It had been love at first sight, about two years or so after I had joined the firm. I happened to be by the window when I saw a beautiful woman crossing the yard. She was too elegant and what we then called 'classy' for any cheeky fellow to risk a wolf-whistle. I had seen her before on various occasions but never as closely as I would have wished. I had been told that she was Mrs Fairchild. Somehow, I found it gratifying that the man I admired should have such a conspicuously attractive wife.

Now, as she walked by, I couldn't help but stop what I was doing to watch her progress. Suddenly, a slim figure in streaming, diaphanous drapes seemed to blow in like a turquoise cloud and, it seemed to me, hardly touching the ground, joined the lady. I knew instantly that she was Imogen Fairchild, my boss's daughter. It was her delicate, fair complexion and her father's platinum blond hair that gave her away. It looked even more fine and silky than his and reminded me of the descriptions of enchanted princesses in ancient fairy stories. At last my innocent, romantic heart had found its idol. From then on Imogen was central to all my ambitions and dreams.

I had heard them talk about her. She was an only child and the apple of her father's eye. At the moment, she was enjoying a short break at home, only to be sent abroad again soon to continue her education. To my delight she quite frequently visited her father during those brief weeks and he appeared rather pleased with the interest she took in the business. A few days after my first sight of Imogen, she came into the rear room of the shop where some of the backing stock was being held. In those days many things that are now pre-packed as a matter of course were then sold loose. By then I already worked mainly in the shop and in the office but, since the stock-room man was on sick leave, I had taken on his tasks of ensuring that none of the many small drawers of the large storage cabinet became empty. I used part of my lunchtime for this. It was the sort of gesture Mr Fairchild appreciated. I hadn't been working long when she appeared. Surprised, I caught my breath but managed to regain my equilibrium by the time she had introduced herself.

'I'm Arnold Forster,' I said. 'I'm an apprentice learning the business.'

'What are you doing now?' Her questioning eyes were of an amazing violet blue and her complexion glowed clear and flawless. I wondered whether she had noticed the two pimples on my forehead I had been fretting over for days.

'Making sure there's enough stock in every drawer. Things have to be handy for quick service, you know.' I spoke with a nonchalance I didn't feel.

'Can I help?'

'If you like,' I said as calmly as I could. 'I am up to letter C. On the top left you'll find the caraway seed drawer. Look inside it and, if it's less than half full, bring it over to me. She reached it easily and I realized that she was of my height, which was very tall for a girl. In a jiffy she was beside me and I quickly scooped the fragrant seeds from my large wooden chest to fill the drawer. She seemed to enjoy the work as if it were a game and appeared sorry when I thanked her and pushed all the chests back into their original positions. She told me that she would have liked to stay in London and help her father; she thought that trading with so many far-flung counties was quite a challenge which she would enjoy. Her father, she said, would have been pleased to let her join the business but her mother had insisted on her finishing her education abroad.

She looked serious, almost sad for a moment then shrugged her shoulders. 'I expect that it will come in useful, especially the languages.' I think it was this conversation that encouraged me to take my study of languages even more seriously. During those few weeks she often dropped in to have a chat with me. Somehow, I nearly always managed to arrange my duties to make it possible. One day she asked me about my parents and whether I was an only child. I told her that my father worked in a bus depot, that my mother was at home and that I had two elder twin sisters.

'You are lucky to have siblings,' she said.

Her reaction surprised me. 'I never really thought about it,' I said, 'but I suppose I am pleased I've got them. Mind, they are quite a few years older than me, and I had to get used to be either fussed over, bossed about, or ignored. They were too old to be real playmates of mine and I could only be an observer when they did their girly things. Still, I think we all loved each other and still do. They say that only children are quicker to grow up.'

Imogen gave a little sigh. 'This may be true if they only live with adults at home, but my mother always made sure I wasn't.' Seeing my expression of incredulity, she explained: 'My father is too fond of me – and she's a very jealous woman. So it was kindergarten, boarding school, educational establishments abroad and, of course, another finishing school to come.'

'I'm sorry,' I stammered, 'I don't know what to say.'

She came closer and touched my arm. 'Don't say anything, Arnold, just be my friend.'

Moved, I nodded, and for a while we stood still, looking at each other in silence until approaching footsteps made us continue with our work. Although I was always conscious that she was the boss's daughter, I found that she made it easy for me to relax and talk to her as an equal. I knew she liked me but feared that I couldn't expect more than that.

It was about a week later that her mother came upon us. We hadn't heard her and I think she must have been watching us for long enough to form an opinion of our relationship. We were busy sorting a consignment of small jars. Although we only talked about the work in hand, there was a feeling of intimacy and close companionship that cannot have escaped her. Of course, I had seen Mrs Fairchild during her brief visits to her husband's office. She would walk through the rooms without lingering anywhere.

Sometimes, in passing, she would nod and smile at some of the staff she knew, but I had never noticed her in conversation with anybody.

And now, there she stood in the doorway, looking at us with the self-assurance of a beautiful woman who always gets her own way. As she addressed Imogen her gaze was on me.

'Ah, here you are, Imogen darling. I'm ready to leave.'

I froze. This was the first time I had heard Mrs Fairchild speak, except that I realized I had heard her before. I could never forget that mellow, beautifully articulated voice that had haunted my romantic dreams at the time. What's more, it came to me in a flash that, after having listened to me talk to Imogen, she must have recognized mine too. My reckless telephone call to the mysterious Mr Morris had been found out.

If Imogen resented this interruption, she did not show it. 'This, Mummy, is Arnold Forster, who will shortly be taking a more important role in the import department.'

'Hello, Mr Forster, I've seen you about doing this and that. Though we never spoke, I could see you enjoyed your work. We are lucky to have the services of a young man with such an enterprising and enquiring mind.'

Ouch! 'Enquiring mind' indeed! I could tell from her mocking look that she knew I knew she knew about the phone call. Smiling, she said to Imogen, 'Run and say goodbye to your father, darling. I'll wait for you in the shop.'

Obediently, Imogen turned and literally ran out of the door. 'Bye Arnold', she called back. She had been quick, but not quick enough. I was shocked to see the depth of anger in her usually gentle face.

Now, alone with Mrs Fairchild, I wondered whether she would openly refer to my indiscretion. But no. She just stood there looking at me. This sounds harmless enough, but actually, she was looking me over. As her eyes examined me piece by piece I felt increasingly more uncomfortable. I remembered overhearing my sisters speak about men who undressed women with their eyes. I blushed, and her little smile widened perceptively.

I pulled myself together and with a slight, formal bow said as firmly and coldly as I could: 'Is there anything I can do for you, Mrs Fairchild?'

She looked into my eyes and, with a low, caressing

voice said: 'Yes, but not at present. Thank you Arnold.'

I watched her leave, my mind and senses in a turmoil.

Later, on my way home, I tried to make sense of it all. I reasoned that since the woman on the phone had said she was Mr Morris's daughter and not Mrs Fairchild, that meant she or they didn't want this relationship to be known. But why? Did this mean that Mr Morris actually lived with his daughter and son-in-law or they with him? Why the secrecy? Perhaps Mr Fairchild didn't want to be pitied for being under old Morris's heel, not only at the office but also at home. I decided to consult my dad. After dinner, with mother and sisters in the kitchen, I started.

'Dad, there's something I want to ask you.'

He lowered his newspaper and looked at me over his reading-glasses. 'Yes, what is it?'

'I've discovered something about the Fairchild family that is important but nobody seems to know about.' Anxiously, I watched for his reaction. It wasn't long in coming.

'Well, son. If it's something important that nobody

knows, then it's because it isn't meant to be known. Don't turn your mouth into an arsehole and spread shit. Nobody will thank you and you'll get yourself into trouble.' With that, his leathery face disappeared again behind his paper. I had to agree that his succinct advice was sound. I would carry on and keep mum.

The next few days at work were much the same as before. No sign of Imogen or Mrs F, as I now called her in my mind. One evening, Mr Fairchild popped into my office. Yes, by then I had a little office of my own down the corridor, having been entrusted with all sorts of clerical jobs such as dealing with import documentation and letters of credit as well as the vetting of all incoming invoices. I had to make sure that everything had actually been received and was in the best possible condition, before payment could be sanctioned. As I said, Mr Fairchild came in, adjusting his scarf and buttoning up his coat as he spoke.

'Pack up, Arnold, you're the last in the building. No need to do overtime.'

'I was just tying up some loose ends, sir. I've finished now.'

He waited for me to put on my duffle coat and together we walked along the corridor and down the steps to the exit. On the way he chatted amiably about some business matters and then mentioned that he was on his way to his club for dinner.

'I have to fend for myself at the moment,' he commented casually. 'Our housekeeper's father had a stroke and she had to go and help her mother to cope over the first week or so. Unfortunately, it happened just after my wife had taken Imogen to her finishing school in Switzerland. The term only starts in two weeks' time but they seemed to be anxious to visit a relation on the way.'

I was shocked. So Imogen had been whisked away immediately after our last meeting. I felt sorry, not only for her but also for her father. At the same time I was wondering about Mr Morris. How was the old invalid who lived with the family managing on his own? I had noticed that for some time now that Mr Fairchild's references to his partner had decreased. He would make quite important decisions on his own and then mutter: 'I'll square this with the old boy later.' There was something odd going on and I couldn't fathom what it was.

'What a pity,' I responded, 'you don't seem to see much of your daughter. I had the impression she enjoyed being at home and in London. And I know she loved rooting about the shop, the stock-rooms and the various departments, always trying to learn as much as she could'.

He gave me a friendly look. 'I know she enjoyed being here, and she appreciated your explanations and guidance.' I was surprised that she had spoken about me to him and that he seemed pleased.

'Remind me to look into the Spanish olive contract tomorrow,' he said as we parted at the gate.

So, after having delivered Imogen to her new prison in Switzerland, Mrs F could be expected back in about ten days' time. To be honest, I dreaded our next meeting and, during sleepless hours, tried to enact in my mind polite ways of escaping her clutches. As it happened, I needn't have worried. She didn't come back. Whether the Fairchilds had agreed to separate or whether she'd gone off with another man, I never found out. Imogen should have returned from Swizerland after a year, but I learned that she had gone straight to cousins in the USA. All this struck me as very peculiar but, of course, I couldn't ask questions.

In some way or other, I had been involved in all departments of the business, especially in the importation of goods. The firm had bought the adjoining terraced house and the intention was to expand the operation to wholesale proportions and supply direct to shops, hotels and restaurants. It was obvious that a deeper knowledge of foreign trading would be an advantage. So it was that at the age of nineteen I was sent by Mr Fairchild to the Globus Import/Export Company in Liverpool, where an old university friend of his was the top man.

I was delighted. What a chance! I knew I had to take this seriously in order to acquire the knowhow that would make Mr Fairchild's new enterprise viable.

It was this comparatively short stay in Liverpool that immeasurably widened my horizon, and it was my knowledge of languages that brought me into contact with the top management. A sudden emergency made them ask me to interpret at a small business meeting and, after that, at ad hoc conferences. My initial apprehension soon gave way to a feeling of satisfaction and even power, as my skill improved with every taxing session. To be treated not as an apprentice lad but as a young man with ambition was very flattering. In fact, I had several job offers that appeared to be an improvement on my position with Fairchild & Morris. These days they call it head-hunting. One American gentleman, Oswald Pemberton, was particularly tempting. He had involved me in conversation on several occasions and finally invited me to dinner at his hotel. Though softly spoken, he was an impressive, distinguished looking man.

In retrospect, I am surprised at the ease with which I had accepted the ambience of a luxury hotel. I doubt whether Mr Pemberton ever suspected that, as a working-class lad, I had never seen a place like this, except in films.

'Well, young man,' he said after we had dined and were sitting comfortably in the huge fauteuils of the smoking room. 'Intelligent as you are, it must be obvious to you that I like you and have a certain interest in you. I think that your personality and aptitude would be an asset in my business. You know, of course, what it is?'

'Yes, sir. You're in shipping.'

He smiled. 'Yes, shipping. But not just any shipping, Mine is one of the two largest freight-carrying shipping companies in existence. At this very moment my fleet of freighters and tankers are criss-crossing all the oceans of the world.' I was genuinely impressed and didn't hide it.

'I know you are very young,' he continued, 'but I can

pride myself in being able to spot talent when I see it.' He paused, no doubt being aware of my eagerness to learn what was to come.

'Will it surprise you to learn that, apart from following your remarkable performances as an interpreter, I have been informed of your training progress here in Liverpool? I even know something about your background at Fairchild & Morris.'

'Fairchild & Morris?' I exclaimed.

He leant back and chuckled. 'Yes, I remember old Morris – came across him decades ago, when I was working in London. What a performer. He could be charm itself. On the other hand, to get his way, he could throw a terrifying temper. When he teamed up with the posh Fairchild, who had money but no business experience, I wondered how long it would last. I was interested to learn that since then Fairchild had married Morris's daughter and that the business is doing quite well.'

Now, this confirmation that Mrs F really was Mr Morris's daughter was of interest.

'Did you meet up with him again in later years?' I asked.

'No. By then he had retired for health reasons – a stroke after an accident, I think. He went up to his sister's straight away, somewhere near Harrogate, and she nursed him back to health. He acquired a taste for country living and refused to return to the business – keeps racing pigeons instead. His daughter has taken over, as you know. She's a keen businesswoman and a smart operator.'

Before I could begin to digest all this new information and its implications, Mr Pemberton continued: 'Let's return to you. I am offering you a job in my company. You'd start at the bottom, fast-tracking through all the relevant departments. With the necessary experience, you could reach the higher ranks of management by your mid-twenties. Further progress depends on your own brains and drive. What do you say?' Waiting, he watched my expression.

I was overwhelmed. This was a unique offer. Yet with the idealism of youth I felt I couldn't desert Mr Fairchild. Above all, I couldn't abandon my only possible contact with Imogen. I was considering how best to word my refusal. The pause was longer than I intended.

'Well, what's your decision?'

'Sir, I am very impressed and honoured by your offer but I find it impossible to desert my present employer. Mr Fairchild has always treated me with kindness and consideration since I was a lad straight from school. I am very sorry, but unless something unexpected happens, I feel I have to stay where I am.'

Mr Pemberton puffed at his cigar and gave me a long look before he spoke. 'Your feelings of loyalty convince me of your innate decency. But, you know, in this world, progress and success have always been built on the shoulders of others, mainly preceding generations. That applies to practically everything, from science to art. One learns and moves on. Even love and gratitude to one's parents doesn't stop the normal child from leaving the nest.'

He leaned forward. 'Mr Forster, I accept your decision but I won't take it as final. If, in the foreseeable future you should change your mind, please don't feel embarrassed – just let me know.'

On my way back to the room that had been hired for me in a little private pension, I was walking on air. I felt elated by the impression I had made on a most important man, the head of a most important organisation. It followed, I reasoned, that I too was important. I, clever Arnold Timothy Forster, had the power to say yea or nay. Chuckling as I walked along, I noticed the curious stares of passersby. I didn't care, they couldn't be expected to understand. Gradually, the feeling of lightness and buoyancy started to drain away and I became aware of a strange fuzziness that had invaded my head. I was glad when I reached my room, a clean, spartan place that only offered one comfortable surface – the bed. Slipping off my shoes, I let myself slump onto it and, within seconds, was fast asleep.

When I woke, I was blinded by the overhead light which I'd never got round to switching off. It hurt my eyes and felt as though it was stabbing my brains. What had happened to me? Gradually it dawned on me that I must have been affected by my unaccustomed intake of alcohol. Had my brain be affected during and after dinner? I wondered. Had I made a fool of myself? I tried to recall the conversation but couldn't remember any gaffs or stupid reactions. I remembered my 'loyalty to Fairchild' speech with satisfaction: but something at the back of my mind kept troubling me. I decided to think about it later and, with some effort got up to get undressed and brush my teeth. Back in bed, I once again fell instantly asleep.

My secondment to Globus Import-Export Co was about to end, so I worked hard to pack as much information as possible into the last three weeks.

After an amiable farewell from my temporary bosses and colleagues, I found myself on the train to London. I was looking forward to be with my family again: I'd never expected that l would miss them so much. Not only that, I had also missed the old firm with its variety of activities and staff members and, especially, Mr Fairchild himself.

That doesn't mean that Mr Pemberton's revelations had been forgotten. In fact I had thought a lot about the whole situation. It seemed to me that in the beginning Mr Fairchild, being young and inexperienced, would be forced to refer to his partner before acting. As far as the staff was concerned, Morris was still the boss and any unpopular decisions were assumed to be his. As time went on, with Fairchild now in sole command, it was still useful to let people think that Morris was strong enough to foil his partner's good intentions. Hence Mr Fairchild's farce of ringing his wife, pretending he was still consulting Morris, who by then was happily breeding racing pigeons in Yorkshire.

Well, I had to admit that this was quite a confidence trick but, on the other hand, it saved a lot of hassle. Who could blame him for taking the easy road? Everything considered, he had always been a reasonable employer, in fact better than most. And so, accepting the situation, I settled happily into my old groove.

One day, Mr Fairchild left the office early. He appeared to be in a good mood and I had the impression he was looking forward to an exciting, or at least pleasurable, evening. Though I was curious, I couldn't ask any questions. In those days you didn't show your interest in other people's private affairs, especially your employer's. A few minutes after I had settled down to work again, the telephone rang. It was Imogen.

'Please don't say anything, just listen. This is important. Meet me in twenty minutes in the alley by the hardware shop.' I could hardly believe my ears. What a way to make contact after all this time. She had sounded almost breathless with excitement, giving the impression of desperate urgency. What had happened? She had warned me not to blurt out her name on the phone in case somebody in the room or the telephonist in our exchange should hear it. Why the secrecy? Was she in any sort of danger?

It never occurred to me not to do as she asked. Having hurriedly locked away all important papers, I grabbed my duffle-coat and half ran to the place of rendezvous. Since it only took me ten minutes to get there I thought I would be early. But no, there she was already waiting. I still remember the rush of pleasure when I saw her face light up with relief and joy. She touched my arm, saying 'quick, follow me. I have a taxi waiting round the corner.' Even inside the taxi she put her finger to her lips: 'Wait. It isn't far.' Indeed, it was only about five minutes' drive, during which I had time to observe her. Her lovely face was flushed but her expression gave nothing away. The taxi stopped in a quiet side street in front of one of those narrow Regency terraced houses that hide a spacious interior and cost the earth to buy or rent.

Imogen jumped out, paid the driver, and ran to unlock the front door. I followed her down to the basement to find myself in a large bed-sitting room. It was comfortably warm and the glow of a gas fire softly illuminated the drawn velvet curtains, the good quality period furniture and the large double bed. As Imogen confronted me, I was at a loss how to read her expression. It seemed an odd mixture of bashfulness and challenge.

'Sorry I had to kidnap you like this, Arnold. But I couldn't just disappear. After all, we're more than just acquaintances whose path crosses now and then.'

I must have looked rather puzzled, for she came

close enough to be within touching distance. 'I .... I love you, Arnold,' she stammered. 'You are the man I want. I want to be yours and share my life with you. But it is not to be.' Her expression was anxious and her eyes were pleading. 'At least, please tell me you feel the same for me.' I drew her close, putting my arms around her. And when I kissed her lovely, sad face it was the realisation of many a daydream. 'You know I love you. I'd do anything for you,' I muttered, 'just say the word.' I felt frustrated by my banal, cliché-ridden response. Why couldn't I express my tenderness, devotion and passion for her in phrases that were worthy of her and this momentous occasion?

But criticism was far from her mind. 'Then don't let's waste time. Let's snatch at least a few hours of happiness, of togetherness.' She stepped back, slipped off her coat and proceeded to take off her clothes. For a moment I stood paralysed, then hurried to catch up with her. In no time we were facing each other like Adam and Eve. Can you imagine how I felt? A healthy nineteen-year-old virgin with raging hormones, seeing his beloved welcome him with obvious desire? Yet despite my passion, my dad's warning words flashed into my mind. 'Don't play around with ignorant young girls or you'll end up with a paternity claim, and if you mess around with a promiscuous little bitch on the pill, you'll risk finishing up with the clap or worse. But if you must indulge, ask our barber for a packet of the best.'

'This ... this is so ... unexpected,' I stammered. 'I'm not prepared ... I have no protection.'

'Don't worry,' she said, coming towards me, 'I am taking the pill.' And as she drew me onto the bed my reservations vanished. Afterwards it was quite clear that we had lost our virginity to each other. The second and third time round was a feast of mutual pleasure, ending in a state of satisfying exhaustion. For quite some time we lay side-by-side, fulfilled, resting. The subdued light of the Tiffany lamp and the gas fire's softly hissing sound seemed to emanate peace, enhancing my feeling of contentment and happiness.

Then she snuggled up to me and started to talk.

'You will have wondered why I suddenly kidnapped you and behaved as I did. The answer is that I am desperate. To make you understand I will have to disclose to you the rather peculiar relationships of the Fairchild family. That's if you are interested.'

'Of course, I am', I assured her. Yet something in the tone of her voice had made me apprehensive, made me fear that her revelations would not be to my liking. She started to speak slowly, with many pauses, as if trying to find the right words that would make her revelations sound less unpleasant.

She told me, that against her father's wishes, she and her mother would spend long periods of time abroad. It seemed to her that her mother was punishing him for something or other with their absence, but also because her mother enjoyed this vagabond life that took her from one house-party to another. All those wealthy socialites who get so easily bored enjoyed her company and were eager to invite her to their holiday villas for weeks at a time. She repaid them by being decorative, amusing and ready to have a fling with any of the other guests. Lately, she had revealed to Imogen that these flings were financially very remunerative and that she made enough money not only to keep them both but also to contribute to the coffers of the firm. I couldn't believe my ears and was about to interrupt her but then decided to listen to her whole story. After a lengthy pause and a sigh, Imogen continued.

'For some time now mother made a point of showing me off, making it clear that I was a virgin, available in marriage to the highest bidder. Well, there has been some interest but she would only be satisfied with a son-in-law who, apart from being wealthy, was willing to be manipulated. She envisaged regular, long visits and the opportunity to organize and run our lives to her liking.

'We were staying in a villa on the Amalfi coast when Wilbour Bollinger arrived. The others had gone off on some sightseeing trip but I had shammed an upset stomach to be left behind in peace. Having been introduced by the housekeeper, we were left alone on the terrace that overlooked the sea. Wilbour Bollinger is American, a middle-aged widower whose quiet, polite manner makes one feel safe and at ease. Yet he also has a good sense of humour that made me chuckle. Our conversation ranged over many subjects, and the long afternoon passed quickly. For the first time since I last saw you, I felt like a worthwhile human being again. He told me that although he had been invited for a week, he had only intended to stay one night. I hinted that I thought he had made the right decision since I couldn't envisage him enjoying the company of our shallow, hedonistic crowd. "Oh, but now that I have met you," he said, "I have changed my mind."

'Of course, mother soon noticed that Wilbour found me attractive. Once she'd established that he was an oil and property tycoon, she was hooked. Taking his reserve and quiet manner to be shyness, even weakness, she felt sure he was a man she could handle. She therefore encouraged his interest, giving him opportunities to be alone with me. He, in turn, continued to stay quietly in the background observing not only the guests, but my mother in particular. I have no doubt that it didn't take him long to form an accurate picture of her character.

'When, with her permission, he proposed marriage, I was taken aback. I told him that, much as I liked him, I didn't want to get married and that there was someone who was very dear to me. "Is there a chance you can marry him?" he asked, and when I sadly shook my head he said gently "I won't push you, Imogen. But if you marry me, I promise you, you'll be in full charge of your own life. You'll be free. I won't tolerate any interference from anybody." I thanked him and asked for time. But mother wasn't inclined to wait. She was afraid he would escape her clutches. The decision had to be made now. You see, Arnold, I can't run away and marry you. I am a minor. I have to do as I am told'.

'But Imogen!' I exclaimed, 'they can stop you from marrying but they can't force you into a marriage. Doesn't your father take your side?'

'No, he always gives way to her. And besides, without Wilbour's money he and the firm will be lost. You see, after granddad Morris retired, father was mismanaging. He messed up in a big way. His incompetence has brought the firm to the brink of bankruptcy. It's up to me to save the situation.'

I couldn't believe my ears. I'd heard enough. I wondered what dad's advice would be. Most likely; 'Stand for no nonsense and tell the truth.' I sat up and bent over her: 'Imogen, you must say no. There's still time to save yourself. You're being manipulated by both your parents. The reason they gave you is a lie: far from careering into bankruptcy, the business is flourishing. Fairchild & Morris have just bought the other two terraced houses on the left and are currently negotiating for a large warehouse in Park Royal. Whether your mother knows the full extent of your father's successful speculations and business deals or not, he is a very wealthy man. There is no need to sacrifice yourself to save the firm. It is all bunkum.'

Open-mouthed and wide-eyed, she stared at me. 'I don't believe you. Daddy would never, never do that to me – not unless he was truly desperate.' And then, to my surprise, she turned on me. 'Who are you to know what is going on? You're spending your time in a little office, now and then popping into the various departments to help out where extra hands are needed.'

Was she belittling me now or was she really not aware how much her father had trusted and advanced me? Though I had only a small office it was adjacent to his and, with the door open most of the time, he certainly didn't keep any developments concerning Fairchild & Morris from me. True, I still spent the odd hour in one department or another, ostensibly helping out, but also to check on efficiency and morale. It was assessment and reporting that very often brought about the necessary improvements. Sometimes, Mr Fairchild would even discuss important points of policy with me and take my opinion into account. I explained this to Imogen, hinting at the same time that my knowledge of his successful outside financial activities had been gathered in a somewhat secret and unorthodox manner. Apart from that, I told her, I had seen bank statements that showed that he gave his wife a very generous regular allowance that made nonsense of her claim that she had to extract money from other men. On the contrary, she most likely gave handsome presents to the young men she fancied.

Imogen seemed to accept my last accusation without protest as if recognising it as a likely fact. She was very serious now, almost cowed. 'This makes it worse, don't you see, much much worse. Her power over daddy frightens me. The greater her cruelty, the greater his love for her. She is capable of anything, Arnold. You know, she threatened to keep me locked up till I am twenty-one if I refused to marry Wilbour. What's more, having me in her power, isolated and helpless, she wouldn't hesitate to beat me if she felt like it. She has done so before until quite recently. She is very strong, you know, and she loves hurting people. I know she beats daddy, I have heard her at it and I've also seen the whips – but he seems to accept it without a murmur. He is a masochist. And I also know he is aware of her having lovers. This must sound like a gothic tale to you but it is true.' She sobbed. 'What a family! you must think. What a horrible pair of monsters.'

I was too shocked to say anything. I needed time to come to terms with all this. For some minutes we lay in silence. When she spoke again her voice had a strange coldness I had never heard before. It filled me with fear for the future.

'I know this will upset you, Arnold, but it has to be. I shall marry Wilbour. I trust him and his promise. He'll be my ticket to freedom. The moment the marriage papers are signed and she is gloating over her victory, I shall tell her to go to hell and never come near me or my husband again. She probably doesn't realize that by giving legal permission to this marriage, they are transferring their power over me to my husband who will then be responsible for me. There'll be no diplomacy, no pretence of a regretful goodbye, I'll make my rejection as hard and as cruel as I can. And what's more, it will include my father.'

I felt sick. The realisation that I had no sound argument against her decision was humiliating and devastating. I didn't know what to say. All I could think was 'I have lost her, lost her forever.'

Then I felt her arm across my chest. 'Arnold, dearest, I know this is a terrible blow. But you will get over it. Eventually, you will find someone suitable to share your life. Don't forget, it is just as hard for me. I'm only glad we could snatch these short hours of happiness. They will have to sustain me for many years to come. It is lucky Dorothy and Vera could lend me this flat at short notice. It would have been much worse to have left you without a final farewell.'

'And Wilbour? What about him?'

'Don't worry. If he turns out to be a good husband, I will keep my marriage vows and be a good wife to him. He will own me and my life but my memories and dreams are mine for ever.' Suddenly she sat up. 'Look at the time. I must get back home before them.'

She leapt out of bed and started to get dressed. I followed suit, still trying to make sense of all the things she had told me.

Hugging me, she pleaded: 'Please go and leave me,

Arnold. I cannot say goodbye in the street.' For some minutes we stood in a tight embrace before I managed to tear myself away. I shall always remember her unhappy, tear-stained face as she watched me leave.

Since this happened to be one of my college evenings, I was not expected home before 9.30. It was just as well: I couldn't have faced my family in my present state of mind. I kept on walking through the dark and empty side streets, not heeding where I was going. I had reached the end of a long avenue of plane trees that flanked a row of old, Victorian houses. Once upper middle-class family homes, they were now split up into numerous flats and bed-sits. A variety of cheap illuminated curtains revealed the status of their owners. From one of those windows, which was partly open, came the sound of a violin. I stopped and listened. I recognized the melody of a well-known classical piece but could not recall its name. The violinist was obviously practising, for I could tell when he or she went wrong. Yet there was passion in the playing and a sensitivity in the phrasing that, in my emotional state, touched me profoundly.

There I stood under a plane tree in front of a broken gate, looking up at a window with washed-out curtains, drinking in every note as if it were a balm for my misery. Tears were streaming down my face as I gave vent to sobs of anguish. Then, silence. The light went out and I was suddenly aware of the mist and penetrating damp. I shivered, put up my collar and started to walk. Somehow, on automatic pilot, I arrived home at the time I was expected.

'I've got an atrocious cold,' I said, to justify the ravages of my weeping. 'I don't want any food, I'll go straight up to bed.' Mother brought me some aspirins and a hot drink of lemon and honey, assuring me that I would be feeling much better in the morning. I did.

But was I really strong enough to face Mr Fairchild? Needless to say, I had spent half the night trying to decide on my next step. I had to face the fact that my revered boss was a masochist and his wife a sadist. If it hadn't been for Imogen, I wouldn't have cared what went on between them. Actually, I didn't have a clear idea what it really meant. Sex, generally, was never discussed in my family, and sexual deviations, as far as they were concerned, didn't exist. Any psychological ramifications or consequences were definitely a mystery. I hoped it would be possible to read up on it in the reference library. I was prepared to accept that, if this was an innate compulsion, neither of them could help it or stop it. What concerned and upset me was their treatment of Imogen.

I still find it difficult to explain why I didn't hand in my notice there and then. Was it a faint hope that Wilbour, seeing Imogen's unhappiness, would release her and that somehow, I could step in as her saviour? Or was it that my loyalty to Mr Fairchild was near indestructible? That I, fresh from the cosy cocoon of my family, entering the outside world like a bird out of the egg, had become fixated on the first impressive figure I came across? Whatever it was, I couldn't make the break. After all, however badly he behaved towards others, including his own child, he was still considerate and generous to me. I decided to stay and see how things would develop.

I was first in the office, hoping that Mr Fairchild would not immediately spot my unease. When he arrived later in the morning he obviously didn't suspect anything. He was his usual urbane and debonair self. I had always admired his appearance. Though good clothes were then hard to come by and I guessed that most of his clothing coupons were probably used by his wife and daughter, he was always well-dressed. I knew that most of his suits dated from before the war. Being of first-rate quality and cut, they hardly looked dated and one was only aware of their casual elegance. His shoes too were bespoke, and I had secretly envied his new, hand-stitched brogues from Tricker's in Jermyn Street, for which I had seen the bill.

He appeared to be in a good mood. 'Ah, Arnold. I'm going up to Yorkshire for my daughter's wedding. My wife is already there overseeing the arrangements. She will then be going to Boston to organise the new couple's home while they're on their honeymoon. However, I shall be back in a few days. In the meantime you will have to hold the fort. I left my contact address on your desk.'

Bracing myself, I offered my congratulations as brightly as I could. As Imogen hadn't actually mentioned the marriage date to me, its immediacy had come as a shock. I just about managed to look attentive while Mr Fairchild gave me some last-minute instructions before leaving. I picked up the note he had left me and saw that the address was 'care of Meadowcrest Hotel'. I then remembered what Mr Pemberton had told me, and that I had subsequently discovered from one of Mr Fairchild's files that he was a main shareholder of Mansion Hotels and that Meadowcrest was one of their properties. I expected he was looking forward to arriving in splendour with his two beautiful women, showing his miserable siblings how wealthy and powerful the runt of the family had become. No wonder he was in a good mood. Revenge is sweet. But, I thought with a good pinch of malice, it won't be sweet enough to compensate for the shock in store for him. I wondered how he was going to cope with his daughter's rejection.

I had awaited his return with some impatience, for in the back of my mind lurked a little doubt as to whether Imogen would really have the nerve to cut her family ties for ever. I don't know how I had expected him to look, but his normal expression, giving nothing away, was a disappointment. I then braced myself and did what I had never done before: I asked him two personal questions. I asked how the wedding had gone off and whether Mrs F was in Boston by now. If my forwardness had surprised him, he didn't show it but answered briefly in a casual way. Yes, the wedding had been a social success, and no, Mrs Fairchild had changed her mind and had returned with him.

'She did it', I rejoiced. 'She really did it. Imogen has gained her freedom.' Though I grieved for myself I was genuinely pleased for her. But Mrs F's return home was another matter and set my alarm bells ringing. Why oh why, I lamented, didn't she go off on her usual travels and console herself with some foreign lovers. At home, I was in her line of fire. I couldn't help but remember our last encounter when she had shamelessly embarrassed me. Try as I did, I couldn't suppress my foreboding that one day soon she would hunt me down.

It turned out to be very soon – in fact the very next morning.

Had I been sitting at my desk facing the door, I would of course have seen her enter. But being preoccupied and bent over a filing cabinet, the touch of her hand on my neck made me jump. 'What the hell!' I shouted, whipping round, nearly knocking her over in the process.

Chuckling, she stepped back. 'My, what a welcome.' She looked what my sisters would enviously have called 'a real fashion plate'. I can now only remember the magnificent silver-fox boa draped elegantly across her shoulders. From under a wide-brimmed hat two beautiful almond-shaped eyes looked mockingly at me. She was obviously expecting an apology. I decided to be barely civil.

'This is a place of work, Mrs Fairchild. We don't do things like that here.' I knew I sounded priggish but didn't care. I had to discourage her. Instead, she came towards me and her hand got hold of my upper arm. I don't know what her next move would have been but I quickly turned towards my desk, where I picked up the internal phone and pressed the button.

'Miss Fuller, can you bring me the listing now, please?'

I saw Mrs F's eyes narrow, and her lips clearly formed the word 'coward'.

Miss Fuller arrived within a minute and, having handed over the lists, waited in case I required something else. I glanced at the pages and said: 'There's something odd about this item. I had better go down with you and have a look.' Turning briefly towards Mrs F I said: 'Please excuse me, Mrs Fairchild, I don't think your husband will be long now.' She didn't reply but I knew she was cross, very cross.

About a week later, Mr Fairchild asked me for a favour.

'My wife is entertaining a friend tonight but I have to go straight to my meeting. I wonder, would you drop off these two bottles of wine she wanted?' The request had been made in his usual relaxed manner, but I knew him too well not to have noticed that something wasn't quite right. 'You don't mind, do you?'

'Not at all,' I said casually. 'I'll make sure they're delivered.'

Before leaving for home, I got hold of Fred who still worked in the stock-room. He never resented my advancement and we remained on a friendly footing. I asked him to take the bottles for me, since it was nearly on his way, giving him a packet of Woodbines for his trouble. I felt pretty certain that Mrs F had specifically asked for me to make the delivery and that this evasion would annoy her. However, the following day nothing was said. About two weeks later Mr Fairchild made the same request, and was pleased when I agreed. Again, I tried to get hold of Fred to do me the same service, but I was told that Mr Fairchild had sent him on an errand in the afternoon and that he wouldn't be back. Obviously, this was no coincidence.

It was therefore with some trepidation that I approached the Fairchild residence. It was a large detached house with a well established garden and mature trees. It stood on raised ground, set back from the road. Since the drive curved and some bushes flanked the first few yards, it wasn't immediately visible from the road. As I approached I could clearly see the large picture-window on the ground floor. A bright light illuminated the curtain from within, creating the effect of a cinema screen.

I rang the bell, ready to hand over the bottles and run. I hadn't expected to be grabbed and pulled in the moment the door opened. What's more, Mrs F immediately side-stepped to block my exit.

'Ah, Arnold, so good of you to come,' she cooed. 'Please take them through for me to the table.' I noticed it was set for two, with a variety of appetizing dishes waiting at the side. 'Unfortunately,' she continued, 'my friend had to call off at the last minute – actually only ten minutes ago. I am devastated. Will you please stay and console me?' She had adopted a gentle, sad expression, her full lips slightly pouting, her eyes pleading. I was furious to have been tricked into this situation. What's more, she wore a gown that revealed more than even a good friend should see at first sight.

'I cannot stay', I said coldly. 'Good night, Mrs Fairchild.' And with a curt bow I turned to go. I was too cross to invent a prior commitment as an excuse. In fact, I wanted to make quite sure she understood that I intended to have nothing to do with her – not now, not ever.

Once again, she physically outmanoeuvred me. She grabbed my arm and swung me round. 'I know you would love to stay. You don't really want to refuse all this lovely food and drink.' She glanced at the bottles I had brought. 'Dear Gerald, he selected the best vintages in the cellar.' She chuckled, 'how kind of him.' As I struggled to free myself from her grasp, she half pulled off my coat. 'Come Arnold, don't be shy, make yourself comfortable,' she urged. 'You won't regret it.' By now we were in front of the large window. I was amazed at her strength. Fighting for my coat, I felt like the Old Testament Joseph resisting the libidinous wife of Potiphar. As I had no intention of leaving my coat behind, I wrenched myself free and pushed her away. She stumbled against the window.

As I fled I heard her scream: 'You'll be sorry! I'll say you attacked me. I'll put a stop to your career!'

Agitated, with my head pounding, I rushed down the drive. It was dark, and even darker by the bushes near the gate. Suddenly, two seconds of bright illumination from the headlights of a passing car. I gasped. There, between the lowest growth of the shrubs, two highly polished shoes were caught in the beam of light. They were brogues of a distinctive design. I knew those shoes – they were the hand-stitched specials from Tricker's. My suspicion was confirmed. Mr Fairchild had set it all up and had secretly watched the shadow-play on the window. God, how perverted can you get? I wanted to challenge him but realized that, in the state I was in, things could easily get out of hand. For my parents' sake I couldn't risk a brawl. So I just dashed silently past. Once more I decided to walk home. I had to calm down, clear my head and decide on my future action.

Well, that was it. Old loyalties had predisposed me to make allowances where I should have drawn the line. He had sold his daughter, his only beloved child, to please this she-devil of a wife. And now, he had acted as her pimp to satisfy her appetite for young men. What masochistic pleasure would the witnessing of my seduction have afforded him? I felt like one of those white mice Imogen and I had seen in the zoo; mice that had been bred and nurtured to become fodder for reptiles. I was surprised by the magnitude of my outrage.

One thing was clear: working for him was no longer an option. Besides, hadn't she threatened me with dismissal? Well, I wouldn't give her the chance. And so, instead of going home, I went back to the office to write a letter of resignation. I knew it had been Mr Fairchild's intention to draw up a proper contract of employment, enforcing three months notice on either side. I was too useful to him for the standard one week's notice. But somehow, to my present satisfaction, he never got round to it. I sat down to write my letter. I decided to give no reason and only stated that since I had not yet taken the annual holiday due to me, I would not be working the notice week. As a gesture, I wished the firm of Fairchild & Morris and its staff all the best for the future.

I left the letter on Mr Fairchild's desk. Apart from the recent happenings, he had been a model employer. I had regrets but knew I would never be able to cope with the dichotomy of his character. Having collected my personal belongings, I left the room where I had spent so many interesting and fruitful hours. I couldn't resist a last sentimental stroll through the shop, restaurant and stock-rooms, inhaling with enhanced appreciation the scent of the various foods and spices. Then came the last locking up and the posting back of the keys. It was a solemn ritual, marking, as it did for me, the end of an era.

There was no use pretending. My parents knew immediately that something had happened.

'I'm leaving Fairchild & Morris.' I announced bluntly. 'I've handed in my notice.'

This was a bombshell which dad received silently but evoked a torrent of questions from mum. In order to calm her, I said I had a better job lined up, rashly mentioning Mr Oswald Pemberton. Then, of course, she wanted further details. Dear old dad came to my rescue. He said he was hungry and ready for his evening meal, making mum retreat to the kitchen.

Alone, I quickly told him the real reason for my sudden decision, and that I still had to apply for the job I hoped was still open for me.

'Rotten bad luck Arnold', he sighed. 'But you couldn't have stopped these goings-on. It would have been hell. Poor old Fairchild,' he sighed, 'I can't help being sorry for him.' Then he gave me a reassuring grin. 'If you're worried about Pemberton and the job, get on the blower to the central post office and send him a telegram.' I did as I was told.

Dad listened as I dictated: 'Pleased to accept offer if still open, A T Forster.'

I had always tried to see myself as an independently minded, confident young man. It therefore came as a shock to me how much dad's understanding and support still meant to me. Was I really fit to go out into the world on my own?

Pemberton's reply arrived next morning. I couldn't tear it open quickly enough. With a sigh of relief I handed it to dad. It said: 'Welcome. When can you start? Pemberton.'

Our reaction was surprisingly emotional. Tears came to my eyes and before I knew what was happening, dad had thrown his arms around me. We hugged, patting each other's back. We both knew that though this meant success, it also was the end of my sheltered life at home. This, indeed, was the start of a new life.

Of course, you will want to know what happened next. I'll just give you the brief facts to round off my story. Oswald Pemberton was as good as his word and I made the best of every chance he gave me. After about a dozen years of hard work I became one of the directors in the top management. By then I had married Clair, Mr Pemberton's niece, and was father of three delightful little girls. My wife not being able to have any more children meant that I would never have the boy I always wanted.

Of course, you expect me to tell you what Clair is like. Well, she is dark-haired and attractive in a slightly plump and motherly way. She also is practical and has no time for sentimentality. Though she never made my innermost being quiver with ecstasy or searing pain as Imogen could do with a word or glance, I soon learned to love her. With her unfailing common sense she is now the solid rock in my life that dear old dad used to be. Sadly, a sudden heart attack took him from us two years ago. It was a hard blow for mum. She now lives with one of my sisters in a granny annexe. My sisters are both happily married and, I'm pleased to say, made me the doting uncle of two nephews and three nieces. So there you are: this is the end of my Fairchild & Morris story. You look disappointed; I guess you want to know what happened to Imogen. Well, perhaps I owe you an epilogue.

Some years after joining the Pemberton empire I was in the process of taking over from my superior, Des Logan, who was about to retire. Luckily I got on well with him and he generously wanted me to do well. Apart from giving me a lot of valuable advice, he invited me for a week to his country place in Vermont. I suppose the idea was that when my future co-directors saw that he considered me to be a regular guy, they would then have no qualms about accepting me as their equal. You see, having been fast-tracked and having married the boss's niece was not exactly in my favour. Des had a log-cabin in the mountains, near the picturesque village of Glenburton, where the locals hold their annual fall festivities. This log-cabin turned out to be a little log-mansion with more than just mod cons.

Des had invited me for the start of October when the autumn foliage would be at its best in this part of Vermont. Just outside Glenburton the end of the valley widens into an area large enough to accommodate the numerous sports and artistic activities, as well as all the farming and craft markets that the neighbourhood usually provides for visitors. Having spent some time looking round, sampling things and socialising, I thought that a walk up the adjacent mountain would give me the full picture. So I took the steep track that led up to a flat promontory overlooking the whole area on three sides. The view from there was so impressive that I felt sure a further climb could hardly improve it. So I remained, looking at the scenery, drinking in its beauty.

The colours of the foliage were truly splendid, ranging from pale yellow through all nuances to rich gold and copper. The reds gloried in flaming crimson and scarlet, and purplish hues and orange patches tried to assert themselves. And in between were the mysterious dark shapes of evergreens enhancing the display. I heard snatches of music drift up on the breeze, reminding me of the little pocket of human civilisation below. But it was the vast, magnificent landscape with its mysterious ancient forests and wild creatures that captured my imagination and wonder. I had been told that moose, deer, bears and beavers, as well as many other animals, were at home there. I surrendered myself to the magic of this impressive world.

I suppose it is only natural that on occasions like these one can sometimes experience the awe of our primitive ancestors, the pantheistic urge to worship the overpowering forces of nature. I must admit, that at that time, I probably was particularly sensitive. Once again I was embarking on an important change in my career. Though confident on the whole, I nevertheless harboured some misgivings and secret fears. It had been a hard climb up the ladder. Oswald Pemberton hadn't spared me and the higher I got the more difficult it had become. I had to watch my step, being aware that he was testing me. Yet quite often I found that the dreaded obstacles were far less frightening than they appeared at first sight. I thought of dad and his down-to-earth wisdom that had so often bolstered my courage. 'Don't be afraid of the monster growling in the dark,' he used to say. 'For all you know it's just an extra-loud fart.' I sighed: I still missed him.

Intending to explore another point of view, I turned round. A tall woman, dressed in white, her fair hair gleaming in the sunlight, stood motionless on the other side of the promontory. Against the colourful backdrop her light figure looked particularly stunning. It was no mirage: the woman facing me was Imogen.

I don't know how long she had been watching me, but now she smiled, stretching out her hand in greeting. This gesture stopped me in my track. I had been about to rush forward to embrace her.

'How are you?' we said in unison, then laughed.

'You have changed,' she said. 'You've filled out. Maturity suits you. It has given you an air of authority.'

'You too have changed,' I admitted. 'You have grown

into a beautiful woman who no longer looks afraid of the world. Are you still married to Wilbour?'

'Yes, he was and still is a good husband and a wonderful father to our two boys.'

'And how are your parents?'

Her eyes narrowed and she said coldly: 'I don't know, and don't want to know.' Then she relaxed and asked: 'I expect you too have a family?'

'Yes. Clair and I have three little girls. The two youngest are twins – the Forster non-identical kind.' Not wanting to admit that there won't be any more and that this meant no chance of a son, I said quickly: 'What a coincidence that we should meet here like this. I'm staying near Glenburton with a business associate.'

'And we are here with friends. Alas, it's back to Boston tomorrow morning.'

Then, for quite a while, we just stood looking at each other, conjuring up memories of a past that now seemed so long ago – memories that were like faded copies of a black and white film, when life moved at a different pace.

Excited treble voices heralded the arrival of her boys. Nearly out of breath, they came rushing up, confronting her. 'Mum, we ran all the way up. We must have beaten a record.'

I was aware of her watching my expression as I caught sight of the boys. I couldn't believe my eyes. One of them reminded me of the old snaps my mother had of me as a boy, and the other one, with his dimples and cheeky look, resembled my sister Betty. Before I could say anything, she introduced them. The one with the features of my youthful self was Andrew, the other one Thomas. I immediately realized that their names started with my initials.

'And this gentleman, boys, is Mr Forster. He is an old acquaintance from London.'

I was taken aback. She had said acquaintance instead of friend, just as she had immediately proffered her hand in greeting to forestall an embrace. It seemed she was making sure I was put into a neutral position.

'Hello! I'm pleased to meet you boys. Which of you is the elder?'

'I am,' said Andrew, 'but only by about fifteen minutes. Though we don't look alike, we're twins. We are both twelve.'

That time-span agreed with my calculation. No doubt, they were my sons. The fact that I had actually fathered sons, and such healthy and attractive looking ones at that, was overwhelming. I managed to pull myself together and continue the conversation.

Then Thomas piped up. 'How's little old England, sir? And London and Big Ben and the two-storey red buses?' It was said with an impish cheekiness that again reminded me of Betty.

'They're all fine, just fine. You'll have to come over some time and see for yourself.'

'Mum and dad say we'll do just that when we're a bit older.'

Imogen then told them to return to the village. I had the feeling she was afraid I might offer them hospitality in London. Politely they said: 'Goodbye, sir,' before running off.

We stood facing each other in silence till the children's voices had faded in the distance. I thought how attractive she looked. Now in her early thirties, she was a woman in her prime who had found her place in the world. Yes, she had changed. She was no longer the unhappy, insecure girl who had found comfort in my love and who needed a part of me to be able to face the future. Was she too now thinking of our last time together? Did she remember assuring me that she was taking the pill?

'You lied to me,' I blurted out, taking it for granted she knew what I meant. I had the impression she was determined not to let anything upset her emotional equilibrium. Yet then I saw her expression soften and her voice acquired the gentleness of her youth. 'Yes, Arnold, I lied – and I'm still glad I did.'

MR DOBSON GOES TO TOWN

Mr Dobson opened the front door and kissed his wife Philida goodbye. Having given her behind a little affectionate pat, he stepped into the sunlit garden. What a day! The air was still morning fresh. He fancied he could smell the damp earth breathing and that the spring flowers in the borders were emitting their perfume especially for him. The front garden, rather over-groomed for many tastes, boasted the obligatory emerald lawn, where the tulips luxuriated in their voluptuous centre bed, their red and orange petals flaming in ostentatious display.

At the gate he turned back. He was pleased to see his wife watching him. She was smiling and lifted her hand for a little wave. He started to walk down the avenue, delighted with the tips of succulent green that enveloped every tree with a diaphanous veil that still left the architecture of trunk and branches to reveal their character. Everywhere he looked, new life and beauty was greeting him. Thus started the first day of Mr Dobson's retirement.

The management had wanted him to carry on: his experience and expertise were of greater value to the firm than the contribution any new, bright whizz-kids could make. But his mind was made up. He wanted his freedom before he was too old and decrepit to make the best of it. Of course, he had consulted Philida and had been rather taken aback when she'd told him to please himself. He was used to receiving definite instructions from her; from what he should eat to what clothes he should buy and what to do generally. In fact, she bossed him mercilessly – and he loved it. First of all, it saved him the bother of thinking about mundane things; secondly, she, being an intelligent and practical woman, really knew best; and thirdly, as long as she troubled to keep tabs on him he felt he could be sure of her love.

'Don't worry about the money,' she'd said. 'Your pension and our investments will be enough to live on. And there is my little private income as well. We're not facing any major expenses, and our children and their families are doing alright without us. I'll go along with whatever you decide.'

And so, today was the first weekday when he'd had a really leisurely breakfast, when he didn't have to rush to get showered and dressed and when he could have more than a cursory look at the morning papers. But after about half an hour of relaxed reading, fate had caught up with him. Philida had placed a piece of paper before him which looked suspiciously like a shopping list. It was.

'I'll not have you loll about all day doing nothing and running to fat,' she said. 'These are a few things I need, so would you be a darling and get them for me?' Though phrased like a question, it definitely was an order. 'And don't take the car, Gerry, the walk will do you good.'

He was a little bit put out, but of course, she was right. He was inclined to be lazy and needed a firm hand to keep him going. Now, walking along the avenue, inhaling the scented air, he had such a feeling of wellbeing and hope for the future that he felt justified in calling it happiness.

This was the superior end of town. All the houses were set well within their grounds behind high hedges, fences or walls, and many of them couldn't even be seen from the road. He stopped for a few seconds to look through the high wrought iron gate of a property he had last visited two years ago. The drive was curving and only a small part of the front lawn was visible. He did, however, remember the layout of the garden and the planting. Every flower or blossoming tree and shrub was white, set in rather severe beds and borders. Lady

Francine Bockingford, the widow of the notoriously sadistic judge, lived here. Prominent in charity circles, she managed to constantly rub people the wrong way with her holier-than-thou attitude. Even now, thinking back to when he had visited her on charity business, he felt uncomfortable and embarrassed. He had thanked God for the unexpected visit of Lady Bockingford's niece. Back home, he had begged Philida never to leave him alone with Lady Bockingford. He must have looked quite harassed because she patted his cheek saying: 'Don't worry, my darling, I won't let her gobble you up.'

Having studied Philida's list, he realised that she was sending him to shops that were quite far apart. What's more, she assumed that he would walk along the circular road as if he were going by car. He chuckled. He knew short cuts and byways she wasn't aware existed. After all, he had grown up here. He reached the gap between two walls he had in mind. It was only about one yard wide, just enough for one normal sized person to pass through. There were high weeds underfoot, a sign of its infrequent use. At the end he turned right and entered another cut between two properties. Two little side streets and he found himself in Paradise Street.

From there on the location changed to one with a definitely lower middle-class ambience. Another few turns and there was Pratt's Row which would lead him into the High Street, close to Philida's favourite greengrocer. He stopped, surprised: the whole length of the street had been resurfaced and the pavement renewed. What a difference it made. The new, clean flagstones with their clear demarcations rekindled in him an obsession from which he had suffered as a young man. The street looked deserted; why not try to reach the far end without stepping on any lines? But there was a difficulty. The slabs were not square but rectangular. Being set with the narrow sides facing him meant they were too long to be negotiated in single regular strides. Somehow, it suddenly became important to him to solve this problem.

Mrs Murphy, glancing down from her first floor window, did a double take, then called into the room: 'Rachel, quick, come look at this.' Silently, the two women watched a well-dressed, distinguished looking gentleman proceed along the pavement in a most peculiar way. He would make a few mincing short steps and then take off in a long leap. The pattern of his progress was not predictable and they watched spellbound until he disappeared round the corner.

'He's from the Ministry of Funny Walks,' stated Rachel in a matter-of-fact tone of voice.

'Well, I never!' said her mother. 'The things you know.'

Mr Dobson felt elated. He'd done it. It showed that he was in pretty good nick, thanks to his wife's strict regime. Also, it was a good omen for the future. Of course, on another level he knew that the latter was nonsense. And now, diagonally across the road was Mr Wittle's green emporium. The terraced display of fruit and vegetables betrayed a feeling for colour and design that was, Mr Dobson admitted, definitely artistic. The artist himself came out to serve him.

'Can I help you, sir?'

Mr Dobson cleared his throat. 'You are Mr Wittle?'

'Yes, I'm Wittle.'

'Well, I am to tell you that I am shopping on behalf of Mrs Dobson.'

'Yes, I recognised you, sir.'

Mr Dobson took out his shopping list. 'She wants two lemons. They should have a smooth, thin skin and be juicy.' Wittle didn't blink, went over to the lemon box and chose the required fruit.

'Two lemons, skin soft as silk, full of 'ealth-giving juice.'

'A string of garlic, please.'

''Ere, arrived from France only yesterday.'

'Has it got a proper loop for hanging up?'

'Sure, all present and correct.'

'And two avocado pears, please. They must be ripe.'

''Ere you are. 'Andle carefully. Them's as tender as a woman's breasts.'

'You don't say … And there are some special herbs she ordered.'

Wittle put the purchases into a green plastic bag. 'It'll be charged to Mrs Dobson's account. Is there anything else, sir? No? Thank you, sir. Goodbye, sir.'

Mr Dobson felt a little bemused. Was he to take all this at face value or was Wittle taking the micky? Whatever, he had to get to Waitrose. As he saw a bus come along, he hopped on and had the pleasure of riding the two long stops.

When he arrived at Waitrose he realised that it would take him quite some time to find the few small items Philida had listed. A member of the staff was about to flit past him. He called her back. She looked very young. Her fresh and friendly face made it easy for him to put his case. His wife had entrusted him with this shopping list, he said, and he hadn't a clue where to find these things. His problem was lack of time as he had to get to an important appointment. Would she show him where to look?

She glanced at the list. 'But they're all over the place!'

He let his face drop and with a hangdog expression pleaded 'But you still can show me, can't you?' He wondered whether he had overdone it, but she gave him a quick look-over, her eyes coming to rest on the grey hair at his temples. 'Give me the list. I'll pick them things up for you. You can wait there, on the bench by the window.' Before making for said bench, he saw her calling to another young assistant before both of them disappeared between the fixtures. He hardly had time to philosophise on the innocent gullibility of the young and the cunning, manipulative wiles of the old, when she was back with the basket.

'I say, you have been quick.'

'I got Arnold to help me. He's a good lad. Shall I take it to the check-out for you?'

'That won't be necessary.' Thanking her profusely, he took the basket from her.

Well, there he was. In and out in a few minutes. He calculated, that with one thing and another, including the planned short cut home, he must have saved well over three-quarters of an hour. This gave him time for a treat. But before turning into the next side street, he had to pick up his wife's watch from Cartier's. Well, not really Cartier. That was what the locals called Carter and Poole, the only jeweller and watch-maker in town. Mrs Poole, the wife of the second partner, was serving behind the counter. She knew him as an old customer and immediately produced the watch that had undergone its annual cleaning.

'Clean as a whistle,' she said.

'It should go like clockwork then,' responded Mr Dobson.

She wrapped the watch in tissue paper, then placed it in a little fancy bag. Mr Dobson paid and slipped the package into his jacket pocket. But he hadn't reckoned with Mrs Poole who would have none of such nonsense.

'Do you realise,' she admonished her customer, 'this is a high-class, solid gold watch on a solid gold wrist-band? With the price of gold now, it's worth a little fortune. Easy enough to slip into your pocket, but just as easy to slip out. You ought to know that now, with the warmer weather and holidaymakers about, the pickpockets have arrived too. It's mostly foreigners that come over special. Can't trust any of them. So let me see you put the watch well down your trouser pocket and your reserve hanky on top.'

Mr Dobson laughed 'You're a woman after my wife's heart,' and obediently did as he was told.

On his way again, he mused how funny life was. Within the span of ten minutes he had been treated like a decrepit grandfather and a silly six-year-old. Truly, everything depended on the eyes of the beholder.

He turned up Norton's Way, to enter an establishment that called itself 'Sunshine Tearooms'. It was an old-fashioned place where time had stood still. He remembered it looking very much the same when he used to come here as a boy with his mother. Only then there were lace doilies everywhere and the china was much more up-market. The superb quality of the cakes and pastries, however, had not diminished since no factory-made items were ever brought in. Mrs

Gardener, like her mother before her, took pride in her first-class ingredients and undisputed skill.

Though the waitress recognised Mr Dobson, she did not know his name. 'Can I help you, sir?'

'Yes, as soon as I've made up my mind.' He had reached the counter where a glass cabinet displayed a variety of goodies. The chocolate fudge-cake and coffee-walnut cake looked a dream. Though he was sorely tempted, conscience got the better of him and he transferred his attention to the tarts and fancy slices. In the end he asked for an Eccles cake which he knew was made with a fairly plain pastry and contained a dried fruit filling which was supposed to be good for you. Having ordered a pot of china tea, he withdrew to the little recess from where he could look out of the window without being seen himself. The only other guests, since it was still mid-morning, were a young couple who were only interested in each other.

The waitress, Mrs Gardener's youngest daughter, had just brought his order, when another customer entered. The newcomer was the sort of man you wouldn't particularly notice in a crowd if you didn't know him. But once you had spoken to him and had personal contact, you'd never forget him. He wore a dark, wide-brimmed hat and a gabardine raincoat that had seen better days. He spotted Mr Dobson immediately and came over to join him.

'Good morning, Mr Goldblatt,' the girl said brightly. 'What can I get you?'

'Morning Betty. Same as usual, please.'

Mr Dobson had noticed her eyes light up. This was people's usual reaction to Goldblatt. Once you got to know the man you couldn't help liking him. What's more, everybody opened up to him and trusted him. This was rather useful since, as the proprietor and editor of the local newspaper, *The Clarion*, he appreciated that innocuous morsels of information could sometimes add up to very interesting news.

'Hello, Dobs,' he said sitting down. 'I saw you from the office window. Stepping out of Cartier's as if you'd just spent a million, then striding up the High like a young Adonis. Is that what retirement does for you?'

'How did you know this is my first day of retirement?'

'Oh, the usual old grapevine.' He spotted Mr Dobson's plastic shopping bags. 'I see that Philida has started as she means to go on. Keep the old man busy and out of mischief. What?'

'That's about it. Doesn't want me to become a couch potato and put on fat.'

Goldblatt laughed. 'Oh, she's a good woman alright. One can tell by the way you're turned out and the condition you're in. I expect you're performing accordingly.'

Dobson knew what Goldblatt meant and said with a smile, 'Well, I've had no complaints.'

Goldblatt changed the subject. 'I suppose your firm said goodbye with a hefty golden handshake? After all you've done for them, you deserve it.'

'Not all that hefty, I'm afraid – but reasonable. And, of course, the usual handsome carriage clock.'

Dobson started to nibble at his Eccles cake, silently contemplating his companion. It seemed incredible that this self-assured, relaxed man was once a shy slip of a boy who was in constant fear of the world around him. He remembered him, the new boy, standing in the centre of the grammar school play-ground, watching two young bullies kick his new blazer around the dusty tarmac. At the same time they called him a dirty little Jew who wasn't fit to be there at all. Then they started bumping into him, trying to push him over.

Having always been fit and athletic, Dobson had never been in danger of being bullied. Though he knew that bullying existed, he'd never actually witnessed it. But now, when he did, he saw red. Conditioned by his family's passionate belief in fairness and justice, he burst into action. He attacked the two boys. They tried to fight back, but his fury had given him extra strength; he gave them a thorough beating and made them apologise. Cowed and humiliated, they'd slunk away. Seeing young Daniel Goldblatt suffering from shock, Dobson had taken him to the school matron. When, an hour later, the victim had rejoined the class, refreshed and in his cleaned blazer, their eyes had met across the room. Both knew then that this was the beginning of a lifetime's friendship.

And, indeed, many years later, when Goldblatt had bought the ailing *Clarion*, Dobson's substantial cash injection had been decisive for the venture to get off the ground. Now, the loan repaid long ago, Goldblatt owned four more local papers, thus covering two counties.

Goldblatt cleared his throat. 'Would you like to know what I'm thinking?'

'Dear Goldie, you know I'm always interested in what you're thinking.' They grinned at each other.

'I think, that with all that spare time you'll be having you should stand for the next council election. We need intelligent, upright men like you. People who are fit for the most responsible jobs.

For a couple of seconds Dobson saw himself before an admiring crowd, wearing the heavy gold chain of mayoral office, with Philida proudly beside him.

'Please, don't bother to butter me up, old boy,' he protested, 'I need a good long spell of rest and freedom before I would even think of going into politics. Besides, what makes you think I'd get in?'

'With *The Clarion* support, you're bound to.'

Dobson knew that his friend wasn't boasting. *The Clarion* enjoyed a very high reputation in this town. Apart from the usual newspaper features and some local tittle-tattle, all public events were meticulously recorded and no council meeting took place without one of the paper's reporters taking careful notes. Sometimes it was Goldblatt himself, or his right-hand man Frobisher or, quite often, Frobisher's daughter Bonnie. She was still under twenty; all long legs and black leather, with bright magenta-dyed hair framing her pretty face. But she possessed the keen intelligence and judgement of a much older person. Though no questions could be asked at the meetings, they were unfailingly asked in the pages of *The Clarion*. No inconsistencies, fudges or evasions went unnoticed, and the good citizens were grateful for this ruthless watch that kept their council up to scratch.

The waitress appeared, setting a mug of tea and a huge egg-and-bacon sandwich before Goldblatt. 'It's your special rye bread, sir. And them eggs were fresh in this morning. Is there anything else?'

'No, thanks, Betty. This looks and smells delicious.' With a mischievous grin at his friend, he cut the sandwich in half and, exposing a beautifully preserved row of teeth, took a large bite out of its middle.

'Does Sarah know this is your usual snack?'

'Heavens, no. She'd kill me. Or at least call Jehovah's vengeance down on my head.'

This came as no surprise to Mr Dobson. His encounters with the former Sarah Edelstein on various public occasions had been only fleeting. Even if his face had become vaguely familiar, he felt sure that he had remained an unknown nonentity to her.

He, however, knew all about her. His sister Olivia,

who had had the misfortune to be in Sarah's class throughout her school years, regularly vented her dislike of her at the family table. Apparently, Sarah, a very spoiled only child, always expected to receive first consideration and the best of everything. To get it she stopped at nothing. Her presumptuous demands, lies and false accusations used to upset the class and even the administration beyond.

With the departure of Olivia to university the stories had ceased and Sarah Edelstein became history. Thus, for years, Dobson had never given Sarah another thought till that fateful evening when he heard about Goldblatt's whirlwind engagement to her. Reluctantly, he told him about Olivia's account of her character.

In Goldblatt's case love wasn't only blind, it was also deaf. He simply laughed it off. 'You're over-dramatising, Dobs. Who can take student rivalry seriously? School intrigues are a basic necessity; they introduce the youngsters to the politics of adult life. Sorry, old chap, you've got this one wrong. I mean to have her, marriage or no.'

Now, decades after the event, watching Goldblatt placidly munching his egg-and-bacon sandwich, he also remembered their first meeting after the honeymoon. Goldblatt had looked at him and, after a short pause, said simply, 'I should have listened to you.' The subject was never mentioned again. Nine months later, like her mother before her, Sarah produced an offspring which was to be her first and last. It was a little girl, Naomi, who turned out to be very much like her father. Dobson soon realised that Goldblatt would never leave the child to the sole influence of her mother. For the sake of the child he was prepared to endure a hell of a home life. He developed a thick skin and disregarded her tantrums.

Nobody was surprised when Naomi, at the age of eighteen, decided to leave home to get married. Goldblatt was delighted when he learned that the groom was a non-Jew, in fact the son of a Church of England minister. As Sarah promptly cursed her daughter and severed all connections, Naomi could now look forward to a peaceful life without her mother's interference. Over the years, Sarah had simmered down. She had developed a passion for cooking and was currently working on another kosher cookery book, her previous one having been a success. At the same time she found romantic satisfaction in an endless email correspondence with a former admirer who now lived in a nursing home. As long as her husband appreciated her food, she no longer cared what else he was up to.

'Another tea, love,' Goldblatt called out to Betty and,

after a questioning look at Dobson who nodded, 'make it two, please.'

How strange, thought Dobson, looking back, he seemed to have endured more anxieties and worries with Goldblatt than he ever had with his two children. Of course, Philida had no inkling of this; she didn't even know of their special relationship. And it really was special. There never had been a hint of sexual attraction between them, but their feeling for each other was deep and solid. Each knew that he could rely on the other whatever the need. Sometimes they would have serious discussions, even arguments, other times they would just sit together without saying much, enjoying each other's company.

'Have another Eccles cake!'

'No, thanks. I daren't spoil my appetite. This being my first lunch at home, Philida is preparing something special.'

Goldblatt smiled. In a peculiar way, over the years, his friend's happy home life had been a comfort to him.

Dobson, in turn, felt that Goldblatt had settled down, had found his groove and level of comfort. He had the occasional mistress, and Sarah was under control.

Every so often he would go up north to stay with Naomi and her family. Since he and Naomi's husband got on well, he was always welcome. Dobson sighed; maybe approaching old age is making us more mellow. He looked at his watch. 'Good heavens, I'll be late!'

'I'll give you a lift,' said Goldblatt. 'Don't worry, I'll drop you out of sight.'

As Dobson walked up his drive, his blousy tulips were waving to him in the breeze.

Philida, charming in a flowery dress and frilly apron, welcomed him with a smile. 'You look well,' she said, handing him an aperitif. 'The walk has done you good.'

Relaxed, Dobson sipped his drink. He couldn't have had a better start to his retirement.

PART THREE:
INNOCENCE AND EXPERIENCE

ʃPLAʃH

One has to hand it to him: he's a powerful figure of a man, an impressive example of mature beefcake. Bearded, muscular, he stands naked at the apex of the baroque fountain. 'Hello there! What's your name, mister? Neptune? Poseidon?'

He doesn't let on, but keeps hold of his trident, looking calmly into the distance. Spread below him in bright sunshine, a carpet of formal geometric flowerbeds forms the vast parterre that leads up to Schönbrunn Palace. This is imperial territory, for centuries the scene of amorous and political intrigues, and where the only game worth playing was the power game. Now, it is a showpiece, history in aspic. Behind the fountain, serpentine paths lead up the steep hill to the glorious, triumphal colonnade, which is in fact called the 'gloriette'. I had intended to climb up to it to enjoy the full panorama, but the heat had exhausted me. Instead, I linger here below the vast basin, staring up.

There he stands, the mighty water god, not heeding

the racket immediately beneath him. What with his exuberant retinue doing their thing, and the water rushing forth and plunging down in sheets, down, and down again into the ornate giant basin, one would have expected some concern. But, of course, he's used to it. I and the other visitors, however, are gaping at the scene, trying to make out what is actually going on. One can almost hear the squealing of the mermaids and the shouting of the mermen as they try to rein in the rearing horses. The gushing, splashing water creates a breeze that lures many of us as close as we can get to refresh ourselves in the drifting spray. Ah, look at that rainbow, and all the sparkling droplets of water like a shower of crystals!

We, gazing up in fascination, are a mixed lot, speaking many languages, just as in the old days of the Austro-Hungarian Empire. He, the supreme one on top, pretends not to notice us. He's seen it all before. Though fashions have changed from silken knee breeches to cotton jeans, the gaping of the crowd remains the same. Everybody is wearing light, summery clothes, except for a group of soberly dressed Japanese. They stroll about in earnest conversation, occasionally permitting themselves a short guffaw or a little giggle. One of their slender ladies in black opens a parasol of shocking pink. She twirls it. It's a *coup de théâtre*, and somehow rather sexy.

Phew, what a heat. My poor feet. I've been traipsing around for hours. No wonder I feel limp and sticky. I'd give anything to be able to leap into this whirlpool. After all, I am a Piscean. Longingly, I look up. That merman on the left, the very young, beardless one, he's smiling and winking at me. He's trying to tempt me. Oh, I can just see myself in the midst of this tumbling cascade, cool, refreshed, exhilarated. I know, water is my element.

Heavens! What's this? A miracle! Somehow, I must have stripped off. A ripple of exclamations runs through the spectators. Rhubarb, rhubarb, rhubarb. I can't pick out what they're saying. I'm standing above them, on the edge of the rim – in the buff. Now, splash, I'm in the water, caressed by waves. Oh, I love it. I stretch my limbs and float. But look, something strange is happening to me. I can hardly believe it: my legs are metamorphosing into a scaly tail!

Hurray! Eureka! I'm my real self now.

I call to my new friends and swim over to them. I'm eager to join the Neptune gang. They welcome me and reach down to help me up, ignoring the chorus of clicking cameras.

CRAIGMORTON HALT

Recent unfortunate events had made me expect danger and pitfalls everywhere. I had dreaded the change over to the branch line, and the worst possible scenario had got hold of my imagination. I feared that the platform we needed was on the other side of a railway bridge, that I wouldn't be able to find a porter and that I would have no chance of coping with an invalid husband and two large suitcases on my own. Apart from that I felt sure that our train would be too late to catch the connection. We would then be stranded in a provincial backwater where, due to the immediate post-war conditions, neither taxis nor hotel accommodation would be available.

As if to mock my apprehension, the transfer couldn't have run more smoothly. Martin and I were now following the porter to the train that started from here. Martin had his arm round my shoulders and I had mine round his waist to give him extra support. The train was already in position with its shiny black steam engine and two carriages. The porter waited for us to catch up, then went up to the first one and started to load our luggage into a compartment.

'They're all the same,' he commented. 'This time of the year the train's nearly empty; running at a loss, I'm sure.' He shrugged his shoulders as if to say: 'What can I do about it?' He was about to lift the cases up onto the rack when I stopped him.

'Please, don't. I wouldn't be able to lift them down, and my husband just had an operation.'

Obligingly, he pushed the luggage further up between the seats and laid our travelling rug on top of it. Then, without being asked, he helped Martin up by half lifting him and then gently letting him down onto the seat by the window. 'There, sir. Not that you'll be able to see much, what with the mist coming down so fast in the evenings.'

The man's eyes lit up when I gave him a generous tip. 'You know,' I confided, 'I'm rather worried about getting off the train in time. We're not going to Craigmorton Town, the terminus, but to Craigmorton Halt just before. I've been told that the train stops there for only a couple of minutes.

Just then, a stocky man in a boiler suit and a railwayman's cap at a jaunty angle walked past us towards the engine. 'Don't worry,' said the porter. 'That is the driver. I'll catch up with him and ask him to make sure you'll have enough time to get off. And I'll get him to give you three bursts on the whistle before he stops. All the best, missus. Goodbye, sir.' And off he ran.

'You're an angel!' I called after him, then settled myself comfortably next to Martin. To encourage him, I patted his thigh. 'This is all a bit much for you, darling, but it won't be long now. Once we get to the castle, you'll be pampered like the king of England.' Martin placed his hand over mine and gave me a wan little smile. He looked pale and drawn and was making an effort not to show his exhaustion.

Suddenly, the door flew open and two women bustled noisily in. The taller and stouter of the two addressed Martin. 'What are these cases doing here? They ought to be on the rack.' She had assumed an air of authority and, by raising her chin, she enhanced the impression of looking down her nose at him. 'Fancy, blocking the way like that. I think that ...'

Quite uncharacteristicsally of me, I stopped her short: 'Sorry. The cases will stay where they are. Neither my husband nor I are capable of lifting them, and we'll have to get off quickly at Craigmorton Halt. If you don't like it, there are plenty of empty compartments on this train.' Martin gave my hand a squeeze of appreciation. We were still holding hands and it was clear to me that he wished to continue.

'Oh, I dare say we'll manage,' said the thinner one in a conciliatory tone. 'Augusta, dear, you take the window seat. I shall be alright beside you.' I nearly burst out laughing when I heard her name. So the good lady felt compelled to live up to her name. I couldn't help wondering what the other one was called. I didn't have long to wait. Augusta took off her sludge green jacket, an expensive waterproof one with umpteen pockets, and passed it, together with her shopping bag, to her companion.

'Here, Peggy, if you don't mind. Just put it along the seat.' Peggy's name was so apt, I nearly chuckled. With her thin, stick-like body and round head, which was enlarged by a mat of permanent-wave frizz, she reminded me of the carved clothes-pegs gypsy women used to hawk from door to door. Sometimes my mother would draw a face on the knobs and by wrapping a strip of material round the rest, make them into little dollies for me. The ladies settled down opposite us and quite openly checked us over, item by item. Needless to say, I did the same to them. Martin had closed his eyes, but I knew he was an expert observer even through the tiniest gap behind his eyelashes.

Of course, they wore the usual thick stockings most of us had to put up with in those early post-war years. But their shoes, to my surprise, were beautifully hand-stitched brogues that would have been at home on the poshest of golf courses. Peggy wore a well-tailored Harris tweed jacket, and Augusta's grey hand-knitted cardigan was a work of art. Their turn-out was in keeping with the current country gentry's preference for quality combined with a generous touch of dowdiness. Too smart or elegant would have been considered vulgar. I was impressed by the fact that these remote regions still had such skilled craftspeople.

It was obvious from their lack of luggage that they were local, and their accent revealed them as being Scottish. It was, however, not a strong accent and I assumed that it must have been modified by a long sojourn in England. I knew immediately that they were sisters, for in spite of their different figures and features, they had one thing in common. Both had large, round eyes with dark circled pale grey irises. And both had that bold, almost unblinking stare which, I must admit, made me feel a little uncomfortable. When they looked from me to Martin, or anywhere else, they did not shift their gaze but swivelled their heads in the required direction ... like owls, I thought.

Augusta, her former belligerence forgotten, addressed me in deep, fluting tones. 'So you'll be staying at Craigmorton Castle?'

I nodded briefly, guessing that there was no other place to stay. Then, Peggy produced a smile, revealing long, rather yellow teeth. 'You will enjoy it, I'm sure. The countryside around here is magnificent. You couldn't find a more exciting place for walking or hunting. The fishing too is excellent. Are you personal friends of Lord Craigmorton?' Martin gave my hand two short little squeezes which was our long-established sign for 'no', 'yes' being one squeeze, or tap, or cough, or whatever was appropriate at the time. In this case 'no' couldn't mean that we didn't know Lord Craigmorton or anybody of importance at the castle – obviously, somebody had invited us. It meant, 'say as little as possible'.

'The reason for our stay is convalescence', I said in a tone of voice that forbade further questioning. I had met Lord Craigmorton briefly. His son Gerald and Martin had become firm friends. They had served the last four years of the war together and had even been wounded together. Now that Martin and I had been invited for an indefinite stay at the castle, it meant that the two friends would have the chance to build up strength and regain their health together. Lord

Craigmorton, a stocky, dynamic man, had been bold and lucky enough to amass a fortune before World War II, when he had bought the vast Craigmorton estate. But he had remained a man of the people, with firm roots in the Yorkshire working class. His intention, so I was told, was to develop the estate in order to create work and homes for the ordinary local inhabitants, which made him unpopular with his Conservative neighbours.

'Peggy,' cooed Augusta, 'it's time you passed the biscuits round.' Peggy extricated a flat tin from the shopping bag, opened it and with a little flourish held it out to us. 'They're flapjack specials', she explained, 'very sustaining when one is travelling, especially nowadays.'

Martin gave my hand two short squeezes. 'This is very kind of you,' I smiled, but we're not biscuits eaters. Besides, we don't want to spoil our appetite since we'll be expected to do justice to the good spread that is bound to await us at the castle.'

'You should be so lucky.' Augusta's voice had turned extra low and sepulchral. 'You don't know whether you'll actually get there.'

'What nonsense, of course we'll get there. We're

being picked up at the halt.' I was getting cross. I saw the sisters exchange a long meaningful look. 'What do you mean?' I demanded.

Peggy pursed her narrow lips, then sighed. 'You see, things aren't what they used to be. In the old days you could rely on everything working as expected and everybody doing what they promised. But since the old laird has gone, people no longer seem to know their place.'

'So?' I questioned, 'what are things like now?'

Of course, she hadn't missed my belligerent attitude, but it didn't deter her from making out that it was her human duty to warn me and tell me the worst.

'Even if the management remember to give the right orders, the staff often say "yes" and then do their own thing. Like imbibing too much of the hard stuff and then sleeping it off instead of, for instance, collecting a party from the halt. You needn't look at me like that, it happened before. Unfortunately, the shed with the lantern isn't much of a shelter. There is a farm track. It is rough and steep but you could walk it in just under an hour.' She swivelled her head to look at Martin and then back at me. 'I must tell you, it's pretty hard going, even for a fit person. Your best bet would be to carry on to Craigmorton Town.'

'And what would we be doing there?'

'Stay in one of the local pubs. The best is the Hog's Head and it's straight across the square from the station. They always have a blazing log fire, the bedrooms are very comfortable and the food is fantastic. Home-grown livestock and vegetables, you know. You couldn't do better. What do you say?'

Martin gave my hand two short squeezes. 'It sounds very tempting,' I said and paused. I saw their heads swivel briefly towards each other. Had this been a triumphal look? 'But,' I continued, 'If people promise to do something for me, I feel obliged to accept their offer as genuine. It would be too bad if they came to collect us and we weren't there.'

Augusta's brow wrinkled and Peggy pursed her lips. 'Well, it's up to you.' She threw a pitying look at Martin. 'Under the circumstances I wouldn't take the risk.' Martin kept his eyes closed but gave my hand a long, reassuring squeeze.

We sat in silence. It was clear that, since I had refused their advice, we were no longer worthy of their attention. I was glad. I no longer had to keep up a conversation and put up a bold front. In fact I was anxious again. Would the driver remember to give me the signal? I had taken the trouble to learn the station names before the halt, but that had turned out to be useless. Looking out of the window I could see only amorphous shapes in the mist. No station name-boards anywhere. I felt sure it couldn't be long now.

Suddenly, a violent jerk and the train came to a screeching stop. In panic, I jumped up. We had arrived. The driver had not only missed blowing the whistle, he had nearly missed stopping at the halt altogether. I almost leapt at the door to open it, when Martin pulled me back by my skirt. A second later Augusta said with exaggerated calmness: 'Deer crossing the line again. Mark my word, Peggy, one of these days we shall have a serious accident.' I sat down again. And now the ladies' pale grey eyes were trained on me, and from the little smirk on their lips I could tell that they had enjoyed my alarm and now my embarrassment. 'To hell with you both,' I thought, and snuggled my hand back into Martin's. After that, silence again. Only the rhythmic rattatatat of the train.

Augusta, who had been playing with the large golden cross upon her bosom, now turned her head towards her sister. 'You know, Peggy, it feels as if we were going a lot faster than usual.' 'How odd,' came the reply, 'I was just thinking the same. He may be trying to make up the time we spent waiting for the deer to cross.' I felt reassured. If we really were going faster, that meant the driver was also making up time for a longer stop at the halt.

When the three whistle bursts finally shrilled in our ears, it was the sisters who were surprised and didn't know what to make of it. I got up and started to pull the suitcases forward, right up to the edge of my and Peggy's seats. By the time I had folded the travelling rug and hung it over my shoulders, the train had come to a stop. I opened the door, then helped Martin get up and, step by step, half lifting him, got him off the train. Then it was back up for the first case, and up again for the second. It was hard work, yet the two women made no attempt to help. They sat motionless; their eyes trained on me like searchlights. Before slamming the door shut I shouted: 'Thanks for your help! May the good Lord reward you!'

I quickly pushed the cases together. They were of equal height and made a safe seat. Martin sat down and I wrapped the rug around him. When I looked up, I saw that Peggy was now in Martin's window seat. The extended stop must have been a surprise to them. Through the mist, and against the dim light of the compartment, only their silhouettes could be made out.

But they were keeping us in view alright. Their heads slowly swivelled as the train started to pull away. 'Those bloody bitches!' I swore, 'They didn't lift a finger to help. They would have tripped me up if they'd dared.'

'Come into the rug with me,' Martin said calmly. It was cold now and the mist was clinging. I should have loved to snuggle up to him and share our warmth, but I refused. 'I can see some sort of light further up. I better check whether anybody is waiting for us there.'

'Don't go, Claire,' he urged. The mist is treacherous. You can see going towards the light, but coming back you'll have nothing to guide you. You could easily step over the edge of the platform.' Frustrated and irritable, I gave way with bad grace. 'Hush', whispered Martin softly, before I could continue. 'Don't talk, don't move.' And then I saw it. A stag stood only about three paces away from us. He was on rough grassland that ran along the platform. Only a two-foot-high iron railing separated him from us. In the mist and semi-darkness he looked gigantic. He towered over us and his huge, spreading antlers seemed to branch up like the crown of a tree. He didn't attempt to step over the dividing rail, just stood and looked. It may only have been for a minute or two, but, believe me, it seemed a very long time. Suddenly he turned and walked towards a dark patch which I assumed to be the edge of a forest.

'Relax, Claire. It isn't rutting time yet, so he isn't dangerous. He was just curious – wanted to check us out.' I was impressed by Martin's calm attitude but remained standing. I felt safer that way. Safer? In fact, I didn't feel safe at all. I've never felt so vulnerable in all my life. What if those owlish sisters had been right? What, if the person who was supposed to collect us was now sleeping off his overindulgence? If he didn't return to the castle with us, they would assume that we hadn't caught that train. I suddenly felt sick. The thought of being marooned in this cold and lonely place was unbearable. Though I was near panic, habit took command. I had to cope. So far I'd always coped, always had found a way in spite of precarious finances, inadequate accommodation and a long period of difficult nursing. I never allowed myself to be seen with red-rimmed eyes, always managed to hold my head high and keep smiling. The solution came to me in a flash: I would have to walk up to the castle and get help. What had Peggy said? About an hour's walk uphill on a rough track. I didn't mind the effort, but what if I got lost in the mist and strayed onto the moors? The horror of Martin deserted, waiting all night in vain for my return, was too frightening to be contemplated any further. Again, I forced myself back to reason. For goodness sake, we've been waiting for barely three to four minutes and there I was again inventing the most disastrous scenario.

It must be the mist, I decided. My eyes were hurting from straining to see, my hearing frustrated by the aggressively muffled silence and, apart from that, the atmospheric pressure seemed to sit heavily and gripping on my head. No wonder that, with normal perceptions not functioning, the subconscious tries to take over. Sight and hearing practically cut off, it made the sense of smell all the more powerful. It is this sense that is most evocative and intrudes with ease into our emotional life. I sniffed. In this all pervading dampness I was aware of the scent of the earth, a concoction of herbs and a faint pungency; the resinous exhalations of pine woods. But underlying it all was the odour of rotting vegetation and decay and, by association, of death.

And then I had a revelation, a recognition of something I should have noticed before; Craigmorton, the name of the place. The second syllable 'mort' meant death. Rearranged, the 'mort on craig' is saying 'death on the rock'. The castle, I had been told, stood on a foundation of rock. Was this name a warning to the world to stay away? Oh God, what fearful fate was awaiting us?

Suddenly, a diffused light came towards us. Behind it was a dark shape. It turned out to be a man of gigantic stature and his voice hit us like a fog-horn.

'Captain and Mrs Lucas?'

'Yes,' came Martin's weak voice.

'I'm Jock Fraser. Craigmorton's estate manager.' Since he had come quite close now, he couldn't fail to notice Martin's pathetic effort to rise from the suitcases.

'Excuse me sir; I think it would be quicker and safer if I carried you.'

I was peeved. Someone else was taking control. 'You are late,' I burst out sharply but almost instantly regretted it.

'No!' Fraser boomed at me. I'm spot on time. The train was nearly eight minutes early.' With that he jammed his lit torch in between the cases, pointing it forward, then picked up Martin and carried him like a child in his arms towards the distant halo of light. 'Follow close behind, please', he commanded abruptly. 'I'll come back for the cases.'

It was an effort to keep up with his long strides. I felt cowed and helpless. Was Martin being carried to his doom?

The car turned out to be an ancient Wolseley with a spacious interior and large, comfortable seats that felt like club fauteuils. Without consulting us, Fraser had put Martin in the front seat, opened the back door for me and then disappeared into the mist.

Martin turned towards me. 'Alright, Claire? Not much longer now, we're nearly there.' I nodded but remained silent. Fraser's high-handedness had upset me enough to prevent me from making a cheerful response. Of course, he was only getting his own back for my accusing him of being late. It seemed no time at all when I heard our luggage being stowed in the boot and Fraser was easing his huge body behind the wheel. I couldn't help noticing his powerful neck and shoulders. His square face had a ruddy complexion and even his bald top, surrounded by fluffy blond hair, seemed very pink.

'I hope the bumpy road isn't upsetting you, sir,' he said after a minute's drive. Our roads have been sorely neglected during the war.' There it was again, he had addressed Martin and ignored me. Still, it was good of him to be so solicitous.

'The car is well sprung – so it isn't too bad,' replied Martin amiably. 'You know, we were advised not to get off at the halt. The local ladies tried to persuade us to make for the Hog's Head at the terminus.'

'Oh, hell!' exploded Fraser. 'Not the three weird sisters again. Bloody hijackers, they are! I told his lordship they'll only stop if we put the fear of the law into them. A strong, threatening letter from our solicitors should do the trick. But he won't do it. "Jock", he said to me, "don't worry, I'll get the better of them bye and bye."' Fraser sighed. 'I suppose he knows what he's doing. You don't become an international tycoon if you're a fool.'

'Interesting,' said Martin, 'but there were only two sisters. Augusta and Peggy. What's the third one like?'

'She looks very much like Peggy and she's a devious bitch. Her name is Maggie and she's in charge of the local telephone exchange. So, you won't be surprised if I tell you that there isn't much she doesn't know about local goings-on.' He gave a little snort. 'We say that the only way of using the phone safely, is to speak Chinese. Now Peggy, she works part-time at the post office. I wouldn't put it past her to do a little letter-steaming of her own. Come to think of it, the envelope of my last bank statement looked a bit dodgy. Augusta, now, she's the eldest. She made a good catch and is now a very well to-do widow. She does the book-keeping for Hamish who owns the Hog's Head. He is the only brother and they all dote on him. Augusta likes to mix with the regulars and listen to their gossip, especially when their tongues have been well loosened and they forget she is there. So, altogether, the three of them know a lot more than they ought to.'

'I'm impressed,' admitted Martin. 'Information and secrets spell power.'

'Indeed, sir. They are being treated with great respect. They will tell you it's because they belong to the MacAlistair clan, but we guess that there is a lot of intimidation and pressure behind closed doors.'

Martin was intrigued. 'A sort of three-women local mafia. Have they actually managed to kidnap any of your guests?'

'Aye, three. And when they tried to phone us from the Hog's Head, they were told by the exchange manager, our Maggie, that recent storm damage is waiting to be repaired. That way the Hog's Head gained another day or two. Mind you, it's not a bad place to be trapped in. It's comfortable and their cook is a treasure. But, of course it causes us a lot of worry. One thing I know. His lordship is making sure we're one of the first areas to get an automatic telephone exchange.'

'How is Gerald?' Martin asked.

'Could be better,' Fraser shook his head. 'His smashed hip is healing but it still troubles him a lot. What is worse, he is listless and depressed. Just can't get interested in anything. He still has nightmares. They say they can hear him yell out in the night. I think, sir, your company will do him a world of good. He often talks about you.' I could see Martin was thoughtful but he didn't comment.

'There are only a few people up at the castle at the moment,' continued Fraser. 'The main ones are Dr Jason and Evie Owen. She's been a field nurse in Africa and Italy. You see, there are another three soldiers his lordship has invited to convalesce here. Actually, he'd offered the Ministry a wing of the castle. He was even prepared to pay for the equipping and maintenance, but they refused. Said it was too isolated for an official establishment. Oh, well ...' He shrugged his shoulders.

Of course, I listened to everything with interest. What a chatty gossip our grumpy Fraser had turned out to be. But then, Martin was a master at drawing information from the most unlikely people. Without saying much himself, he would do it all with a sympathetic smile, an encouraging nod or two, and a look in his eyes that made them think that at that moment they were the centre of his world.

Suddenly, conversation ceased. We had come out of the mist. An enchanting landscape rose up around us. Bathed in the silvery light of a star-studded sky and an almost full moon, we saw hills of wild moorland rolling up to distant mountains. Here and there were dark patches of forest, and in some places sinister pinnacles of rock seemed to be clawing upwards through the vegetation like fingers of a desperate hand. On the largest and highest rock before us, humped like a whale and partly covered with stunted trees, stood the castle. In this eerie light, with its towers and turrets silhouetted against the stars, it looked like a Scottish valhalla that had magically risen from a sea of mist. If this was valhalla, was Lord Craigmorton its Wotan, the macho God who welcomed the wounded heroes home and into his capricious power?

When we had reached the top of the winding track I could see the building more clearly. Castles had stood on this rock since the Dark Ages, one replaced by another in due course. The latest edition, I saw, was in fact nineteenth-century Victorian with added crenellations and other Gothic features and trimmings. In fact, an architectural mongrel. And yet, I had to admit, it was an impressive pile. Whether its exalted position or the luminosity of the night had increased its impact, I don't know. I felt intimidated. I couldn't help wondering how Martin and I would fit into this strange setting.

On arrival, Jock Fraser took possession of Martin again, carrying him up the few steps to the grand entrance. I had been left to scramble out of the car by myself and was once again trying to keep close behind them. Being aware of the fake medieval exterior, I imagined an interior full of appropriate martial ironmongery, as well as numerous hunting trophies such as stuffed stag heads with glass eyes that stare down from every wall.

We first entered a sort of anteroom. Then the inner door opened and we were ushered into the great hall. My attention was immediately drawn to the blazing logs in the huge fireplace. The flames enhanced the soft lighting of the room surrounding it. The encircling gallery above, though visible, was not sufficiently lit to reveal the details of the paintings between the off-leading doors. The place had obviously been refurbished in the 1930s, just before the war. The sofas and armchairs surrounding the fireplace, like the rest of the furniture, had a clean and uncluttered line. The odd antique pieces seemed to fit in well enough, and the various art nouveau touches, like the bronze figures, glass vases and Tiffany lamps, added softness to the decor. I noticed that the upholstery as well as the many oriental rugs on the wooden floor looked slightly worn which gave the room a well-used, homely feel. There were some portraits and landscape paintings on the walls, but no swords, lances or ancient shields. Nor were there any clanking suits of armour and, though I looked specially, there wasn't a single pair of antlers on display.

I made myself concentrate on the details of my surroundings rather than on the people who were now watching our arrival. I didn't want to face a lot of strangers. I didn't feel like standing up to their scrutiny. I was tired of playing a part, tired of everything.

Lord Craigmorton, a jovial man with shrewd eyes, was the first to greet us. Then Gerald, his son, limped forward and he and Martin embraced silently. It was a moving sight, for we all knew that this was their first meeting after they had nearly died together. A large, lean dog rose from the rug in front of the fire. It was a deerhound. He came quietly up to me, sniffed, and then raised his head to look straight into my eyes. 'This is Percy,' said Lord Craigmorton. I put my hand on his head and faced his quiet, searching look. Satisfied, he wagged his tail and returned to his rug.

'Percy says you'll do,' announced his lordship,

'and so say I and all of us.' It was then that I really looked at the people around me. They had smiling, welcoming faces that expressed genuine interest and warmth. And I, who had been psyching myself up for another bold and cheerful-front performance, couldn't take it. I couldn't cope with kindness. I burst into convulsive sobs, and though I tried, I couldn't stop the tears from gushing from my eyes. Martin stepped forward towards me but Gerald stopped him. Lord Craigmorton had put his arms around me. 'There, there, lass. Don't worry, let it all out.' As my tears kept flowing onto the shoulder of his Harris tweed jacket, he kept patting my back. Gradually, the sobbing ceased and the tears started to flow quietly and soothingly. It felt as if all my worries and fears were being washed away with this gentle stream.

Lord Craigmorton stroked my head and murmured into my hair: 'There, it's starting to feel much better, isn't it? I know. I've been there.' His paternal embrace and the patient goodwill of the people around me made me realize that I was being accepted as one of them. My lonely worries would from now on be a thing of the past. Martin would be well again, a new life was awaiting us. A great sigh of relief summed up my feelings. Everything, yes everything was going to be alright.

VERISIMILITUDE

'You're early,' said Nina. It sounded sharper than she had intended. After rushing about to buy snacks for tonight's gathering, she had hurriedly arranged everything ready for serving. Now, after a quick shower, she was still in her bathrobe, anxious to get dressed. Besides, she liked to apply her make-up at leisure, and relax a few minutes before facing guests. For a moment, she wondered whether to explain this to him, but decided she couldn't be bothered.

'Just go in, Paul,' she said, 'pour yourself a drink.'

Normally, he would have hung up his raincoat and done just that. But he was still standing there. She found it strange that he should ignore her request. Somehow, he seemed different tonight. She knew him as a self-effacing man who, at their meetings, would only speak when someone asked him a direct question. He was the proverbial grey man who melted into the background. But now he looked at her with unaccustomed boldness. His salt-and-pepper hair falling unkempt over his forehead, he seemed to grow in stature as he walked towards her. His steps were slow and deliberate. There was a strange glint in his eyes. Sensing in him a peculiar tenseness and excitement, she felt uncomfortable. It suddenly struck her that he could be thinking of her naked in her bathrobe. Surely, he wouldn't try to force himself on her?

'Sorry to put you out, Nina,' he said softly. She recoiled inwardly as he stepped closer. 'Let me deliver the obligatory, welcoming little pecks.' And with that he kissed her lightly on both cheeks. She felt relieved. But instead of retreating he remained, his face close to hers. She tried to step back but was trapped against the telephone table. Suddenly, his hands were round her neck. He seemed amused by her surprise. 'Nina, dear,' his voice was low and oddly melodious. 'What would you do if I strangled you?'

She felt a tightening of his grip. Felt, to her horror, that he was wearing gloves. Panic struck. Her reaction was instant. Her hands flew up. In split seconds, strands of his hair were round her fingers and her thumbs pressed on his eyeballs. 'You'd be blind before I'm dead,' she gasped and started to dig her hard, long nails into his eyelids. With a curse he tried to shake her off, but her hands were anchored in his hair and her nails did not budge. Not till he let go of her neck did she release him and let him step back.

She must have hurt him, but he laughed. 'Quite a tigress! This really was interesting.'

She was still glaring at him.

'Can't you take a joke?' He tried to sound light-hearted but it didn't quite come off.

Though she stood there, apparently collected and haughty, she was afraid. She had no idea why he should want to kill her. They weren't lovers. They were not even close friends. He was just a member of the small literary circle who met now and then to discuss practical issues of interest to professional authors. Since he was a travel writer, she wasn't even in competition with him.

It would be half an hour before the others were due to arrive. Half an hour of danger. She saw him walk towards the hallstand. Good God! Her late father's walking sticks and golf clubs! The lethal possibilities nearly paralysed her. No good running upstairs. None of her doors had a lock. What could she do?

The telephone rang. Before he could rush back to reach it, she had picked it up. Without waiting to listen who was calling, she shouted: 'Paul is here. Come now. Help! Philip!' She stopped. Paul had pulled the lead out of the socket.

Again they confronted each other. He knew as well as she did that Philip lived just round the corner, and that he could appear within minutes. The trouble was, that calling out Philip's name had been a tactical move, an act of faith. She had no idea who had phoned. It could have been a double-glazing firm. She saw he was thinking. He couldn't risk killing her now, even if he smashed Philip's head with a golf club, should he turn up. The police were bound to check her telephone records. They would trace the caller and learn that she had been in fear of Paul.

He was smiling as he took off his gloves. 'Sorry if my bit of play-acting has upset you. But you see, I was anxious to learn how a young woman like you would behave in the face of danger. Why don't you get dressed now?'

She was about to swear at him, when Philip stormed in. 'What on earth is going on here?' He was without coat, just in his old cardigan and slippers. Obviously, his reaction had been instant.

'Paul tried to kill me,' she said simply. 'Your phone call saved me.'

'Utter nonsense,' laughed Paul. 'It was an experiment. I can explain.'

'You had better!' growled Philip. He put his arm round Nina's shoulders. She wasn't the kind of woman who needed a man to take care of her. But now, the protection of this blond giant was a real comfort. She felt shaky. The shock reaction was catching up with her. He helped her up the stairs. 'I'll bring you a cup of tea,' he said soothingly. 'There's plenty of time to lie down for a while before getting dressed. Don't worry. I'll see to the others as they turn up.'

When Nina looked back, Paul was unbuttoning his Burberry. He was no longer smiling.

The first thing Nina noticed as she came downstairs was the coats and jackets on the old-fashioned stand. No hats were topping the hardwood branches, so that they curved up towards the stuccoed ceiling as if in competition with the giant deer antlers on the panelled wall. Although her father had died four years ago, she still could not bring herself to get rid of his many beloved monstrosities, of which these antlers were but one. She caught whiffs of unidentifiable French perfume, probably Gwendolyn's and Roberta's combined, as well as the scent of Adrian's Turkish cigarettes. Muffled voices came from behind the parlour door. She stood still, not to listen, but to collect herself fully. She felt much better now; the rest had done her good. She knew that, once in there, she would have to keep her wits about her and control her emotions. She had to make them believe her story. If they, her friends, did not accept it, what chance had she to convince the police? She was determined to see Paul punished.

Taking a deep breath, she opened the door. Conversation stopped. Five faces turned towards her. The excitement and tension were palpable. As expected, they all sat in their usual places. Over time, they each had acquired their own special spot, like birds coming back to roost. Though not looking at him directly, Nina was aware of Paul sunk deep in his armchair. She forced herself not to react to him, to keep calm. One person was missing. Partly because she wanted to know, but mainly because she wanted to break the tension and introduce a note of normality, she pointed to the vacant chair.

'Hello, all. Where's our Stanley?'

'Couldn't come,' answered Philip, stopping the slight movement of his rocking-chair. 'He phoned. He's still in New York. Has to sort out some unexpected financial sharkery.'

'I see,' said Nina. She also saw that none present had been upset by this, although the absence of Stanley Goldberg's expertise had wiped the tax and business item, which had in fact been the main item, off their agenda. Obviously, the gap was now to be filled by an inquest on a case of attempted murder. How grand this sounded. It was a once-in-a-lifetime opportunity for some of them to meet the real thing. Nina could tell they were eager to get their teeth into it.

Philip's huge hand touched her arm. 'Are you all right, Nina? Sure you can face this?'

She nodded. 'Yes, thanks.' She was aware his words expressed polite solicitude, which everyone here would take for granted. The warmth of his gaze and the gentleness of his touch, however, told her it was more. She had met Philip when, after having been injured as a war correspondent, he had given up his job to live with his sister and her family just round the corner from her. While recovering, he had taken up writing. His adventure stories, intended for youngsters, had soon become popular with boys of all ages. She remembered her father chuckling over them during his long confinement in hospital. Philip had stood by her after her father's death, just as he was trying to support her now. She was acutely aware of the dichotomy of her feelings: on the one hand grateful and comforted, on the other, a trifle resentful that he should think her incapable of coping on her own.

She could have sat in Stanley's vacant chair, which was the one furthest away from Paul, but fearing to appear weak, she chose her usual place facing him. She ignored him, looking instead at Roberta Pennington who had leant forward, her finely chiselled features alive with interest. From the cut of her short, dark hair to the cut of her tailored trouser suit, she gave the impression of almost aggressive stylishness. She was a crime writer whose cool and lucid prose would tease her readers most entertainingly through subtly convoluted plots. Her voice was clear and self-confident. 'Nina dear. Philip told us about his phone call to you, and what took place when he arrived here. He told us you said that Paul had been trying to murder you. We were horrified. He insisted we shouldn't question Paul or discuss the matter without you. So please tell us now. What happened? Do you want to call the police? Believe us, we're all agog to know.'

'We are an' all,' confirmed Gwendolyn Bradley, who sat opposite Roberta at the other end of the curved sofa. Gwendolyn – never to be called Gwen – was a woman whose fresh and rosy plumpness made her look years younger than her actual early sixties. She was a successful writer of refined historical romances. Amongst friends, however, she liked to play the down-to-earth lass, varying the strength of her Yorkshire accent according to mood. Her bright blue eyes focused on Paul. 'Aye, an' we want to hear both your stories.'

'Nina darling, do tell. I can't wait to hear all about it,' drawled Adrian Fitz-Giffard, sinking into himself again after Nina had motioned that he should not bother to get up. He was sitting between the two ladies in the centre of the sofa. His long legs were drawn up, so that his arms partly embraced his knees, and partly wound up to his waist and towards his neck. Nina always marvelled at the fancy positions he managed to adopt. He seemed to be all limbs. Her secret nickname for him was spaghetti-man. Unwound and upright, he was even taller than Philip, his narrow-chested thinness exaggerating the appearance of his height. Pale, sharp-featured, with auburn hair brushed forward, he looked like Aubrey Beardsley, a resemblance he made much of.

Roberta addressed Nina. 'If you give us your story first, then Paul can give us his.' Nina didn't know whether to be annoyed or amused. She's putting herself in charge again, she mused, and none of us can be bothered to protest. Oh well.

'Dear friends,' she started, looking at each one in turn. 'I'm sorry we can't have our planned meeting. The unpleasant scene, which occurred before your arrival, is now leading to this – I don't know what to call it – discussion, inquiry?'

'Inquisition,' muttered Paul, but only Philip heard him.

She then narrated in detail what had happened, exactly as she remembered it. There were no interruptions, but general surprise at what sounded an incredible account. When she had finished, they turned to Paul. His face was impassive. He remained silent. Philip's eyes narrowed. 'Come on, Paul. Utter!'

Paul looked round, then shrugged his shoulders. 'What can I say? The account of the action is correct, but the interpretation is wrong.'

'Is it?' said Philip sarcastically. 'Do you mean you were trying to cheer her up, make her laugh?'

Paul ignored the remark. 'As you all know, I am a writer of travel books. They are realistic accounts of what I see and hear. I report in detail, making a virtue of necessity. The truth is, I have very little imagination. I can only record and mirror life. For years now I've been flitting from place to place, living out of a suitcase. I'm sick of it. I want to give up and settle down. Unfortunately, I have no other skills but writing. I thought I might try my hand at crime novels.'

'How interesting,' interrupted Roberta sharply. 'So

you think this is the easiest option?'

'For me, yes. I can't see myself writing romances, like Gwendolyn, or fantastic tales exploring the occult, like Adrian. Nor could I tackle the complicated emotional relationships of suburbia that Nina writes about. But with crime, I can get newspaper accounts, court reports, case histories and the like. Even so, my lack of imagination is a handicap. I thought it would be a good idea to test myself. So I started a novel with the murder of a young woman and described her reaction. Then, tonight, I faked a similar attack to see what would really happen.'

Among the general exclamations, Nina's voice rang out. 'And how did your fictitious damsel react?'

'She nearly fainted and begged for mercy. Her face was distorted with fear.'

'A far cry from nearly having your eyes gouged out,' commented Adrian. 'As a matter of interest, what did our Nina look like? What was her expression?

'A poker face,' Paul said dryly. 'She looked as cool as a cucumber.'

'A cucumber with a poker face,' chuckled Gwendolyn,

making her bosom shake.

Paul continued. 'I put it down to my inadequate acting and tried to revive the threat by pulling out the telephone lead. No use, she stood her ground.'

'Bravo, Nina. Good lass!' cried Gwendolyn.

'What on earth did you imagine would happen after this scene?' asked Roberta. 'Did you really expect her to laugh it off, when you'd gone to all this trouble to scare her to death?'

'Well, I thought I'd explain my reason to her, as I've just done to you, and she'd understand. But I see now, the more realistic my performance, the less likely she'd be to believe me.' He sighed. 'It just brings home to me the magnitude of my lack of imagination.'

Nina couldn't help realising that this had been the longest speech she'd ever heard from Paul. And what's more, that everybody had paid the closest attention.

Roberta started to speak again. The others did not interfere. After all, Paul was invading her professional territory. 'I hope,' she said with her neat little head held high, 'you will realise that a good crime novel needs even more imagination than an ordinary novel, not less. All the plotting and development of the characters must be based on realistic probabilities and must, above all, be psychologically plausible. If you can't imagine what your protagonists are feeling and are likely to get up to, forget it. You can't kitchen-test crime without ending up in jail yourself.'

'But what else could he do?' asked Philip.

'Goodness, lad, there all sorts of chances in t'non-fiction line,' said Gwendolyn. But we can't tell 'im what to do. We know nowt about 'is background, 'is specialities or, come to think of it, owt else. Aye, we know nowt about him.'

'That's right,' confirmed Philip, 'he's never told us anything about himself. He never expresses an opinion on anything.'

It struck Nina that they were talking about Paul as if he weren't present, and that they seemed to be quite unaware of doing so. She realised, that before his attack on her, she too used to ignore him, the invisible man in their midst. But now he was, apart from her, the main protagonist. Impatiently, she interrupted. 'For heavens sake, he's still here. Why not ask him?' Astonished, they stared at her, making her wonder whether she had embarrassed them.

Adrian unwound himself and leant back. 'If there's any close questioning to be done, I suggest Roberta does it. After all, she has dabbled in law in a previous incarnation.'

'Thanks for the "dabble", Adrian. But I am prepared to do it just the same. I will ...'

To everyone's surprise, Paul stopped her: 'If you intend to stage some sort of court performance, then I should be allowed a defence.'

Before they could discuss this point, Gwendolyn signalled her approval, her full, rosy lips in a benevolent smile. 'Of course you can. It's only fair. Whom would you like?'

'Philip,' was the prompt reply.

Nina had to admit the brilliance of Paul's move. From Philip's attitude earlier on, Paul was well aware of his antagonism. At the same time, of all the people present, Philip was the one who would conscientiously fight his own dislike, and give voice to any facts and considerations in favour of the accused.

Finding himself the centre of attention, Philip stroked back his mass of blond hair to gain time. 'This comes rather out of the blue, folks, but if you'd really like me to do this, I'll have a bash at it.' As it happened, all were concerned that 'justice should be seen to be done', and that a quasi prosecutor and defence, in a very loose sense, could be an advantage.

Nina and Paul did not take part in this discussion. They sat opposite each other, waiting. She couldn't help feeling that the four others were playing a game for which they were making up the rules to their own advantage. All this meeting had to decide, was whether there existed enough evidence of guilt for Paul to be handed over to the police. She had no doubt that, if by any chance this were to result in a high profile trial, some of them would find it a lucky publicity windfall. The question was, who would gain from a public court case, and who would try to avoid it? Roberta, for instance, could make quite a meal of it. And Philip, as a writer of adventure stories, could also gain a lot.

She wasn't so sure about Gwendolyn. Her high public standing as a lady of refinement could be stained by association with a strangler. Also, she had to consider the danger of zealous journalists rooting about in her past. They would discover, not the proverbial silver spoon and the posh ancestral mansion, but the overcrowded back-to-back in the slums of Leeds, from where plucky young Gwendolyn had escaped. After a certain amount of horizontal work, she had found a besotted lover to married her and, in the fullness of time, make her a wealthy widow. No, thought Nina, Gwendolyn was too cautious to risk exposure.

As for Adrian, she couldn't imagine him welcoming sordid publicity. Though, come to think of it, he might find performing in court rather satisfying. Still, he had to consider the generations of Fitz-this and Fitz-that, who would definitely frown upon such vulgarity. Nina was amused to realise that both she and Paul would probably gain from such publicity. But Paul would have to be judged 'not guilty' in order to enjoy his fame. Nina saw him watch her and wondered what he was thinking. In a strange way, it felt that being outside the general discussion, they were somehow thrown together. For the first time, she looked at him critically and found that he had rather fine eyes: light grey irises with dark outside rings, under a fringe of thick eyelashes. It was a lean face of good proportions. If he had a decent hairstyle and shaved the grey stubble, which is so ageing, he'd be quite good looking. She couldn't help thinking of some of the ugly men she had come across, who nevertheless managed to attract friends and lovers without apparent effort. But they had what Paul lacked: self-confidence and charm.

She knew that he knew she was thinking about him. Within this little enclave of privacy, it almost felt like some form of intimacy.

'Well, that's it,' she heard Adrian say with a tone of finality. 'That's settled.'

'What's settled?' she asked, alarmed, suddenly returning from her musings.

'Nina!' Adrian's hooded eyes opened fully with a reproachful look. 'I thought you were attending our deliberations.' Then, he instantly changed tack to prevent her from assuming that he was being judgemental. He smiled at her sweetly. 'Nina, darling, as you know we all admire you for many reasons. One of the important ones is your integrity.'

'There's no need to butter me up, Adrian. If you have anything unpleasant to tell me, please just say it.'

'No, no!' He protested. 'Nothing unpleasant. I just thought that Stanley Goldberg would have been the ideal judge. But since he isn't here, the six members present should all act as jurors and decide on the verdict.'

'This is ridiculous. I am the plaintiff. I'm not likely to vote "not guilty".'

'You might, darling. By the time we have considered everything, you may find the accused's intention to have been harmless. It gives you the chance to follow your conscience and vote against yourself without letting on. In Paul's case, on the other hand, if he is guilty, remorse may prompt him to face an official court.'

Nina laughed almost hysterically. 'This is a lot of nonsense, and you know it. Anyway, our two votes will cancel each other out. What you are telling me in so many words is that you are a bunch of cowards. That you haven't the guts to declare your opinions and stand by them, that you ....'

'Stop it!' Philip's voice was commanding. She had never heard him speak to her like this. 'Remember, Nina, we are your friends. If you don't trust us, we'll go. You are free to do what you like.'

General alert. The atmosphere was electric.

'Philip, old man,' soothed Adrian, 'let the girl blow off steam. After what she's been through it'll do her good.' Then he turned to her: 'If you have any other suggestions, we'll be happy to discuss them.'

Nina shook her head. In a low voice she said: 'No, let's do it your way.'

Adrian gave a sigh of relief. 'Your comment is being noted.' She watched him turn his gaunt face towards Paul. Under his fringe of auburn hair he seemed paler than usual to her. How heavy his drooping eyelids looked, and his long, narrow hands that had waved, flapped and floated to accompany his speech now lay in elegant repose on his lap. Nina reflected that he managed to wear his decadence like a badge of honour.

Meanwhile, Roberta rummaged in her huge crocodile handbag which she always declared to be imitation leather. She found her handkerchief and daintily dabbed her nose.

'Philip is right,' she addressed Paul, 'we know nothing about you. If we are to assess your story, we should know something of your background. Over all these years you never told us anything.'

Paul looked at her coldly. 'Over all these years you never asked.'

'But,' Gwendolyn stopped him, 'I remember we asked you quite a lot of things.'

'Yes, assorted general knowledge facts, but nothing about me and not my opinions'.

Gwendolyn fell silent, her little rosebud mouth pouting between her plump, pink cheeks. She was thinking, trying to remember, but couldn't come up with anything to contradict him.

'Well, then,' prompted Philip, 'where do you hail from?'

Nina wondered whether Paul resented being questioned in this manner. But he sat up, his expression impassive as usual. He spoke with a slightly gravelly voice. 'I spent my early years in Chichester where I was born. Later, my father who was a consultant specializing in abdominal surgery, moved to various hospitals in turn, taking his family with him. There were four of us; I had a younger sister. He was successful and we were pretty well off.'

Nina didn't know why she was surprised. Somehow, in the back of her mind, she had believed him to be a working-class boy who had had to struggle to become a professional writer. Philip must have thought very much the same, judging by his comment.

'So you come from a happy upper middle-class family.'

Paul slightly raised his eyebrows. 'I didn't say happy.'

Gwendolyn immediately picked up this point. 'What upset you? Was it sibling rivalry? Sibling jealousy?'

'No,' he said flatly, 'it was father's buggery.' Nina guessed that their combined intake of breath must have given him some satisfaction.

He continued. 'I remember one Saturday afternoon arriving downstairs after father had been hard at me. Little Evie was noisily running to and fro, laughing. I, hurting and distressed, told her to get out and shut that bloody door. Before I knew what was happening, mother had got hold of me and dragged me through the hall to the kitchen sink.

'"I'll give you using that word in my house!" she screamed hysterically, while pushing the carbolic soap into my mouth. I started to retch and dear little Evie, begging and crying, tried to pull her off me. A short time after, I was sent to boarding school.'

'Was your mother aware of the abuse?' asked Adrian.

'She knew all right, but pretended not to. At the same time she took her anger out of me as if it had been my fault.'

Philip's face expressed compassion. 'Hell,' thought

Nina, 'his soft heart will now make him commiserate with that murderer.'

Instead she heard him say: 'Poor woman, she must have felt trapped. With no other means of support, where could she go with two children? And imagine the shame of it all in those days.'

For the first time Paul showed emotion. It was surprise. 'You know, I never thought of it from her point of view. But then, she didn't see it from mine either.'

They were amazed to actually hear him chuckle. 'Obviously, lack of imagination is a family trait.'

'And what about school?' Adrian persisted. 'Were you bullied?'

'They tried to start with, but I was so angry, so wild and aggressive that even the older boys were afraid to tackle me. They left me alone but I was never popular. Since I hated sport, the teachers didn't like me either. But I had a quick and retentive mind, so they were forced to give me good marks. After that it was straight to university. Then, having passed in modern languages, I worked for a shipping company, both in the UK and abroad. After some ups and downs I became a travel writer of sorts.'

'Not of sorts,' protested Roberta. 'You're one of the best in that field. But I don't understand how you can write about scenery and happenings without imagination. Everything you narrate is solid and believable.'

He allowed himself a little smile. 'Thanks. It all sounds true because it is true. I cannot invent. Everything from nature to architecture and even people and conversations is observed and recorded in detail. My main chore then is editing.'

Adrian refused to be side-tracked. He wanted to complete the picture of Paul's background. 'What happened to your family? Did you ever go back?'

'No, I never saw them again. I hated my parents but was seriously worried about my sister.' Nina watched him intently. She became aware of the sudden narrowing of his eyes and hardening of expression. There was an almost imperceptible pause during which he seemed to draw in extra breath but then continued with the same level, gravelly voice as before.

'I was still at university when Evie drowned herself. They found her body caught in the bulrushes. The week after, my mother too committed suicide. She'd cut her wrists and trailed blood all over the house till she finally collapsed on dad's bed. I don't think it affected him very much because he just moved away and soon after married again. I kept dreaming of revenge, of what I could do to make him suffer. But instead of being shot or having his head bashed in he died of a heart attack while fucking his new young wife. What a great way to go! Is this justice? I ask you. Is it?'

They sat in silence, digesting Paul's information. Could this fantastic tale be true? Since he obviously was incapable of invention, it must be. Must it really?

Nina had always prided herself on being exceptionally perceptive where emotions and deeper feelings were concerned. That was why she had become a writer who could successfully explore complicated family relationships. As she always put it to herself, the eddies, currents and storms of human existence, the turbulences of the mind and the anguishes of the soul were all stuff that put wind in her sails. Though in her writing she favoured an elegantly restrained style, capable of convincing her readers of her innate sensitivity, in her private thoughts she sometimes indulged herself with expressions that were highly dramatic, even vulgarly overblown.

As she sat there, listening to Paul, watching his face and body language, she was waiting for a clear signal from her inner, hitherto infallible monitor. Confused, she tried to reason. The bare facts of Paul's sister's and mother's suicides as well as his father's subsequent marriage and demise could easily be verified, but the father's secret, criminal activities and the suffering of the family could not. She had to admit, however, that nobody was likely to commit suicide without overpowering pressure. Also, the matter-of-fact, almost brash manner of Paul's narration didn't quite ring true – the man was at pains to hide his emotions. But why? To her annoyance she could not plead ignorance. Her sensitive antennae had picked up the reason. The hiding of his feelings and emotions behind conspicuous coldness had become the habit of a lifetime. It was a lonely, unhappy man's standard weapon of defence. Oh, hell. What was she to think now?

Meanwhile, Gwendolyn had set the ball rolling again. 'I suppose we're all influenced by our background, but we got to pull oursen up and leave all the bad luggage behind. I, mesen, I've come from poor folks. Seven childer and a dad boozin' away the wages e's earned down t'pit. The life me poor mum 'ad! I wasn't goin' to be like 'er! Noways.'

For goodness' sake, thought Nina, I hope her lingo won't get any broader, I just couldn't bear it. Aloud, she asked: 'What did you do?'

Gwendolyn produced her signature chuckle and bosom bounce. 'I decided to choose a life worse than death. I was quite an eyeful in them days.'

'You still are,' interjected Philip.

'Well, I let mesen be set up by a mill-owner. 'T was a luvely little house – I even had a skivvy. What was I to do with all them spare hours? Well, I studied English and literature. And then I left that bloke 'cause I landed Leo, a rich widower who was willin' to make an honest woman of me. Well, he knew all about money, so I kept me eyes and ears open. I secretly read all his documents and correspondence and played daft while listening to him and his cronies discussing business. Yeh, I took every chance to learn about finance. When he died, 'is friends tried to get me to invest in their shady joints, in fact, they tried to cheat me.' This time she bounced with laughter. 'I never enjoyed mesen more than telling them bastards where to get off. Since then I dabbled in finance, spent some time writing me novels and 'ad some fun on t' side.'

There were expressions of surprise all round but Nina knew them to be phony since Gwendolyn's horizontal history was already well known to them. And the reason why the good lady made no secret of it amongst her colleagues, was because they knew that she had enough information about them to make betrayal unwise.

'You're the proverbial merry widow. Good for you,' exclaimed Roberta. 'I'd call this a success story. Mine is more commonplace; happy family, good education, good job, unhappy marriage, good divorce and then a lucky break with my crime novels. I must be content with that.'

Nina had listened patiently. She was aware that all this sidetracking had a purpose: it gave them time to sort things out in their minds, to decide on a verdict that was as fair as could be, while taking account of their own personal interests.

'Let us return to the business in hand. Are you ready to vote?' asked Roberta.

To the general murmur of consent, she dived once more into the jaws of her crocodile bag and retrieved a small notebook from which she tore some back pages. She handed them round. 'Since we know each others' handwriting, we had better use symbols: Nil for innocent and X for guilty.'

'She's in full command again,' thought Nina and, after some hesitation, obediently marked her paper, folded it and put it into the bowl.

Roberta now arranged the unfolded papers in two columns. The result: two guilty, four innocent.

Lisa watched Paul's face. He was looking at her with the ghost of a smile and his eyes were suspiciously shiny. She then countered the gaze of the others, wondering who were the two that had voted guilty.

THE MAGNOLIA GOWN

Mrs Gibbon

When he returned with the second rail of gowns he knew immediately that she was on the warpath. He recognized the stance: poker-straight, tummy in, chin high.

'I am speechless, Mr Green. I would never have believed it!' Her pale sapphire eyes bored into him. 'You don't really think I will accept this merchandise?'

'What do you mean, Mrs Gibbon? What's wrong with it?'

'What's wrong?' she snapped. 'Good God, man, are you blind?' Her long, pearly claw stabbed into the first rail. 'Look at the workmanship: wobbly stitching, shoddy finish. And here, look how the sequins have been put on. Atrocious!' She snatched the garment off the rail and held it up. 'This is a rag, not a Lady Patricia gown!'

'Mrs Gibbon, please, it ain't that bad.' With one

glance he had taken in the faults and the pink sequin chrysanthemum that looked like a crab on the run. 'My girls are skilled operators,' he protested, 'they work hard to give satisfaction.' His voice went husky as he tried to plead for sympathy. 'With small kids they're stuck at home. They need that money real bad and, believe me, Mrs Gibbon, they love working for Lady Pat.'

'Cut out the sob stuff. Your precious girls are leading you by the nose.'

'Nobody's taking me for a fool, madam. True, I'm like a father to them, but I'm strict and they respect me. They'd do anything to ...'

'Listen, Mr Green,' she cut in, 'I'm not interested. I cannot be bothered with outdoor workers; that's your job.' Now the claw was stabbing at him. 'YOU have accepted the contract and YOU deliver the goods. Half the work is below standard; this gown is quite unusable and I won't pay for it.' She flung it onto the counter. 'And what's more, I will debit you for the spoiled satin. You can keep it.'

'Crikey, Mrs G.!' He calculated that if he gave way on this piece she might accept the others. 'OK, Mrs Gibbon. I will get a remake just to please you ...'

'No remake. You keep the rag.'

'But madam, I must consider ...'

'And I, Mr Green, must consider my partners. She drew herself up. 'If you cannot deliver, I shall have to engage another contractor. This is business – not charity.'

Mrs Kopel

The reception, sorting and storerooms of S H Green, Ltd were untidy but clean.

'Good morning, Mr Green. Lovely morning. Where do you want this lot?' The speaker was a brisk, no-nonsense sort of woman.

Mr Green, fated to cope with women of strong character, could handle her. 'Over there. Now, Mrs Kopel, I have a bone to pick with you.'

'Me, sir?'

'Yes.' She saw he was cross and no mistake.

'I don't like being taken for a sucker. Look at this rubbish!' He held up the magnolia gown. 'Either you were too bloody lazy to check it it properly or you saw the lousy workmanship and thought you could get away with it. Make a fool of me, hey? And that after begging me to give you a chance in better class trade.'

'Lord, what did you expect me to do?' She faced him, fierce with resentment. 'You wanted them things in a hurry – double quick, you said. Well, Mrs Lishinsky had to go into hospital, so I had to give extra work to Mrs Patel. But her mother too was took bad, so she had to get little Tare to help her.'

'Shut up, woman!' he bellowed. 'We don't use child labour!'

'Mr Green,' she snapped, 'you know damn well the girls have to help ...'

'Shut up, I say. I know nothing about this. It has nothing to do with me. Understand? If those blasted women can't turn out proper work, sack them. There are plenty others glad of a job.' He stood there, eyes flashing. He had managed to work himself up.

'Mr Green.' She was exasperated but kept her temper. 'I can't work miracles. Have a heart. It takes time to train a new one. Besides, Mrs Patel is usually a good worker but, as a widow with a sick mother and three kids ...'

'Time folks stopped breeding like rabbits,' he grunted. 'Here, get her to re-make it – and I want to see no stitch holes in the satin.'

'But you'll pay her something, won't you? She can't ...'

He had simmered down but said sharply: 'Mrs Kopel, if she doesn't do it, she's out. This is a business – not a charity.'

Mrs Patel

In its heyday it had been a fashionable town residence but now, dilapidated, every room housed a whole family.

Mrs Kopel climbed the familiar staircase. The spice-laden air vibrated with the noise of fretful infants, foreign voices and the plaintive twanging of oriental music. She sniffed. She did not hold with curries. 'It ain't nice,' she thought, 'all them smells hanging about, even sticking to those old walls. If ever it gets into our materials, that'll be the end.'

When she entered the room, Mrs Patel was surprised to see her. Her beautiful dark eyes were red-rimmed, and Mrs Kopel wondered whether it was from crying or lack of sleep. Most likely both.

'Oh, Mrs Kopel, I thought you said Friday.'

'I did, but this 'ere is urgent. Mr Green is doing his nut.' She unwrapped the magnolia gown. 'I'm in real trouble, I am. You'll have to remake it.'

The young woman frowned and bent over the garment to examine it. She remained silent.

'How could you turn out a job like this, Mrs Patel? I thought I could rely on you.'

Still Mrs Patel said nothing. Mrs Kopel noticed how thin she had become. Some of her workers, she knew, just wanted pocket money, but this one needed the work to survive.

Little Tara, who had been sorting sequins, joined them. 'Granny made this one before she collapsed – she was in such pain.' Her little pinched face was anxious. 'I can easily unpick it,' she volunteered.

'No, you can't,' said Mrs Kopel. 'If you nick the satin and make a hole, your mother will have to pay for it.'

'I will use a pin and pull out the thread stitch by stitch. Please let me.' A worried ten-year-old, she looked as if everything depended on her.

'Well, alright then,' conceded Mrs Kopel, and turned to Mrs Patel. 'Mind you work on the inside of the old seam. No pay for this, I'm afraid. As it is, I had to stop Mr Green from sacking you.' When she saw the fear in the child's eyes she wished she had not said it.

Mrs Patel collected herself. 'I will put it right.'

Mrs Kopel sighed. This educated young woman could get a decent job outside if only her mother could look after the youngsters. 'How's the old lady?' she asked.

'Still very ill.'

'Are you going to see her today? Do give her my best wishes.'

'Thank you, no. I have to be in when Mr Ramshid calls for the rent.' At the thought her chest tightened. She dreaded the gaze of his hooded eyes all over her.

'It's not my business,' said Mrs Kopel, sensing something unpleasant, 'but I hope he isn't pressing you for money just now.'

'No, no!' exclaimed Mrs Patel, 'he is a distant relative and charges us very little. We are fortunate to have such a spacious room.'

'Glad to hear it.' Mrs Kopel thought it was indeed lucky that there was enough space to keep the work separate and clean. 'Next week is wedding dresses,' she warned. 'Take special care.'

'We shall be very careful,' Tara piped up.

'I'm thinking of the boys.'

'Don't worry, Mrs Kopel, they know this corner is out of bounds.'

'I hope so. They seemed to be getting pretty grubby as I came in.' Checking from the window she saw that the Patel twins were still playing among the refuse bins and dusty ivy. 'At least they're healthy and lively.' She gave Tara a gentle pat on the head and smiled at Mrs Patel before turning to go. 'Keep your pecker up, dearie; I'll see whether I can get something out of Mr Green. Cheerio.'

Alone again, Tara's wise little face turned to her mother. 'She's very kind, really.'

'Yes,' sighed Mrs Patel, telling herself that so was Ranshid in his peculiar way, and so were the Indian cousins who left little envelopes on her sewing machine. But she was sick of having to accept charity. Oh, God, how she hated charity.

Sally Weiss

The guests at the charity dinner were sipping their aperitifs, socializing and getting friendlier by the minute.

'Cor, look Sam, look at her!'

Mr Green followed his brother-in-law's leer. 'I'm looking.'

'Ain't she smashing, the way she stands with her hip out?'

'Even better in the horizontal,' thought Mr Green. He had recognized Sally instantly – a flame of the not-so-distant past. But he kept mum. Daniel couldn't be trusted. What's more, he had also recognized her gown – Mrs Patel's rejected creation. It still wasn't perfect but only an expert would notice.

'Sam, she's making straight for us,' hissed Daniel.

Indeed she was. As her breasts swayed gently with every stride, Mr Green noticed that the sequin artwork had metamorphosed into a sort of octopus. Sally had obviously attempted a further improvement, and the new creature seemed to float quite happily on the swell of magnolia satin.

'Sammy!' she cried. 'Surprise, surprise!'

Heads turned after her. She was a curvaceous blonde. Mr Green's taste ran to the opulent and voluptuous in everything and he especially liked flamboyant women. A sparkle came into his eyes but, remembering Daniel, he just played the jovial businessman.

'Sally, good to see you. Here, this is my wife's brother, Daniel Birnbaum. And this lovely lady, Dan, is Sally Weiss from Leeds, one of our former wholesale connections. What are you doing in London, Sal? Business or pleasure?'

'Oh, just a visit. Helping with the charity work.' She

smiled at both men, slightly favouring Daniel, who started to glow and felt he had to react somehow. 'What a super evening dress, if I may say so', he gushed. 'It must be a designer.'

'It is. We're not out in the sticks up north, you know. Actually, I ordered it specially for this do.'

Daniel marvelled. 'You must be a wealthy lady.'

She shrugged her shoulders and the octopus leapt up in alarm. 'I'm just a working girl, Mr Birnbaum, and I worked hard for this gown.'

'Bet you did,' mused Mr Green. He had sold it at cost price – the sum Mrs Gibbon had debited him with, plus the few pounds he had allowed Mrs Patel against his better judgement. Sold it to that ginger-haired traveller of Tuckers who had wanted it for his niece. Some niece!

'Now, gentlemen,' cooed Sally, 'can I add your names to my list of contributors? Say fifty pounds each?'

'Fifty quid!' gasped Daniel.

Mr Green intervened. 'We're already on the chairman's list, Sal. But look who's coming.'

It was Mrs Gibbon. With her new hairdo and slinky, pearl grey evening dress she looked very elegant – in an enamelled sort of way. She betrayed no recognition of Sally's gown but Mr Green knew that after having put two and two together she was sure to have made it seven, at least. There was nothing he could do. Damn that randy old ram from Tuckers.

Introductions over, Sally held up her list. 'I see you're not on it yet, Mrs Gibbon. May I ask you for a donation?'

Just then the reverend Mitchell, C.of E. and Rabbi Polensky stopped by. They were nursing their glasses of wine in amiable companionship, radiating goodwill.

'Such a worthy cause,' Sally fluttered her eyelashes at them for support. 'Shall we say one hundred pounds, Mrs Gibbon?

Daniel guffawed. 'She thinks you're loaded.'

They all laughed and the octopus on Sally's bosom went berserk.

Mrs Gibbon managed a smile. By now three local bigwigs had joined them: two councillors and one MP. They looked at her expectantly. The reverent gentlemen too were willing her to give.

She was still smiling but it seemed to hurt.

'Come on, Mrs Gibbon,' cajoled Mr Green, his voice oily with bonhomie. 'This is charity, not business.'

ƧAY CHEEƧE

When, after many years of absence, I found myself again in the temple of luxurious living, namely Harrods, I made straight for what I consider its inner sanctum – the Food Hall. There, the splendour of the art nouveau decor helps to elevate an already impressive display of food to the level of an artistic experience. The beautiful tiles on walls and ceiling depicting plants, birds and animals, as well as some hale and hearty country folk of yore in their quaint smocks and gaiters, create an impression of wholesomeness and dedication to nature. They somehow seem to sanctify the shoppers' greed and gluttony, by turning the purchase of luxury fare into almost an act of worship.

All the food on display is beautifully, sometimes even dramatically arranged – for instance the fresh fish counter. Just imagine suddenly encountering the stare of a bright pink fish over one metre long, artfully arranged among other exotic inhabitants of the deep. I almost had the notion I was snorkelling along one of those famous, fancy barrier reefs beloved by producers of nature films. I would hardly have been surprised to hear David Attenborough's breathy commentary.

As I passed the long cheese counter I couldn't see the one I used to buy on previous visits. True, time was too short for a thorough search but I feel sure I would have easily noticed the semi-transparent discs of the Austrian 'Quargel' – I cannot remember its French name. These discs, when kept long enough to ripen and reach their full potential, become so smelly that I used to keep them in the garden shed. But, believe me, they are delicious.

The subject of stinky cheese triggered my memory and I am about to share with you an account given to me by a schoolfriend of long ago. She was Mrs Anthea Bentley, nee Bolton-Frisby, from Hampshire. Being of a somewhat romantic disposition she had let herself be swept off her feet by a handsome and charismatic foreigner who promised to rescue her from the tedium of a conventional existence. His origin was in the wilds of some Balkan or Middle-Eastern country, but as soon as he had arrived in England he had the good sense to change his long, unpronounceable name to the simple but quite distinguished one of Bentley – Andrew Bentley. Her upper middle-class family didn't think him good enough and tried to deter her by belittling him as 'that swarthy dago'. Anthea broke with her family, left home and married him. I never learned how he made his money, but make it he did. I heard various rumours about obscure deals in foreign countries and, to be sure, he did make frequent journeys to the continent and the Middle East. Anthea usually accompanied him and he seemed to enjoy showing off his English lady. This was in the mid-1920s before air travel became the norm.

The incident in question happened on the Orient Express, on which they had booked a compartment. Knowing from experience that the restaurant car would only join the train at their first stop in the morning, they had a light meal at their Istanbul hotel before boarding the train in the evening. Wagons-Lits passengers did not travel with just one medium-sized suitcase that could be put on board by the railway porter. No, they often had several large trunks, bags and cases, most of them to be stored in the special luggage wagon. Assorted personal servants and Wagons-Lits officials were frantically milling around to ensure that every item destined for personal use on the journey arrived in the right compartment: trying to retrieve one of those from under a mountain in the baggage van would have been a nightmare.

Unaffected by all this hubbub and excitement, Mr and Mrs Bentley boarded the train to be greeted deferentially by a man wearing the company's smart blue and gold uniform. He was the conductor responsible for the comfort of the Wagons-Lits passengers. His name was Lucien Duval and they called him Duval. In fact, since he knew them as regular passengers and generous tippers, he always made sure they received privileged treatment. This meant amongst other things that the compartment allotted to them was close to the usual amenities and never above a wheel.

Anthea told me that she was aware that though the other travellers on this type of train were usually people with aristocratic or academic titles, they did not receive as much attention as her plain Mr Bentley. She realized that Andrew's self-confident bearing and aloof politeness made him appear to be a man of power and influence. This was reinforced by his impressive looks. He was tall, broad-shouldered, and the expression of his coal-black eyes in his sharp-featured face left no doubt that he took it for granted the world owed him respect. Thus, everybody assumed he was a very important person who, for reasons of his own, had chosen to travel incognito.

I think that at this point of the account it would be useful to mention that under the influence of constant travel and her dear Andrew's guidance, Anthea's conservative taste had changed considerably. Gone was the placid acceptance of her youth that a monthly menu with a range of only about six to ten dishes was acceptable, especially since leathery meat and washed-out vegetables were its regular feature. For generations her family had been active church people who gloried in denying themselves what they called the excessive pleasures of the flesh. This comprised not only many entertainments but also physical comfort and the decadent gratification derived from rich food and drink. Anthea couldn't remember that this had ever been spelled out to her with clear orders to abstain from this or that. It just was integral to their way of life and any deviation from it became instantly obvious. Needless to say, the whole family had harboured the most grievous foreboding when she had allowed herself to be whisked away by a mysterious foreigner to face what they considered degradation and the perils of a dangerous, unknown world.

The truth was that Anthea not only enjoyed travelling and discovering new countries with strange peoples, cultures, customs and food, she had actually developed a passion for trying out and tasting whatever was on offer. She particularly appreciated the variety of textures and flavours of cheeses which, over time, had become an obsession. Andrew was only too happy to indulge her and whenever he discovered a new speciality of cheese it landed, to her great pleasure, on her plate.

On this particular voyage, having had a very active last day in Istanbul, they decided on an early night and asked Duval to make up their beds and let them know in the morning when the dining car had been coupled on and was ready to serve breakfast.

The head waiter, known to them as Jean-Paul, greeted them with friendly deference and led them to their favourite table on the scenic side of the train. One would have needed an astonishing appetite to cope with the whole déjeuner menu served in those days, which featured seven to eight substantial courses. There was a fish and a meat dish, both with speciality sauces, a capon prepared with truffles, a fancy egg dish, and a variety of choice vegetables. There was also plenty of fruit, and a choice of desserts and cheeses. No doubt, if by any chance one had hankered for some item not featured on the menu, the obliging head waiter would have tried his best to conjure it up.

They had the table to themselves. Eating leisurely, they savoured their food whilst watching the landscape flitting by. They smiled at each other and Anthea made a convincing pretence of savouring the moment to the full.

I remember that it must have been about that time that, overcome by curiosity, I had casually asked Anthea about Andrew's business. Her answer had been vague and I couldn't make up my mind whether she was being evasive or really didn't know much. It seemed that he dealt with a variety of merchandise ranging from food to machinery. Over time she couldn't fail to realize that his contacts were with global corporations and government department of various countries. He was, however, not prepared to reveal any details even to her, not because he didn't trust her or thought her incapable of grasping the facts, but because he knew her to be a cautious and highly sensitive person who would be inclined to worry and feel apprehensive about every deal. He wanted her to be carefree and relaxed, not just for her own sake but also because, after the cut-and-thrust of international trading, he needed her to be his harbour of peace and tranquillity.

I don't think these answers satisfied her. But what could she do? Constant nagging was not her style and would have damaged their marriage. If Andrew thought he could keep her in a bubble of quiet contentment he was mistaken. Without being told she guessed that some of his enterprises were on the risky side and could even be illegal. She continued to worry, and having to pretend she didn't made it worse.

Of course, it wasn't all travelling and living out of a suitcase. Several times a year they would stay in some beautiful place, sometimes for weeks, and enjoy a life of leisure. It always was a top-class hotel or a flat or villa belonging to one of his mysterious and absent friends. She certainly never had to rough it. Before their visit to Istanbul they had stayed in an ancient Venetian palace. Having recently been restored and refurbished it looked magnificent. It was the ancestral home of one of Andrew's business connections, a fabulously wealthy aristocrat. But it turned out that this had been only partly a holiday, since Andrew kept excusing himself in order to attend meetings and business discussions.

During his absence, she spent her time sightseeing, visiting art galleries and arts and crafts places like the famous glassworks of Murano. Though there was a lot of cheap tat about, the up-market boutiques stocked designer goods that compared favourably with any to be found in the capital cities of the world. She enjoyed wandering along the narrow streets and over the innumerable little humped bridges that crossed the backwater canals. Venice certainly had a lot to offer. Being a romantic soul, she found the combination of its fascinating, turbulent history and almost dreamlike beauty irresistible.

A young, attractive woman, strolling pensively along, couldn't fail to attract male attention – especially in Italy. Every so often men would try and pick her up but she was feisty enough to send them packing. One day she had the distinct feeling that she was being followed. Because it seemed to be the same shady figure over a lengthy period it felt somehow different. She therefore decided to keep to the more populated areas for a while.

Sitting under an umbrella in one of the waterfront cafés opposite San Giorgio, she contentedly sipped her ice-cold spritzer while watching the passing crowds. Two gondoliers were waiting for fares along the nearby landing stage and further on a vaporetto was churning its way towards the island.

Suddenly, a man stood by her table and said something which was drowned out by a child's noisy hooter. He sat down opposite her. Since there were still two empty tables she assumed he was another johnny trying to pick her up. She turned aside and ignored him. But then he started to speak and her heart missed a beat.

'Hello, Mrs Bentley. I have wanted to meet you for some time but I know that my old friend Milan, you call him Andrew, wouldn't allow me to do so officially.' His voice was rough, somehow ingratiating and insolent at the same time. She looked at him and didn't like what she saw. His face was round and puffy with the unhealthy complexion of a person who lived on junk food and drank too much. The two-inch long scar on his left cheek looked rough and puckered though it must have been quite an old one. As he continued to speak, with what she recognised as a Slav accent, his gaze wandered all over her in a way she found insulting.

'Milan and I were childhood friends, belonged to the same gang. Street kids scavenging in the slums of Zagreb. We had to fight to stay alive, you know. So it was all for one and one for all. Except that Milan struck it lucky and got out of it. Got an education, didn't he, and then never came back to help us, not once. But some of us think it's time he did. Better late than never, hey? Besides, we've done our homework and we know quite a lot about him and his business. I want you to tell him to meet me.'

Her chest had tightened with apprehension and she felt sick. But she slightly raised her eyebrows and gave him a haughty look. With his cheap straw hat and crumpled linen suit he looked insignificant enough to melt away in a crowd, except that his loud red-and-green checked tie made a claim to individuality. His expression became more insolent.

'I'll be waiting for him at 10 o'clock tonight, at the back of Luigi's trattoria by the little dolphin bridge. So you'd better tell him.'

'I won't,' she said curtly and rose to leave. She didn't look back as she wound her way between the tables to the waterfront.

'You'll be sorry if you don't,' she heard him hiss behind her. 'Very sorry.'

She took the next vaporetto to the stop near her palazzo, all the time almost trembling with outrage and fear. Unsuccessfully, she tried to imagine what he could do to Andrew. If he was one of a gang, anything could happen. She had no choice, she had to tell Andrew. But, of course, she would have to be diplomatic. She was surprised that the revelation of his deprived childhood had not upset her. If he really had been a feral boy, fighting and thieving for his existence, what a magnificent achievement to have become the man he was.

After taking a shower, she dressed with care. She felt she had to look as good as she possibly could. It wasn't for him, really, but for herself. She needed all the self-confidence she could muster. As she stood on the balcony, watching him pay a gondolier before making his way up the landing-steps, she forced herself to take deep breaths and calm herself. She heard his footsteps. He was light on his feet and graceful for a man of his size. It always gave her a thrill to see his eyes light up when he approached her.

'You look more lovely than ever! I've just the thing to go with your new gown.' 'Another piece of jewellery,' she thought without enthusiasm, but when he produced a large opal pendant she found it easy enough to respond with a show of delight. It obviously was a rare specimen: the colours in it were deep and rich and their iridescent play produced a mysterious fire that more than hinted at the miraculous pressure and power that created such beauty in the bowels of a young, developing planet. But then she remembered the common saying that opals were cursed and brought bad luck. Though she tried not to be superstitious, she couldn't help being apprehensive.

The pendant was on a thin gold chain and he carefully fastened it at the back of her neck. 'There,' he said proudly and gently kissed her ear. 'What did you do this afternoon? Anything interesting?'

'Oh, the usual sightseeing. I started near the Accademia and dropped in at the art gallery further on. We went there last year, you remember? Signor Berlotti himself showed me some interesting etchings, fine detailed work of ancient carved doors and architectural details, very reminiscent of Ruskin's work.'

'Did you buy anything?'

'Of course not. You know I prefer to do that with you. Then I ambled along some back streets to San Marco where I had another look round inside. I always find something new I missed before. Then round to the café near the Hotel Metropole opposite San Giorgio. While resting there enjoying a long drink, a man accosted me. Apparently, he'd been following me.' Anthea took care to speak as calmly and casually as she could.

'Oh, these randy Italians!' he exclaimed.

'Actually, no. He knew my name and asked me to give you a message.' Andrew's interest increased.

'Why ask you? Did he say who he was?'

'Not really. Just asked me to tell you he'll be waiting for you tonight at ten o'clock at the back of Luigi's trattoria, the one near the dolphin bridge.'

'The nerve! What did he look like?'

'Round face with a scar on his cheek. Ashen skin. Altogether rather sickly and unpleasant looking.'

'Did he talk about anything else?'

Anthea was wary and shrugged her shoulders. 'His main concern was this meeting. I guessed from his appearance that he wants to touch you for some money or maybe a job. Anyway, I left as quickly as I could and, thank God, he stayed behind.' She was pleased with herself. She felt she'd struck just the right tone. 'Are you likely to meet him?'

'Of course not. I can't be bothered with every lazy layabout who thinks I give handouts to spongers. That reminds me, tonight Count Alberti has invited us to a dinner party, followed by a concert. I'd like us to go. That's if you agree.'

'What sort of concert?'

'Mainly works by Vivaldi, played by a ladies' string ensemble – just as they used to during his lifetime.'

'That's lovely,' she said brightly.

'I have to leave now for a business meeting but I'll be back in time to change for dinner.'

The evening was a success. The other guests were pleasant company and later on the lady musicians in their period costumes made a charming picture in the palatial setting. She had enjoyed herself and was aware that Andrew had never left her side. She remembered the man's malevolent hissing. How would he revenge himself for being ignored?

The following morning Andrew stayed in. He was working, studying documents and making notes. They had a light lunch on the balcony after which he dashed off. It was a beautiful day for sightseeing again; sunny but not too hot. By late afternoon she found herself in St Mark's square, relaxing in one of the arcade cafés. It was a popular place for foreign visitors and, indeed, the two young women at the next table were English. Anthea, always interested in people and their lives, couldn't resist listening to their conversation. It appeared that they were old friends and that the brunette one, Sofie, had married an Italian and was living in Venice, whereas the blonde one was her visitor. Suddenly, an exclamation of surprise. Sofie had picked up a newspaper from the vacant chair beside her.

'Good God,' she said. 'Listen to this. They found a body floating in the canal next to ours – under the dolphin bridge which is only two minutes from us.'

'Probably got drunk and tumbled in,' suggested Blondie.

'No, he wasn't. They say he was murdered, strangled with his own tie – one of those jazzy harlequin ones.'

Anthea caught her breath. Could it be that sponger? She had to know more.

'Excuse me, please,' she said, 'did I hear you say there was a murder not far from here?' Looking what she thought was suitably shy and embarrassed, she continued: 'You see, I've been walking quite a lot in that area, exploring the narrow canals and admiring the lovely little bridges. I had no idea this could be dangerous.'

Surprised, the two young women looked at her but since she was obviously a respectable English lady, they accepted her instantly.

'Oh, you needn't be afraid, unless you are wearing expensive jewellery or look as if you were carrying a lot of money. More often than not, these murders are due to political or business rivalry.' They obligingly moved their chairs apart and she accepted their invitation to join them.

'Are you saying that people of that calibre resort to murder?'

'Oh, yes, but they're never caught. You see, they don't do the dirty work themselves, they hire an assassin.'

Anthea was shocked. It seemed the fact that Andrew had not left her side all evening didn't prove he was innocent. 'I don't understand,' she burst out, not hiding her surprise. 'How would one get hold of a hit-man? They don't advertise in the papers! I wouldn't know where to start.'

'Neither would I,' agreed Blondie.

Sophie was obviously enjoying her role as the person in the know. 'I can't say that I would either, but there are quite a number of bars and eating places that are frequented by so-called agents and facilitators. And they aren't just low dives either. It is usually the head waiter or bar attendant that requires just the vaguest hint to make the introduction to a middleman. I understand that a successful assassination costs quite a bit of money since every intermediary has to receive a commission.'

'But what about the police? Surely they know all this. Why don't they watch out and act?'

'They say they do,' said Sofie laconically. 'But you

must remember, this isn't England.'

Just then, two middle-aged ladies were passing by. Both were elegantly attired and were walking arm-in-arm. Sophie had stopped talking till they were well past. 'The taller one in mauve is a well-known surgeon. He specializes in liver and kidney problems.'

'Did you say HE?'

Sophie grinned. 'Yes. He's an open transvestite. The lady beside him is his wife.' Blondie, truly intrigued, followed this up with more questions. With the subject of the murder having thus been eclipsed, Anthea was at a loss how to return to it without raising some sort of suspicion. In any case, there probably was no further useful information to be gained. She thanked the two young women for their company, and they parted amicably.

Anthea was deeply worried. What if her suspicion were true? Would Andrew be ruthless enough to rid himself of a menacing enemy in such a fashion? Whatever she felt and thought, she had to keep it to herself and pretend that she was content and happy. To face him openly was just unthinkable.

And now, sitting opposite him after a luxurious

meal, with the landscape flitting by, she was displaying a placid contentment she did not feel. She saw him look at her and smile in the special way that seemed to be reserved for her alone. However friendly he showed himself to other people, it was never the same. Assuming that she was playing her part well, she did not expect what followed. He reached across the table and gently but firmly took her hands in his.

'Anthea, love, why are you unhappy?'

The shock made her gasp. 'What do you mean?'

'I may appear to be a tough fellow. Most people wouldn't credit me with great sensitivity. But, you know, the success of all my enterprises depend on the minute observation of people and their reactions. And as far as you are concerned – you, who are the most precious thing in my world – I am attuned to every fibre of your body and to every one of your thought-waves and vibrations of feeling. This may sound highfalutin' but, believe me, it's true. So, please, tell me what's troubling you?'

Of course, she couldn't reveal her suspicion regarding the assassination and the nature of his business ventures. Yet she suddenly realized that this sudden turn of events may be her opportunity to persuade him to change their way of life completely. She now didn't mind him being aware of her anxiety.

'You see, I was and still am afraid of upsetting you. Until recently I enjoyed our nomadic life and everything connected with it. But now I feel the time has come to settle down; I am longing for a permanent home and a circle of close friends. But I didn't have the courage to ask you to retire. You keep telling me we are well off yet you seem to be driven to make more and more money.'

Andrew looked very serious, still holding her hands. 'Go on.'

'Well, for years now we have been buying the most beautiful furniture, carpets, pictures and objets d'art, only to hide them away in some warehouse. I've never seen any of them again so, frankly, what use are these treasures to me? The years are passing and that fabulous dream home is still a distant mirage. I want to settle down, Andrew. I want to live a normal life with a circle of friends and become a member of a local community. I'd like you to buy a house in the country, near a little town. There should be enough ground to build a new garden to our design. That should be fun. And, perhaps, we could start a family? There is still time but if I wait much longer, my chance will be gone.'

He could see she was upset and near tears. 'My God! What a blind, selfish brute I've been. You should have spoken sooner. Darling, I'll do exactly what you say: I'll find a suitable house and you'll be able to enjoy all the things we collected. I'll make sure you'll have everything you want. Mind, I shall miss you terribly but I'll join you as often as I can.'

'No!' she cried, aghast. 'You don't understand. I want you to retire and live with me, otherwise the whole thing makes no sense. How can you be so short-sighted?'

He let go of her hands and sat back. He was obviously struggling to grasp the full implications of her demand. As he continued to sit there with an expression she couldn't fathom, she rose. Forcing back her tears she stammered: 'Forgive me. Don't worry, we shall carry on as before.'

He caught up with her just as she reached their compartment. 'Anthea, we won't carry on as before. Now that I know how you feel it would be unthinkable. Of course, I cannot retire immediately. Things have to be wound down, contracts adjusted, new arrangements made. With any luck I should be able to call myself a gentleman in retirement within the next month or so. Will you be satisfied with that?'

She threw her arms round his neck and burst into tears, but they were tears of joy.

He looked relieved. 'As soon as we get to London, we'll ask Crosby & Burton to get onto the best agents to find us a property. And while I wind up my affairs you can view the various offers. When you come across a possible choice, you just let me know and we look over it together. During that time, where would you like to stay?'

'Oh, somewhere in Mayfair – the Partridge Hotel should be handy enough.' Anthea was delighted: Messrs Crosby & Burton the solicitors were an old established firm and she had dealt with them concerning minor matters before. In fact, quite some time ago Andrew had told her to get their help in case anything should happen to him. They had instructions concerning his financial position and last will. Sitting side by side, his arm around her, they discussed the type and size of house that would satisfy their needs.

The train stopped. When Anthea looked out she saw that it was just a small station and that nobody had got off or on. However, a uniformed man who looked like the station master approached the wagons-lits and handed up a parcel. The whole process took just about one minute. 'How strange,' she said, only to find that

Andrew gave an amused chuckle. A few minutes later Duval, their conductor, appeared with the very same parcel. When they were alone again, Andrew opened it and passed the contents to Anthea. There were three primitive balsa-wood boxes, each topped by a label with an equally primitive drawing. The scribbles bordering the labels looked like mysterious runes and she guessed they could be Turkish. The simple line drawing however was perfectly clear. She was confronted by a goat with huge udders and a broad smile on its face.

'Oh, a cheese! Is it a gorgonzola type?' she was delighted. 'Quick, let's taste it.' Andrew produced some plain biscuits and a knife. They cut out a wedge and found it to be so ripe that the vacated space in the box started to refill immediately with the oozing, gooey substance. At the same time its odour filled the compartment and became increasingly more pungent and intense. As the prepared morsel passed her lips and her tasting buds made contact, she closed her eyes and a low, sensuously vibrating hum expressed the depth of her pleasure.

'Oh, Andrew,' she almost moaned, 'this is divine. This is the best cheese I ever tasted.' Praise couldn't be higher.

He obviously felt well rewarded by such depth of appreciation. 'When I came across it,' he explained, 'I thought it would please you. One of my contacts succeeded in tracking down the maker and, since he had some business in this area, we managed to arrange this somewhat unusual delivery. But look, we can't keep the opened box here, the pong is overpowering.'

'We could hang it out of the window, that would solve the problem.'

As seasoned travellers they always carried string for emergencies and in no time at all the precious cheese was dangling securely outside their compartment window.

Anthea was happier than she had been for a long time. The problem of their future home and Andrew's retirement would soon be settled, and now this exceptional cheese felt like a good omen of things to come. As usual, he had gone to great lengths to please her. Whatever her worries about him, his love for her had never been in question. She had never seen him look at other women: he was not a philanderer. She suspected the reason for his devotion was that he valued her not only as his wife but in a strange way found in her a replacement for the loving mother he lost in early childhood. This realisation did not upset her. His emotional stability confirmed her opinion that he really was a man who had a lot going for him.

They were sitting companionably together, not bothering to look out of the window, as the train was still speeding though vast stretches of the Hungarian plain. Long past Budapest they were nearing the Austrian frontier. Suddenly the door was flung open. Two men in uniform barged in. Their attitude was aggressive. The elder of the two barked at them: 'Are you Mr and Mrs Bentley?' Seeing them nod he continued. 'Well, Mr Bentley, your little game's over. We've at last caught up with your criminal activities.' Anthea gasped and Duval, the conductor, standing behind the men, shrugged his shoulders to convey his bewilderment to his favourite passengers.

Anthea was terrified, believing that the men's allegation could be justified. But Andrew slowly rose and, towering over the official, made it clear that he considered their accusation ridiculous. 'What's all this about? You had better be careful what you say and do. The consequences could be very serious – for you. Who are you, anyway?'

The man, somewhat taken aback, drew himself up. Just under average height with a portly figure and florid complexion, he sported a rather large walrus type of moustache which was an obvious attempt to make himself look more important. One could see that he considered himself to be quite an imposing personality in his smart uniform with all those gold buttons, braid and epaulettes. As this was taking place not all that long after the end of World War I, the traditions of the old Austro-Hungarian empire were still very much alive. If you wore a uniform, you were somebody. Every postman in his plain uniform would consider himself superior to the average civilian.

'I am Inspector Varga. Senior inspector of the railway and border police. This is my sergeant. We have power of arrest.'

'And what's your problem at the moment?' asked Andrew in a relaxed sort of way.

The inspector seemed put out that his attempt at intimidation had failed. 'Diamond smuggling,' he replied curtly. 'But now, as you will know, we have found our man.'

'Interesting. Well, if you are accusing me you had better prove your case. Please feel free to search our trunks in the luggage wagon as well as our case and valise in here.'

The inspector gave a sarcastic laugh. 'I see you want to sidetrack us, waste our time. No such luck. We are smart enough to go straight to your hiding place.'

Anthea relaxed. She was certain that Andrew, if he were involved in some diamond smuggling business, would not do so himself. He certainly wouldn't take such a risk when travelling with her. She saw the inspector signal to the sergeant who went across to the window, opened it and triumphantly pulled in their suspended cheese. What followed was pure farce.

The inspector watched his man open the box and tentatively prod the firm skin-covered part of the cheese. Not feeling any relevant, firm resistance underneath, he looked at his chief with a slight shake of his head.

'You stupid clot! Can't you look properly!' shouted the inspector and tore the box out of his hands. Whereupon his thumbs went right through the bottom of the box, churning and mauling the soft gooey contents till they oozed over the rim onto his splendidly braided cuffs and down the front of his uniform. He didn't seem to be able to stop – he just couldn't believe that no diamonds were hiding in its depth. Almost hysterical and seemingly oblivious to the overpowering odour that now impregnated the room, he tried to carry on. At last, the sergeant wrestled the box from his demented boss and pushed him out into the corridor. He turned back and, with a sheepish grin, handed it to Duval, who had watched the scene with amazement.

Leaving the window wide open, they went to the dining car for a comforting drink. Though this episode had been ridiculous and absurd, they had not found it funny. The man's hysterical clinging to his self-importance and delusion was almost tragic. Anthea regretted the loss of her precious cheese, but decided not to open another box but to save both of them for a future celebration.

They had intended to spend a week in Vienna before returning to London, where they would initiate their arrangements for retirement. They had booked in at the Hotel Astoria at the back of the Opera. While Andrew went out again for what he said would be well under an hour, Anthea started to unpack. Since Andrew had not arrived back yet, she decided to have a quick bath for a little soak and rest. Afterwards, she remained in her negligée. She was uncertain how to dress until she found out what sort of plans Andrew had made for the evening. He loved to give her cultural surprises and she was looking forward to them. But now well over an hour had passed, and this turned into two hours.

She was worried: he was usually meticulous in letting her know whenever he was delayed. Perhaps he had phoned and she had not heard it in the bath? She rang down to reception in case he had left a message for her, or whether they knew of any serious traffic problems or accidents. She got dressed. And now, hours later she was frantic with apprehension. Where was Andrew? What had happened to him?

The hotel management were anxious to alleviate her distress. They knew the couple from previous visits and took the matter seriously. After contacting the police and all the main hospitals, the truth emerged. Andrew had had an accident. He had been walking along the pavement when a little dachshund suddenly dashed across his path. He had lost his balance, fallen and crashed his head against a bollard. The ambulance had arrived without delay but he had died on the way to the hospital.

It was at this point that I appeared on the scene. When the hotel manager saw that Anthea was almost mad with grief and incapable of dealing with anything, they asked her whom they could contact to help her. Without hesitation she gave them my name and address. She was determined not to involve her family in any way. Luckily, I had no commitments at the time and was therefore able to take the very next plane to Vienna. I spent the following two weeks sorting things out for her.

When I asked her whether she wanted to take Andrew's body to England and have him cremated or interred there, I was surprised at her response. 'I don't care what you do with his remains,' she said flatly. 'Without life and spirit the carcass means nothing to me. He might as well be buried here in Vienna – he was more at home in any place on the Continent than he ever was in England.'

And so the flamboyant adventurer for whom most people would have foretold a dramatic death engineered by some powerful enemy, was laid to rest beneath a simple unpretentious cross in Vienna's Zentralfriedhof, the victim of a petty accident. Anthea and I were the only attendants as the coffin was lowered into the grave and the first trowelfuls of earth clattered down after it. Ashes to ashes, dust to dust. Anthea did not weep but said simply, as if speaking to Andrew: 'I know you are not here. I won't come here again.'

I invited her to live with me in Surrey until she felt confident to face the world on her own. She stayed two months and then moved into the Partridge Hotel in Kensington where she took an apartment on the top floor. I learned that she was very well-off indeed but since she couldn't face running an establishment just for herself, this was the ideal solution. Without household responsibilities she had time to join a bridge club and various other clubs and societies where she acquired some associates who were culturally on the same wavelength and could provide company when needed. But she seemed also to have made real friends with the hotel's permanent staff, especially with Elsie, the chambermaid.

Of course, her family tried hard to get into her good books. They couldn't bear the thought of losing all that wealth. Her elder brother Julian and her cousin Elvira in particular made repeated efforts to get close to her, and Flora, her eldest niece, made the mistake of being aggressively persistent. Of course, Anthea, remembering their past behaviour, would have none of it.

Every so often we would meet for little jaunts together. We even shared the odd holiday, mainly in England. I was intrigued by one of her habits – her frequent visits to delicatessen shops, Harrods food halls and specialist cheese shops. She would stand in front of the counter and contemplate the display, almost like an art lover in front of a painting at a special exhibition.

I wouldn't say Anthea was happy but I think she was

reasonably content. It seemed the close proximity of high-class shops and places of entertainment suited her. Of course, I have no idea what sort of role the memory of Andrew played in the rest of her life. I was surprised and upset when she suddenly died from a stroke. This was the cue for her family to descend like locusts to badger her solicitors. But Mr Burton of Crosby & Burton would not be rushed. In the fullness of time a meeting was arranged for the reading of Anthea's last will and testament, to which I too was invited. It took place not in the partners' cosy old-fashioned office with its solid mahogany furniture, velvet curtains and ancestral portraits, but in a sort of impersonal meeting hall on the floor above.

When I arrived I found that all members of Anthea's family were already present. This puzzled me, as I knew she hated the lot of them for the way they had treated her when she had insisted on marrying Andrew. Surely she couldn't have made them beneficiaries. They sat round a large conference table, at the head of which sat Mr Burton himself. Two of his clerks were standing behind him in attendance. Though I had been punctual, I was the last to arrive. Room was made for me at the table and Mr Burton began. I had half expected a short sentimental eulogy of the dear departed, but he obviously thought that unnecessary. He started with an outline of the estate's assets, comprising an amazing number of stocks and shares as well as a long list of valuable properties in prestigious parts of London, Paris, Rome and even America. There were gasps all round when he mentioned their estimated value: it was a fabulous sum.

I looked round the gathering. Some had turned pale, others were flushed, but all were in a high state of excitement. I could see their eyes sparkle with greed. Most conspicuous were the three who considered themselves first in line of inheritance: Anthea's brother Julian, her cousin Elvira and her eldest niece Flora.

The inventory continued but the contents of the warehouse where all the furniture, pictures and other works of art were stored were not listed in detail. The same applied to the jewellery. The reason for this was to emerge later. The rough value estimate, however, made everyone gasp again, myself included.

'And now, ladies and gentlemen,' said Mr Burton in his most formal and starchy voice, 'I will read to you Mrs Anthea Bentley's letter which represents her last wishes. You will perceive that she has carefully thought of all of you and that her wishes are perfectly clear.' He managed to increase the tension by taking a long, slow draft from his glass of water. Even I wished him to get on with it.

'My dear friends and family. I, Anthea Bentley, being of sound mind, have decided to share out my possessions as follows: To my dear friend Mary Anderson, I wish to express my gratitude for her staunch friendship and help. It gives me pleasure to think that she will be wearing my large opal pendant and emerald ring.'

I was amazed that I should have been the first on the list. By the way the others stared at me, I knew that they were, too. I realized that though these two pieces were very valuable, they were only a token of her goodwill. Sensitively, she had been at pains to assure me that she was not paying me for my friendship.

No more jewellery was mentioned, but handsome money bequests were made to the staff of the Partridge Private Hotel as well as, oddly enough, some employees of the Wagons-Lits Orient Express.

Mr Burton cleared his throat and continued: 'In appreciation of the love and understanding my dear family have always shown to me and my husband Andrew, I am leaving you all a keepsake that will help you treasure my memory.' The tension was now almost unbearable. It also was the cue for the two clerks to take the dust cover off some stacks on a side table that turned out to be framed photographs.

They were handed out to every family member and I saw that they depicted Andrew with his arm round Anthea's shoulder. It was a good likeness and the pair looked well and happy.

The beneficiaries were bewildered. They didn't know what to make of it. Of course, they had to wait in order to find out what else would be coming their way.

Mr Burton continued with Anthea's letter. 'I wish to assure you, my family members, that I have the highest opinion of your intellect, enterprise and industry that makes you more than capable of dealing with the practicalities of making a living. And since you have always taken great pains in impressing me with your moral superiority, I decided not to insult any of you with any further bequests that are ultimately based on filthy lucre. Complying with your moral outlook, I have instructed Messrs Crosby & Burton to sell or auction all my possessions, be they stocks and shares, property, jewellery, or the goods stored at Portland's warehouse, the proceeds of which are to be distributed to the charities all over the world. If you require a list of these transactions, Mr Burton will supply them on request.'

After a few moments' stunned silence, the outcry was ear-splitting. I sat back with utter satisfaction. What a revenge! The greater the uproar, the more I enjoyed it.

I would never have believed that I could ever delight in such a crescendo of decibels. Perhaps Mr Burton did as well because he made no attempt to put a stop to it. He waited patiently till calm was restored.

But then Flora cried out: 'The will is invalid, the woman was insane. There is a legal rule of family entitlement. We will fight this in court.'

'That is up to you,' said Mr Burton placidly. 'I think it is only fair to mention that Mrs Bentley had a consultation with two very prestigious specialists, one of them the royal family's physician, who certified that the lady was of sound mind. This is dated one day before the signing of the will.'

Mortified silence.

Mr Burton continued: 'There is a codicil which entitles ten of the closest family members and Mrs Mary Anderson to visit her apartment in the Partridge Hotel and distribute any of the remaining possessions amongst themselves. I have arranged with the management that every assistance should be given to you. They will be in attendance tomorrow afternoon.'

After a heated argument amongst themselves they finally accepted the proposal.

Knowing Anthea, I realized she was providing me with, so to speak, a front stall seat to the final scene of the drama. Of course I was aware of the family's suspicion. The following afternoon I assembled with the others in the Partridge Hotel lounge. Not until everyone was present did the manager take us up to Anthea's suite. The large sitting room occupied the south and west facing corner of the building and overlooked a part of the adjacent park. I could imagine her watching the locals come strolling down the street with their dogs straining excitedly at their leads, eager to reach the freedom of the green.

The others had no time for such useless speculations. They were on a treasure hunt. But before they could rush about, the manager introduced Elsie, who had been Anthea's personal attendant: she would be able to tell them which items were hotel property. These were in fact all the furniture and hangings and even some of the vases, ornaments and pictures. I had realized long ago that, as long as she was physically comfortable, my friend had become to a great extent indifferent to her surroundings. I guessed that she had lived in her imagination, in a world of the past where Andrew was to be the centre of a home of their making.

Over the years I had learned quite a bit about Elsie, a pleasant-looking Filipino woman in her mid-forties.

She was married to an English mental hospital nurse and they had two girls at university. Since she also tried to support her poor relations back in Manila, Anthea's legacy to the hotel staff had been like a gift from heaven. Always active and full of energy, she was a happy and caring person and I knew that Anthea had become very fond of her.

The brief attempt of proceeding in a civilized manner was soon followed by an undignified rifling through wardrobes and drawers. Rejected items were scattered all over the place whereas others were physically fought over. I saw two matrons almost rip a cashmere shawl in half and shoes were literally flying through the air. Anthea had been a tall lady and her shoe-size was proportionately larger than average. Thus, although beautifully designed and made, they were of no use to anybody here. The contents of the wardrobes were pulled about and ended up in piles on the splendidly large bed. Once again, the expensive garments that had been made to measure were of an unsuitable size. Besides, these model-gowns, creations of the long-past twenties, were no longer wearable. Great frustration all round.

I was sitting on a chair against the wall and Elsie, across the room, was leaning against the door-post. We kept looking at each other, sometimes in horror, sometimes in amusement. What a spectacle!

'There must be some bracelets, necklaces, rings she was wearing every day!' exclaimed Julian in despair. But I knew better. The only items she wore constantly were the opal and emerald ring bequeathed to me.

Just then, Flora lifted an Impressionist-style landscape off the wall. 'This belongs to the hotel,' cried Elsie. Too late. Flora nearly dropped the painting while everybody, with exclamations of surprise, stared at the vacated spot on the wall. A safe! The solid metal front and dial of a wall-safe.

I jumped up and raced across the room, I thought the furious pack were about to murder Elsie. Their angry shouts were quite terrifying. Julian had his hands around her neck: 'The combination, you know the combination!'

'Yes,' breathed Elsie. He released her and bade her enter the number. She did so with a trembling hand. Slowly, the door swung open. Deathly silence. Then an awed breath of wonder. There, alone within the ample space stood a wooden casket. About the size of a shoe-box, it looked quite splendid, with its carvings, brass lock and corner fittings. Julian grabbed it and, holding it against his chest with his left arm, tried to open it.

Flora sprung forward and nearly attacked him. 'No, you don't! I know your tricks. This has to be opened on the table with everybody watching.'

So, there it was now in the middle of the table but Julian couldn't open it. He turned to Elsie who had been watching without betraying any emotions. 'There is no key. Have you got the key?'

'It isn't locked,' she said flatly.

But Julian still couldn't open it and neither could Elvira. Then Flora was going to have a try but changed her mind. Turning to Elsie she said: 'You're playing a game with us. There is some trick mechanism and you know how it works. Open it. Now!' she commanded.

'Please,' said Elsie gently, and remained where she was.

Flora bit her lip. After a few moments several of the others said 'please' in unison.

Elsie stepped up to the table and, after a few deft movements, raised the lid. Everybody had crowded round and I too moved forward and joined them.

'Tip everything out,' they cried, 'let's see, let's see.'

They expected a cornucopia of wonderful jewels to spill from this splendidly worked casket. The tension was excruciating as Julian slowly upended it.

There were exclamations of amazement all round. Unbelieving, they stared at the pile of faded, yellowed and stained cheese-wrappers and labels. A cheaply made balsa-wood box sat on the top of the pile. Everyone leaned forward as greedy, desperate hands tore it open. It was empty but a most horrible odour made them almost leap back. They stared at the lid that bore the primitive drawing of a goat in full udder. And as if to mock them, the goat was smiling.

LO/T FOR WORD/

Though Martin was trying to give up smoking, he lit another cigarette. He needed the extra few minutes in the car outside his gate to collect himself. The Mimi affair was getting him down: he felt cornered, trapped. For the umpteenth time he wondered whether she really was pregnant, since he'd always been so meticulous in taking precautions. Perhaps he wasn't her only lover. Or she could have cooked up this story to make him leave Elisabeth. Of course, if it were true, he would accept the financial responsibility. He realized that, selfishly, he had wanted it both ways. He had felt rather flattered to be seduced by a much younger woman, but he still didn't want to sacrifice Elisabeth and his home.

The fact was that his marriage could still be considered a happy one. Though over the years their physical relationship had simmered down considerably, the affection was still there, and their friendship and comradeship was as strong as ever. They always shared their thoughts and experiences as a matter of course, enjoyed discussions on all sorts of subjects, and they never got bored with each other. So why couldn't he tell her about his infatuation with Mimi, about his unsuccessful struggle to get this young siren out of his system? And now, having regained his senses, of his difficulty in ending it all? He believed Elisabeth would understand, but at the same time he couldn't face the likelihood that she'd be deeply hurt.

What made it worse was Mimi's attitude. Before he had left her flat half an hour ago, she had treated him to her usual routine: flattery, wheedling, reproaches, and finally, threats. Still in her negligée, she had glared at him through the gaps in the long blonde hair that hung about her face. 'You must ask her for a divorce. You can't keep on putting it off. If you haven't the courage to tell her, I will.' Enraged by his silence, she had screamed at him: 'I'm warning you, Martin, you can't just throw me over. I'll make you sorry you ever touched me.' There was no point in telling her that he already was sorry, but his disgust with her performance made him blurt it out just the same.

He'd expected a strong reaction, but the table lamp and vase hurtled in his direction came as a surprise. Without waiting for more, he had fled.

He parked on the drive, then walked mechanically up to his front door without looking at his favourite roses, as was his wont, and found himself in his armchair, not knowing how he got there. Wrapped in a cloud of depression, he kept reliving the horrors of the past few hours.

He started. Elisabeth had entered the room. 'Hello, darling, you're early. Did they cancel the meeting?' she asked sweetly. Guilt-ridden, he could barely look at her. She was her calm and amiable self. The mauve shantung blouse suited her, and he couldn't help noticing how attractive she still was. Oh, hell, what had he done? He'd be lost without her. His chest tightened. His stomach knotted. He tried to confide in her, confess his deceit, but the words wouldn't come. It was all too much. He buried his head in his hands, presenting a picture of despair.

She sat down on the arm of his chair and patted his shoulder. 'There, there, you poor old thing. Don't fret. I already know all about it.'

He lifted his head, stared at her in disbelief.

'Martin, dear, I know you too well not to have guessed that something was amiss. I didn't know the details, of course, but they were revealed to me on the phone twenty minutes ago.'

He groaned and tried in vain to fathom her expression. It wasn't disappointment, or grief, or anger. The uncertainty made it worse.

'What, what did you tell her?' he stammered.

'I told her she should go ahead and have the baby; that I'll give you a divorce for the sake of the precious new life.'

'No, you can't do that!' It came out like a scream. He was devastated.

She ignored the interruption. 'Mimi – she told me her name was Mimi – Mimi was delighted. After all, she said, a child needs both its parents. "Oh, he's pretty good with children," I admitted, "but are you sure you can afford him?" "What do you mean?" she asked. "Well," I said, "he's pretty expensive to keep. You must have noticed that everything he has is of the best – bespoke clothing, hand-made shoes, Rolex watch and quality jewellery, not to speak of his taste for luxurious cars."

'"But he's wealthy", she cried. "He has property. He's a director and main shareholder of the Occidental Electrical Incorporation!" "My poor child," I said. "You obviously don't know the way of the world. Men will say anything to get what they want. In fact, dear Mimi, he doesn't own a thing. And his job at the OEI is entirely dependant on my brother's goodwill. So, obviously, if he leaves me, his job too is gone.'"

He jumped up. 'What a bundle of ridiculous lies!'

'I know, darling. Isn't it cruel. And now,' she said firmly, 'please sit down and listen. It won't surprise you that from then on the conversation acquired a different aspect. Mimi said that she wasn't a home-breaker, that she'd hate to rob an older woman of her life's companion. But once the baby was born she would be helpless and in need of financial support. She thought a guaranteed maintenance commitment would be the fair thing. However, if I were to give her a lump sum, she would renounce all claims on you and the matter would be closed in one fell swoop.'

Elisabeth now sat opposite him, her expression inscrutable. 'Mimi named a six-digit figure which I instantly rejected. "You know," I said, "I don't need to lay out sums like that. I can pick from a wide selection of men, just for the day-to-day luxury I'm able to offer. True, I'm used to Martin and we get on, and, like a white horse, you can take him anywhere. But he certainly isn't worth that much."'

Martin stared at her aghast. Undeterred, Elizabeth continued. 'Well, darling, there followed a heated auction in reverse and, finally, we settled on a figure. She paused for effect. 'The sum of ... £ 5,000.'

'You can't be serious,' he exclaimed, 'that's peanuts!'

She paused again, letting the humiliation sink in fully. She watched him calmly as he fumed and squirmed. He was suffering alright. Still inscrutable, she continued: 'Of course, I pointed out to her that I would only pay after a reputable laboratory had made the DNA test and confirmed your paternity.'

Suddenly, Elisabeth crumpled up; the whole top half of her body slumped forward, her head almost touching her knees. Alarmed, he saw her shoulders shake as she seemed to be fighting a choking fit, gasping for air. He panicked; he didn't know what to do. Obviously, all this stress had been too much for her. Then, she lifted her head. Red in the face she spluttered: 'Her language! You should have heard her language! Ever, ever so ripe!'

It was only then he realised that Elisabeth was convulsed with laughter.

€GG/ FOR /ALE

I opened the envelope. The invitation, in a copperplate font, informed me that only the Tsar could order one, only royalty could own one, and only members of the aristocracy could see one. I, however, had the opportunity of purchasing one. Thus, I was respectfully invited to peruse the stock of Fabergé eggs in their shop, which was located in the jewellers' precinct on the fifth deck. I couldn't believe it. Real Fabergé eggs on an American cruise ship? Pull the other one! But since I had no plans for the evening I thought this could provide a little diversion. I had visited that shopping area before and had been struck by the abundance of jewellers. Their wares seemed to range from cheap tat to what appeared quite valuable and elegant pieces.

The ship's emporia had one thing in common: they had wide entrances. In fact, one was hardly aware that they were entrances. When looking at an item in one of the continuous display windows, one's gaze would be drawn from one object to the next and the next, till suddenly one would find oneself in the centre of the shop – lured, so to speak, and trapped in the spider's web. The spider, in the shape of a welcoming shop assistant, would then enfold one with smiles and skilful sales talk that made a quick escape difficult.

I had no problem in locating the right shop. A young man stepped forward and invited me to take one of the two unoccupied chairs arranged around a low table. My first impression of him was a pleasant one. He was quite good looking, well groomed and obviously eager to please. I found myself flanked by two girls on the left. For a split second I thought that one of them was topless but it turned out to be a tight-fitting, flesh coloured t-shirt. She looked a cheerful, relaxed sort of person and I felt sure that had the table been of normal height, her arms would have rested on it, cradling her generous bosom. She had a pink, fleshy face and her bright, little eyes examined me in a flash. When she turned to speak to the girl beside her, I realized they were friends. She too wore a t-shirt but it was dark green with white stripes. Both had dyed blonde hair dangling around their neck. I promptly named them Miss Pinky and Miss Stripey. They probably were in their early thirties, but I looked upon them as girls because their get-up made it clear that they wished to look young, which made both the staid categories of 'women' or 'ladies' inappropriate. They certainly did not appear to be the kind of people who would buy Fabergé eggs. I assumed that they had been sucked into the shop by its cunning geography. From the few words they exchanged I guessed they were Americans.

The gentlemen on my right, however, did not speak. I perceived an almost tangible wall of silence between them that made it clear that they were strangers and wished to remain strangers. My immediate neighbour was one of those huge, florid men who make a virtue of their size. He was sprawling in his chair, his mid-blue jacket and trousers crumpled loosely about him, his blue shirt open at the neck. Obviously, a man who liked his comfort. I saw that his suit was a good quality, bespoke one (had to be for his stature) and that its creases were part of the natural linen look. Though he had not spoken, I assumed he was American after noticing the rings on his fingers. His massive left hand displayed two wide gold rings, covered with sparkling stones that could have been diamonds. And on two fingers of his right hand another two rings proclaimed that might was right. I had seen these rings on other Americans at my dinner table. They were silver, also wide and massive and heavily embossed with tendrils, leaves and flowers. No Englishman would want to be seen with knuckle-dusters like these. However, I was unable to guess the nationality of his neighbour – a dapper old man who had dressed for dinner and looked impeccable in his black suit and white shirt. He was one of those dessicated, lean types who manage to look the same for decades. My guess put him in his late seventies or early eighties. I watched as he casually took note of everything around him, his expression remaining inscrutable. Well, I thought, both chaps could be sufficiently loaded for a luxury purchase. But surely, they didn't expect real Fabergé eggs? I have seen some genuine ones in prestigious exhibitions and in the Queen's collection in Buckingham Palace. The whole idea was ridiculous and I felt sure the two men knew it too. So what was it all about?

Obviously, the person to enlighten us was the young shop assistant whom I instantly named Carlos because of his Latin good looks. He welcomed us in good English with an American twang, while hopefully scanning the shop's precinct for late-comers. Actually, I was surprised that so few people had been expected since there were just six chairs around the table and only another four in the corners of the room. After a few more minutes it became clear that he would have to content himself with an audience of five.

He started to tell us how Gustav Fabergé and his son Peter Carl established their jewellery business in St Petersburg in the mid-nineteenth century, and how eventually the Russian Tsar became their patron. Being familiar with the story, my mind started to wander. I looked at the showcases that encircled the room, at the sparkling exhibits on glass shelves, multiplied by the reflecting mirror backing. There were many rings and bracelets and several important-looking necklaces studded with rubies, emeralds and diamonds. I even detected a tiara. Of course, I couldn't tell whether these dazzlers were the genuine thing or not.

My attention returned in time to hear the summing up. Carlos impressed upon us the fact that every one of their Fabergé eggs was created by skilled artists and artisans and that they were genuinely unique. I wondered how his firm was entitled to claim that their creations were Fabergé, but realized that I may have missed this information during my spell of mental absence. Then, with an air of importance he approached one of the display cabinets. Although their upper parts were all glass, their lower quarter appeared to be solid wood. He went down on his haunches and unlocked one of the doors. He did so with the natural ease of one whose joints are still strong and supple. I couldn't help noticing that his light grey suit was of a shiny, artificial fabric. Since the jacket pulled across the back and the hang of the sleeves wasn't quite right, it was obvious to me that it had been bought off the peg. Nevertheless, he looked well groomed and stylish enough. He brought out a large casket, carefully locking the door again before bringing it to the table. We watched him doing this twice more.

Now, all the Fabergé eggs I had ever seen in reality and in photographs were the size of hen's eggs. The miniature aspect clearly enhances the difficulty of the execution. From the precious decorations to the exquisitely crafted contents they are undoubtedly a miracle of craftsmanship. Apparently, Tsar Nicholas II ordered two Fabergé eggs every year – one for his wife and one for his mother. They were special presents for Easter, Russia's main festival of the religious year. They had to be a total surprise. It was said that not even the Tsar himself knew what Peter Carl Fabergé would come up with for the occasion.

Somehow, the giving of eggs rings an emotional bell for me. Not so much because it symbolizes the resurrection of Christ, but that since pagan times it celebrates the burgeoning of new life and the arrival of spring. It is a Slav tradition which was followed by my mother's family who lived in the highlands of Moravia. It was their custom to cover a hard-boiled egg with a design drawn with melted candle-wax. When immersed in a cold-water dye, the waxed parts would remain white. If one wanted to enrich the pattern, one could wax some of the coloured parts and put it in another dye-bath, thus creating a third colour. Throughout my childhood, my mother always managed to paint a few eggs for me.

And now, Carlos started his presentation. As he opened the caskets one by one, he adopted the solemn dignity of a high priest revealing a sacred relic to the faithful. First to emerge from its luxurious padding was an egg covered with a textured satin enamel. I am not sure, but I think it is called *guilloché*. It was decorated with elaborate garlands of foliage and flowers. But no hen could ever have produced this symbolic egg. Its mother must have been an ostrich.

Carlos looked at us, trying to assess the effect of his first revelation. We were obviously interested but not bowled over. Then, from the second casket emerged an egg of the same size. It was made of pale, green glass. Suspended in its interior was an assortment of pretty little flowers. Pinky on my left exhaled an appreciative 'ahh', but the rest of us remained shtum.

And now he turned to the third casket. Somehow, I found it quite pleasurable to watch this ritualistic performance. It reminded me of ancient fairy stories and fate-laden mythological dramas. Another ostrich-sized egg appeared, this time of pale blue glass with multi-coloured, patterned little fishes looking saucily out at us. After again drawing our attention to the wonderful workmanship and artistic merit of the pieces, Carlos did something to the top decoration of the green glass egg, whereupon the performance started. The little flowers began to move in a pattern of up and down, to and fro, interweaving and round and round. I sat motionless, observing, evaluating, trying to judge - aware that the others would be doing likewise. The two gents in their own fashion revealed nothing. The big man, his thick lower lip voluptuously protruding, sprawled with half-hooded eyes, whereas his neighbour sat rigidly upright, his face a mask of stern alertness. I could imagine him at a board meeting, causing apprehensive junior executives to weigh every word carefully before daring to speak. Only the two girls responded with warmth. As the contents of the first glass interior started to move, they freely showed their admiration.

Thus encouraged, Carlos increasingly addressed them, even though they would seem to be the least likely buyers. I supposed he thought or felt that their appreciation would produce a positive atmosphere that could stimulate us three poker-faces. As I watched him, I became increasingly aware of the hidden effort he was making. Also, on further observation, I had to modify my first impression of youthful vigour. His pale olive complexion lacked freshness and there was a slight flabbiness of cheeks and jaw. Also, there was a puffiness below his fine, dark eyes, which could look quite soulful during his rare moments of repose.

He activated the second glass egg and the little fishes too started to come alive. As I watched them perform it struck me that an obvious trick had been missed. This was crying out for a musical-box effect. Perhaps the dance of the flowers from Tchaikovsky's *Nutcracker* ballet would be appropriate. And for the fish? After some thought I came up with 'We joined the navy to see the world, what did we see, we saw the sea.' As I watched the bright little things swim round and round, I was searching for a word that would describe their wide-eyed look and winsome expression. Suddenly, I heard Stripey sigh, 'Ah, aren't they cute!' It hit me like a jovial slap on the back. 'She's got it, by Jove she's got it,' I shouted to myself. I felt like Professor Higgins in *Pygmalion* when Eliza Doolittle finally came up with the right pronunciation. Stipey had hit the nail on the head – 'cute' was *le mot juste*.

Carlos had remained silent during the initial moment of the dancing display to allow us to contemplate and appreciate the performance. But now he was off again, impressing upon us for the umpteenth time the high artistic quality of the workmanship. 'And, ladies and gentlemen,' he continued, 'I must stress most emphatically that every one of our Fabergé eggs is unique.' And in case we didn't know what unique meant, he proclaimed dramatically: 'There isn't another egg like it in the whole universe.' It occurred to me that they could produce a multiplicity of the same design and that by removing one leaf or changing the colour of just one flower or stripe on a fish they could still uphold their claim of uniqueness.

'Many firms are trying to manufacture this product' he continued, 'but we are in a class of our own. Only we can justly claim to do full justice to the spirit of Peter Carl Fabergé.'

I could hardly believe my ears. He'd admitted they were not the only producers of Fabergé eggs. And what's more, this fact hadn't come as a surprise to my companions. It appeared that I had been the only one to believe in their exclusiveness. How naive can you get! My pride had been thoroughly punctured.

As I watched Carlos draw himself up into a stance of authority but at the same time adopting an expression of bonhomie, I realized that he was preparing us for something. He was moving in for the kill. Would he be able to give one of us the *coup de grâce*? He started to address me and the men: 'Ladies and gentlemen, can you guess the price of these works of art?' Carefully, he picked up the enamelled egg and held it close to Mr Paleface.

'How much do you think this will cost you?' The gentleman thus questioned did not change his stern look, just gave a short shrug of his shoulders in reply.

'Well,' said Carlos with the air of one who was bestowing a bonanza, 'This will only set you back $15,000.' The girls gasped but the gentlemen remained impassive.

'A bargain!' exclaimed Carlos. 'At 15,000 bucks it's an absolute bargain! Just imagine yourself the owner of one of these precious eggs – the lifelong aesthetic enjoyment you would be bestowing on yourself, your family and your friends. The world would have to acknowledge you as a person of discernment and culture.' Turning to old Paleface again, he adopted a confidential man-to-man approach. 'This is not all. This is not an indulgence in luxury. It is ....' and now his voice became clear and firm to suggest the hard-headed, far-seeing businessman, 'it is an investment – the best and soundest you can make. It will not only maintain its value but, like other works of art, it will increase it manifold.'

'The poor chap is working really hard,' I thought. 'Top marks for effort.' I could sense his gradual disappointment as the impossibility of a sale became more and more obvious. The two girls, though now completely ignored, were impressed and appeared to be willing the men, one or the other, to open their mouths and buy.

I couldn't help remembering a conversation with my state-room attendant who hung about from early in the morning till late at night, ever ready to serve and oblige. To my surprise I had learned that the staff were not faithful, permanent employees of the shipping company – almost, I had imagined, like the members of a large family – but that they were hired on a six-month contract only and that they had to share a bunk-bed cabin with others deep in the bowels of the ship. I wondered whether Carlos had to work under similar conditions. For all I knew he might not even get a wage, just food and lodging and commission on sales. For this he had to be smartly dressed and groomed like a gigolo to impress the fat-cat ladies. So I too was rooting for him to make a sale. Alas, the men continued to sit there like stone Buddhas and refused to react.

At last he gave up, using the rest of his energy on hiding his frustration and bidding us a polite farewell. The big man heaved himself out of his chair and left without a word, and Mr Paleface, after rising stiffly, treated Carlos to a quick nod before disappearing. I realized that from beginning to end neither of them had uttered a single word. And, of course, neither had I. The girls gave Carlos a friendly smile and thanked him before walking out. I, having a mobility problem, was the last to leave. Somehow, I couldn't suppress a feeling of guilt for having expected free entertainment from a person who was struggling to make a living for himself and possibly for a family as well. It moved me to offer him a more extended thank you. 'I enjoyed your informative talk,' I said. 'I now appreciate all the thought and effort that goes into the production of such objets d'art.' And before I could stop myself I heard myself say: 'I wish you better luck next time.'

Suddenly, the whole experience which I had expected to be an amusing diversion really turned sour on me. He stood there motionless. His face muscles tightened. I knew he was clenching his teeth. His eyes narrowed and stared at me with what could only be interpreted as hatred. His expression said clearly: 'You can stick your bloody understanding and effing sympathy, the only thing I want is a sale.'

As I hobbled away, rather chastened and upset, I thought I could feel his malevolent gaze burn into my back.

As soon as I arrived back home I consulted the oracle, my arch-enemy, the computer. He came up with a multitude of firms who all manufacture 'unique' Fabergé eggs. These were made of a variety of materials, right down to painted tin eggs that were presented in tin boxes, six at a time. I ask you, how much more unique can you get?

BRIEF ENCOUNTER

Though the sun was shining in a cloudless, almost Mediterranean-blue sky, some of the early morning freshness still lingered pleasantly in the air.

I was ambling along a Yorkshire lane, enjoying the vibrant green of vegetation on my left and, on my right, beyond the loose stone wall, the undulating grazing land and distant view of the woods. On the verges, the show of colourful wild flowers with the soft hum of insects and the dancing butterflies seemed to complete the picture of nature at her peaceful best.

Suddenly, out of the corner of my eye, I caught a movement. I turned my head. There, along the top of the stone wall, a fox came trotting towards me. Having drawn level he slowed down and, to my surprise, adjusted his pace to mine. It was a dog-fox; large, confident and in his prime. He carried his bushy tail with pride and his thick, glossy coat flamed like burnished copper in the rays of the sun. I was stunned by his beauty.

We were practically at eye-level as he continued partnering me on the wall. His eyes never left me. But he was not just looking AT me, he was looking me OVER.

What did he think of me? Not much, I gathered, for his bright, intelligent eyes seemed to echo his rather mocking smile. How is it that, of all animals, foxes appear to be smiling? I could not help feeling a twinge of disappointment as he resumed his former, faster speed. He was moving with springy, graceful steps, placing one foot neatly in front of the other as foxes do. He had judged me as being of no importance, I thought, not even worthy of a backward glance. Soon he would be out of sight. My sense of loss was ridiculous as I watched his progress with a heavy heart. But then, some distance away, he stopped. Stopped and looked back at me. It was a long, deliberate look before he disappeared down the other side of the wall.

What delight! He must have been thinking of me all the time he was moving away. The pantheistic part of me was elated for this had not been about nature-watching, a sort of spying on wild animals. No, I had enjoyed a one-to-one contact, a personal encounter when one living creature consciously meets and respects another. This fox had not been afraid of me, nor had he wanted to attack or harm me. He had felt curious just because I happened to be there, a fellow traveller.

I should like to think that in his short life he may have had the odd flash of memory of a young girl in a lane quietly going his way. As for me, this episode happened three quarters of a century ago but it is as alive and fresh in my mind as if it had happened yesterday.